The Midnight Special

A THOMAS PURDUE MYSTERY

BY
LARRY KARP

A WRITE WAY PUBLISHING BOOK

The Thomas Purdue Mystery Series:
The Music Box Murders
Scamming the Birdman

The Midnight Special is a work of fiction and any relation to persons living and real is purely coincidental.

Author photo courtesy of Jimi Lott, Seattle, WA

Cover photo courtesy of Christian and Kathleen Eric, Costa Mesa, CA

Write Way Publishing
PO Box 441278
Aurora, CO 80044
staff@writewaypub.com
www.writewaypub.com

First Edition; 2001

ISBN 1-885173-51-2
1 2 3 4 5 6 7 8 9

This one's for:

Bill, J.B., Tammy, Karen, Susan and Sandy
at the Seattle Mystery Bookshop, Seattle, WA;

Bob and Norma at Mystery Books, Bryn Mawr, PA;

Bonnie and Joe at the Black Orchid, New York City;

and all those dedicated mystery booksellers
who work long hours for little money
because they love the stuff we write.

Thank you.

And now abideth faith, hope, charity, these three;
but the greatest of these is charity.

—I Corinthians, XIII, 13

1

When she said, "Thomas, I've got a problem," I knew it was trouble. Trouble with a capital T, which rhymes with E, which stands for Edna. Twenty-plus years practicing neurology at a big New York hospital does that for you. A nurse at the other end of a phone line only has to say, "Dr. Purdue ..." and I know whether my patient needs a sleeping pill, an emergency tracheotomy, or a body bag.

"Can you come over?" Edna said. "I mean *right* over."

I started lacing my shoes. Morning sun poured over my face through the ceiling skylight. June in New York. Shakespeare in Central Park. Mets in first place. Girls in summer dresses. Great time to be alive. "Sure, Edna," I said. "I'm on my way. Are you all right?"

"Yes, *I'm* fine," she said. "It's that tinhorn Marcus Wilcox who isn't."

Who? I thought. Who's Marcus Wilcox? And why is she calling *me* about him? I flipped my half-read issue of *The American Journal of Neurology* onto the coffee table, snatched the portable phone off my shoulder where I'd been balancing it, jumped out of my chair, scooted toward the door. "Is Marcus sick?"

Short pause. Then Edna said, "Not sick, Thomas. Dead. I killed him."

Edna Reynolds lived on Lexington between 69th and 70th. At least a 45-minute hike from my place on West 16th and 8th Avenue; by subway, two trains with a transfer at Union Square. Better be a sport. I waved a cab over, and as the driver veered to the curb I hopped in before he stopped.

The cabbie, a small toad with a flat tweed cap low on his forehead, chuckled as I slammed the door. "Y'in kind of a hurry, Mac."

It wasn't a question, but I answered yes, then added, "I'm a doctor. Sick patient. Move."

He flipped the flag on the meter, chuckled again, chirped, "Man, I don't believe this. A doctor makin' a house call? Didn't think you guys did that no more."

"Special patient," I said. "Over to Lexington—go! Pedal to the metal."

"Ho-ho—money talks, huh, Doc?" The cabbie veered back into traffic, shot up 8th, cut off a UPS truck, then zipped in front of a moving van. "Sorry I ain't got no si-reen," he called over his shoulder. "Where to on Lex?"

It occurred to me I'd be smart to get out a block or two away from Edna's building. "Lex and Sixty-seventh," I said.

"Gotcha, Doc. Mercy Mission on its way." The cabbie floored the accelerator, weaved crosstown on 23rd, damn near clipped a woman who'd zipped across the street in front of a Don't Walk signal. "Pinhead moron!" The cabbie extended his head out the open window as far as it would go. "Next time I'll take your goddamn *ass* off for you."

I tried to keep my eyes off the scrambling vehicles and pedestrians, mind on the situation at hand. Edna Reynolds murdered some tinhorn? Didn't compute. When I went to my first meeting of the New York Music Box Collectors' Association I was a freshman med student, and Edna was serving her second term as president. She spent hours talking to me about the history of mechanical music, showed me how to intelligently evaluate machines for purchase, even taught me restoration techniques. "It's because you're for real, Thomas," she said. "You love these silly things as much as I do. Otherwise, I wouldn't give you the time of day."

On the New York antiques scene Edna Reynolds was known as the Doll Lady. Not that there was anything doll-like about Edna; perish *that* thought. She was an imposing woman, Gertrude-Steinish in appearance and manner, with a penchant for setting her feet and speaking her mind in language salty enough to send any blood pressure in earshot skyrocketing. Edna's nickname came from the fact that she collected automata: elegant dolls and whimsical furred animals that move in charming and funny ways, usually to musical accompaniment. Edna was also an accomplished repairer and restorer, had even created her own line of modern automata.

Edna was also my patient. Seventy-three years old, she'd been hypertensive for years, and after a couple of small strokes, a big one nailed her around the end of April. She spent a few weeks on Manhattan Medical's neurology service, then went back home with a nonfunctioning right arm and hand. The good news: Edna was a southpaw. The bad news: she needed two live hands to work on her automata. Edna never did have much patience with ineptitude, particularly her own. She was the terror of the Rehab Ward. The smiley-faced little tech who tried one morning to get her to weave a potholder refused afterward to go within three doors of her room. No question, Edna was a force to be reckoned with. But a killer? I couldn't see it.

At Lexington and 67th I paid the cabbie, jumped out, waited a moment to let him peel away from the curb and disappear into uptown traffic. Then I coughed away his exhaust and walked briskly up to 69th Street.

Edna's neighborhood was mixed residential-commercial, apartments above street-level specialty shops, lawyers' offices, agents' dens, lairs of investment brokers. Here and there a full-fledged apartment building, holdover from days when people thought it made sense to live close to where they worked. Edna's building was one of these, a twelve-story brick structure that had once been light in color, consistent with the art nouveau canon under which the place had been constructed. In a swoopy sandstone oval above the entry, *The Warburton* was embossed in stylized letters. I sailed through the outer doorway into the vestibule.

Edna lived in Apt. 4F: 4-in-the-front. EDNA REYNOLDS, said the name tag next to her bell. Not Reynolds, not E. Reynolds—no linguistic fiddling to put off the burglar, rapist, or grifter who might prey on an elderly woman living alone. Edna Reynolds lives here, said the tag. Just try something funny.

I rang the bell. Practically before I removed my finger, Edna's voice came through. "Yes?"

"I'm here, Edna," I said.

"Oh. Good." The buzzer sounded.

I opened the door, trotted into the little elevator, began my slow ascent to the fourth floor.

Edna was waiting in her doorway. Tan silk blouse, red-and-brown plaid pleated woolen skirt. No old-lady cotton print sack for our Edna. Hair up in the customary gun-metal bun; face powder and just a bit of lipstick faultlessly applied. Large brown eyes, narrow nose, firm round chin. But her hands were clasped in front of her, and it didn't take anything like 20/20 to see how badly they were shaking. "Thank you for coming," she said. "I'm sorry to impose on you, but ..."

She reached for my hand. Like a mackerel at Gristede's flipping up off its bed of ice into my palm.

"No problem," I said, and walked past her into the apartment. I looked around. "Where is he?"

Edna closed the door. Her face was unusually red, and she seemed to be having trouble looking directly at me. "He's, uh ..." She pursed her lips once, twice, then blew out a mouthful of exasperation. "Well ... he's gone."

I began to feel a trifle exasperated myself. "Yes, I know he's gone, Edna—you killed him. Where's the body?"

"Oh, *shit*, Thomas." She stamped her foot, sending a picture of a French automaton, a girl selling flowers, to a crooked angle on the wall. "He's not gone, dead. He's gone, *gone*. Left. Got up and walked away." I stared at her. She patted my arm. "I *didn't* kill him," she said, her voice softer now. "I just thought I did. Come in; I'll tell you about it."

She took my elbow, guided me through the living room into

the kitchen, where she aimed me at a chair in front of a small white table. "Sit," she commanded. "I'll cut you a piece of my chocolate cake; no argument, please. You do drink regular coffee, don't you?"

I laughed. "Why should I argue about your chocolate cake? And yes, you know I drink regular coffee. Now, talk. What the hell happened here?"

Edna set up a pot of coffee.

Her apartment was Wonderland, packed with the beguiling automated figures she collected and restored—lasting testimony, most of them, to the whimsical humor and ingenuity of a small number of French manufacturers a century ago. Beautiful bisque-headed dolls that played the harpsichord, or did a tambourine-dance, or lifted the top half of an egg shell to reveal a feathered, peeping chick inside. A white, furry rabbit who rose out of a cloth cabbage to chew a leaf with supreme arrogance. Dancing bears. Fiddling cats. Mephistopheles playing a mandolin as he does in *Faust.* Pierrot sitting cross-legged on the low edge of a crescent moon, strumming a guitar and every now and again sticking out his tongue, whereupon the moon would wink one of his blue, glass eyes. Hidden within the wooden bases or inside the bodies of the figures themselves were small comb and cylinder musical mechanisms. Edna's huge exhibit was near-magical. Whenever I left her place I needed to stand a moment and blink my way back before I could remember where I was going next.

The vigor with which my hostess was slashing off my piece of cake impressed me. "I'm in bad shape, Thomas," she snarled, taking care, I thought, not to look at me. "This goddamn stroke ... I make my *living* restoring old automata and building new ones, but for the past month and a half, I haven't done squat. And I've got very little in the way of cash reserves—"

"Edna, didn't you ... er, come into a little money last year? Same time I did?"

She looked as if she'd just taken a big bite from an unripe persimmon. "It came in, it went out." Light shrug.

"Excuse me, shouldn't have asked. None of my business."

"When I called you over here I made it your business," she snapped. Deep sigh. "Amazing how fast a pile of money can vanish. I gave some to my niece and her husband in Peoria: nice kids, why should they have to struggle? I paid off some money my husband once borrowed from a friend for an emergency. Emergency, spelled H-O-R-S-E."

As long as I'd known Edna this was the first she'd mentioned her husband. She saw me staring at the dull gold band gnawing into the flesh of her left ring finger. "Interest piles up after thirty-two years." She gestured toward her collection. "And of course I bought a few toys. Biggest bite, though, was to bail out Casson's son and granddaughter in Switzerland."

A half-century ago, Casson was the acknowledged world master in automaton restoration. Edna lived with him and his family while she was learning the trade.

"They'd opened an automaton museum, went in way over their heads, were about to lose the works ... along with their shop, tools, home. No way I could let that happen. But it pretty well wiped out *my* windfall ... so here I am, damn near broke. I always told myself I could sell my collection if I needed to ... and of course, I can. I *could*. Not very much longer and I'll just plain *have* to ... but the problem is, I don't *want* to." She looked around the apartment. "It'd be like selling off pieces of myself."

Edna slid the slice of cake onto a plate, set it in front of me. "Here, eat."

I picked up my fork.

She lowered herself into the chair opposite me at the table. The glance she shot at her right hand, resting on the table top, would have paralyzed it if such weren't already the case. "I need to get back to making money damn soon," she growled, "or I won't have any choice. Unfortunately, that little goober Wilcox found out."

I let a mouthful of cake slide blissfully back and down, titillating every taste bud along its path. "This goober's someone I know?"

"Huh!" Snort of pure scorn. "Better you don't. Better I didn't. Little bastard runs one of those shamelessly frou-frou interior design shops; he found his way to me when one of his clients wanted a broken automaton fixed. Wasn't a whole lot of work, but I'll bet he charged the client through the snoot. After that he started picking up damaged automata cheap, and bringing them over. I fixed, he sold. And when he needed something in antique fabrics—drapes, chair covers—there he was at my door, could I help him? Well, sure I helped him. I didn't *like* him, but can you like everyone you do business with? Then while I was in the hospital he came by with some work, and Bigmouth next door"—Edna jerked a contemptuous finger toward Apartment 4R—"old Mrs. Wolper, gave him a complete medical rundown on me."

I chewed, nodded.

"So for the last three weeks, starting the day I got back from the hospital, here comes Marcus Wilcox, pitching a daily fawn and grovel. He's heard about my 'misfortune,' oh dear, and he is *so* sorry. But maybe he can help. 'You know what, Edna—I could sell some of these automata for you ...' As if I'd need his help for that. One phone call and I could sell any piece, and for full value, not the sixty or seventy percent I'd get from him on consignment. As many times as I told him no, there he was back the next day. 'Just dropping in to see how you're doing, Edna: any feeling coming back in the hand, any movement? No? I'm *so* sorry. But maybe I can help.' Oh, Thomas, I could just kill ..." Edna's voice faltered, "him."

"So I understand," I said. "What convinced you to try?"

"The way he behaved today. From the minute he walked through the door he was practically twitching. No foreplay, not a word about how's my hand and arm. He's been *thinking*, he said; he has a great idea. I should consign my collection to him—my *whole* collection. He knows he can sell it fast; then I'll have enough money to keep me the rest of my life. He's *worried* about me, all alone in this apartment with my useless right hand and arm. I've already had one stroke; what if I had another? Wouldn't I be better off in a ... oh, God, Thomas! In a goddamn 'care center,' one of those hellholes stinking of piss pots and Lysol. Marcus, the darling, would feel *so* much better with me there."

I shrugged. "Why didn't you just tell him no?"

"What do you think I did?" Edna seemed to expand in her chair. "Of course I told him no. But he kept right on talking.

Without my automata to worry about, I could have my own apartment—my own *little* apartment. Wouldn't be any trouble for me to keep up. 'Because you've got to face facts, Edna: you're not going to be able to take care of yourself very much longer.'"

My mouth full of cake, I rolled my eyes. This Marcus Wilcox had to be more dog-brained than dogged. Anyone who knows Edna Reynolds should know never to say anything like that.

"That did it. I told the little bastard to get the hell out of my apartment *and* out of my sight, and then I ... well, I gave him a shove. And you know what he did, the idiot?"

"I can't begin to imagine."

"He made a grab—actually put his scuzzy hands on Josephine Baker there. I guess I didn't stop to think. Just picked up St. Cecilia and hit him, hard. Right on top of the head."

I glanced over to a small table in the living room where a foot-high bronze statue of the patron saint of music stood demurely next to a plaster image of Josephine Baker, smiling and resplendent in a sequined bra and feathered G-string. Wind the key in Josephine's back, music plays, sequins rotate, and feathers gyrate to a lively musical accompaniment. I burst out laughing, couldn't help it.

Edna chuckled. "You should've heard the thud. He went down like I'd poleaxed him."

"She conks to stupor," I said. "I gather you enjoyed that."

Edna nodded firm agreement. "Won't even try to deny it. But then I thought, my God, he's not breathing, and when I tried to find a pulse, I couldn't. That's when I called you; I came in here for the phone. But by the time I went back inside, he was rolling around and moaning. A few minutes later he was awake. Before he left he said I hadn't heard the last from him. I was a danger to myself and society."

I laughed again. "To yourself, no," I said. "But society? The man may have a point."

"Funny. He said he was going to file assault charges."

With reluctance I swallowed the last bite of cake. "I don't really think so. Remember, he owns a fancy decorator shop, probably caters to wealthy women. Imagine having it come out that he tried to pressure a poor disabled lady into selling her valuable collection, then actually grabbed one of the pieces. Bet his fingerprints are all over Josephine."

Edna couldn't help grinning. "Little bastard really did seem desperate. Bet you anything he's in a money bind, a big one."

"If he is, pressing an assault charge just for spite'd be about the last thing on his mind."

Edna sighed. "I hope you're right. Well, I'm sorry to've dragged you over here like this. I tried to call you again after Marcus left, but you were already on the way."

I reached across the table, patted her hand, said, "Forget it. I was just hanging around, waiting 'til the shops'd be open so I could run an errand. *And*'—I pointed at my empty plate— "where would I get a better piece of chocolate cake?"

Edna's eyes went watery. I was embarrassed, hadn't intended that. "You're a good friend, Thomas," she said softly. "Very few understand what it means to be a friend, but you do. I don't know how I'd have managed the last three years without you. Let alone the last six weeks." I started to say something but Edna held up a firm left hand, palm toward my face. "No, I mean it, Thomas. I'm grateful to you and I want you to know it."

"Fine." I waved off her obligation. "You brought a little excitement into my day. It's been routine, routine, routine for months now; I've been getting bored."

"Well, I'm sorry to disappoint you—not having a corpse on the floor." The right side of her mouth curled slyly upward. "Particularly Marcus Wilcox's corpse."

"Don't give it another thought," I said. "I'm sure I'll find one soon. I'm overdue."

If I ever put together my top ten Wish-I'd-Never-Said-That List, those lines will be number one.

From Edna's I hiked down Lexington, worked my way through the lunchtime crush of office workers and shoppers. No rush now. No need for lunch, either: Edna's cake would keep me fueled until supper.

At 63rd I turned east, strolled a block to Third, then half a block downtown, where I stopped in front of a shop-width plate-glass window displaying tables that could warp the heaviest floorboards, chairs capable of inducing lower back spasms within a ten-minute sitting, bronze statues of barely draped men and women twisted into postures unattainable by any living vertebrate. To the left of the window was a narrow doorway; above the window were curlicued gold letters: *The Palais Royal.* More than a bit pretentious, but that wasn't important. What was important was Broadway Schwartz's report of a music box inside worth checking out.

Schwartz had called just before five the afternoon before to tell me to scope this music box. "Not what you usually buy," he said. "But worth a gander. Definitely quality ... and different. Gorgeous burl walnut case on top of a matching stand, big enough to bury my Aunt Sadie in, and she's pushing three-fifty. I tried to get a look inside of it, but the dealer was one nasty Joe, slammed his hand on the lid, told me get lost. Still and all, I thought I'd better tip you."

Schwartz is an antiques picker, one of those gifted people who can spot a diamond in a pile of rhinestones, or a 2,000-year-old Grecian urn on a table full of modern reproductions. He's the antique world's equivalent of the dowser, the book scout, or the top-level medical diagnostician. Most of my best antique music boxes have come my way thanks to the perspicacity and loyalty of my energetic little friend. He knew if I saw the music box, liked it, and bought it, ten percent of the purchase price would be in his hands within twenty-four hours.

And even if I am partial to the smaller, key-wound music boxes, lovingly manufactured as one-offs during the 1830s, '40s, and '50s by skilled Swiss clock and watchmakers, I had to respect my pal's judgment. The instrument he'd described sounded circa 1880, likely a factory-produced musical ho-hum. But Broadway Schwartz said different, said quality, so I thanked him, hung up, called the shop. When the machine clicked in I clicked off—no point advertising my interest. Better to just go by in the morning.

I walked through the open doorway, looked around. The shop was smaller than I'd have thought, filled with massive furniture and statuary like the stuff in the window display. To the right, swoopy maroon drapes between two plaster colonnades struggled to create the illusion of a separate room behind. Clearly, the merchandising keywords at the Palais Royal were big and klutzy. Even the ceramic and glass pieces were huge: giant urns, pots, and oddly-shaped receptacles I couldn't begin to identify.

I spotted the owner—I guessed it was the owner—seated at a desk toward the back of the shop, studying me. As I studied back, I realized why the shop seemed so small: on the wall behind the dealer was a door. Back room—storage? Special customers only?

The man acknowledged me with a tentative nod. Round face, lots of freckles, red hair. Open-necked white shirt, gray ultrasuede jacket. "May I help you?" he called in a high-pitched simper.

I walked over to face him across the desk, noticed a couple of small red objects on the floor next to his chair. Cinnamon red hot candies. "My friend said you have a music box I might be interested in. Schwartz. *Broadway* Schwartz."

When you've been picking as long and successfully as Schwartz, your name becomes an Open Sesame, grabbed up the instant it's dropped. But not this time. The man shook his head. "I'm afraid I don't know any Broadway Schwartz," he whined, giving the clear impression that such knowledge might fairly be taken as evidence of moral turpitude. "And in any event I rarely have music boxes; they're terribly hard to get anymore. Haven't had one in, oh, more than a year. Sorry, sir; I don't believe I can help you." He looked down at the papers on the desk in front of him, saying without words the interview was over.

"Were you here yesterday afternoon?" I asked. "Late in the afternoon, right before closing. Maybe one of your employees—"

"I don't *have* 'employees,'" the man said. "And yes, I was here yesterday, all afternoon. Now, let me tell you once more: I have no music box; I had none yesterday. Your friend, whoever he may be, is in error ... or perhaps having a little fun at your expense."

He reached into his jacket pocket, then popped something into his mouth. A wave of cinnamon washed over me.

"Listen," I said. "I've known Broadway Schwartz for almost twenty years and he's never yet sent me chasing geese. If he said there was a music box here, there *was* a music box here. You don't want to show it to me, that's your call. But I *am* a serious collector, and if a music box is worth it I pay the going rate."

That got me the answer I was looking for. The dealer's cheeks reddened, eyes flashed anger and embarrassment. "Are you calling me a liar?" he snarled.

I had to restrain a snicker. With his unruly reddish hair, round, blotchy, freckled cheeks, and lips twisted into a sneer, he looked like Howdy Doody gone over to the dark side.

"Not necessarily," I said. "You might just have a bad memory. Maybe I can help it along."

While I was talking, the phone on the desk began to ring. Howdy flipped me a quick fish-eye, then grabbed the receiver and said, "Hello ... oh, Mr. Dunbar." His face went the color and consistency of library paste. "Yes ... yes, I know I said— hold on just a minute, would you, please?" He lowered the phone, put his hand over the mouthpiece. "Get out of my salon," he hissed. "Immediately. Otherwise I'll call the police." The receiver in his hand seemed to be vibrating.

No point pursuing further. If he did have a music box—and I was convinced he did—he had no intention of showing it to me. Sometimes a dealer finds an item he knows he can sell to a particular customer, usually one who never argues price. Another prospective buyer may make a nuisance of himself—as I was doing right then. Or maybe this music box was hot. Such things do happen and Howdy didn't strike me as a man inclined to muddy the waters of commerce with unnecessary questions. Whatever the explanation, after Schwartz made him nervous yesterday he probably hid the box away in the room behind his desk. Bottom line: lost cause.

I nodded, turned, and started to the front of the shop. Behind me, Howdy started talking again into the phone, softly. Too softly for me to be able to make out any words.

Just inside the front door stood a little gold-incised Eastwood table, holding a scalloped silver tray full of business cards. Automatically, I picked up one of the cards, scanned it. *The Palais Royal*, it said. PERSONAL LIFESTYLE DESIGNS FOR THE DISCRIMINATING. MARCUS WILCOX, PROPRIETOR.

I glanced toward the back of the shop. M.W., Prop. was still engaged in earnest phone palaver. Marcus Wilcox—how about *that*, Mel Allen? Small world, New York.

From Howdy Doody's Royal Palace I wandered up to the Seventh Regiment Armory on Park at 66th, to meet Schwartz and walk through The Midsummer Antique Show. Opening time was one o'clock; I was three minutes late. From down the block I could see Schwartz wearing out the sidewalk in front of the building. God forbid he wasn't first in; someone else would pick off all the good stuff. I sprang for two tickets, then rode my friend's wake through the door and into the hall.

After more than two hours we'd covered half the show. Schwartz looked disgusted. When a picker as sharp as Broadway Schwartz has empty hands after two hours of sniffing, you know you've got a lousy show.

For me, though, it was still entertainment. We stopped in front of a booth to size up merchandise; the dealer, a heavy man with pink-shot watery blue eyes and rouge-red jowls, ran eye-tape over us. Customers? Tire kickers? "Come on in, take a look," the man wheezed. "I sell things with peoples' names on them." He picked a glass paperweight out of his display case, held it out toward us. "Nice gold lettering, huh? Wilbur Rommel Dry Goods, Topeka, Kansas. Hey, see the phone number, seven-four-nine—had it easy those days. And here"—he put Wilbur down on the counter, snapped up a small bronze paperweight, a standing lion—"Edwin Herman, fifty years. Guy must've been a Lion for half a century, can you imagine? And over there, see—doctor's sign-shingle, came off of a house in Red Bank, New Jersey. Got lots of autographed pictures; guess you could call them my bread and butter. But y'know what're the *best* sellers—go out as fast as I can get 'em in?"

I told him I couldn't imagine.

From beneath the brow of his ever-present black fedora, Schwartz's dark eyes shot me a warning. Suffering fools patiently is an important part of a picker's job description. Fools sometimes part with valuable items for peanuts, or pay through the schnozz for dreck. In addition, the antiques gossip network is wired better than any Bell System. Let a dealer put the kibosh on a picker for being a wise guy, and that picker might as well go downtown and file for unemployment.

"Pictures of dead people—in their coffins," said the dealer, *sotto voce*. "*If* the name of the person's on the back. And babies, *especially* babies. Couple of weeks ago I went to an estate sale, picked up this five-by-seven of a kid in a coffin, had 'Our Dearest Little Jackie Womrath' written on the back. I put it out here, and just an hour ago two collectors damn near come to a fight over it. So I did a little auction, just the two of them. Got a hundred and a quarter—how d'ya like *that?*"

"Cool," I said, and tried to visualize people who'd take up arms over photographs of dead babies, but my beeper interrupted my train of thought by vibrating against my left leg. I picked it off my belt, checked the red numbers. 555-6837. Man Med Emergency Room.

Who was calling from the ER? Med school semester had just ended; I was officially off-duty for two weeks. I always leave my beeper on, though, in case Sarah, my wife, needs to reach me in a hurry. Or Schwartz happens to spot something wonderful at a flea market.

I hoofed out to the pay phones in the lobby, called the ER. The receptionist put me through to Room 3, where Linda Martin, a tough, capable nurse from San Antonio, was allegedly in dire need of talking to me. "Oh, Dr. Purdue, thank *goodness!*" Linda breathed through the wire. "We got ourselves a li'l problem heah—friend of y'all's, a Mr. Frank Maar."

More trouble with a capital T, this time rhyming with C, standing for Crank. Frank the Crank, my good friend and sometime co-conspirator, owner and operator of Wind Me Up, a hole in the wall on West 12th just off 7th, crammed with the finest musical antiques, collectibles, and novelties. Aside from his occupation, Frank owes his nickname to the most impressive bipolar disorder I've ever seen, and remember what I do for a living. My stomach did a barrel-roll. Frank hadn't attempted suicide, had he?

"Blunt trauma," Linda continued. "Ah know y'all're on vacation but he aisked me ... well, actually, *tol'* me ... to call y'all. Says he won't let anybody else touch him. Po' li'l X-ray tech was scared spitless."

Nuts! That was Frank in the grip of his Black Angel, as he called his depressive episodes. But blunt trauma? Did he trip in his shop and go sprawling? Get conked on the bean with a burglar's pistol? Take a total body bashing from a sadistic mugger, pissed at finding only a quarter in Frank's pockets? "What shape is he in?" I asked.

"Oh, he'll be okay," Linda drawled. "No loss of consciousness, looks like nothing's broken. But he's gonna hurt a while. Bruises all over his body, a few cuts. And burns—looks like cigarettes."

"Be right over."

Schwartz came along, happy to be sprung from the Booth of the Living Dead. Besides, Frank was also *his* good friend. My wife Sarah insists that anyone who puts the three of us into a room together should be prosecuted for reckless endangerment of the community. When I tell Sarah that seeing people having a good time seems to make her nervous, she snorts and says yes, if it's people like Frank and Schwartz and me, I'm absolutely right. That makes her *very* nervous.

The sight of Frank in the ER nearly broke my heart. He was on his left side on an exam table, curled fetus-like, wearing only jockey shorts. An intravenous tube dripped saline into a right-arm vein. His arms and legs were masses of lumpy red abrasions and contusions, shoulders and abdomen dotted with angry, blistered burns. Nothing from the neck up, odd. I touched his shoulder lightly, said, "Hey, Frank."

He turned his head just enough to take me into his gaze. Black eyes beamed hostility. "Go fuck yourself," he mumbled. "Le' me alone." Then he looked away again.

I knew not to be put off by Frank's downtime behavior. He wanted me there, all right, but he wasn't about to tell me that—or more accurately, he couldn't. His Black Angel took no prisoners.

I'd tried for years to get Frank onto maintenance medication, some pharmacological concoction that might keep his keel a bit more even, but to Frank's way of thinking, chemicals are poisons and drugs are chemicals, so he'd have no part of them. I was tempted there in the ER to take advantage of the situation and start Frank on an antidepressant, but knew that'd run counter to his wishes. Besides, Frank spent much more time up than down, and when he was up he was cheerful and energetic in a way few of us can even begin to understand. How would I feel if I made him over into a bland, blah, Mr. In-between? And in any event, as soon as Frank realized what he was getting, he'd refuse to take any more.

So no antidepressants—settle for short-term, pragmatic treatment. With one eye keeping Frank in clear view I said to Linda, "I'm not going to give him any drugs—he wouldn't want any, and really doesn't need any." I pointed at the IV. "You've got the admission blood work?"

"Uh-huh. Drew it when we started the IV. But it took three orderlies to hold him down."

I rested a hand ever so casually on Frank's shoulder. "Poor old Frank," I said. "He must *really* be feeling bad. Usually he's the nicest guy in the world ... and funny? He'd have you in stitches." I bent over to talk into Frank's ear. "Tell you what, old buddy. You need some X-rays, a CAT scan. Dr. Schwartz and I'll go along with you, won't leave you alone for a minute. You've got nothing to worry about."

As I patted Frank's shoulder, it heaved beneath my hand. Frank let out a honk, then started crying. Good. If he had to be depressed, let him at least be compliant.

I looked at Schwartz. "Got any better ideas than that, Doctor?"

Schwartz waved off the possibility. "Sounds right to me."

Linda fixed a highly dubious gaze onto Schwartz.

"Linda Martin," I said lightly. "This is Dr. Schwartz, from Mt. Sinai Neuro. He and I were up there, going over one of his cases when you called—so I brought him along."

Linda's expression said if she and I were the only people in the room she'd tell me she'd grown up on a Texas ranch, and had no trouble identifying bullshit at first whiff.

"I'll give him a physical," I said. "Then we'll get X-rays, a CAT, check out the blood work. If he's neurologically stable we'll send him up to the ICU, twenty-four-hour observation—and I mean *observation*. Someone keeping eyes on him every minute."

Her expression said she heard me loud and clear. Depressed people have nasty habits of jumping out windows or wrapping IV tubing around their necks.

"They should call me if there's any sign of internal bleeding or any other trouble—otherwise I'll see him tomorrow afternoon. I know Frank. In twenty-four hours I'll be able to talk to him, find out what happened."

"You're going to be the responsible physician, then?"

"I'll write orders before I go."

Nearly seven o'clock before I got Frank tucked safely away. None of the tests showed serious damage. "Worries me, though," I said to Schwartz as we walked down the steps from the hospital. "That wasn't anything like your usual going-over: nothing broken, no head injury, just a whole lot of really painful stuff on the body, arms and legs. Someone was torturing Frank—why?"

Schwartz shrugged. "Beats me."

"Broadway ..."

"Huh? Oh ... sorry, Doc. Unintentional."

"All right. Problem is, I won't be able to keep him in-house more than twenty-four hours. Utilization review, good old insurance companies. But I don't like the thought of him going home, being by himself—what if whoever worked him over comes back for another try? Think we can get Mick the Dick to stay with him for a while?"

Our friend Mick McFarland, aka Mick the Dick, was a young private detective with a build that made Arnold S. look like a 98-pound weakling. "Yeah ..." Schwartz began slowly. "But I think I got a better idea."

In Schwartz I trust. "Shoot."

"Mick and Sandy live over on Second Av now, up in the Seventies. Nice new high-rise ..." he grinned wickedly. "They went yuppie, big-time. How about Frank goin' over there—they got plenty of room, and the goons won't know where to even start lookin'. Then when he feels good enough to open the shop, Mick can go along with him."

Sandy was Mick's wife, as well endowed in the female manner as Mick was in the male. She worked part-time as an actress in soap operas, part-time as a pickpocket—hence Schwartz's moniker for her: Soapy Sandy Stickyfingers.

"Makes sense to me," I said. "Want to give them a call?"

"Leave it to me, Doc. By the time you spring Frank, I'll have 'em on board."

Schwartz hopped a First Avenue bus uptown to Yorkville. Edna's chocolate cake was now an eight-hour memory; my furnace needed stoking. I trotted across 30th to 2nd Avenue, took a downtown bus to 10th, scorched into the Second Av Deli.

An hour later, my arteries pleasantly coated with fallout from corned beef, stuffed derma and cheesecake, I hiked up 2nd Avenue to 14th, then turned crosstown. Almost nine o'clock, daylight fading, warm evening air heavy with the perfume of flowers. All right, that was only because I was passing a florist shop, but so what? I gulped at the atmosphere as if it were ambrosia. A pretty young woman going east in a minimal silk frock smiled at me; I smiled back. Summer's gentle evening breeze, 78 degrees warm, tickling the city's happy bone with heady *nachtmusik*. Raw cold a thing of the past, drenching humidity something to bitch about in August. For now, just listen to the city's Ode to Joy.

A crew was filling potholes at the corner of 7th Avenue; I breathed in the tarry fragrance. A bouquet not to everyone's liking, but a whiff of tar on a warm summer evening always takes me back to the boardwalk at the Jersey shore, to the Garabedian Auction Gallery in Asbury Park where at the age of eighteen I bought my first music box, a lovely Swiss cylinder instrument that played six tunes on its twin combs. Cost me seventy-five dollars, at the time a pile of money. I paid for my treasure, carried it onto the boardwalk, found an unoccupied bench facing out to sea, sat down, put the music box on the seat next to me. Then I pushed the start lever. As the waltz from *Faust* began to play I inhaled the pungent, tarry smell of the pine boards beneath my feet. Waves rolled in over the sand, retreated, came in again. Sun dropped into the water, colored the ocean orange; a breeze off the water cooled my face. The music box played "I Dreamt I Dwelt In Marble Halls." My life stretched before me like the flaming Atlantic Ocean: for every step I might move forward, the horizon would recede. I had all the time in the world.

Edna, Wilcox, Frank. A bum day, but as my late, New Age pal Shackie might've put it, maybe The Forces were about to hang me a U-ie. By the time I got back to my building I was feeling noticeably more cheerful. I slapped a fiver into the palm of an old guy lounging across the sidewalk from my door before he could even ask, then charged up the steps and inside. Up four flights to my apartment, two stairs at a time. As I pulled out my key, my upper lip was stiff, my pecker up. Go in, do a little work on a fantastic Reymond-Nicole overture box Schwartz rooted out of a west-side estate a few months before, then fall into the sack smiling.

But as Fats Waller used to say: one never knows, do one?

I turned the key, walked into the room ... and found myself looking into the barrel of a handgun.

Behind the pistol was a young man with a scared but determined look on his face. Behind *him*, a rope hung down to the floor from the big hole the young man had obviously bashed through my skylight.

Some days are just no good. We should be able to declare them null and void, like misdirected checks.

2

The gun-holder was shaking so badly he could hardly keep his weapon pointed where he wanted it. He wasn't much past twenty, tall and slim, with a round face, flattened nose, large, high-set ears, and a generous mop of light woolly hair. No tracks on his arms, no pop-marks below the short sleeves of his black T-shirt. Maybe he snorted his fixes, or swallowed them.

Wide brown eyes darted glances everywhere; arms, head, legs, and trunk were in constant motion. He looked like one of those vibrating battery-powered children's toys; way he was shaking, he might've pulled the trigger unintentionally. I felt even more scared than he looked.

The kid extended his right hand. "Give me your wallet." Voice hoarse, tone almost pleading.

"I've got personal things you can't possibly use," I said. "Pictures, cards , like Triple-A—"

"Keep your hands up." The kid waved the pistol.

"If I keep my hands up, how the hell am I supposed to give you my wallet?"

He didn't come even close to smiling, just waved the gun again. Something funny about the way he watched me speak.

"I ... I don't care about the *wallet*. Just get your money out and give it here. But move your hands slow."

This kid was no pro, at least not at armed robbery. He was more than confused; he was in a major emotional snit. That and the way he was watching me talk ... wait a minute. *Watching me talk.* And holding the gun in his *left* hand.

In my momentary hesitation the kid glanced at the workbench directly to my right. *Carpe diem*, Purdue.

"Antique music boxes," I said. "I restore them." As I spoke I reached over—*very* slowly—and pushed the start lever on a nice Nicole Freres forte-piano box. It began to play, an exquisite arrangement of sumptuous chords backing impressive up-and-down-runs in the treble.

As the instrument swung into a striking sequence of alternating question-answer passages between its loud and soft combs, the kid's jaw went slack. "Wow!" he breathed, then leaned forward to get a better look. His eyes bulged, pupils went large and black. Whatever he was high on, it wasn't narcotics. His hand wavered. Gun barrel lowered ever so slightly.

My hope had been to distract him but I wasn't about to argue with a full-blown trance. I launched a short chop to his left wrist with the edge of my hand; the gun sailed up over our heads, then clattered to the floor. The kid howled, grabbed his wrist. I snatched the pistol.

"Don't shoot." The kid's hands flew up over his head. He looked like a bowl of Jell-o in an earthquake.

I motioned to the chair in front of the workbench; my young visitor slid carefully into it. We listened in silence to the remainder of the tune, the kid gawking, strangely enthralled. Could he be ..?

Stop-tail clicked music to a halt. The kid shook his head as if trying to clear cobwebs from his mind. Then he stared at me. "You gonna call the cops?"

"Let's see your wallet." I made a give-here motion with my free hand.

He stared as adenoidally as if I'd addressed him in Latin.

"Your wallet," I repeated. "You know—that thing you wanted *me* to give *you*. Come on, hand it over."

"Mister, what are you, retarded? I ain't *got* a wallet. And if I did, you think I'd bring it along on a job like this?"

"Turn your pockets inside out. All of them. Slowly."

He did as I said, not taking his eyes off me. Slowly was the word, all right. I thought the sun might set and rise again before he got four white flags hanging from his pants, one from his shirt. The shirt pocket held three one-dollar bills, that was it. With a sullen look, the kid extended the money toward me.

"Put it back," I said. "Doesn't look like you're exactly flush ... uh-uh-uh! Hands back up for now, that's a good boy. What's your name?"

"For me to know, for you to find out."

"Suit yourself. This really the best way you could think of to put a few more bills in your pocket?"

Will wonders never cease? He started to cry. Talk about shaking.

"Put your hands down," I said. "Relax a little—*just* a little." I waved the gun at him, gentle reminder. He didn't know I'd never fire it, but that was for me to know, him to find out. Down came the hands. "Okay," I said. "Why?"

Small shrug. "I do skyjobs." He pointed backward at the jagged hole in my ceiling. "Y'know ... get up on a roof, bash the skylight, come down on a rope, clear out what I can carry—money, jewelry, light stuff. Then up the rope and I'm gone."

"You get up ... on roofs?"

"Sure. Back alley wall, ground-to-roof usually less'n a minute. Heights don't bother me. I've got strong arms and legs, and I know what I'm doin'."

"You're a Spiderman."

The kid showed a mouthful of yellowed teeth. "Yeah. You could say that."

"But no one's ever walked in on you before."

He swiveled his head, glanced from windows to door.

I waggled the gun. "Don't even think about it."

Message received. The kid shook his head. "No ... this's the first time. I ring the outside door buzzer first; anyone answers, I split, come back later. No answer, I go topside and in; I'm out in not more'n five, ten minutes. Alarm goes off, I move a little faster, but that doesn't happen much. Be surprised how many people have only a sign, no alarm. Or they got an alarm but don't bother turnin' it on."

Almost a year now since Sarah and I moved in, and getting an alarm system was right up there, high on the to-do list. Another fine road to hell, courtesy of Purdue Paving. "Bad luck, kid," I said. "But don't take it personally. I've had a rough day too. Here ..."

I reached over, still keeping the gun on him, and turned the Nicole back on. Music played; the kid sat stone-agog. If I'd set off a grenade right next to him, he wouldn't have so much as flinched. That boy just watched the Nicole—*watched it as much as listened.*

Now I was sure.

"What do you see?" I asked. No answer. "Kid—*what do you see?*"

"Icy white poles," he murmured, eyes glued onto the music box—or better, onto the music. "With, like, streams—deep blue and shiny black—running down them. Orange flashes ... the high notes. And purple and gold ... waving ... like a flag."

Bob's your uncle and I'll be a monkey's! Score, Purdue. My Spiderman Kid was synesthetic.

In all my years of neurologic practice I've seen only a few cases of synesthesia, an odd condition where sensory nerves seem to cross-communicate. In the most common form of synesthesia, sounds produce visual response patterns as real and constant as their auditory counterparts. When someone says S-A-M, you and I and the synesthetic both hear Sam, but the synesthetic also sees a specific visual pattern which may be pleasing or not: he may tell you Sam is a good name, clear, bright and amber, while John is disgusting, all crumbly and bile-colored. When a synesthetic says, "I see what you mean," he's being literal.

Synesthetics tend to have exceptional memories, and more than half of them are lefties. There's also a general heightening of emotional response: where you and I might be happy or sad, synesthetics are delirious or devastated. Where we get angry, the synesthetic is furious. And where we may be nervous, a synesthetic is a willow in a hurricane.

But it's music that has the most extraordinary effect on synesthetics. The joy you or I might feel at hearing a lovely clarinet solo or operatic aria is as nothing compared to the intense emotion of the synesthetic as he watches the music flow past his eyes. When I talk about golden chords and silvery arpeggios they're no more than figures of speech, but for this kid they were as real as the brass cylinder he saw turning slowly, its pins bringing forth music from the teeth of the comb.

The cylinder clicked to a halt, final notes faded. "You see sounds, don't you?" I asked.

No response.

"What's my voice look like?"

Small smile. "Hot fudge. Like flowin' down over a mountain of vanilla ice cream, meltin' the ice cream, mixin' in with it."

A boy after my own heart. "You don't like to tell people what you see, right?"

"Uh-uh." Headshake. "They make fun of me."

At best. Parents of synesthetics sometimes punish their children for "making things up" or even lying. But you can test synesthetics on different sounds one, two, ten years apart, and they'll always give identical answers. Just as S-A-M always *sounds* like Sam, it also always *looks* like Sam.

"I won't make fun of you," I said. "I wish I could see what you do, feel what you feel. It must be great."

That's called one-downsmanship, a useful way of dealing with neuropsychiatric patients. Make them comfortable, keep them talking. And it's not necessarily insincere. I meant every word of those three sentences.

The kid nodded toward the Nicole. "I never heard anything like that in my whole life. I always thought music boxes were those dumb little things, y'know, got a plastic ballerina goin' around on top, sound like puke. Ugly brown shapes, red knife points, sharp enough to cut me, so bright they're like burning my eyes. But this ..."

"Is a real music box. The McCoy. It's actually a musical instrument that plays itself. When the pins on that brass cylinder pluck those steel teeth, the teeth vibrate and make the music. Wooden case is the amplifier. No other musical instrument sounds like a music box."

The kid shook his head. "You ain't whistlin' Dixie, mister." He scanned the workbench, pointed at the assortment of parts and half-assembled mechanisms. "You fix these things up? When they're broken?"

I nodded. "On the side. My day job's medical work—I'm a doctor over at Man Med, specialize in the brain and nerves. Which is how I know about your condition. You've got a gift, kid. Learn how to use it, you'll be grateful for it, not sorry."

"Huh!"

"You don't believe me?" I waved my hand at the music boxes on the workbench. "You like these little toys?"

The kid nodded, wariness smeared on his face thick as movie makeup.

"And you're not punching a clock anyplace, are you?"

He laughed, the wordless equivalent of You-gotta-be-kiddin'-mister. "Just do skyjobs ... and stuff."

"Be a bigger crime than skyjobs and stuff to let a gift like yours go to waste. How about this: I'll teach you music box restoration. You won't get rich but you can earn a decent living ... and you'll listen to music boxes all day, every day."

The kid bit on his upper lip, studied my face, waited for the second shoe to clunk. Finally he said, "You serious, mister?"

"Serious as I ever get. What do you say?"

He shook his head, looked at his black gum-bottomed sneakers. "I don't know ..."

"What do you mean, you don't know? You'd rather do skyjobs ... and stuff?"

"It ain't that. Problem's how my grandpa and me're gonna live while I'm learning." But the boy glanced at the Nicole, a brief look full of longing.

"Grandpa ..?"

"Yeah." The kid's cheeks flared. "My grandpa's old, can't make money himself no more; it's all up to me. Landlord's the world's biggest shitsack, don't care nothin' except about his lousy rent money first of every month. So ..." He aimed a rueful glance at the pistol in my hand.

"Where'd you get it?" I asked. Silence. "Going to have trouble if you don't give it back?" I saw something like hope in his eyes. He shook his head. "Good." I cracked the barrel, emptied the bullets onto my worktable. Then I stood up. "It's going for a swim. You want a job or not?"

"Huh?"

"What, are you deaf? I asked, 'Do you want a job?'" I pointed at the Nicole. "Fixing these. Look at the back wall, what's on the shelves—see how many jobs behind I am? I'll teach you a skill you can use the rest of your life. And I'll pay you enough to take care of you and your grandpa. From day one."

The boy squinted at the Nicole. "You ain't just fucking with my head?"

"Headfucking's not in my line," I said. "Trust me, I'm a neurologist." I grinned, held out my hand. "Thomas Purdue."

The kid grasped it, gave me an automatic handshake. He looked like someone who'd just that instant checked his lottery ticket and seen six winning numbers. He tried to smile, couldn't quite pull it off. "Yeah, well ... okay, Dr. Purdue. Hey, what can I lose, huh?"

"Only some prison time and a bad case of despair," I said. "But call me Thomas, all right?"

"Sure. Thomas."

"Now I'll ask you again. What's *your* name?"

A smile took root, then spread outward from the corners of the boy's mouth and eyes. "Henry, Henry Levitsky. But you can call me what my friends do."

"Which is?"

"Jitters—but that's another thing. These music boxes're pretty old, aren't they? Like I bet over a hundred years?"

"Some are close to two hundred."

Long, low whistle. "So they got to be pretty valuable, right?"

"Some are *very* valuable, right."

Jitters held his still-trembling hand out toward my face. "What about *this*? I shake, like whenever I get the least little bit nervous. What if I mess one up 'cause I got the shakes working on it?"

"Then you'll fix it," I said. "What man can break, man can fix. But don't worry: those shakes aren't going to be any problem. Didn't I tell you to trust me? Come on—let's get started."

I walked to the rear of the shop, stood in front of the wall of wooden shelves I'd pointed out to Jitters a few minutes earlier. "Here." I took a small box from the second shelf, blew off the dust, handed the box to the boy. "This's a pretty nice one, circa eighteen-forty ... wait a minute." I picked up a pen and pad, wrote an address, passed the paper to Jitters. "Where do you live?"

"One-Ten Rivington. Apartment six."

"Good. Take the music box to this address; it's right on your way home. The lady you'll talk to there, Sophie Soleski, is a good friend. I'll call her, tell her you're coming. She deals in antique music boxes, and she'll give you a thousand bucks or damn close, for this one. That'll take care of you and Grandpa for a while, won't it? Oh—your pay'll be two hundred a week. All right?"

Jitters looked at the music box he was cradling in his arm, then back at me. "You're *giving* me this? Why?"

"Call it a show of good faith. You have to give one, too."

His eyes narrowed to slits. "Like how?"

"Like a promise. No more skyjobs ... and stuff. I'm not about to waste my time teaching you if all you're going to do is end up in stir. Now, promise."

Jitters looked back at the music box. "Yeah, okay," he said to it.

"No more skyjobs."

"No more skyjobs."

"And stuff."

Embarrassed snicker. "And stuff."

I felt as if I were my wife, Sarah, doing to Jitters what she's forever doing to me. Shoe on the other foot, but for a hike through uncertain country it's smart to put on heavy footwear, even if it's a little ugly. I clapped Jitters' arm. "Good—go on, now. Better get home before Grandpa starts worrying. Won't take you long to stop at Sophie's—whoops. Wait a minute."

Sarah! My wife'd be back tomorrow. Let her walk in cold on my new apprentice at the workbench and I'd be dealing with a four-alarm disaster. "Just remembered," I said. "I'm going to be tied up all day tomorrow. But the day after we start at eight o'clock. Sharp. Be here."

Jitters nodded solemnly, tucked the little music box under his arm, then made a move toward the rope hanging from the smashed skylight.

"I'll take care of that," I said. "Take off."

Another nod. He double-timed toward the door and out.

3

Next morning I nailed plastic sheeting over the jagged sky-light hole, then called a glazier. Tomorrow, the earliest. That'd work. Radio weathermen were saying it ain't gonna rain no more, no more.

Quick call to Man Med's ICU: Frank was still neurologically stable and moving into a better frame of mind. "Any change, ring my beeper," I told the nurse. "Otherwise I'll see him late this afternoon."

From one battered patient to another. I went to my work-bench, sat down in front of a marvelous three-tune overture box by Henri Reymond-Nicole, son-in-law and protégé of the great Swiss master, Francois Nicole. Music boxes by Nicole and Reymond are in a class by themselves, peerless sound quality, mechanical design and musical arrangements. When Schwartz found me this gem he got a triple commission; we both celebrated for days.

But every ointment has its fly. All music boxes I've ever seen by Francois or Henri have shown severe deterioration of the lead weights soldered beneath bass comb teeth; this metal rot makes a disaster of tuning. Worse, Nicole and Reymond did not stamp tuning scales under their combs. So the poor restorer, tediously shaping new lead weights, can only infer proper tuning by reference to pin patterns on the cylinder, and scales in already-restored boxes of the two genius makers. Like doing a tedious jigsaw puzzle with key pieces hidden all over the house.

I clamped the comb into a vise, started plucking teeth. Cut lead strip, solder it into place, listen, snip lead, listen, snip lead. Next tooth, same process, *d. c. al fine.* Only the thought of the music I knew I'd eventually hear kept me from heaping hideous curses on the memories of Father Nicole and his son-in-law for being so undiscerning in their choice of lead suppliers, and leaving their successors no tuning cheat-sheets.

By noon I had sixteen more teeth in tune, enough for one sitting. Time to make rounds in the city.

One-Ten Rivington Street, down on the Lower East Side. First American home for many European immigrants during the early 1900s. Squalid and dangerous then, squalid and even more dangerous now. I took the crumbly concrete steps two at a time.

An elderly Puerto Rican man, sitting on the top step enjoying a cigarette, waved me over. "Who you lookin' for?"

I almost said Henry Levitsky but realized just in time that would clearly mark me as an undesirable: bill collector, probation officer, cop. Instead, I came out with, "Jitters. Apartment six."

"Eh, Jit." The old man cackled. "You got something for him?"

"Yeah, a job."

The old man dragged at his cigarette, loosed another cackle, then glanced at the roof of the apartment building across the street. Apparently Jitters' skyjobs were not considered classified information on Rivington Street. "'Fraid you're just a little bit too late, mister. Jitters and his grandpa, they got evicted."

I pulled a twenty out of my wallet, extended it. "Know where they went?"

He shook off the bill, shook his head no. "Like to help you, mister, but ..." He waved a hand in all directions. "It's a big city, y'know?"

I was a little disappointed but not surprised—and not discouraged. But I would be if I got the wrong answer at Sophie Soleski's.

Sophie lived in a small apartment building on Bleecker Street close to Sixth Avenue, less than a half-hour's stroll from Jitters' former digs. She and her late husband Peter were classic cultured Europeans, able to talk rings around most people in literature, music, art, world politics, or Freudian psychology. Peter restored music boxes, Sophie sold them; by the 1970s they were the grand old couple of NYMBCA. Along the way, Peter made a restorer of my late friend Shackie; Shackie passed along this workshop know-how to me. And Purdue begat ... Jitters? Peter died in 1987, but Sophie's still there, still the grand old lady of NYMBCA, selling her magical (as she's always called them) music boxes.

Soph greeted me at her door with a face full of amused skepticism. "The mysterious seller has not appeared."

"Great! What I wanted to hear. Let me in, I'll tell you all about it."

Sophie stepped aside to let me pass, then shut the door and turned an extra-wry smile my way. "You know I love you dearly—

but I'm eternally grateful you're not my son. If I'd had to bring you up there's no question in my mind I'd not still be here."

Sophie turned eighty-four last year, but she could easily be fifteen or even twenty years younger. Her face is virtually un-lined, and she stands very straight, just an inch or two short of my height. I dare you to look at her well-groomed gray hair and not think of steel. NYMBCA members argue whether Sophie's debt is to genetics or estrogen preparations. I say it's determination.

Soph led me into her parlor, a sunny room with a mahogany dining table at the center, her collection nicely displayed around the walls. Not a large number of pieces, but every instrument she and Peter had kept over the years was a prize. A huge, long-playing music box with interchangeable cylinders. Five or six superb early cylinder boxes by top makers. Opposite the long-playing box, a Symphonion Eroica, a magnificent proto-stereo-phonic instrument that played three metal discs simultaneously. To the right of the Eroica, a life-sized acrobat-automaton in colorful circus silks who inverted himself to balance on one finger atop a ball while a fine comb-and-cylinder mechanism in the base played "Twinkle, Twinkle, Little Star"—which might strike you as ridiculous, but you'd be wise not to offer that opin-ion to Sophie. Some years ago a terminally pompous British visitor did just that, citing the apparent incongruity as "incon-trovertible evidence" that the original music-works had been replaced with a modern, inferior mechanism. Whereupon Sophie proceeded to skewer and roast him. "The tune is actually '*Ah Vous Dirai-je Maman,*'" she informed him, "a French folk melody whose origin is lost in antiquity. The Danish composer Peter Heise didn't think it was so ridiculous—he used it as the major theme in his *Triumphal March.* And Mozart? *He* must not have thought too badly of it either; perhaps you should sometime listen to his Piano Variations ... K. Number two-sixty-five, I believe it is." She told Peter to dismantle the base and show the Brit the fine circa-1870 mechanism inside, but her red-faced guest threw in the towel, said that would not be necessary. For the remainder of his visit, he kept his opinions, as they put it on that side of the pond, severely to himself.

We settled in at opposite sides of the table, Sophie watching me as if I might be concealing a dangerous weapon in my mouth. Finally she said, "I'm listening, Thomas."

When I finished telling her about my encounter with Jitters she flashed me a heavy dose of eye heat. "Let me understand, Thomas. A boy drops through the skylight into your apartment, holds you up at gunpoint, and as a reward you decide to teach him music box restoration?"

"Sure," I said. "Figure I gave him an aptitude test, and not one person in a million could've scored so high. The way he sees sounds; the way he *feels* about them! Soph: he's been evicted from his apartment, he's looking a thousand bucks square in the eye—and has he shown up here to sell you that music box? The real question is, how could I *not* do what I did?"

Sophie ran her tongue across her front teeth as if erasing words she'd decided to keep to herself. After a moment she said, "Thomas, the way you live on the edge. One day you are going to fall and hurt yourself."

"May be. But remember the expression on Peter's face whenever he heard music from a wreck he'd resurrected? Well, that was this kid's face when he heard my music box."

She inhaled deeply, blew out a chestful of resignation. "What's this condition of his, Thomas? What did you call it?"

"Synesthesia. Greek: a joining together of the senses."

"How strange it seems. I can't imagine."

"Try this. You and I live in black-and-white; synesthetics live in Technicolor."

"My!" Soph shook her head. "You really do think he'll stay on the straight-and-narrow?"

"Can't promise, but yes. I'm betting as soon as he gets into music box work his old skyjobs're going to seem dull."

"That's really what he called them?" Sophie chuckled. "Skyjobs? Oh my. If you don't mind my saying so, you must've had fun selling this one to Sarah. Was she with you when—"

"The kid dropped in? Fortunately, no. I'll have to tell her later today. She's been away the past week, visiting her sister in Monta-a-a-a-na."

Sarah's sister Anne is a neat woman—funny, sharp, generous—but she lives in a place called Jordan Falls, Montana. Picture endless skies, miles of rolling range land, trees as far as you can see. Nearest neighbor more than five miles away, unless you count the sheep—which is about all there is to do there. If God has His Little Acre, Jordan Falls is Satan's Big Spread. Pollens to make you sneeze, bees to sting you, range fires to fry you, bears and cougars to maul you to bits and devour your body, hawks and vultures to eat the leavings. I spent a year in Jordan Falls one week, Sarah telling me all the while I was like a bored, naughty little boy. Since then, by mutual agreement, when Sarah and Anne are trooping across the numbing western landscape, I take a week to savor the pleasures of my city, reveling in the feel of hot asphalt beneath my feet.

Sophie chuckled. "Better have a good story ready."

"Count on it, Soph. But there's more I wanted to tell you. Something about Edna Reynolds."

Soph leaned forward over the table, hands clasped before her. "Yes?"

A one-word question. When you get to Sophie's age and hear someone's name brought up like that, it very likely means you no longer know that person. "Relax," I said. "She's not dead. Just wants to be."

Soph listened through my tale of Edna's woe, all the while shaking her head sadly. "Poor Edna, so proud. So independent. You probably don't understand yet—it doesn't hit a person until he's on the cemetery side of his semi-centennial. How little there is left ... and where *did* it all go so fast? Yes, of course I'll call Edna. Maybe I can figure some way to help."

"Thanks, Soph," I said. "I thought if anyone could, it'd be you."

Home again, home again, jiggedy-jog, to the custom pad Sarah and I designed for the married couple who couldn't stand living together but couldn't bear to live apart. For M'lady, a trim, tidy sitting room and bedroom to the west; for the gentleman, a disorderly music box repair facility with elevated sleeping platform to the east. A common kitchen-dining area in the space north of the Great Wall of Purdue served as the only east-west border crossing, while at the southern extremity of the wall a tiny vestibule provided entry from the outside hallway. From the vestibule, a doorway to the right led into my chambers, one to the left into Sarah's.

Sarah was in my workshop, lounging across the sofa like a tuckered-out Cleopatra. I leaned over to kiss her cheek.

"Welcome back—long plane ride?"

"It's the changing planes." She pulled herself up to sit. "Drive to Helena, fly to O'Hare, wait an hour, fly to Kennedy." She poked a finger into her left ear, popped the finger out. "Up and down, up and down. My ear just won't stop buzzing."

"Take an antihistamine, maybe some nose spray. Should clear it up."

She nodded. "I will in just a minute."

She cocked her head, the better to give me that look. You know the look I mean: men get it all their lives. First from their mothers, later from their wives. "I shudder to ask, but what sort of trouble did you get into while I was away?"

Ever wonder why that warbling, tremolo organ stop is known as Vox Humana? "Trouble? Come on, Sarah. I caught up on some repair work, went to a few antique shows with Schwartz. What kind of trouble would I get into?"

"Give me a break. I could've spent my entire week in Montana ticking off possibilities."

Which she probably did.

"And with Schwartz to help you, the possibilities were endless," she added.

I raised my right hand. "I was perfectly well-behaved. Scout's honor."

"You're not a Boy Scout; you never were." Reluctant little smile. "If you couldn't be good, I hope you were at least careful."

"I was good, I was careful; don't worry. I even made a new ... friend. You'll appreciate him."

Like I'd appreciate a loud fart in a fancy restaurant, said Sarah's face. "I'm listening," said her voice.

I told her about Jitters and his synesthesia, how he reacted to music boxes, and especially how dedicated he was to looking after his poor infirm old grandsire. Sarah Socialworker's eyes went shimmery. As I knew they would. "How did you meet him?"

Story time. "No job, needed money; poor kid was really up in the air. He heard on the 'vine there might be something here for him, so the other evening he dropped in. I played the music boxes; he was ... well, enchanted. *Enthralled.* I offered him an apprenticeship; he'll start day after tomorrow."

The truth and nothing but. Sure, I left out a few details, like the gun and rope—so it wasn't the whole truth. Two out of three's not bad.

"Hmm." Sarah, searching for holes, couldn't find any. "Well, I guess I'll look forward to meeting him. What do you say we go out to dinner when it's time? I'm not up for cooking."

Home free—but better have a word with Jitters about never mentioning his drop-in route in front of Sarah. I checked my watch: 4:30. "You can rest your eyeballs while I run up to Man Med, check on a patient."

"But I thought you were on vacation."

"I am. Special patient. Frank the Crank."

"What happened to Frank?"

"Got worked over in his shop." Two out of three again. The truth and nothing but.

"Oh, *no.*" Sarah's hand flew up to cover her mouth. For all the word "care" has been overused, abused, abased, and cheapened, Sarah *cares.* And if the canvas upon which she paints her concern is a bit wide for my taste, I can't argue that her art is anything other than genuine. "Is he ..?"

"He'll be fine," I said. "In fact I'll probably send him home after I look him over. Go on, take a nap, see you about six, six-thirty. I said I'd be there by five."

I didn't bother to tell her to whom I said I'd be there by five. She'd only have wondered, why Schwartz? Three in a row—that doggone whole truth's a real bugger, it is.

Sarah started toward the kitchen; I headed for the vestibule. Before I got there, though, I heard, "*Tho*mas?"

Prickles on the neck. When my name becomes a one-word question, alarms go off. "Ye-e-s?"

She pointed toward the ceiling, to the sheet of plastic stretched over the hole in the skylight. "I saw that when I came in, then forgot about it. What happened up there?"

"Oh yeah—I forgot, too. Came in and found it a couple of days ago. Somebody must've started out to do a robbery, then changed his mind. Glazier'll be here tomorrow."

"Oh." She nodded dully, then disappeared around the corner.

Four in a row. Was I on a roll or what?

4

A round little nurse's aide snickered as Schwartz and I came up to the nursing station. "Oh, Dr. Purdue, thank God you're *here*. Dr. Allstate—that's what Mr. Maar calls Dr. Ralston, the resident—checked your friend over at four o'clock. Since then he's been pacing in there like a hamster in a cage."

More like a squirrel, I thought. I thumbed through Dr. Allstate's notes in Frank's chart. "Multiple abrasions, contusions, first- and second-degree burns to arms, legs, chest, abdomen. Treat symptomatically. Injuries painful but not serious." "Painful but not serious"—that's like "minor surgery," an operation performed on a person other than the speaker.

"He's driving us batty." The little aide groaned. "'When can I go? When can I go?' Like a kid in a car: 'Are we there yet?'"

"Your day of tribulation is over," I said. "Praise the Lord."

The aide rolled her eyes. "You know something, Dr. Purdue? You're as bad as he is."

I didn't answer, just waved Schwartz in the direction of Frank's room. Shoes fit, wear them. I've been called a lot worse than bad as Frank the Crank.

Frank was sitting up in bed, staring out the window. I coughed. "Mr. Maar ... I understand you're ready to go."

He wheeled around, big smile. Up-Frank today, Black Angel on leave. Sing glory, hallelujah. The high-intensity fixture in the ceiling beamed off his shining dome, accentuated the hollows in his cheeks. On his arms and legs, where the hospital gown didn't cover, big purplish bruises and smaller blistered burns ran riot. "Ready and rested, Doc—least as rested as a person can get in a hospital. Two a.m. they're takin' your blood pressure; three a.m. it's a thermometer in your trap; four o'clock they're givin' you a handful of pills for pain; five o'clock it's do you need a sleepin' pill, you don't seem to be sleepin' so good."

"Codeine doing anything for your pain?" I asked.

"Dunno." Frank's voice lowered into conspiratorial range. "They're givin' but I ain't takin'. I wait 'til the nurse goes out, then I flush the damn pills down the crapper. No way I'm puttin' *that* stuff in my body."

Allopathic, homeopathic, naturopathic, it doesn't matter. As far as Frank is concerned, any pill is a chemical, and we know what chemicals are, don't we? A bit of lithium here and there would do wonders for his mood swings, but Frank would as soon eat a nice lettuce, tomato, and cyanide sandwich. Disordered as his own body chemicals may be, they're still his and he's sticking with them. I've long since given up trying to persuade him otherwise; I take Frank as he is, being grateful for up-Frank, making a quick getaway when the mood of the moment is down.

Frank nodded at Schwartz. "Hey, Broadway."

Schwartz couldn't seem to take his eyes off Frank's injuries. He acknowledged the greeting with a weak salute.

"Frank ... what happened?" I asked.

Shrug. "Two gorillas came in the shop, big one, little one.

Little guy was a dude, fancy white shirt with monograms and them buffoon-type sleeves. He stayed by the door; the big guy gave me a massage."

"Whyn't you just give them the dough outa the register?" Dr. Schwartz's two-penny contribution.

Frank glared at him. "That's what the cops said ... but these guys weren't after dough. Dirt's what they wanted. They were askin' where I got a certain fancy music box I supposedly sold."

"You *supposedly* sold," I echoed.

"That's what I said, Doc. Supposedly. But I never set eyes on it, not ever. Way they described it, I sure as hell *would've* remembered it. Great big thing, fancy burlwood case with a matching stand, beautiful painting on silk inside of the lid, six cylinders on a carousel—"

"A revolver box," I said.

Frank's face lit. "Hey, Doc, double-bingo. Yeah, that's what they called it. Something else, too, but definitely that. A revolver."

Revolver boxes are marvels of Swiss engineering ingenuity, four or six cylinders mounted into a carousel-like mechanism. To play a different set of tunes, unlock the carousel, rotate it so the cylinder of your choice faces the comb, lock it back into place. Understandably, these intricate mechanical wonders were expensive to produce, and unfortunately, the wealthy folk who could afford such luxurious toys did not always operate them properly. Too often, a careless rotation of a carousel sent a hail of comb teeth flying across the sun parlor. Not many revolvers were made; few survived. Rare as they are, they're eagerly sought after by collectors.

I gave Frank the fish eye. "What made them think *you* sold it?"

"Hey, search me, Doc." Wide-eyed Frank, the Soul of Honesty grievously and wrongly challenged. "If I coulda told them anything, you think I'da laid there and let 'em do what they did to me?"

I had to agree there was logic to that.

"If I'da really sold that box to Marcus Wilcox, don't you think—"

"Sold that box to *whom*, Frank?"

Four eyes stared at me. Schwartz had obviously made the connection. Frank looked puzzled. "You know the guy, Doc?"

"Only slightly, which I'm not complaining about."

"I know what you mean. I've never been able to stand the little twerp and I always will."

"You've got a rare way with words, Frank. Point is, Schwartz sent me up to his shop yesterday to look at a music box—"

"Which I saw there the afternoon before ... and at least from the little bit he let me see of it, it looked one hell of a lot like the one you were just talkin' about," Schwartz said.

"And which wasn't there—or he *said* it wasn't there—when I dropped in on him," I said.

Frank rubbed his chin, memory lubricant. "Funny thing," he said, slowly, looking at the ceiling as if the information he sought might be inscribed there. "Month ago maybe, I was talkin' to Lucas Sterne, and he told me something about a super music box, which I swear he called a revolver. Said the old guy who owned it and a snotty little designer showed him pictures, they wanted to have it fixed so it'd look decent and play right, and then they were going to sell it. But they weren't about to consign it to him, so Lucas got his ears out of joint and blew them off."

No one mangles metaphors, slays similes, and strangles syntax like Frank the Crank. Lucas Sterne was the proprietor of The Lucas Sterne Music Box Emporium, located on 56th Street, just southeast of Central Park, precisely at the center of the music box universe (as defined by Lucas Sterne, Prop.). A talented restorer, highly knowledgeable in his field, Lucas took umbrage the way some people take heroin. Nothing for him to throw out a client who dared suggest he function as a mere technician. Thanks to a mega-collection he'd brokered a couple of years before, Lucas could afford to be as snotty as he liked to just about anyone he didn't like.

"This Wilcox seems to be getting around," Schwartz said. "Him and this music box. If it *is* the same one."

"There's more," I said. "Wilcox has been bugging Edna Reynolds, wants to grab her collection to sell in his shop. Edna thinks he's in a big money bind. She said he really put the screws to her yesterday."

"Ho-ho-ho." Never mind the pain, Frank chortled. "He put the screws to the Doll Lady—*not* a smart thing to do. She must've been foaming at the mouth."

"Enough she cold-cocked him with St. Cecilia."

Schwartz was clearly appalled; I realized I hadn't told him about the beaning. Frank looked confused. "St. Cecilia?"

"Patron saint of music—bronze statue in Edna's living room. She got so sore she picked it up and brought it down on Wilcox's beezer."

Frank waved his hand like a second-grader with an acutely full bladder. "Edna figures maybe somebody's got this Wilcox's balls in a vise, okay. But what's that got to do with a big, fancy music box?"

You know about blinking-amber moments. You're barreling along life's highway when you notice a flashing yellow light on a sign at the shoulder: *Dangerous Road Conditions Ahead.* My mind's eye saw Sarah sitting on the edge of the bed next to Frank, pointing first at the sign, then at the turnout so thoughtfully and conveniently provided. "Say 'It's probably nothing, and in any case the police will look into it,'" Sarah insisted. "Then *turn around* and let's go have a nice dinner."

Backseat Driver Sarah, maybe she was right. But the wheel was still in my hands, and on I sped, past the amber light, picking up speed, zipping down that hazardous highway. "What'd the cops say, Frank?"

"Huh! Said they'd check things out with Wilcox. Then, just a couple of hours ago a dick came in and asked was I *sure* I heard right, and I said sure I was sure. Well, he said, he went and talked to Wilcox, and Wilcox didn't know thing one about me sellin' him a music box. So the dick figured maybe it was a buncha weirdos having a kick or two, maybe they didn't like Wilcox and made up a cock and bull story just for a little fun. He took down my description of them, said he'd 'look into it.'"

No missing the sarcasm in Frank's voice—but how many muggings, bashings, and strongarm jobs are carried out every day in New York? To leave no unturned stones above them all, the police would need a hundred times their actual manpower, and even then, good luck trying to find a particular basher in the City of Eight Mill that never sleeps.

"See?" Sarah said into my mind's ear. "It's a fool's errand. You can still turn around. Please?"

The leadfooted fool floored the pedal. "Makes *me* wonder."

Schwartz flipped me his classic shrug. "Want to go talk to Wilcox?"

"Not 'til we get more information—or he'll just tell us what he told the cops. Let's start with Lucas, hear the whole story straight from the beginning." I started to motion Frank to lie down, but my hand froze mid-gesture. "Wait a minute. When I was at Wilcox's shop he got a call from somebody named Dunbar, and I thought he'd wet his pants. Wouldn't want you to get bored the next couple of days, Frank—why don't you see whether you can find out who Dunbar is and why he's terrorizing double-tongued sleazeball interior designers."

Games are meat and drink to Frank the Crank. He likes to say he might one day go into politics because he's always got his ways and means. The antique-world grapevine is a marvel of intelligence-gathering, its thoroughness and accuracy unchallenged by the professionals of any government agency. Frank's shop, Wind Me Up, is one of the major informational crossroads in the system, Deep Throats forever coming through the door or ringing the phone, giving Frank the latest, taking it away.

"I'll see what I can do, Doc."

"Good. Now lie down. I'll check you over, then sign you out. After that I've got to go; Sarah's waiting. Schwartz'll take you up to Mick and Sandy's, get you settled in."

"Mick and Sandy's ..?" Frank on the razor edge of mood reversal. Careful, Purdue. I gently edged him onto his back.

"Don't worry, Frank—let's get you out of here; then Schwartz'll explain everything on the way. Right, Broadway?"

"No sweat, Doc. Meet you at Lucas' shop in the morning?"

"He opens at ten. We'll be his first visitors."

***

I took Sarah to Rossetti's, a six-table Italian storefront on 8th between 21st and 22nd. Her ear was bothering her and she had a nagging headache. Rapid travel across two time zones upsets people who prefer their days structured into a predictable routine, and Sarah's definitely a schedule freak. I did most of the talking at supper, told her a little more—a *very* little more—about Jitters, and assured her Frank was all right. When I started talking about Edna, Sarah's interest perked. "How terrible—I just can't imagine anyone behaving like that Wilcox person. Edna doesn't need a care facility, does she?"

"Not at all. She can look after herself just fine. But she really does need two hands for her restoration work, and I don't think she's ever going to have two working hands again. Which she knows. Not being able to make a living's probably only the tip of a damned big iceberg."

Sarah swallowed a forkful of spinach. "Well, of course. Restoring and creating those automata ... that's been her life for what, fifty years? Easy to understand why she's so down."

"Easy to understand," I echoed. "Tougher to know what to do about it. I'll stop by tomorrow, see how she's doing. Maybe I'll get a bright idea."

Sarah put down her fork. "Let's go tonight."

Let's? Short for let *us*. "But you're—"

"Tired? Yes, I am, a little. But it won't be time to go to sleep for another three hours."

I forced a sigh back into my chest. My wife may be hungry but she won't eat if it isn't mealtime. My wife may be tired but she won't go to sleep until bedtime.

"And I certainly want to do whatever I can to help Edna.

Why should I just sit around the apartment and read?" Sarah crumpled her napkin, laid it on the table next to her half-eaten salad, pushed away from the table. "Well, come on. Get the check; let's go."

"No dessert? No coffee?"

"Thomas, for goodness sake. You're like a little boy. If I know Edna she'll have cake and coffee on the table five minutes after we're in the door."

Actually it took Edna nearly ten minutes to set out the last of yesterday's chocolate cake and coffee for us. As we sat around the kitchen table chewing and drinking, I told the women about the strange travels of Marcus Wilcox and his music box, about Lucas, about Frank. Dubiety accumulated like a mud pack on Sarah's face. Edna, though, just stared at me with mild tolerance, and as I came to the end of the story she nodded—wearily. Didn't say a word. This was not like Edna. "What's the matter?" I asked.

She waved me off. "Nothing."

"Edna!"

Her eyes flared. Fine. Antipathy is better than no pathy. "Thomas, god*damn* it," she snapped. "*Look*, would you, at my fucking right hand. Lying on the table there like a dead cat. I've been repairing and restoring automata since nineteen fifty-five, and I'm the best—excuse me, *was* the best in the business. Now I'm an ass-up one-armed paperhanger in my own repair shop."

"What happened?"

Unblinking eyeball ice.

"I'm as stubborn as you, Edna, maybe more so. *What ... happened?*"

She sighed. "That little prick, Marcus Wilcox—the *nerve* of him, telling me I ought to put myself away. I decided I'd show him. I went into my repair shop ..."

For the first time I noticed the door to Edna's repair shop was closed. I'd never seen that before.

"... where I used to feel more at home than anywhere else in the world. I looked on the worktable, and there was the Japanese tea-server automaton I'd been restoring when I had my stroke and called you, talking like I was drunk. But that tea-server was a big job, and I thought maybe I should try something easier first, see how it went. 'Like I was drunk' gave me an idea. I'd fix the little drunkard automaton. It didn't really need all that much."

I knew the one she meant, had seen it in the living room on our way into the kitchen. A man slouched on a park bench in front of a lamp post, derby set at a jaunty angle, bottle clutched in his right hand. Above him stood a grim-lipped policeman, brandishing a club. I walked into the living room, pulled the start button on the side of the base. The little man raised his bottle to his lips, whereupon the cop clouted him across the shins with his billy stick. The drunkard's arms and legs flew out in surprise and anger, his mouth opened, and he proceeded to give the cop a solid piece of his mind; for this he was rewarded with another dose of billy, this time atop his head. All this to the music of Offenbach's "*Gaieté Parisienne*," played by a small music-works concealed in the base.

I trotted back to the kitchen, automaton in hand. "You fixed it," I crowed, then pushed the empty plates and cups aside to set the little drunkard down on the table between Edna and Sarah. "It's perfect."

Long sigh. "It was an easy fix ... or it should've been. The wire that links the drunk's arm to the raising-cam came loose so he couldn't get his drink—and hell, if a cop's going to give you a sore head and legs you might as well have your booze. Should've taken me ten minutes, tops, to clean the joint with steel wool, brush on flux, set the wire in place, lay down the solder. But this job took me over an hour. The hardest part was getting the wire square up against the cam and holding it there. I finally got it set with a little alligator clamp. Sweat was pouring over my face, into my eyes, onto the automaton."

She reached over, gave the winding key a couple of turns, pulled the start button. I could almost hear that little drunkard glug as he drank. "But Edna—you did it," I said. "What the hell's the problem?"

"Huh. The problem is, I didn't quit while I was ahead. I figured one down, try the tea-server. I needed to work inside her body, and the last thing I'd done before my stroke was open up the back. So there she was, still lying face-down on the table. I thought maybe I could do the work one-handed if I used that self-retaining retractor of yours."

Not exactly mine. I'd quietly liberated it from Man Med's Surgery Unit. A self-retaining retractor is two steel half-circles, each with a curved projection angling downward, 180 degrees apart. Lower the projections into a patient's abdomen, pull the half-circles apart, and a ratchet holds the instrument open, giving you a nice clear surgical field. Edna's retractor was a small one, pediatric size, equally useful for treating abdominal emergencies in a young child or a doll.

Pain of recollection twisted Edna's face. "I got the retractor into place but when I tried to open it my right hand wouldn't do shit; I just kept pulling the doll to the left. So I set my shoulders, leaned down against the doll and yanked—and the retractor flew up into my face. The doll went sailing off the table."

I held my breath.

Edna rose from her chair, motioned Sarah and me to follow. Out of the kitchen, through the living room; Edna's limp was barely noticeable. She'd've been a ton better off losing the leg and keeping her arm and hand ... but she didn't get to choose.

She opened the door to her workshop and led us inside, past the worktable, to where the tea-server automaton lay on the floor. We stood staring like witnesses to a grisly accident.

The doll looked as if a small bomb had gone off inside it. The papier-mâché body, fully open now in back, lay amidst a mess of gears, wires, and pulleys originally inside the body and presumably properly connected. The ceramic head was nearly a yard farther away from the table, split neatly front-to-back.

The look Edna turned on her right hand might have withered it to a stub. "Stupid goddamn rehab tech at the hospital," she muttered. "Pinned a yellow smiley-face on my blouse and told me I needed to 'acknowledge my limitations.' But I was such a creative person, she was sure I could learn some new, useful skills. Like crocheting potholders to sell at the hospital gift shop. *Shit.*"

She turned away, unable to look further on her disaster. Sarah and I each put an arm around her, led her back into the living room. She stopped short of her chair, looked up at us, groaned. "Thomas, Sarah ... what am I going to *do?*"

"I'm not sure, Edna," I said, then added quickly, "Yet."

She moved off, made her way to the window. Finally she began to speak, slowly, softly, as if addressing the pedestrians flowing through the slanting evening light, four stories down. "You know how long I've been buying distressed automata, the more distressed the better. That wonderful Chinese opium-den automaton behind you: I've never seen another one like it, not even in a picture. When I bought it at auction it was in a cardboard box, in probably a hundred pieces. As I was carrying it out, a certain wealthy collector we both know sneered—actually *sneered* at me. '*I* don't buy damaged goods,' he said. Close to two years I worked on that piece, and then one day he was here to visit and saw it on the table. Didn't recognize it, of course, but he had to have it. He offered me the sun, moon and stars. 'Sorry,' I told him, 'I wouldn't dream of selling you any of my damaged goods.'"

She turned away from the window to face us. "The first time I ever saw an automaton I knew what I was going to do with my life. I went to Switzerland, worked more than five years with Casson. Since then I've been restoring damaged goods ..." Her voice rose, sounded like a cracked reed. "But now *I'm* damaged goods. Who's going to restore *me*?"

"You are, Edna," I said. "You're going to be your own masterpiece."

She sighed, then mumbled, "Excuse me a minute," over her shoulder as she walked past me to the bathroom. Then the door closed behind her. *Slam!*

Sarah pointed at the table next to the chair Edna had been sitting on when we came in. A three-ring album lay open, eight inches of pages. I sat down, picked up the heavy book, plopped it into my lap.

Each pair of open pages was an entity, several pictures of an automaton before and after Edna's restoration, along with a description of her work. I was holding a career-long documentation of passion and accomplishment, balancing the life of a seventy-three-year-old woman on my crossed legs.

It was staggering. Hundreds of musical automata, porcelain dolls and furred animals, brought to Edna in boxes and baskets, sent out from her workshop in glory. If Edna were a doctor she'd have been a top-level consultant, someone who saw only patients with advanced cases of disastrous illnesses. Looking through that album would've caused Jesus to turn away in embarrassment from the raised Lazarus.

"I see you're reviewing my triumphs."

I levitated from the chair, grabbed at the album to keep it from falling.

"Sorry. I didn't mean to scare you."

"I was lost in Wonderland."

Edna hummphed. "No picnic being a has-been, kiddos."

I started to object but she waved me silent. "That's what I am, Thomas—a diddledamn has-been. My head knows what to do, but when it gives my right hand an order it's like saying giddy-up to a dead horse. The night I had my stroke ... longest night of my life. Lying there in that hospital bed, feeling like half my body was gone ... not a prayer of falling asleep. I didn't think morning was *ever* going to come. All night long, sweating like a hog, thinking okay, Edna, wake up now, enough. Move your arm and leg. But I was stuck in a nightmare ... and I still am."

She pressed her lips together, nodded by way of punctuation. "Do you believe in God, Thomas?"

Sarah snorted. "Believe in God? Why, Edna: the real question is whether Thomas believes in *anything*."

Edna and I exchanged a glance. Nothing for Sarah to give me a lick with the rough side of her tongue, but never in front of witnesses. I shook my head, hoping not to upset her further. "Whether there's a God is one of the many things I just plain don't know."

"Well, I just plain don't *believe*," Edna snapped. "Never have. But right now I hope I'm wrong—I hope there *is* a God. Because then when I die I'll be able to tell Him what I think about the way He runs His business. He treats His beloved people shabbily. At best He's goddamn careless; at worst He's a cruel son of a bitch."

I had no trouble seeing Edna, wings sprouting from her back, giving the Lord both barrels, maybe threatening to clout Him one with her harp. I smiled, couldn't help it.

Neither could she. She took the album from my lap, deposited it gently on the table top. "You're a good friend, Thomas," she said. "You too, Sarah. I want you to always remember, I appreciate everything you've both done for me."

Nice sentiment, but too much of the valedictory about it. "Works both ways," I said cautiously. "I appreciate all *you've* done for *me*. And are still doing."

She didn't take the bait, just sighed again. A thought popped into my head, one I didn't care for in the least. I got up, stretched, said, "My turn," then headed off to the bathroom.

When I came back a couple of minutes later I was holding a small brown bottle in each hand. "Edna ... look what I found in your medicine cabinet. A hundred Amytal; a hundred Nembutal. Could put a person to sleep for a long time."

Sarah's eyes were like flying saucers. Her cheeks looked chalked.

I made a show of examining the labels. "The Leisure Years Home, Long Island City ... wonder how these got into your medicine cabinet."

I thought she was going to give *me* both barrels, right between the eyes, but all I got was a small, sad smile. "I call it The Seizure Years Home," she said quietly. "My friend Sadie Moskow's spending the last of her golden days there. I ... uh ... well, shit. I noticed they're not overly careful about keeping their pill cabinets locked. So last night when I went to see Sadie, I ran out to the nursing station and hollered at the nurse, 'Get in there quick, my friend is choking to death.' Soon as she was around the corner I grabbed the pills." Edna extended her hand. "Now please give them back."

"No way," I said, and slipped them into my pants pocket.

Once again I thought I was going to get a major league what-for, but Edna's face softened. Almost in a whisper, she said, "It's time for my ride on the Midnight Special. Please give me back my ticket."

"The Midnight Special?" I asked. "As in Pete Seeger? Midnight train shines its light on a prisoner in his cell, he goes free by morning?"

Edna looked as if I'd plopped a half-pound of raw, dripping hamburger into her hand and she couldn't figure out what to do with it. I settled myself into a faded green wingback chair, tapped fingers on the armrest. Edna lowered herself by degrees onto the sofa. Sarah sat at her side, rested a hand on the old woman's shoulder.

"Tell us, Edna," I said.

Quick chew at her lip, then Edna started to speak, slowly, softly. "I was born in Tremont, Oregon ... tiny town east of Portland. Railroads ran through, into and out of Portland every day; lots of freights, and three passenger runs. The Midday Regular and the Evening Limited stopped in Tremont, but the Midnight Special just whistled at the crossing and blew right on past. I never fell fast asleep 'til I heard the Midnight Special go by."

Edna's fingers clenched. "An old couple lived next door, Mr. and Mrs. Svengaard, and just about every day that's where I was, watching Mister do his woodwork. He built tables, chairs, cabinets, anything. He showed me how to hold a saw to get a clean cut, how to drive a nail without leaving hammer marks on the wood." Edna shook her head. "One morning, I was six years old ... I woke up and Mr. Svengaard was gone. Mother told me he was up in the stars with God and the angels."

Edna's voice went husky. I leaned forward in my chair.

"Less than a year after that, Mother and Dad decided to move to Pennsylvania. Dad's brother owned a farm near Harrisburg; he wanted Dad to come work it with him. So we sold the house and furniture, packed up our things, and rode into Portland late one evening on Mr. Dahlgren's wagon. Dad got a sleeping compartment on the Midnight Special, four nights and days to Philadelphia. We went aboard, the whistle blew, the train started rolling ... and I fell asleep.

"When I woke up it was dark. I pulled back the curtain and looked out. The train was rushing along through a bowl of stars—I'd never *seen* so many stars. They danced around me like they were playing hide-and-seek. We must've been going through a town because the engineer blew a long, loud blast on the whistle. So that's how it works, I said to myself. You buy a ticket on the Midnight Special and ride up into the stars. I looked for Mr. Svengaard, called his name, but next thing I knew it was bright light, all the stars gone, and my mother telling me if I wanted to go to the dining car and have breakfast I'd better not be such a sleepyhead. I got up and went along, but I couldn't talk, couldn't say a word. Dad thought I was just dozy; he gave me sips of his coffee. That was more than sixty-five years ago but it's as fresh in my head as the night it happened. I never heard Pete Seeger sing that song without seeing Mr. Svengaard."

She pointed at my pants pocket. "I'm ready for my ride, Thomas." Voice back to normal. "Bad enough to be the way I am now—but what if I have another stroke and end up like Sadie, lying in a pissed-up bed at Seizure Years?" She held out her hand. "Now please: be a *real* friend. Give me back my ticket."

No sweet chariot swinging low for to carry our Edna home. Her long journey would be by express train, and heaven help any fool who ignored warning gates to try to flag it down.

I took a deep breath, shook my head. "Your train's not in yet, Edna. Sorry."

Edna of the gimlet eyes. "My train's not in yet? It's *my* diddledamn train, not yours."

"But it's not your train. You got upset and misread the date on the ticket. Now listen, Edna. Promise me you won't get on that train and I'll make you two promises back."

I thought she might tell me where to stuff my two promises, but her mouth curled into a curious little smile. Good; this was the Edna I wanted to see.

"Okay, Promise One: If you ever get to be nursing home material I'll make sure you never go."

I could see she knew I meant it. "And Promise Two?"

"I'll help you get back to doing your restorations. I admit, right now I don't know exactly how. But—"

"You 'don't know exactly how.'" Edna mimicked me viciously. "You don't even have a goddamn clue. My arm and hand are dead, so what do you think you're going to do—say a few magic words and sprinkle a little holy water—"

Sarah bounced to her feet, mouth twisted, fists clenched in front of her chest. She glared at me, then turned full heat on Edna. "The two of you!" she snapped. "Playing word games about trains and stars and tickets. I've come to expect that sort of thing from *you*, Thomas, but Edna ... well, I didn't think I'd *ever* see Edna Reynolds trying to take an easy way out."

I held my breath. Had anyone ever talked to Edna like this and lived to tell about it? I didn't dare look at her, though Sarah right then was no visual picnic herself.

"I've known you a long time." Sarah clipped each word like a surgeon excising a particularly offensive bit of abnormal tissue. "And I would've expected better from you. Yes, you've had a stroke, your hand won't work, and that's not easy to take. But your life is *not* over. How long have you known Thomas? If he says he's going to think of something, do you have any doubt he will?"

As if someone were channel-surfing behind her eyes, Edna's face flickered between dubiousness and hope. Yes, I did have her ticket in my pocket but I knew she could easily get a reissue. I needed to keep her out of the terminal.

"Give me a month," I said. "For one month, promise me

you won't do anything drastic. If I can't convince you by then to put off your train ride I'll give you back your ticket and you can jump aboard whenever you want."

A moment's pause. "You mean that?"

"Would I lie to you?"

Sarah looked stricken. Edna started to chuckle, then broke into a full-throated laugh. I joined her. Sarah stood there, hand to mouth, as if she couldn't figure what to say to two such naughty children. But I knew our laughter was as good as a handshake, gave me a promise of a month. Without that, I'd've bet the farm Edna would've been speeding through the stars that night, one-way ticket, no return.

5

Next morning, five minutes before eight, knock-knock. Jitters, right on time. When I opened the door he scuttled crab-like into the room, music box tucked under his arm.

"Ready to work?" I asked.

A nod. "Yeah."

"Grandpa's happy?"

"Sure."

"Nice subway ride up from One-Ten Rivington?" Silence. "Or did you hoof it? From One-Ten Rivington?"

"Yeah."

A young man of very few words. "Jitters?"

"What?"

"Look at me."

From the time he came into the room he'd been looking everywhere but into my eyes. Slowly, he turned his head, met my gaze.

"Know what's up, Jitters?"

"Whuzzup?" His hands twitched, quivered; he took a tighter grip on the music box.

"The jig, Jitters. That's what's up. You and Grandpa don't live at One-Ten Rivington anymore, do you?"

Pause. Stare. "You went and checked."

"Can you blame me?"

Embarrassed smile. He set the music box down on the work-table, then moved toward the door.

"Jitters, where're you going?"

He turned, made confused motions with his hands. "Back ... I don't know. I figured—"

"You figured you flunked the final," I said. "But that was only the mid-term." I pointed at the music box. "You had every chance to dump that, if not to Sophie, to somebody else, but here it is with you—"

"I'd *never* sell it," the boy blurted. "I never *heard* nothin' like—"

"Right! You pulled it out, Jitters, big A-plus on the final. If anyone owes apologies I do: where you live, who you live with, that's none of my business. Here." I slipped two bills out of my wallet, handed them to Jitters.

Which left him thoroughly confused. "What's this?"

"What's it look like? Two hundred dollars, your first week's pay in advance. I should've given it to you when we met; you obviously needed it. What'd I think—you dropped in on me the way you did for a little exercise?"

Jitters tore his eyes away from mine, looked at the work-bench with such anguish my own stomach knotted against my throat. "What's the matter?" I asked. "Don't you want to learn how to restore music boxes?"

Like turning a switch. His eyes flashed. "Sure ... well, *sure* I do. But—"

Lights out. He'd gone one small word further than he'd

intended. "But what?" I said. "Come on, Jitters, talk. What's the big problem?"

"I'm sorry," he howled. "I feel bad, I mean ... how I came in here with a gun, going to rob you and all ... and you give me a job and a music box worth a lot of dough ... even give me *money*. I don't deserve—"

"Don't worry," I said. "We usually don't get what we deserve, and most of the time we should be grateful for that. As for the money, I'm not giving it to you; you're going to work for it. But not quite yet. We've got to wait 'til tomorrow to start." Jitters looked like I'd slapped his face. "Emergency," I said. "I'm sorry. I really am."

The boy forced a wan smile. "Guess emergencies happen with doctors, huh?"

"Sometimes." I picked up the music box, handed it back to him. "Hold onto it for another day—unless you'd like to leave it here." His face said he'd sooner leave both his arms. "Fine. See you at eight tomorrow. And oh, yeah ... one other thing. About my wife."

Eyes wide with anxiety scanned the room. "What?"

"Relax, she's not here. She goes out to work about a quarter to eight, isn't back 'til about five-thirty. Sarah's ... oh ... let's say she's straight as they come. She knows you're going to be working here, but not ..." Jitters looked frantically at the skylight. "Glazier's coming any time now," I said. "I told Sarah I thought it was a break-in that never went any further—didn't lie, did I?"

The boy wasn't sure whether to smile or look scared.

"But if she connects you with it, we're both dead. Far as

she's concerned you heard about my music boxes from some antique dealer, you came over, we hit it off, I offered you work. Got it?"

Poor Jitters was in full-body palpitation. "Yeah ... sure. Whatever you say."

A little after ten, Schwartz and I were sitting with Lucas Sterne at the back of his showroom. Don't call it a shop, worse, a store. Not if you want Lucas Sterne, Prop. to continue on speaking terms with you.

From behind his desk Lucas studied us, tried some quick mental arithmetic. "You must forgive me," he simpered. "But when I walk up to my showroom door on a lovely June morning and find the Hardy-Har-Har Boys waiting to 'talk to me,' I can't help feeling just the tiniest bit, shall we say ... apprehensive?"

Slim, trim Lucas in his crow suit: black pullover, black slacks, the better to set off his wide, dark eyes and cascades of black curls—though with Lucas now creeping reluctantly up on forty, I suspect he spends more than a little time in front of his bathroom mirror, brushing away salt. No less black and white is his personality, a curious blend of the highly admirable and darkly contemptible. Lucas is an expert re-storer, highly conversant with mechanical-music history; I've seen him choke up at the sound of a particularly fine early cylinder music box. On the other hand, he's Lucas-at-the-Rathole for elderly NYMBCA members. Local legend holds that before a collector's corpse reaches room temperature Lucas has the spouse's signature on a sales contract.

"Apprehensive, Lucas? I can't imagine why." I zapped him with a big smile. "Maybe we've made you sweat just the tiniest bit here or there—but considering how well you always came out in the end I thought you might roll out a thick red carpet for us."

Schwartz snickered.

A burgundy mantle worked its way from the sides of Lucas' nose toward his ears. "Don't push your luck, Thomas. I don't have all day; I really do run a business here. What do you want to talk to me about?"

"A music box, of course, what else?" I pointed toward the front of the shop, where an elderly man and a young woman were quietly browsing the machines. "Want to look after your customers? We'll wait."

Lucas shook his head. "Tire kickers." Then he called out, "If you'd like to hear any of my wonderful music boxes, just ask; I'll be delighted to play them for you." The woman acknowledged him with a forced smile and a nod, the man with a noncommittal grunt.

Lucas flashed a nasty little smirk. "You want to talk about a music box, Thomas? Surely I have nothing here to tempt a collector of your advanced standing."

Surely he was right. Lucas' stock ran to the common and flashy: late nineteenth century production-line music boxes with lots of nickel plate and case inlay, with bells to clank and drums to roll, thereby drowning out musical arrangements so dreadful they rightfully should've been strangled at birth. Price tags on these gaudy garbage boxes ran about double knowledgeable-collector value—because knowledgable collectors

never shopped at the Lucas Sterne Music Box Emporium. Lucas'
clientele ran to the un-knowledgeable wealthy impulse-purchas-
ing noncollector. "No, there's *not* anything here to tempt me," I
said. "I'm interested in a box you apparently did *not* get to put out,
a revolver box. An elderly gentleman, the owner, and a frou-frou
interior designer wanted you to patch it together so they could
sell it. But sadly, not to you."

The more I said, the more Lucas looked as if he'd taken a
whopping bite of curdled cottage cheese. "Thomas, I can't see
that this is any of your business. Can you tell me—"

"Sure I can tell you. Schwartz noticed this music box a few
days ago, sitting in Mr. Frou-frou's shop. First thing next morning I went in to scope it, and guess what. Not only was it gone,
but the designer—Marcus Wilcox?—"

Lucas nodded.

"—told me it never existed."

Schwartz looked about to burst. "And I ain't exactly in the
habit of hallucinating music boxes—especially one *that* size."

"Then a couple of goons beat up Frank the Crank. They
were looking for information about a revolver box he'd supposedly sold to Marcus Wilcox. Frank told me he'd never
seen the box, but he remembered a little talk he had with you
about a month ago. That's why I'm here."

Give Lucas this: he looked genuinely concerned. "Is
Frank ... all right?"

"Basically. No major damage, but he's going to hurt for a
while—body's covered with bruises and cigarette burns."

Color drained from Lucas' face. He watched the young
woman go out the door; the older man was obviously working his way along the same path.

"Who knows, Lucas?" I said softly. "Help me, you may be helping yourself."

Lucas leaned to his right, pulled open the bottom drawer of a metal file cabinet, flipped through folders. A puff of air shimmied the curls on his forehead; automatically, he shook them back into place. He plucked a file from the drawer, laid it ceremoniously on the desk in front of Schwartz and me. He arched an eyebrow. "Go ahead. Open it."

Inside was a single sheet of paper, headed Appraisal: Antique music box by Paillard, six-cylinder plerodienique-revolver, circa 1875.

Lucas picked up on my expression.

"Plerodienique-revolver?" I croaked.

"Mmm. Yes, indeed. Ever see one?"

I shook my head. "I've seen a plerodienique, and I've seen a revolver, but not in combination. Never heard of one either."

"Nor had I."

Schwartz looked like a spectator at the World Series of Ping Pong.

"P-l-e-r-o-d-i-e-n-i-q-u-e," I said. "Rarer, even, than a revolver. Cylinder's in two parts—left half keeps playing while the right half shifts, then vice versa, so you can pin a single tune to play through several revolutions of the cylinder. The one I saw was at Randy Stockton's in Chicago. One cylinder played the whole *Barber of Seville* overture, gorgeous. Even when Randy got the shorts a few years back, no one could pry that box away from him. He could've got, oh, fifty-K, I'd guess, same as for a revolver. But a plerodienique-revolver"—I looked down to the bottom of Lucas' appraisal page. "Two hundred thousand, Lucas? You're serious?"

"I'd hardly put down such a figure casually." His tone suggested ice was creaking beneath my feet. "A piece that unusual wouldn't even have made it into my showroom. One phone call to any of four or five particular collectors, and it would've been gone. But Wilcox and his friend just wanted me to clean it, make it shine and play properly, then take my hourly fee and say thank you. Apparently they had their own ideas about selling it. 'Fine,' I told them, 'if all you want is a technician, I'll tell you where to go.' "

"And where might that have been?"

Lucas mugged as if on camera. "I referred them to Barton Moss."

Schwartz coughed, choked.

"I *can* be a son of a bitch," Lucas murmured.

Handsome is as handsome does. Barton Moss calls himself a music box restorer, but most NYMBCA members call him a garage mechanic—derogatory moniker for a hack with no respect for either his own work or that of the Swiss makers who created these marvelous instruments from parts machined to ultra-close tolerances. When a good restorer runs up against a mechanism that won't go back together or won't play as it should after reassembly, he looks for his own error, something he missed. Barton Moss just grabs a mallet and gives the recalcitrant machine a couple of stiff whacks. That's bad enough—but Barton also tends to drink more than is good for him, whether on the job or off. In his over-lubricated state he's destroyed more than one machine entrusted to his care. Few NYMBCAns will give him any work beyond the repair of a broken spring; what living he makes comes from people who don't know any better—general antique dealers and one-box noncollectors.

I was horrified. Being a son of a bitch is one thing, but to steer a plerodienique-revolver to Barton Moss? "Lucas, how the hell could you *do* that?"

Lucas waved off my concern. "It didn't need much: clean, polish, a little damper work, a broken spring. I told the idiots what that work *should* cost, and suggested they offer Barton twice as much to get it done—to their satisfaction—within a month."

"That could go a long way toward explaining why somebody's backtracking," I said. "The box might've blown up in the buyer's face ten minutes after he got it home."

Lucas made a languid, not-my-problem wave, then continued the movement into a greeting for someone at the front of the shop. "Be with you in a moment," he crooned.

I looked around, saw Derrick and Rochelle Mendota just inside the front door. Derrick and Shelly were NYMBCA members, in their mid-seventies, not all that active for the past few years. "Thomas, Broadway," Shelly called out. "Hel-*lo*." Derrick acknowledged us with a nod and a tight smile.

"I didn't know they were still buying," I whispered across the desk to Lucas.

"People do sell, Thomas. Sorry, but we need to finish up."

I looked back at the appraisal sheet. Serial number: 67032. Owner: Rudolph Hartmann, address down on Perry Street, phone number. "Mind if I write some of this down?" I asked Lucas.

"I'll make you a copy," he said. "If Frank got beaten up because of some game that moron owner and his designer friend are playing, I'm only too glad to help you sock it to them."

Lucas trotted off to the copy machine at the rear of the shop. Schwartz and I walked in the opposite direction, shook hands with Derrick and Shelly. "Lucas tells me you're selling some of your collection," I said.

They looked at each other. You tell him. No, *you* tell him. Finally, Derrick spoke. "We're ... uh, selling the entire collection, Thomas. Everything."

If not world-class, their collection was still a nice assortment of good-quality cylinder and disc music boxes, acquired over some thirty years of picking and choosing. I gave them a doctorly up-down. "That's a surprise. You're both ... all right?"

"Oh yes, yes, certainly." Derrick moved his hand rapidly back and forth in front of his face, as if that would dispel any possibility of impending illness or death. "It's just ... well, none of our children have the least interest in music boxes ... and we thought it would be best not to burden them ..."

Derrick fell silent as Lucas came forward, copy in hand. "Here you are, Thomas—just one favor, if you please. This is for reference only, *not* for circulation. Promise."

I folded the paper, tucked it into my shirt pocket. "No sweat, Lucas. Thanks for the privilege of your communication."

Sour smirk. "I'm sure you're an excellent physician, but I'd just as soon not find myself in need of your tender ministrations."

"Thanks, Lucas. Makes two of us." I nodded to the Mendotas. "Hope you'll still come to NYMBCA meetings."

Derrick's face tightened. Shelly bit her upper lip. "Well ... yes," Derrick finally managed. "Yes ... of course."

Barton Moss lived in New Rochelle, the last house on Randall, a short, dead-end street. Schwartz and I pulled up a little after noon, parked the Vee-Dub in front of Barton's bashed chain-link fence. Schwartz doffed his black fedora, wiped a handkerchief over his forehead, then clamped the hat back on and whistled. "Place makes Tobacca Road look like Fifth Avenue."

No argument. The small house facing us looked as if it had been done over by the Decorator for the Damned. Lengths of siding sagged away from the structure as if in re-vulsion. Once—long ago—it had been painted white. A front window was covered with a sheet of carelessly-applied plas-tic; the roof shingles looked anemic. Behind the house to the left was Barton's workshop, a squarish slat-sided shed ham-mered into existence over a couple of drunken weekends. House and shed were surrounded by a map-like array of foot-high weeds and bald dirt. I didn't come often to Barton's, but every time I visited I swore it couldn't look worse—and ev-ery time I came back, it did.

I opened the car door. "Let's get it over with, Broadway."

We pushed past the rusty gate, walked up the cracked concrete path to the front door. No bell. I knocked once, then again, harder. Nothing.

Schwartz pointed to the shed. "Maybe he's workin'."

We picked our way through the piebald meadow, trying to keep to bare spots, the better to avoid the dog turd concealed in the high grasses. Barton didn't own a dog, never did, but it was as if the neighborhood pooches had gotten together and designated Barton Moss's yard as their regional drop point.

I put my ear to the shed door, heard nothing. Then I knocked, taking care not to splinter the fragile wooden panel. From inside I heard a scraping noise, then footsteps. The door opened, and there in all his repellent glory stood Barton Moss.

Picture Ichabod Crane immediately after his encounter with the Headless Horseman. Lank black hair, not cut or even combed for weeks. Last shave probably three days ago. Behind swollen lids, eyeballs like street guides of metropolitan New York City. Filthy white T-shirt, equal measures of grease and food. Ratty, grimy jeans. No socks, left shoelace untied. I congratulated myself on putting off lunch until the return trip.

Barton blinked into the sunlight. A sour smell washed over us, whether from the workshop or Barton himself, I couldn't tell. Schwartz tried not to wrinkle his nose.

"Hi, Barton," I said. "How's tricks?"

Barton glanced at Schwartz, then back at me. He worked his tongue over his lips, looked thoroughly bewildered, as well he might. What the hell were Thomas Purdue and Broadway Schwartz up to now? I've never gone to see Moss on anything other than a mission of harassment, whether to worm information out of him or reclaim a music box some innocent had left in his hooch-headed care. Which was it today?

"Can I ask you a couple of questions?" I said.

"'Bout what?"

"A music box. What else?"

"Don't know if I got the time."

"You'll find the time if you make me come back here with a cop," I said. "Or a lawyer. Or both."

I had no grounds to justify either approach, but Barton didn't know that. He also didn't know why I was there, but you can bet there's always something going on in Barton's life that would turn unpleasant in a hurry if an attorney or a policeman happened to get involved. Barton flicked a coated tongue over his scabby lower lip, then stepped outside and pulled the door shut. "Make it quick," he muttered. "I ain't got all day."

The notion of spending all day in the company of Barton Moss left me far closer to nauseated than enthusiastic. "I'm interested in a certain music box you worked on just recently," I said. "A plerodienique-revolver."

Swillbellies don't play good poker—no missing the flash of fear in Barton's eyes. "Don't know what you're talking about," he mumbled.

"I told you—a plerodienique-revolver, six cylinders. Might be a little tough, considering how many of those you've worked on during the past two months, so let me help you. Paillard, number sixty-seven, oh-three-two. Clean-and-polish, broken spring, some dampering. Lucas Sterne sent it your way."

Barton rubbed his chin between thumb and forefinger. "Lucas Sterne told you I worked on it?"

Well, not quite. Lucas said he'd made the referral, but not every music box owner who gets the name of a restorer follows through. I shrugged. "Sure Lucas told me. That's why I'm here."

The intensity of Barton's reply surprised me. "Well, Lucas

is a lying prick, okay? That little faggot wouldn't send me work
if I kicked him back half." He jabbed an index finger into my
breastbone. "I ain't about to take any fall on accounta Lucas
Sterne. *Fuck* Lucas Sterne. Okay? You finished?"

I took a half-step backward to get beyond the poke range
of Barton's finger and the aura from his armpits. "Not yet.
The owner of the music box was an elderly gentleman, a Mr.
Rudolph Hartmann. He was working with an interior designer
named Marcus Wilcox. That help you remember?"

Barton's hands fluttering in front of his face made me
think of butterflies on mescaline. "I don't know what the
hell you're talkin' about," he shouted. "I never saw any
plerodienique-revolver music box; I never *worked* on one. I
don't know any Hartmann or ... or ..."

He half-turned away; I was losing him. "Marcus Wilcox,"
I said quickly. "*He* told me you worked on the music box,
too."

"Then they're botha them liars," Barton screeched. "I
don't know anything about that music box and I don't know
those guys from Adam. Now fuck off. I got work to do."

The shed door slammed behind him.

"He's just a poor dumb music box restorer," Schwartz
mimicked. "Don't know nothin' about nothin' or no one.
But the way he looked when you mentioned the music box
and those two names? I bet he's in there changin' his under-
pants right now."

I charged across the narrow stretch of weeds between concrete path and shed, crouched under the single grimy window to
the left of the door. Slowly, I straightened up, shaded my eyes,

peered inside. Sure enough, Barton was on the phone, and to describe his end of the conversation as animated would be to grossly understate. Free arm waving, feet stamping, head bobbing. No question I'd hit home. Who the hell was he jawing at? I put my ear to the wall, then to the glass, but no dice. Oh, for a stethoscope. I motioned to Schwartz, next best choice, and stepped aside. Dropping his fedora to the ground, he applied right ear to window, plugged the left with a finger, beetled his face in concentration. After a moment he shook his head. "He's upset, all right, Doc, big time. But I can't make out why, or who he's lettin' go at."

I thought of blowing into the room and grabbing the phone away from Moss—but no point. Whoever might be at the other end of the connection, Wilcox or Hartmann or someone else, would hang up the instant he heard my voice. "Come on," I said to Schwartz. "Time to bark up a different tree."

On our ride back to town we decided to give Hartmann's tree first bark. We left the car in my parking garage on West 15th, monthly rental more than Sarah's sister pays for her house in Jordan Falls, Montana. Then we hoofed it to 8th, turned downtown, stopped at 14th long enough to pick up a couple of potato knishes and Dr. Brown's Cel-Ray sodas from a vendor, munched and swigged our way past 11th to Perry.

The address on Lucas's appraisal was just east of Washington Street, a low apartment building with the appearance of a dyspeptic hippo. Its façade was of those dark brown and yellowish-tan bricks they seemed to favor in the early 1900s. Built to last, probably with plaster walls a foot thick. Across the street, an elderly couple studied us from their second-story deck, a triangular platform just large enough for two canvas chairs, cut from the corner of the '60s red-brick building. No landed English gentleman and lady on their spacious veranda ever turned a haughtier, more proprietary eye upon their domain.

We swallowed our last mouthfuls, did a little facial house-keeping with napkins, threw paper and bottles into a receptacle on the corner, garishly painted with the message **NEW YORK IS NOT SQUARE OR A GARBAGE CAN**. Then we climbed the three concrete steps to the stoop, checked the names above the door-bells. HARTMANN was neatly lettered above Number One.

I pushed the buzzer.

"Yes? Can I help you?"

Schwartz and I both jumped a foot; the words had come from behind us, rather than the speaker-box above the door buzzers. The voice was loud but not abrasive. Hearty.

I turned to face a man leaning out an open window to our left. Two huge hands practically covered the sill. Mid-seventies, big but not fat, a geriatric jock. Full head of wavy white hair brushed pompadour-style high off the forehead. His facial skin was rough, cheeks ruddy. Eyes blue, clear, questioning.

"Can I help you?" the man repeated.

I nodded. "My name is Thomas Purdue; this is my friend Broadway Schwartz. Are you Rudolph Hartmann?"

"Yes?" There was a clearly-understood "So" between the one-word reply and the question mark.

"We'd like to talk to you ... about your music box. The plerodienique-revolver."

At my elbow I felt Schwartz freeze. I held my breath, hoped

Hartmann'd be sufficiently curious or concerned that he'd give us a better reception than Moss had.

The old man ran eye tape over us. Finally he nodded. "I'll buzz you in. First door to your left, directly inside."

He vanished, then the buzzer sounded. I pushed through the doorway, Schwartz right behind me. By the time the door closed Hartmann was waiting for us in his open doorway.

He *was* big, six-two or three, about two hundred well-packed pounds. Nicely dressed: light-blue silk shirt, crisp dark-blue summer worsted pants. But I noticed the shirt cuffs were just a bit thready, the pocket slightly frayed to either side of his pen clip. "Come in, come in," he said. Again, that ingratiating tone, odd. Almost too eager to please.

Hartmann closed the door behind us. More surprises. We stood in a large living room made to look even larger by the spareness of its contents. A few stark black-and-white prints hung on whitewashed walls. Furniture all chrome and white cloth, but strikingly little of it: love seat on the east wall, sofa between two straight-backed chairs on the south, low coffee table in front of the sofa. On the table stood a clay sculpture, two and a half feet tall, with an ebony base, male and female figures in loving embrace. Two spindly rubber plants framed the front windows. At the back of the room was a glass-topped dining table surrounded by four chrome-and-white chairs; to the left of this eating space I could see into the kitchen: refrigerator and stove. The place had the appearance of transition, someone either moving out or in.

From behind the back wall I heard a child-like voice, sing-song, as if reciting a nursery rhyme. Schwartz's face told me he also heard the voice, but if Hartmann picked up on our silent communication he didn't tip. "You said you wanted to talk to me about some sort of music box, Mr. ..."

"Purdue," I said. "Thomas Purdue." My extended hand disappeared inside Hartmann's massive paw. "My friend, Broadway Schwartz. Yes, we *are* interested in a particular music box, a quite rare, valuable plerodienique-revolver."

Hartmann worked his lips up and down, side to side. "What makes you think you'll find it here?" He extended his arms as if to take in the apartment. "I'm hardly a music box collector ... as you can see."

Singsong, singsong in the background. Could get to you. "I didn't really think we'd find the box here," I said. "But I hope we can get some information about it. Look, Mr. Hartmann: not to play games with you. Schwartz saw that music box in an interior design shop, the Palais Royal, over on Third. Owned by a man named Marcus Wilcox."

Hartmann's body stiffened, all pretense instantly gone. His hands clenched into bomb-like fists. Harsh whisper, one word: "When?"

"Just a couple of days ago. I'm a collector, would've been interested in buying it. But when I went to see it, Wilcox swore it didn't exist, said he hadn't had a music box in months."

"That lying son of a bitch!"

Someone gives you a giftie, take it with thanks. "Mr. Hartmann, I'm really concerned about what might be going on over this music box. Day before yesterday, two goons worked over a very good friend of mine, an antique dealer; they were trying to find out where he'd gotten a plerodienique-revolver he'd supposedly sold. Happens my friend never laid eyes on the box—but someone wanted somebody else to think he had. Which led me to ..."

Go on, said Hartmann's eyes.

"Lucas Sterne. The antique world's a tight little group. Lucas told me about you and Wilcox, how you got his appraisal and asked him to repair the box, but didn't want to sell to him. So he sent you to Barton Moss. I've known Barton a long time and it's no trouble to get information out of him. Just add a little alcohol and squeeze judiciously."

Hartmann, clearly teetering on the cusp, dog-eyed Schwartz and me. I pulled my wallet, flipped it open to the card section, showed Hartmann my medical license. "I'm a neurologist over at Man Med, collect and restore antique music boxes for fun and games. And as long as I've been at it, I've never seen a combination plerodienique-revolver. So figure the odds that two of them are moving around New York right now, let alone that Marcus Wilcox is involved with both. If *I* can find you, so can someone else—and judging from what someone else did to my friend, your visit with him isn't going to be nearly as congenial as this one."

Hartmann swallowed, an audible gulp. "All right, gentlemen. Maybe we can help each other."

He turned and strode toward a door at the back of the room, stopped halfway, motioned us forward. "I was going to get some pictures of the music box to show you," he said. "But I think you need to know the whole story. Come along with me—just don't ... well, don't be put off by what you see and hear. You ... *are* a doctor."

"Maybe *I* ain't, but I pretty much seen it all." Schwartz, never to be considered chopped liver.

Hartmann smiled. "Come on, then."

As we approached the door, the singsong got louder. Now it sounded like a little girl, but I still couldn't make out words. Hartmann, hand on doorknob, paused, then turned the knob firmly and pushed the door open. Schwartz and I followed him into the room.

If the living room was odd, this space was bizarre. Strategically located ceiling spotlights illuminated immaculate white walls. I wanted to shade my eyes. Across the room stood a filing cabinet, a small desk with an electric typewriter, a large wooden slideout shelf unit, and a table of light wood such as an architect or draftsman might use, strewn with paper. All around the perimeter, dolls perched on tiny chairs or sat on miniature Victorian sofas. Next to the door stood an impressive red-roofed dollhouse, three stories high, each room filled with toy furniture and accessories, and peopled with peewee dolls. Hartmann saw me staring at a large black perambulator more than three feet long, in mint condition, a hundred years old if a day. He nodded, then reached to push a steel lever which folded back the head-cover. Now I could see a striking life-sized girl-doll with sparkling blue eyes, creamy painted-porcelain skin and a luxurious blonde wig beneath a red and green knitted beret set jauntily to the right.

Seemingly oblivious to us, a small figure hunched over a table in the far corner. It was moving its hands and arms, and apparently singing itself a song, though not one I could come close to recognizing. Hartmann walked over, rested a hand lightly on the person's shoulder. "Lettie, dear," he said softly. "We have company. Would you like to say hello?"

The figure turned slowly, regarded Schwartz and me with feral eyes, wily and uncomprehending. Her face twisted into an expression of apparent pain, then horror-tinged loathing, finally tentative amusement punctuated by a silly giggle. She began to gesture with her arms like Circe in the process of turning Ulysses' crew into pigs. I thought of a little girl auditioning for the heavy role in a first-grade play.

When the old woman started to speak—or better, screech—waves of gooseflesh flew up and down my arms and across the back of my neck. "Lettie, Lettie, eat spaghetti, never fretty, sweaty Betty, hello, hello, mellow fellow, I want Jell-o, give me Jell-o."

Lettie was as disconcerting as any patient I'd ever seen. The skin of her face was like alligatored varnish on an ancient piece of furniture, eyes those of a cruelly tortured animal. Her hair, white as the walls around her, was gathered into a red-ribboned ponytail and topped with a maroon artist's beret set as jauntily as the one on the perambulator-doll. She had long, graceful fingers, even covered as they were with gray clay, and she held them out in front of her chest like a symphony conductor wielding ten batons. A flowered apron tied behind her neck and at her waist had only been partially successful in preventing her from clay-smearing her white cotton summer dress. Mounds of grayish clay, haphazardly and irregularly shaped, stood on the table before the old woman, who continued to dart bright green eyes from Schwartz to me, then back. Her lips moved incessantly but I could hear only the softest murmur, probably a mishmash of nonsense rhymes and clang associations, her own private background music. Schwartz shuffled from one foot to the other. Maybe he really hadn't seen it all.

Hartmann smiled gently at the woman; he must have squeezed her shoulder because she turned her attention up to him. The air in the room seemed to have palpable weight. "This is Dr. Purdue, Lettie," Hartmann said, pointing my way. "And his friend, Mr. Schwartz. Gentlemen, my wife."

"Wife, knife, strife all my life ..." Lettie squeezed her eyes shut, then a hand shot out as if she were trying to catch an insect in flight. For a moment she went back to playing ocular tennis with Schwartz and me. "... Purdue, derpoo, screw the stew, defend, commend the friend, Mister-Pister Schwartz-Quartz in shorts." At that point the old woman turned around in her chair and began to knead the closest lump of clay, accompanying herself with that private singsong.

Hartmann held up an index finger in our direction, then went across the room, opened the top drawer of the file cabinet, took out a large brown envelope. He pointed toward the door; I followed Schwartz out.

With the door closed behind us, and Lettie's self-directed conversation again barely audible, Hartmann motioned us to the far end of the room. Schwartz and I sat on the sofa, Hartmann on one of the straight-backed chairs. He sighed, smiled weakly, finally got himself going. "As you can see, gentlemen, my wife is ... not well." His voice was soft, throaty. "Not getting better, either, nor will she ... though they tell me she could live several years, deteriorating all the while. Her doctors have advised me to put her away ..." His voice rose on the last word, cracked; he wiped at his eyes, swallowed hard. "But Lettie deserves better, gentlemen. She was a sculptor, you know. *Very* well regarded."

He inclined his head to indicate the clay man and woman in embrace on the coffee table beside us. "She and I," Hartmann said. "A gift to me on our twenty-fifth anniversary ... more than twenty-five years ago. She always said I was her inspiration, her muse ... which to tell the truth is about all I really ever *was*. I made a good start in life, but turned out to be one of these promising young men who never do keep those promises. Decorated war hero, BMOC-football player at Penn State ... then I graduated and had no idea what to do with myself. So I fiddled around in the art world, became a gallery gofer—a promo man, drink-buyer, doer of lunches. Then I met Lettie and she became my career. I was her manager. She created, I marketed. Have you ever heard of her, gentlemen? Lettie Hartmann?"

Schwartz coughed. *Chutzpah*-loaded as my little friend is, he's the last person to hurt someone's feelings. I shook my head. "No reflection on your wife; visual art's just never been my thing. If she'd been a musician I'd have heard of her. How prominent was she?"

Hartmann smiled openly: nice even white teeth. "Truthfully, Dr. Purdue, not in the very top rank—but right at the front of the second. She had shows galore in the 'sixties, 'seventies, right through the 'eighties. But then as she began to deteriorate, it all went by the board. You see, that's where the first and second-rate are really defined. When first-raters stop producing, their work skyrockets in value because there isn't going to be any more. Second raters are forgotten. While Lettie was productive we lived well ... all right, *too* well. We spent a lot of money on art, saved nothing. So for nearly ten years now it's been up to me to see us through. I drew on my connections to open a small mat-and-frame business; that's what you saw at the far end of what used to be Lettie's studio there. But I've also had to sell our collection of paintings and Lettie's sculptures for whatever they'd bring. 'Lovers' here is the only Lettie Hartmann original we have left."

Schwartz looked around the room. "That's why it's so ..."

"Empty, Mr. Schwartz?" Hartmann chuckled. "Not quite. Lettie was quite a collector herself, dolls and doll accessories. This room was full of them. The irony is, as Lettie's own work fell in value, her doll collection went up. So I've sold them too, all but her very favorites."

"The ones in her studio," I said.

Hartmann nodded. "Not that I think she even knows whether they're here—but I can't bring myself to dispose of them. That dollhouse is a Schoenhut, extremely rare and wonderful. The perambulator's British, highly valuable considering its size and condition, and the doll in it is incredibly rare, a life-sized Jumeau. Lettie knitted the beret; she couldn't walk past that doll without smiling. I can't help hoping one day I'll see her do it again. Bad odds, I know, but still ... Well, though, to get to why you're here."

Hartmann's face went ultraserious. "To put it bluntly, gentlemen, I'm rapidly running out of two important commodities: money and time. Probably the second is more important." He paused, flicked lint off a trouser leg. "I'd been having what I thought was indigestion; finally I went to see my family physician over at the Delancey Street Clinic. He sent me to a specialist who did some tests and found I've got colon cancer—unfortunately, too far gone for any chance of cure by surgery. Radiation or chemotherapy might prolong my life, but not for very long, and in a weakened condition where I couldn't be much help to Lettie. We have no children to help, so my only hope is to lay aside enough money that with my life insurance there'll be enough to maintain Lettie here with a full-time companion for the rest of her life. And ..."

Hartmann took the brown envelope from his lap, waggled it at Schwartz and me, then turned it upside-down to dump a bunch of photographs onto the coffee table. "... this represents my only hope."

Schwartz whistled. "Hey, Doc. That *is* the one I saw at Wilcox's."

"And the one Lucas Sterne appraised," Hartmann murmured.

I studied the pictures. Impressive didn't half say it. A huge case, elegant burled wood with magnificent central lid inlay of brass, ebony, mother-of-pearl, and pewter, sat atop a matching table. An inside shot showed the classic revolver setup, shiny carousel holding six cylinders; easy to see the mid-cylinder plerodienique lines. Set into a narrow ebony frame on the inside of the lid was a painting. Not easy to make out details but it appeared to be a small village, mountains behind it, with people working in the foreground.

Another photograph showed a colorful embossed card, decorated with bright lithos, within a black leather cover. The card listed the six tunes played, one per cylinder over six revolutions. All operatic overtures: *William Tell, The Thieving Magpie, Semiramis, Zampa, Alessandro Stradella,* and *Ines de Castro.* One very common, three well-known, one unusual, and one I'd never heard of. A mechanism this rare, with such a range of operatic music, must have been manufactured on special request for a person with both an outstanding musical background and a very fat wallet. A nobleman? Member of a royal family? Certainly a patron of the arts. The lid painting was fudge icing on the *Sacher torte,* a touch sometimes added to the very finest of the larger mid- to late-nineteenth century music boxes. All of a sudden, Lucas's estimate didn't seem ridiculous.

"A family heirloom, gentlemen," Hartmann said. "Ac- quired in France by my grandfather right after the First War. Supposedly a very fine example."

"Never mind supposedly," I said. "It's magnificent—and probably unique."

"So I learned ... recently. But one day perhaps thirty years ago the spring broke. I had no idea where to take it to be fixed, and I didn't really want to sell it ... so I stashed it away in the back of a closet and forgot about it. Until just a few months ago."

Common story. From outside the hobby, trying to find your way to a qualified antique music box restorer can be a nightmare. You may get sent to the right place by a helpful antique dealer or clock restorer, but more likely you'll be told or finally conclude it's a lost cause, and either dispose of your instrument or—as Rudolph Hartmann did—put it into long- term storage in a closet, attic, basement, barn, or chicken coop.

"When it occurred to me the music box might be the answer to my problem," Hartmann continued, "I called Wilcox. Back while Lettie was still active he sold some of her sculptures. I've also done framing for him. With his clientele, I thought he could get a good enough price to justify paying him a commission. He's not the most pleasant person but I had no idea he was dishonest. Fortunately I insisted we get an appraisal. I checked the phone book, found Sterne's ad, and Wilcox and I went over there with the photographs. When Sterne came up with his estimate I nearly hit the floor. The catch was, he wouldn't do the repairs the box needed unless he could also sell it, and his commission would've been forty percent. I thought that seemed excessive, especially since Wilcox said for twenty percent he was sure he could sell it to one of his high-roller clients."

Schwartz looked at me, grinned.

"Did Lucas tell you The Lucas Sterne Music Box Emporium is not listed as a charitable organization?" I asked.

Hartmann chuckled. "His exact words. I see you know Mr. Sterne."

"Very well. What else did he say?"

"That we could take the box to a Barton Moss in New Rochelle. Which I did, in a rental truck. I have to say, I wasn't impressed; what a slob, what a dump! But I thought if Sterne recommended him he was probably all right. I left the music box around the end of April; Moss said he'd have it ready in a month—but didn't. I started calling him, oh, once or twice a week, and then last week he called me to say he had bad news. There had been a break-in at his place and my box was stolen, along with some others. He said he hoped I had insurance for it."

"Do you?"

Headshake. "My homeowner's doesn't cover antiques, and art and antiques premiums are unaffordable. But wait, it gets worse. I have no receipt from Moss for the music box. I just left the box there; I didn't think ..."

Some music box restorers give clients receipts, but this is a relatively new development. Most restorers who go back a while simply take in work, often not even labeling it with the owner's name. If the owner thinks to ask for a receipt, it may be given, if grudgingly, but far more often than not, the owner *doesn't* think and doesn't ask. Just as Hartmann didn't.

"So when I notified the police," Hartmann said, "they weren't very helpful. They told me I had no evidence."

Schwartz pointed at the table. "What about those pictures?"

"What about them?" Hartmann shrugged. "I had pictures ... of a music box. But Moss denied ever having it in his shop, I had no receipt, and the police wouldn't even talk to Wilcox or Sterne. The detective said, 'Suppose Mr. Sterne did refer you to Mr. Moss? He can't testify that you actually did leave a music box there.'"

"How about Wilcox?" Schwartz was fairly giving off steam. "*He* saw you leavin' it with Moss. He'd be a witness."

"I'm afraid not." Hartmann reddened, looked more sheepish than ever. "Wilcox didn't come with me to Moss'; he said it didn't take the two of us to do that, and besides he had a busy afternoon. So I hired a couple of young men to load the music box and table in and out for me, but ..." He held out his hands, palms up, helpless supplication. "I hired them off the street—for cash. Now try to find them. I know how stupid I sound. The policemen made no secret of that."

Sometimes there's just nothing to say.

"So there I was," Hartmann said. "I accused Moss of misappropriation but hadn't a shred of proof. But *you* say you saw the music box in Wilcox's shop."

"Just a couple days ago," Schwartz chirped. "Maybe you oughta have another talk with him."

Hartmann shook his head slowly. "He'd only deny everything. You didn't take a picture, did you?"

Schwartz tapped the side of his noggin. "Only up here."

"Hard to get that developed," I said.

Hartmann raised a cautious finger. "Dr. Purdue, Mr. Schwartz ..."

Schwartz beamed me a quick eyeball alert. Here it comes.

"... maybe *you* could help me—I mean to get back my music box. You said you're a collector, Dr. Purdue. And that you were interested in owning it."

"Guilty on both counts," I said. "But knowing the price now, fair as it is, I'm afraid I'm just not in that league. Few collectors are."

"Well, we could talk price. We could *talk*." I started to smile; the old drink-buyer and lunch-doer was coming through loud, clear and persuasive. "I'd certainly expect to give you proper consideration—without your help I suspect I'm going to end up with nothing."

He turned slowly to look toward the back room where Lettie's incessant singsong came softly through the closed door. I wondered how he managed to put up with it, day after day after endless day. He was either a saint or a con artist; tough sometimes to tell one from the other. Or he and Lettie might've both been grifters—but if they were, they were good. *Really* good.

"And Lettie will end up in a home—a municipal nursing home ..." Here his voice broke, cheeks went red, eyes filled. He wiped a shirtsleeve across them.

Was he putting me on? Didn't think so. His pictures were undeniably those of the music box Lucas Sterne appraised and

Schwartz later saw, spruced up, in Wilcox's shop. That little cinnamon-chomping slimesack must have cuddled up with Barton Moss, certainly anyone's match in an oozing contest, got Hartmann's music box spiffy, then sold it on the spot to a Mr. Deep Pockets. Now you see it, now you don't. Sorry, Hartmann, it was stolen. Sorry, Purdue, don't know what your picker's talking about.

Hartmann took my silence as reluctance. "Please, Dr. Purdue ... Mr. Schwartz ... if you don't want to buy the music box I'd still pay you a substantial reward. I was going to give Moss five thousand for his work, and Wilcox's commission would've been twenty percent—that's a total of forty thousand dollars. I couldn't in good conscience offer you less. What do you say?" Hands clapping together on the last word, Hartmann made an impressive hail-pleading-fellow-well-met.

"I guess we can give it a try," I said. "But no promises." I held out my hand, palm up. "Be helpful to have those pictures."

Hartmann slid the photos into the envelope, then paused. "They're my only proof—"

"How far have they gotten you?"

He nodded reluctantly. Slowly, deliberately, he placed the envelope into my hand.

Outside, strolling up Seventh Avenue, Schwartz broke the silence. "What was with the missus, Doc? Alzheimer's?"

"Don't think so. She's a live wire, not a dead connection. Rhyming speech, strange gestures, inappropriate giggling; all that compulsive clay-play—her mind's not shutting down, just shifting into a different reference frame, one that makes sense only to her. Without doing a physical, with no lab work, my best guess is it's some unusual kind of schizophrenia, probably a hebephrenic variant. They used to call schizophrenia *dementia praecox* because most often it appears in young people. But sometimes it does pop up later, in old age—"

"So then it's *dementia altecox*?"

Broadway Schwartz, the Henny Youngman of medical nomenclature. "You might say that."

"How about Hartmann. Think he's for real?"

"I'd put my chips on yes. From Lucas to Barton Moss to Wilcox makes sense. Wilcox must've had that box in his shop just long enough to call his fat customer and get him down there to see it. But timing's everything, Broadway, and you happened to drop in at the Palais Royal before the customer did. Bad timing for Wilcox, but maybe good for Hartmann."

"And also maybe for you?" Schwartz looked like a mischievous cartoon animal.

"Come on, Broadway—I can't even think about paying that kind of money for a music box. But why not pick up a quick forty thou, make sure Frank doesn't get another visit from the Goon Squad, *and* maybe get Wilcox off Edna's back? Be time well spent. You got that kind of time?"

Shrug. "Sure, Doc. Like always—you're in, I'm in. Your games usually end up bein' more profitable than pickin'. And besides, by the time you're gonna want me to do anything, I'll already have a good half-day's work done. Figure it's overtime."

Pickers—at least good pickers—are out before the sun, even in June. They scope flea markets while vendors are unloading cars and trucks, check out estates before the heirs go off to work, rummage through the previous day's arrivals in junkyards. The watchword of Schwartz's faith is "Y'snooze, y'lose."

"How 'bout you, Doc. *You* got the time?"

"Two weeks—final exams at Man Med're done; new residents don't report 'til June twenty-fifth. Got nothing better to do." I checked my watch: 4:15. "What do you say we go up, have another talk with Wilcox. Together this time."

Schwartz grinned again. "Can't exactly say it's my pleasure—but I guess it's what to do."

6

We pushed through turnstiles at the Eighth Avenue cross-town station, trotted up to the train. Its doors were shut but a man stood on the platform, one hand extended into the car between the rubber door bumpers. "O-pen da *door*," he chanted, "o-pen, se-sa-me." As we approached he pointed with his free hand at a small red light one car forward. "Light's on, they gotta open," he said over his shoulder. "They ain't allowed to go if the red light's on ... hey, o-pen da *door*. O-pen—se-sa—"

As if in frustration the train let out a hissing sound, then doors clattered open. "Y'see—*told* you." Basking in his triumph, the Maven of the Underground motioned us aboard. He grinned at us all the way to Lexington, where we got off, took the uptown train to 59th, then danced across to Third through the late afternoon sidewalk crowd.

By a quarter to five we were in front of the Palais Royal. The carefully lettered sign inside the door said the shop was open Tuesday through Saturday, 9:30 to 5:00, but the locked door, barred windows, and dark interior said otherwise. "Don't exactly keep regular hours, does he?" Schwartz muttered.

"Busy little bugger," I said. "Too busy to keep his shop open.

Guess we'll have to try him again tomorrow—meet you back here at one?"

"Fine with me, Doc."

I was home by five-thirty, found Sarah stretched out on the sofa in her living room. I bent over her, kissed her nose lightly. "Tired?"

She nodded. "First day back's always rough."

Sarah's a nurse-social worker in a Planned Parenthood Teen Pregnancy Prevention Program. More specifically, she runs the program, so when she returns from a vacation there's always a deskful of bucks no one was willing to stop for her. "Maybe you ought to wait a day or two after a trip before you go back in," I said.

Helpful Thomas Purdue. Sarah made a sour face. If she's home and able to go to work but doesn't, that's no different from calling in sick when she isn't. And telling lies is not in my wife's *modus operandi.*

"We've been through this," Sarah said.

"I know that. But jet lag still—"

"Is *not* an illness. Enough, Thomas; I don't feel like arguing."

"Feel like going in to Jersey?"

Heavy duty fish-eye.

"Dad's having an exhibit. I told him I'd come in tonight, walk through it with him."

Sarah blew air out of the corner of her mouth. "Do you think he'd be upset if I—"

"Not at all. I'll explain, he'll understand. Dad's good that way."

She nodded. "Yes, he is. And I know you'll make it convincing." She got up slowly, stretched. "How about dinner?"

"It's almost six—I'll grab something along the way, otherwise I'll be late ... What're you doing?"

"What does it look like I'm doing—I'm putting on my shoes. I'll walk downstairs with you and go have a bite at Italo's. Better than cooking for one."

As we came down the steps, there was the man I'd given a fiver a couple of days before. He was across the sidewalk, hunkered down against the pole of a No Parking sign. Hard to tell just how old he was, but I thought around seventy. His white shirt was ratty, pants baggy and threadbare. He needed a shave—hardly surprising—and his sparse, gray hair hadn't been combed for a while. I reached into my pocket, took a fin out of my wallet, handed it to him. "Good luck."

"Thank you, sir. Thank you very much." He struggled to his feet, made a little bow, almost Japanese-style, then turned and shuffled off down the sidewalk.

"Oh, honestly!" Sarah's foot went tap-tap-tap on the sidewalk. "You're really *not* helping him. Inside of an hour your money's going to be in the hands of a bartender and that poor man's going to have a stomach full of alcohol. If you really wanted to help, you'd give money to a mission. Then you'd know it'd go to providing proper food and shelter."

Talk about unresolvable conflicts. I say if someone needs money and you can help, give him the money. Far be it from me—or you—to tell him what he needs it for; that's his business. Institutional charity doesn't flip my switch, especially when I figure the percentage that goes to the house. Not to mention how the poor so-called beneficiaries are not permitted to eat their proper food or lie down on their proper beds until they've mouthed proper words of praise and thanksgiving to that gracious Deity from whom they drew short straws. Some charity. More like having your nose rubbed in your own misfortune.

But Sarah looked tired and I needed to get on my way. Quick wave, friendly smile. "See you in a few hours."

"You are impossible."

"Just highly improbable. Don't wait up."

Fifteen minutes later my VW and I were moving westward through the Lincoln Tunnel. In the dim yellow underground light, faces in the other cars looked jaundiced. I tried to gear up for what lay ahead. It wasn't going to be easy.

My relationship with my father has always been defined by roughly equal measures of skepticism and love. Dad spends words the way a pauper spends nickels, dispenses smiles the way a bindle stiff might hand around dollar bills. Situations that set him fuming usually start me laughing; he tells me I don't take matters seriously enough. But Dad's an exceptional diagnostician—and I was in need of a consultation.

Dad lived in Hobart, a medium-sized city about a half-hour's ride along Interstate 80 from New York. I got off 80 where the Passaic River divides Hobart from Grassville, chugged around the little traffic circle, then drove up 33rd Street to Roosevelt Avenue where I turned right. Dad's house was just a few blocks down Roosevelt, between 28th and 29th.

This was Doctor Row, had been forever, one of those

neighborhoods seemingly preserved in amber within an airtight cocoon of modern high-speed motorways. Practically every house featured a ground-floor office, living quarters above, and a gold-lettered sign out front, hanging from a little wrought-iron gibbet. When I was a kid the names on the signs were roughly half-Jewish, half-WASP: L. R. Goldstein, MD, Diseases of the Eye and Ear. E. C. Remington, MD, Urology. Now they were mostly Hispanic: J. N. Martinez, MD, Women's Care. Dad's friends tried for years to get him to relocate in one of the tony lake towns in Bergen County, but this was his house, his neighborhood, his practice. Will Purdue, MD, Internal Medicine. The gold lettering was faded; the man was not.

I pulled to the curb, killed the motor, then looked up the hill at the big wood-sided house with its wrap-around screened porch. Fresh brown paint, white trim. Lawn closely mowed, edge-clipped, cleanly weeded—not by a gardener. I thought about a summer evening when I was seven or eight: Dad and I were pulling weeds on that front lawn. Below us on the sidewalk, a burly white man in a red and black checkered shirt snarled, "Move, nigger!" then shoved a black man out of his path. Dad dropped his trowel. When the black man turned and yelled back, "Who you callin' nigger, white-trash son of a bitch?" the white man pulled a knife from his pocket and slashed, catching his opponent on the cheek. What looked to me like gallons of blood splashed onto the concrete sidewalk.

Dad was already down the hill, moving like a rocket-powered tank. With the black man on his knees, hand to his cheek, the white man turned to go after his new attacker. Dad barreled into the guy's left rib cage, grabbed his right wrist, shook the knife to the ground, then fetched the man a clout to the nose that sent blood spraying in every direction. The white man wobbled, dropped to the sidewalk next to his victim. The black man made a move toward the knife. Dad stopped him with a single word: "Don't!"

I ran down the grassy hill to stand at my father's side. The two men knelt in their blood, looking furtively upward at Dad. "See the blood, Thomas?" Dad said, looking not at me but at the fighters on the sidewalk. "Can you tell me which part of it came from which man?" Without waiting for an answer he hauled the gladiators up by their shirt collars, marched them up the steps into his office, where he gave the black man a tetanus shot and sewed up his laceration, then attended to the white man's sprained right wrist and fractured nose. "Life's tough enough," Dad said as the men walked meekly out the door. "Why do you want to act like idiots?"

As I walked up to the house, Dad opened the screen door. Required to give up his hospital privileges at seventy, two years earlier, he still saw patients in his office, five mornings a week. Afternoons, he painted, whether in the little studio he'd set up in what had been Mother's sewing room, or out somewhere on location. Evenings, he admitted, dragged. He'd been sitting on the screened-in porch watching for me.

He strode down the wooden steps, took my hand, shook it earnestly. Pearly-silver hair, suit, vest, tie. At six-four and with a stair's advantage, he towered over me, a gray eminence. "Glad to see you, Thomas," he said. "I'm pleased you wanted to come to my exhibit."

"Your first art show," I said. "I wouldn't miss it."

Eye tape took careful measure through slitty lids. "You're not in some kind of trouble, are you?"

Talking to my father can be like dealing with Sarah. "No, of course not. What would make you think that?"

Dad beamed me a healthy portion of visual applesauce, then pulled his car keys out of his pocket. "I'll lock up. Meet you at the car."

"Still driving the 'sixty-six Pontiac?"

"It gets me where I want to go."

There's enough broken in Dad's world that needs fixing. A car that works reliably is to be treasured. I cut across the lawn and up the concrete driveway at the side of the house, back to the garage.

Mendenhall Galleries was a small, glass-fronted building in white stucco on River Road in Grassville, just north of Hobart across the Passaic River. Why "Galleries" I have no idea: it was only one, fair-sized room. But this month the walls of that room were hung with thirty canvases from the brush of Will Purdue, so I was not about to quibble.

A stork of a woman in a dress that would've made a fire engine look faded leaped from behind her desk and gushed greetings as we came through the door. There was an un-natural light in her brown eyes; close-cropped black hair topped an egg-shaped head that bobbed alarmingly on her long neck. "So good to see you, Doctor."

Dad accepted her light cheek-buss with surprisingly good grace. The storky woman turned to me. "And this is?"

"My son. Dr. Thomas Purdue, Jo Mendenhall."

"Dr. Purdue, Junior; how *won*derful." She clasped my hand with her ten spidery fingers. "I'll bet you're proud as you can be of your father."

I could have told her I'd always been proud of my father, long before he'd developed his painting skills to the point of justifying a public exhibition. But I just said, "I'll bet you're right."

Appreciative chuckle, "Heh-heh-heh. I'm just *so* pleased, Doctor; this has been one of my most successful shows ever." She took in the room with an expansive arm-sweep. "Just look—we've already sold nearly seventy-five percent of the pieces, and with more than two weeks still to go. We might sell out; then you'll have to do another show. Heh-heh-heh."

I hoped my smile didn't look as forced as it felt. Dad regarded her with genial tolerance. "I'd be glad to."

"Wonderful!" She clapped her hands. "Well! Let me get out of your way. I'll go back to my paperwork and you can show your son the exhibit."

I picked up a tan brochure from a small table. Below a photo of Dad's face was the title, A MEDICAL VOYAGE: THE ART OF DR. WILL PURDUE. A couple of paragraphs explained that Dr. Purdue, who'd practiced medicine in Hobart for nearly a half-century, had combined his personal holistic vision with his long experience in healing and wellness to produce an artistic expression in oil on canvas, as his predecessor, Dr. William Carlos Williams, had done in words on paper.

"Who the hell wrote this crap?" I muttered out of the corner of my mouth.

Dad inclined his head toward Jo Mendenhall, whispered, "Who do you think? You should've read it before I went over it." He snatched the brochure out of my hand, returned it to the pile. "Come on—let's look at the work."

As far back as I can remember, Dad had puttered with paint and brushes, but about the time I hit high school he began working in earnest—stopped doing still-lifes and seascapes, started to record his days' work in paint. It was as if this process helped him understand what was otherwise incomprehensible, or at least accept what he couldn't make sense of. Sometimes I wondered whether he could've continued in practice without his brushes and paint.

I moved counter-clockwise around the room, absorbing Dad's panorama of human affliction. My father's painting was like his speech: straightforward, spare, direct. "Lung Cancer" showed an emaciated man sitting up in bed, skin and eyes yellow with jaundice, right index and middle finger stained almost orange with tobacco. He gazed at the half-full pack of Lucky Strikes on the bedside table, and in his expression I saw longing, hatred, self-disgust—and above all, despair. I knew as soon as I turned my head he would snatch another coffin nail from the pack and light up. "Elephant Boy" was a small, resentful-eyed collection of lumps, bumps and hanging tumors. In "Stillbirth," a mother in her delivery bed held her limp, pallid baby in a blanket; the father leaned forward over her right shoulder, staring into the child's face as if to will it back to life. "Chemo" showed a hairless man in a wheelchair, his face puffy from steroid therapy, reaching up tentatively to shake hands with his visitor, a tall, muscular black man in a basketball uniform, whose shaved, shining head gleamed in eerie counterpoint to that of the doomed patient. Even the group paintings: "Operating Room," "Kidney Dialysis," "Rehab Center," were unsettling. The surgeons' faces made it clear they were going to lose their patient. The shrunken woman on the dialysis machine didn't have long to go. Nor would the convalescents slumping and lurching through their prescribed exercises make any significant improvement in the time left to them. Dad's work was unsettling, distressing—but not depressing. In the contrasts of bright colors, in the bold brush strokes, I saw determination tinged with hope, and beyond that defiance, a mass fist-shaking at eternity. Go they all must, go they all would, but they weren't about to go quietly.

Dad shook me out of my thoughts. "Not the sort of thing you'd think people would want to hang on their walls, is it? I wonder who bought them all."

"*Memento mori* in *fin-de-siecle* Grassville," I said. "More class, more expensive, and a whole lot more pizzazz than a skull on a desk."

Dad zapped me with an icy glare. "Thomas, sometimes you're just a little too clever for your own damn good."

No point objecting. If the shoe fits ... "Does it really matter who buys them?" I asked.

Dad shook his head, kept me firmly in view. "Just curious ... like I'm curious about the real reason you hauled yourself out here on an evening in the middle of the week."

"The *other* reason," I said. "I really did want to see your exhibit—but I also need a consultation. Tell you about it when we get back to your house."

We sat in matching beige and gray armchairs in Dad's living room, trying to read each other across a small mahogany pie table. Faint smell of horsehair, tinged with a sharp wax odor from the hardwood floor. Nothing in that room had changed since my boyhood; like marriages in those days, marriage gifts tended to last. Furniture was '30s: chairs, sofa, love seat with mahogany arms and button-tufted cushions. Behind Dad was Mother's baby grand piano, unplayed, untuned, unopened since her death. To my left, a square ebony table with lyre-shaped cutouts at either end held a cylinder music box, a six-tune, thirteen-inch instrument in a modestly-inlaid wooden case, manufactured a century before in one of the factories of the Swiss Family Paillard. That music box was the foundation of my addiction, made me a sucker for the Garabedian Auction Gang in Asbury Park; then when I went to med school in New York and fell in with the big-time collectors I was a goner. I tried many times to give Dad a top-quality music box but he always said no, one music box was plenty, and he was satisfied with his good-but-not-great Paillard which he'd "set right"— whatever that meant—when he was a boy.

Soft light from the floor lamp on Dad's left fell over his face, making his features look like the work of a master stone-carver. Long legs fully stretched, crossed at the ankles, he sipped at his Manhattan (easy on the whiskey, heavy on the bitters) and listened as I told him about Edna, including her pill-theft and the deal I'd made with her. He hummed softly, a tune I called "Dad's decision grease" when I was a kid. It seemed to get him through difficult differential diagnoses, whether on patients or cars; helped him weigh the relative merits and attractions of cheddar and Camembert in the supermarket. One day when I was ten or eleven and had a nasty case of stomach flu, I lay on Dad's office table, watched him draw medication into a syringe. When I heard the familiar hum I asked if there were words to that music. Dad cocked his head, held up the syringe to the light, shot out a bit of the fluid through the needle. "Sure. '*Sweetest little feller ... everybody knows ... Don't know what you call him, but he's mighty like a rose ...*'" Then wham! right in the ass, hypodermic fire. As nausea edged into blissful drowsing, Dad's decision grease diffused through my brain; the music was still there next morning when I woke, free of heaves and trots. It's been there ever since, more tenacious than any microbial invader.

When I finished my story, Dad stopped humming, then said, "Why do you imagine I can help your friend?"

"Dad ... do I have to tell you to look at your own paintings?"

He put down his glass, came to the edge of a smile. "Think about it, Thomas. We go through our lives a blood clot away from total disability, a skipped heartbeat from dissolution. Keep that on your mind, you don't *need* a stroke to be paralyzed. Now, your friend ... what's her name?"

That's Dad. Down to cases. "Edna," I said. "Edna Reynolds."

"Right. Edna's got to see herself as a clever, talented woman who happens to have a disabled hand. Do two things for her. Get her attention off her handicap and back where it belongs— on her work. Then convince her she can find a way around her problem to keep doing that work. Remind her death's just a statistical probability; get her wondering how she'd like to sit through eternity staring at a paralyzed hand. Get her doing something every day that leaves her feeling ... well, *necessary.*"

"Every day in every way," I said. "Edna'll just love that."

Dad shrugged. "Did I say it'd be easy? People are good at hiding their weight: you don't realize what you're up against until you've stooped and are trying to lift them. Maximize your leverage, Thomas. Whack her with a two-by-four between the eyes, twitch a feather behind her ear—whatever it takes to show her she's still alive and has work to do. Just get Edna onto the right track. Then get the hell out of the way."

Dad picked up his glass, drained it, then chuckled, not with cheer; his way of closing a conversation. "It's no walk in the park, Thomas. And if you think it's tough watching someone get old, wait until you're doing it yourself."

7

Eight o'clock next morning, knock-knock, there was Jitters, holding his music box out in front of him like a propitiatory offering to a god. Mouth slightly open, eyes wide and expectant: "*Oh, please—no emergencies today.*"

I took him by the arm, led him to the workbench. "Put the patient on the table."

We dismantled his treasure, a fine instrument to launch the career of a restorer. Nice little circa-1840 cylinder box with no serious problems; cleaned, polished, dampered and adjusted, it would reward its owner with six fine arrangements of Italian operatic arias.

Under my direction, Jitters unscrewed and removed the comb from its brass bedplate, then took off governor, spring barrel, cylinder, and finally control levers. He looked up at me. "Now what?"

"Now we take these main components down into their basic bits and pieces. Every little spring, every tiny screw."

Jitters' hands went into sustained vibration. "I told you—" he began, but I held up a palm for silence, then reached to the shelf above the workbench. "Here you go," I said. "Your crutches."

On the edge of the table in front of him I fastened two ball-joint vises, each of which held a five-inch-long metal bar atop a vertical post. Jitters stared at me. Was I putting him on?

I handed him the spring barrel assembly and a pair of small pliers. "What the hell you waiting for?" I said. "Pull that pin and slide off the winding ratchet."

Jitters laid his hands across the metal bars, set plier jaws around the pin, tugged gently, then sat staring at the pin in the pliers. In his perfectly motionless hand.

"Works, doesn't it? And once you get the hang of things, pick up some confidence, you probably won't even need it. Now, the ultimate weapon ..." I pulled a small brown bottle out of my pocket, set it on the table in front of my apprentice. "This is called Klonopin—for when you're having an especially bad day and the hand rests aren't enough. Take one only when you *really* need it, every now and then. Use it regularly, you'll get killer convulsions when you stop. Also, if you drink while you're taking this stuff, you'll get sicker than you ever want to be. Kapeesh?"

Jitters looked at the bottle as if it might explode in his face, then slipped it quickly into a pants pocket and went back to the barrel assembly.

If Barton Moss was a garage mechanic, Jitters was a neurosurgeon, working screwdrivers and pliers over that fine geriatric brass-and-steel body the way a good doctor would apply scalpel, scissors, and clamps to flesh. Respect was written all over his face, reverence in the light yet steady touch of his hands. You can teach restoration techniques but this attitude can only come to the job with the apprentice, and whether or not it does makes all the difference.

By a little after ten we had six carefully-separated piles of greasy brass bits on the table. "Clean and polish time," I said. "We'll run the cylinder and bedplate through the ultrasonic wash and rinse, shine 'em up, then grab a quick lunch out of the fridge. After that I've got some stuff I need to do the rest of the day, so while I'm gone, you clean and polish the rest of the components. Take you easily the whole afternoon; we'll pick up from there tomorrow. Just make sure to lock up when you're done ... and better be out by five. Before my wife gets back."

Jitters looked at me as if I'd laid the keys to Fort Knox in his hand. "You're gonna leave me here ... by myself?"

"How else you going to get your work done?" I punched his arm lightly. "Sure I'm taking a chance—but I've been watching you work and I just don't think you're going to grab and run. If I'm wrong, you'll never work on another music box, ever, anywhere. I'll find you, count on it; use you instead of a monkey for some of the brain experiments I do over at Man Med."

Jitters went white. "Come on," I said. "Introduction to Useful Solvents and Mild Abrasives One-oh-One."

As I strolled up to the Palais Royal a few minutes before one, I saw Schwartz hoofing hard from the north. When he chugged up to the door, he was puffing. "Whew!" He mopped shine off his forehead with a crumpled handkerchief. "Had to wait through two full subways before I could get on."

When Broadway Schwartz is on time he figures he's late. I jerked my thumb at the open shop door. "Our friend's here today. Catch your breath—then let's see how enlightening he wants to be."

Marcus Wilcox was in the back of the shop, showing a

massive mahogany credenza to a well-dressed young couple. Schwartz and I pretended to browse near the front. If Wilcox's prospective customers were of average height—and they appeared to be—then Wilcox was impressively short, five-three tops. Surprised me for a minute but then I realized, this was the first time I'd seen him on his feet. Not once during my earlier visit to the Royal Palace had the little king gotten up from behind his desk.

Wilcox followed the couple past us to the door, assuring them with every step that their taste was impeccable, that such marvelous furniture does not grow on trees—Schwartz couldn't stop a quiet snicker—and that nothing would give him more pleasure than to arrange safe delivery to their apartment.

Once the pigeons fluttered around the corner out of eye-shot, Wilcox cocked an eye on me. For an instant his face bent back into the same bootlicking smile he'd used on the young couple. "And what might I be able to do for—" Right there the penny dropped.

He reached into the pocket of his light blue ultrasuede jacket, opened the left corner of his mouth, popped in a couple of cinnamon red hots. Only then did he glance at Schwartz ... whereupon the second penny fell with a thud.

Tight parentheses sprang up in the pale terrain between his nose and lips; his hands went all a-fidget. Howdy Doody, ratings gone to hell, facing the possibility of being fuel in Buffalo Bob's furnace that winter. He glanced at his desk, then at us, then back to his desk as if gauging his odds of getting there in one piece. Suddenly he took off at a canter. Schwartz and I followed at a more leisurely clip. Wilcox grabbed the phone, started punching buttons.

"Thanks," I called, "but we don't need a cab."

"I'm calling the police," he whined.

I've never been much of a card player but if offered a high stakes poker game with this twerp, I'd've jumped. "Fine," I said. "Great, in fact. Go right ahead—I'm sure they'll be interested in hearing about a stolen music box ..." I waved the brown envelope like a flag of war. "that I've got pictures of."

Down went the receiver. Wilcox glanced streetward, then jackstepped over to shut the door, throw the bolt, flip the window sign around to CLOSED. Cinnamon red hots, pop, pop. "All right," he snarled. "Who are you guys and what's the game?"

Schwartz laughed; I came close. Picture Howdy Doody trying to play Jimmy Cagney. "We're friends of Rudolph Hartmann," I said. "Who's not awfully happy with you right now."

"I don't know what you're talking about." From arrogant Cagney to craven Peter Lorre in one conversational turn.

"Let me show you." I pulled one of the photos from the envelope, held it out to him. "I'm talking about this plerodienique-revolver music box. Hartmann's music box. Schwartz saw it here in your shop the other night. You and Hartmann took it to Barton Moss for repairs so you could flog it high to a certain Mr. Deep Pockets. *That's* what I'm talking about. And if you'd rather tell your story to the cops, we don't mind at all."

Pop-pop-pop through near-bloodless lips. This guy was teetering on the edge of a breakdown.

I pushed a rude foot through the conversational crack. "You can see how your story goes down when Lucas Sterne swears you were in his shop with Hartmann, heard the appraisal, and got worked up over how fast you could sell it. Lucas will also swear he referred you to Moss for the repair work. Wonder what *Moss*'ll say to the cops." I looked at the phone. "You want to call or should I?"

I reached for the receiver. Wilcox grabbed my wrist in fishy fingers.

"Or on the other hand," I said, "you can just tell the two of *us* what's going on. Entirely up to you."

I hate liars. Sarah would tell me I'm hypocritical, but she doesn't understand. If people who live by the lie are abominable, people who live by the truth, the one-and-only truth, are more than flesh and blood can bear. Walt Whitman said truth is whatever satisfies the soul, which is to say we're surrounded by any number of valid truths that the straight poop can never bring into focus. That, only stories can do.

I gave Wilcox the look I usually reserve for med students or residents who're trying to fake their way through case presentations they were too lazy to prepare for. Blessedly, the little creep pulled his clammy digits off me. Pop-pop. "All right," he muttered. "Hartmann *did* come to me, the lying old bastard. And yes, I did tell him I had the right connections to sell his music box. But only if it was looking nice and playing right. I don't sell defective merchandise."

"No damaged goods in the Palais Royal," I said quietly.

My sarcasm either flew over his head or bounced off his hide. "Absolutely not. We went to talk to that snotnose Sterne, but he didn't want to do the repair job. '*I'm* not about to put in all those hours for five thousand dollars so you can get two *hundred* thousand,' he told us. Take it to Barton Moss."

"And then?"

"And then, Mr. ...?"

"Purdue. Thomas Purdue. My friend, Broadway Schwartz."

Pop-pop. "And then when Hartmann heard that appraisal he got dollar signs in his eyes. What did he need *me* for? He told me, well, now he'd have to *think* about it. That was a lot of money. Maybe he ought to leave the box to his sister. And so on. I've heard it all before: twenty percent commission on two hundred dollars is one thing, the same percentage of two hundred *thousand's* something very different. That's all I can tell you. If the music box went to Barton Moss, Hartmann took it there himself and made his own arrangements." Pop-pop. "Maybe you ought to talk to Moss."

"We already have," I said. "He doesn't know a thing about the music box, never saw it. But Schwartz did spot it in your shop here just a couple of nights ago, and by the next morning it was gone, presto change-o. Amazing how such a great big music box can make itself invisible."

Wilcox's face went scarlet. Every muscle in his body contracted. He shifted his bulging eyes to size up Schwartz, must've liked what he saw because he let fly a nasty right chop. Poor judgment. Schwartz may be small but he's survived close to a half century in New York's antique pits. He casually raised a hand; Wilcox howled as his fist bounced harmlessly off Schwartz's forearm. Before Wilcox could get off a second shot I grabbed his hands, pulled them together behind his back. "Behave," I snapped.

One surprise after another. Wilcox relaxed to the point of collapse. From wannabe bantamweight champ to alleged assault victim in the blink of an eye. "Let *go* of me," he whined.

I relaxed my hold on his arms. Wilcox stepped away, shot

me a glance of unalloyed hate. I've never seen a wharf rat cornered by snapping pooches but I'll bet it'd look a lot like Marcus Wilcox looked right then. He shrugged his jacket back into proper fit, reached into a pocket, pop-pop. "Your Mr. Schwartz may *think* he saw that music box here," Wilcox sniffed. "But I'm afraid he was mistaken. I've told you all I can tell anyone; now please excuse me. I've got a business to run." Pop-pop. He walked to the door, opened it with a flourish. "Good afternoon, Mr. Purdue. Mr. Schwartz. I don't expect to see either of you here again. *Ever.*" Pop-pop-pop.

We stopped at a Hebrew National Deli a couple of blocks down Third. Poor starving Schwartz, on the go since six AM, did a demolition job on a giant Reuben sandwich and a massive slab of apple strudel. I settled for a frank, salad, and coffee.

"Guy who thinks we're gonna believe that stuff oughta run for president," Schwartz mumbled between swallows.

"He doesn't care if we believe him or not," I said. "He went with Hartmann to talk to Lucas? So what? You saw the music box in his shop? *I* know your eyes are better than any camera, but so what? And remember, Hartmann did say *he*—not they—took the box up to Moss', that Wilcox was busy. Smart move, Wilcox. If we didn't know he was lying from the get-go, who *would* we believe, him or Hartmann?"

"Guy's a weasel, Doc. I'd still go with Hartmann."

"Who might just be a better liar. Come on, eat up. I hate to do it on an full stomach but I think we need to go spend a little more time with good old Barton."

We got to New Rochelle a little before three, pulled the VW to the curb in front of a confectionery a few blocks from Moss' place. Schwartz followed me inside, to the phone in back, then browsed paperbacks while I checked Bell's city government pages, dialed my number, waited through the ring, finally heard, "New Rochelle Police Department, Third Precinct," a growl.

I pictured Barton Moss temporarily in charge of my vocal cords. "Yeah, uh ... this's Barton Moss, over on Randall Street ... I was wonderin' y'know, about that robbery at my place, couple of days ago—you guys find out anything yet?"

"When did you report this theft, sir?"

"Jeez, I ain't sure exactly—but it happened just a coupla days ago, like I said. Guy broke in, ripped off some valuable antique music boxes. I want to know if you got him, or at least if you got any leads."

"What did you say your name was, sir?"

"Jeez all man! Moss! *Barton* Moss, M-o-s-s. On Randall Street. Okay? Got it?"

"Just hold a minute, sir."

My indignant objection was cut off by a recording assuring me the New Rochelle Police Force was committed to preserving my safety and that of my possessions, and a representative would be on the line as soon as earthly possible. That turned out to be about thirty seconds later. "Sorry, sir," the gruff voice said. "I can't find a file on any Moss case; nothing at all on Randall Street. You *are* sure you filed it?"

"'Am I sure'—'*course* I'm sure," I blubbered into the phone. "Jesus Christ, this is where my tax money goes, huh? I work one hour out of every four so a bunch of guys in blue suits can sit on their fat asses and fart into their chairs all day instead of findin' the bum who ripped me off. You ain't heard the end of this,

Dickhead Tracy. I got friends close to the mayor." Then I slammed down the phone.

Schwartz eyed me over the top of an Agatha Christie paperback. "Hey, Doc—you sounded more like Moss than Moss. Get what you were lookin' for?"

"Yep. Barton never reported any robbery. And if we can't loosen him up now, maybe he'll be more flexible after the cops pay him a nice visit about a nonexistent report of a nonexistent robbery." I tapped the paperback lightly. "Pick up any pointers?"

"Nah." Schwartz chuckled, returned the book to its holder. "That Herculee Poy-rot's pretty sharp, but when it comes to antiques he don't know shit from shoe polish. Gimme Lovejoy any time."

Like the day before, no answer at Moss' front door. Like the day before, we walked around the side of the house and trooped through the wild greenery to the workshop. Unlike the day before, the workshop door was wide open. Schwartz tapped the panel once, then again. No response.

I peered around the corner. "Oh, shit!"

"'S'matter, Doc?"

I stepped inside, motioned Schwartz to follow. The place was a shambles, desk and cabinet drawers pitched willy-nilly, contents all over the floor. Tools, machine parts, papers everywhere, tossed salad, heavy on the black grease dressing. Lids on most music boxes stood open. The only wallhanging, a 1950 poster of an automotive calendar with a scantily dressed girl holding a pair of pliers, and saying she'd love to lube your pistons, was ripped off its nail, frame broken, pulled to pieces.

"Barton?" I called out, not with a whole lot of hope.

Schwartz grabbed my sleeve. "Hey ... *Doc.*" He pointed to a lathe near the middle of the room. On the floor to the right of the giant tool, a scuffed pair of black shoes extended into view. No question, they were occupied.

Lucky again: we hadn't touched anything. I followed Schwartz to the lathe, and yes, there was Barton Moss in the shoes, face-down on the floor. A massive pipe wrench lay near his outstretched right hand. From beneath him a goodly stream of dark blood had worked its way along an irregularity in the concrete floor to pool at the far side of the lathe.

I squatted over the body. Cause of death was obvious, a huge gaping wound in the upper back, to the right of the spine. "Nice job," I called up to Schwartz. "A monster knife ... or maybe a pair of bazooka scissors. Entered from the right, maybe clipped the liver, then smack into the heart, could've cut it right in half. He was dead before he hit the floor."

"Thanks for sharing, Doc." Schwartz pulled back his fedora, wiped with the wrinkled hanky.

"Another thing—wound runs side-to-side, almost horizontal. Not downward, the way you'd expect if somebody just happened to take a swing and nailed him. It's as if they knew exactly where to aim the weapon."

"Like if the killer was a doctor?"

I raised an eyebrow Schwartz's way. "Or a short person."

"Funny, Doc. Hey, you ask me, I think we'd be smart gettin' outa here. Like fast."

I stood up. "In a minute. Try to remember: did you see anyone walking or driving away from Barton's as we came up?"

Eyes squeezed shut, Schwartz shook his head. "Don't think so."

"Neither do I." I looked around the disaster scene. "Either some first-class vandalism or someone was looking for something. Bet number two—and just for the record, I'm damn glad you got Mick to babysit Frank."

Schwartz was practically to the door. "Hey, Doc, come *on.* The way you wised off on the phone to that cop? He could be just about here by now, and better figure he's loaded for bear."

Thomas, sometimes you're just a little too clever for your own damn good.

Thanks, Dad.

As I turned away from Barton something caught my eye, an irregularity on the floor next to the body, right at the edge of the pool of blood. I stepped back, crouched down.

"Hey, *Doc!*" From the doorway, Schwartz was making like a third-base coach waving a runner home with the winning score. "What the heck you doin'?"

"Broadway, look at this."

"Doc ..."

"Come over here a minute."

I could hear the sigh all the way across the room. Then he was at my side. "What's so interesting that we gotta stand here like pigeons in a shootin' gallery?"

I pointed at the floor. "What's that?"

Schwartz leaned forward, squatted. "Looks like ... little candies. Maybe three or four of 'em? In the blood."

"Cinnamon red hots?"

"Son of a gun. Wilcox."

"Must've fallen out of his coat pocket when he swung the knife, scissors, whatever. Probably he and Barton were having a major discussion; we know about what. Barton must've gone for that pipe wrench, turned just long enough for Wilcox to grab the blade and give it to Barton in the back."

"Unless ..." Schwartz cocked an index finger in my direction, then pulled the trigger. "Unless it's somebody wants everybody else to *think* Wilcox. I mean, Wilcox didn't make any kind of a big secret about eatin' those candies."

Count on Schwartz for full measure every time. "Possible," I said. "But then there's the fact the wound's track is perfect for someone as short as Wilcox. We can sort it out later, somewhere else. Got a little piece of paper, quick?"

Schwartz pulled out a pocket notebook, tore off a page, passed it to me. Very carefully, I slipped the edge of the paper under the red hots, making sure to take along a bit of blood, then folded the paper around the bloody candy. "Okay, Broadway—now let's get out of here."

"Not too fast for me, Doc." He studied my left hand. "Especially figurin' now we've gone and tampered with evidence at a murder scene."

"Not exactly. More like removing, I'd say."

"I'd say it don't matter exactly *what* you want to call it." Going through the doorway, Schwartz looked like a fox sniffing for dogs. "Cops'd call it Jail Time."

We made our way quickly through the shin-high weeds. "Not if they never find out," I said. "Besides, it's going to come in mighty handy. When we show it to Wilcox—"

"Oh, *nuts*." Schwartz lifted his right foot, gave it the evil eye. "Dog shit, all over my shoe."

"Means good luck," I said, then looked at the trail Schwartz was leaving on the concrete. "Good luck for the shoe stores, anyway. Soon's we get back, we'd better get you another pair and feed these babies to the sharks in the East River."

Schwartz was not pleased. "Ain't gonna smell so hot in the car."

"Leave the windows open." I looked at my watch, nearly five. "We'll never get Wilcox in the shop again today. Mañana."

8

Light traffic into the city, Beetle parked by a quarter to five. Schwartz and I hustled up West 16th, and damn if there wasn't my same old beggar chappie, leaning against the No Parking sign across the sidewalk from my door, eyeing that door like a cat waiting for Mousie to skip from the hole. I pulled out a fiver, slapped it into the man's hand as Schwartz and I jogged past. "Good luck, old-timer," I called over my shoulder.

He jumped as if I'd goosed him, then croaked a thanks and took off down the sidewalk. "Guy's getting to be a regular," I said to Schwartz. "That's three times this week." We started up the stairs side by side. "Strangest street person I've ever seen—just stands there like a Buckingham Palace guard. Never puts out a hand, doesn't say a word."

I swear I saw Schwartz's nose twitch. "You're sure he *is* a street person? He ain't staking you out for some reason?"

"Sure he's staking me out—a fiver a day keeps the shakies away. Don't think he's FBI. *You* try living on Social Security."

As we walked into my workshop Schwartz stopped to stare at Jitters, hunched over the workbench. "My new apprentice," I said. "Hey—Jit. I didn't think you'd still be here."

He turned slowly, raised the magnifying visor, blinked like someone waking from a dream. "I ... I'm not done yet."

"Be surprised if you were—let's see what you've ... wait a minute, where the hell are my manners? Jitters, this is my pal, Broadway Schwartz, guy who finds these little toys for me. Broadway, Henry Levitsky ... Jitters. He's learning restoration."

They shook hands. Schwartz looked Jitters up and down, side to side. My apprentice just looked awed. "You find music boxes?" he whispered. "How?"

"Picker," I said. "If there's a good one in a building he's going past, he'll smell it. He's got a gift ... like you've got one for restoring."

"Cool!" Jitters glanced at the table top. "Sorry I couldn't get it all done."

He damn near had. Bedplate, control levers, governor parts, cylinder assembly, all lay in neat groups, gleaming like gold. Only the spring barrel was still dull and dirty. I leaned forward to check the work more closely. "Nice—very nice."

Jitters' face glowed with happiness. "Hey, thanks. I hoped it was okay." He lowered his voice. "I probably *coulda* got it all done but I cheated a little bit." He pointed toward the floor-to-ceiling shelves at the back of the room, some crammed with books, others with music boxes waiting for repair. "I took a break, read some of the books ... looked at some of the boxes ... played a couple of 'em. I ain't never in my life heard ..."

Schwartz chuckled. "Sounds like you got a true believer, Doc."

"One thing," I said, and picked up the left governor side plate, holding it gingerly by the edges so as not to leave fingerprints on the gleaming surface. "Look close."

Jitters peered through the magnifying lens at the piece of brass. "See in the bearings and screw holes?" I said. "White powder? Polish residue. It'll eventually grind brass away and stop the gears from running. When you're done polishing here's what you've got to do ..." I took a wooden toothpick from a little box near the back of the table, set it into the hole, twirled it, pulled it out. "Now the polish is on the toothpick, see? Bearing's clean."

Jitters nodded, then picked up the other governor side plate, reached for a toothpick.

I touched his shoulder. "Not now."

He looked up, eyes asking a silent question.

"I've got someone else I want you to meet—can you spare another couple of hours?"

Brief pause. "Sure."

"Edna," I said quietly to Schwartz. "Then I want to check in on Frank. You up for that?"

Shrug. "Sure. Lemme just give Trudy a call."

Trudy is Schwartz's wife, and if it's only by the common law I still challenge anyone to show me two people more admirably married, or for that matter just plain more married. Schwartz and Trudy finish each other's sentences, know each other's every next move, invariably regard each other with affection and respect.

As Schwartz disappeared into the kitchen, I said to Jitters, "You want to call your grandpa, let him know you're going to be late?"

He shook his head. "We ain't got no phone. It's okay, though. He won't worry."

"Up to you. I'll go leave my wife a note."

***

Edna knew something was up, but not what. Old hat for me to walk in with Schwartz, but who was this kid with the wide eyes and sandy Brillo-pad hair? "My new apprentice," I told her after I'd introduced Jitters. "I wanted you to meet each other." I pointed at her tightrope-artist automaton. "Play it for him."

Edna tapped a foot, narrowed her eyelids.

"Go ahead, Edna. Play it."

Jitters, Schwartz and I stood in front of the automaton while Edna, beaming gamma rays of suspicion at me, moved slowly to its side. She turned the winding key, pulled the start button.

Music began to play. The little ropewalker stirred to life, moved forward on the wooden platform, balancing pole at the ready. First one foot, then the other glided out onto the rope, which in reality was a half-tube, open at the top to enclose vertical projections from the undersides of the walker's slippers. Guided by fine wires running in a groove below the tightrope, the miniature aerialist moved forward in fits and starts, shifting his pole one way, then another. Jitters' mouth was open, but he seemed not to be breathing.

A step or two from the far platform, the little figure suddenly lurched leftward, looking for all the world as if he were going to plunge to the floor. Jitters let out a cry, then smiled as the man recovered his balance and moved swiftly to the safety of the platform, where he wheeled around, ready to repeat the walk in the opposite direction. But Edna pushed the button, shutting down the performance.

Jitters stood still, breathing heavily. He blinked, shook his head, clearing mental smog.

I'd picked this particular automaton for a reason—its

music. An outstanding comb-and-cylinder mechanism concealed within the wooden base played four superb operatic arias. We'd been listening to a gorgeous arrangement of "*Ah! non credea mirarti,*" from Bellini's *La Sonnambula*, full of trills, perfectly-timed grace notes, and cascading runs up and down the length of the comb.

"Tell her what you saw, Jit," I said.

Edna locked eyes with the boy. "What the hell's going on here?"

"Don't worry, Jit," I said very quickly. "She's all right."

"It was different." Jitters began slowly. "I mean, different from anything I ever saw anywhere. Like one of those heavy cloths with weaved-in pictures of people from the Middle Ages, knights and—"

"Tapestries?" Edna asked.

Jitters' face lit. "Yeah—that's it. A tapestry, but swaying, kind of like it was in just a little bit of a breeze. Blue mainly, real deep blue, with orange threads and some round shiny-silver decorations. The little guy there was walking through it ... I ..." He stopped, looked as if he was going to cry.

"Synesthesia," I said.

Schwartz said, "Gesundheit."

Edna looked at me curiously.

I draped an arm around my apprentice's shoulders. "No sweat, Jit—you're among friends." Then I told Schwartz and Edna about the boy's condition. "It's as if his acoustic nerves were linked to his eyes as well as his ears: he doesn't just hear sounds, he also *sees* them. Our voices, a bird singing, jack-hammers in the street, ambulance sirens—"

"I like them." Jitters grinned. "Sirens're fireworks, getting lighter and darker all the time the sound's rising and falling. Neat."

"And as you noticed ..." I watched Edna closely, "good music grabs him and won't let go."

The astonishment on Edna's face told me I was moving down the right road. "Edna restored this piece years ago, from a bunch of parts in a basket," I said to Jitters.

Edna punctuated Jitters' awed "Wow" with, "Thomas did the music mechanism."

Jitters didn't know which one of us to gawk at.

Edna grimaced. "Damaged goods."

"Not any more." I nodded toward Mephistopheles with his mandolin. "Play him that one."

Without a word Edna let me know loud and clear that whatever I was up to I wasn't going to get away with. But she played Mephistopheles, then five or six more enchanting musical automata. Jitters watched, transfixed.

The last showpiece was a little furry rabbit inside a head of lettuce, who chewed at the leaves while cheerful music played. As Edna pushed the stop button Jitters said, "Did you restore him, too? All of these?"

"Every one," I said. "The more damaged Edna can find 'em, the happier she is. She makes new body parts, new clothes if she needs to—but only with old fabric. She fixes motors, makes new wire linkages for the movements"—I pointed at the Chinese opium den. "Tell him the damaged-goods story, Edna."

"Thomas, for Christ's sake—"

"Come on, Edna, tell him. He'll love it."

She rolled her eyes, but then told Jitters about the wealthy collector who never bought damaged goods. The boy shook his head. "Jeez—what an asshole."

Edna burst out laughing. Jitters went scarlet. "Sorry, Mrs.— I didn't mean to—"

"It's Edna," she said, her eyes more animated than I'd seen them in weeks. "And don't worry. An asshole by any name's still full of shit."

Jitters allowed himself a tentative smile.

"Show him your workshop, Edna," I said.

Jitters looked as if he were about to be escorted into the Kingdom of Heaven, but his expression shifted quickly as Edna said one word. "*Thomas!*"

I pretended not to notice. "He'll eat it up," I said, and started toward the closed door at the back of the living room. Edna charged after me. Schwartz and Jitters, both no doubt thoroughly confused, brought up the rear.

The workshop was unchanged from my last visit, tea-server automaton still on the floor behind the worktable. "Edna's having a little trouble right now," I said to Jitters. "She had a stroke and—"

"Thomas, shut your goddamn mouth!"

Under usual conditions that would have pushed the stop button on my monologue, but not this time. "Relax, Edna," I said, more firmly than I usually speak to her. "*You're* among friends, too." I looked back to Jitters. "Edna's stroke paralyzed her right arm and hand; she can't do repairs one-handed. That head in two pieces on the floor—an accident. She dropped it."

Jitters' big brown eyes expressed more sorrow than any possible words. He seemed not to want to look at Edna, instead squatted over the doll, studied the split head.

"Edna's been doing this work for more years than you've been around," I said. "She's the best in the business. But she needs a right hand."

Jitters looked up. Dawn was breaking. So was Edna's patience. "Thomas, you know good and goddamn well I'm not about to take charity."

"No one's giving you charity," I said. "This kid with his one-in-a-million talent happened to drop into my workshop, no job, no money. I gave him a little test—sent him off with a music box, told him he could sell it to Sophie—"

"Oh, to Sophie!" Edna tried not to look amused. "She was by last night to tell me to keep my chin up. What've you done now? Figured out a new con game and got Soph to play roper?"

Close. Doctors and con men both spin yarns to capitalize on a listener's sense of self-interest. Only the intended beneficiary differentiates the two.

"Never mind," I said. "Jitters *didn't* sell Soph that music box. Empty pockets, empty stomach, and he walked away from an instant thousand bills. What do you make of that?"

All the time I was talking, Jitters watched Edna. Now she turned slowly toward him, and as their eyes met, hers narrowed.

"He took apart his music box today," I said. "Cleaned and polished it. His first restoration job."

"You're not ever going to sell that box, kid." Edna sounded like Mae West with a chest cold. Jitters smiled shyly, then glanced back at the mutilated tea server.

"People with his condition have incredible memories," I said. "You only have to show him how to do something once. Bet any money you want that after five years with me he's the best music box restorer in New York; in ten years, best in the world. But he can also be the best at automata ... if you'll take him on *with* me. Time and effort's what I want from you, Edna, not charity. Teach this kid how to restore automata, I'll teach him about music boxes. We'll take him to the next NYMBCA meeting, make him a member."

Left hand on hip, Edna looked me up and down like a mother giving it to a kid who wasn't anywhere near the cookie jar when it came crashing down onto the kitchen floor. "And if that just happens to give me the right hand I need to get my work done, isn't that nice?"

"Sure, nice. Nice all around. Jitters learns a trade. You earn a living. Your customers get their automata fixed. And a hundred years from now, people in the hobby are grateful Edna Reynolds decided not to sit in her chair with her useless arm, and take her knowledge underground with her—oh, by the way, forgot to tell you. Schwartz and I ran into Derrick and Shelly Mendota, down at Lucas'. They're selling their entire collection."

"Their entire—they're not sick, are they?"

"Not that they're saying. Just their kids aren't interested in music boxes so Derrick and Shelly don't want to burden them with having to dispose of the collection. This way, there'll be nice, easy money in the bank or a stock account—"

Edna exploded. "And what are they going to do the rest of their lives? Derrick and Shelly, I mean. Sit around and stare at each other, just waiting for ... oh, you son of a bitch."

"Just waiting for the Midnight Special to roll in? Sure sounds like it."

"Hey, *Doc* ..." Streetwise Schwartz, so savvy and tough, was also a prize tenderheart. He'd been making faces at me all through the exchange; now he couldn't stay silent. But Edna waved him off. "It's okay, Broadway—he's right, the bastard." She wheeled to face Jitters, skewered him with eye darts. "You sign on with me, it's not going be a walk in the park," she snapped. "And if you start and then quit, I'll tear out your liver. Thomas'll tell you: I'm not Priscilla Patience."

Jitters' eyes stayed level. So did his voice. "You teach me how to fix these musical dolls 'n animals, I don't care if you're the Bitch of Bleecker Street." He stooped to pick up the tea server's carcass, laid it on the table as if it were the body of a battered little girl. Then he turned back to Edna. "When you want me to start?"

"Let him come here tomorrow morning," I said to Edna. "I'm going to be busy all day. Has to do with your friend Wilcox, actually."

Edna Reynolds, Lord High Justice in the Court of Contempt. "What's that little fucker up to now?"

Schwartz coughed politely, looked away.

I didn't want to get into the matter of the late Barton Moss right then; I had another patient to check. "Figure he's up to his scrawny neck in trouble," I said. "I'll come back tomorrow morning, make sure you haven't eighty-sixed Jitters. Fill you in then."

From Edna's on Lexington to Mick the Dick and Soapy Sandy's Second Avenue yuppie pad. First thing this strongarm private eye and his pickpocket wife did last year when they came into a pile of money was move out of their sagging old house in Flatbush into a spanking eastside high-rise condo. Then came the designer-lady, and when she was done the place looked fit for a young venture-capitalist and his attorney-wife. Furniture, cushions, carpets, artwork—*everything*—perfectly color-coded in peach, pale blue, and mauve. Lamps and light fixtures of stainless steel. Languid plants in pots, hanging from chains. Tables, chairs, sofas: uniform golden oak. Mick and Sandy always sat stiffly in those chairs and sofas, wearing their store-bought respectability like itchy woolen trousers. Eventually they'll realize they're still Mick the Dick and Soapy Sandy, plenty good enough.

This evening, only Mick was sitting stiffly, looking as though he might, if not careful, soil the nubby fabric on the arms of his chair. "Sandy's up in Pelham, dinner at her mom's. Usually I go with her, but ..." He grinned, arced a nod in Frank's direction, explanation enough.

Frank, wearing his cheerful face, perched on the hideous light-blue leather sofa and told us how much better he was feeling. "We're gonna go open the shop tomorrow, me and Mick," he said. "Both of us're gettin' more'n a little sick of just sittin' around here."

Mick's wide face creased into a lopsided grin. "We stay here another day, I think I'll have to tie him down."

"We don't want that," I said quickly. "But you need to be careful. A lot's happened, most of it ugly, and that little clot of mucus, Marcus Wilcox, is right in the middle."

I told them about the visits Schwartz and I had paid on Lucas, Wilcox, and the Hartmanns, and our two excursions to New Rochelle to see Barton Moss. Frank rolled his eyes, whistled. "Hoo-boy! Them candies could make it red-hot for Wilcox, couldn't they?"

"I'm counting on it," I said. "Sounds to me that once Moss

got his hands on the music box, Wilcox made a deal with him to fix it and then tell Hartmann it had been stolen, tough luck. Just hide the box a few months, wait out the sick old man. Then sell, put the money right into their pockets. Poor Lettie wouldn't be any threat."

"And you figure Wilcox iced Moss?" Mick jabbed punctuation with an index finger. "Why?"

"Not sure. Moss may've gotten nervous after Schwartz and I came snooping, and Wilcox decided to shut him up once and for all. Or maybe Wilcox figured from the beginning to get rid of Moss. A one-way split's better than two, and then again, no chance of Moss' talking to anyone. Especially when he was drunk."

"But one thing I can't figure." We all looked at Schwartz. "Wilcox killed Moss, okay, whatever reason. But that workshop was tossed like a Caesar at Sardi's, and I don't figure they were chuckin' stuff at each other. What was Wilcox looking for?"

"That I don't know. If you hadn't seen the music box at Wilcox's, I'd wonder whether *Moss* got greedy and decided to cut *Wilcox* out. Be kind of hard to hide something that big, but—"

Frank put the caboose to my train of thought as only Frank can. "It don't make no nevermind. The point's mute." In other words, shut up and stop wasting time. "I got some stuff you'll want to hear, though." Frank's dark eyes glittered with fun.

"You do, huh?" I said. "Like what and from where?"

"From this guy and that one. What do you think, Doc, I been sittin' around here, just watchin' the tube all day?" Frank inclined his head toward the phone on the end table next to him. "I been on the 'vine like you told me to do."

"All right, Cute Man, good. You've had your jollies; now give."

Frank grinned at Mick. "See the stuff I gotta put up with?"

"Frank ..."

"Hey, easy, Doc. It's like this: basically, Wilcox is not exactly the most honest guy a person might want to do a deal with."

"That's not news, Frank."

"Gimme a chance, would you? You want news, here's news. You asked about a Dunbar—well, Wilcox sold some artwork to a guy, name of Prescott Dunbar, runs a poshy designer pit up in the greenbelt, East Fifty-ninth between Park and Fifth. Dunbar paid through the snoot and then afterwards found out the whole lot was a fake, every piece. He even sold some before he tumbled, which as you can imagine must've been very embarrassing, what with the clientele *he* sniffs up to. Word is, ever since Dunbar tipped, Wilcox has been turning the city upside down trying to raise big dough."

"Restitution time," I said.

"Maybe more. There's dough and there's big dough. Dough's four zeros with a low number in front—what Wilcox'd have to give Dunbar back to cover the purchase price. *Big* dough's what our boy's been trying to get his hands on—someplace up in the middle *five*-oh range."

I thought a moment, then said, "I give up, Frank. Hit me with the punch line."

"Well, it's only a thought ..."

"Forget the fine print."

"... but the interesting thing's that Dunbar's doin' all his chasing on the QT, no cops, no shysters. Big question's why. And if Dunbar wants, say, a thirty-K refund for the dreck, why is Wilcox out there hustling like a maniac to raise maybe two hundred-K? A seven-times premium?"

Schwartz raised a hand like a kid asking teacher for a hall pass. "Dunbar must be shakin' Wilcox down for every nickel he can get. Blackmail."

"More like extortion," I said. "But same principle."

"Way *I* see it, Doc." Frank nodded emphatic agreement. "These are nice guys."

"Interior design's a tight little business, Doc, whole lot nastier than antiques. Competition—whew!" Frank fanned the air in front of his face. "Designers're like them little ratty yap-yap dogs, never miss a chance to bite each other in the ass."

Schwartz broke the brief silence. "Might fit, Doc. Wilcox sells that music box for two hundred-K, it gets Dunbar off his back."

"And his commission from selling Edna's collection would pay the refund for the dreck, as Frank put it."

Frank clapped his hands. "Maybe you want to go have a talk with Dunbar?"

I shook my head. "If Dunbar *is* blackmailing Wilcox he wouldn't be about to admit it, and besides—why would he send goons to beat you up? Why would he kill Moss and tear his place apart? If Dunbar's in this equation I'll bet he's only the catalyst. What I'm going to do is take your information along with my pocketful of bloody candy, have another talk with Wilcox. Broadway, meet me at his shop a little before twelve tomorrow?"

"I can get there earlier, Doc. For me, that's late afternoon."

"Just my point. He's hardly keeping regular shop hours right now and that might be the best time to catch him—middle of the day. Which means you can get your work done first. Besides, there are a couple of things I need to do."

Just a few minutes' walk home from the subway. Almost eight, rush hour a thing of the past. Sun lowering over the Palisades, glinting pink off skyscraper windows, lending fiery copper brilliance to a fabulous punk hairdo on a young man waiting for a bus. Rose reflections glowing on every face moving past me. Soft evening breeze fluttering skirts on pretty women in pairs and threes as they stepped along 14th Street, laughing, chattering, hands in constant motion. Wouldn't you live in New York if you could? Wouldn't *everyone?*

No sign of Sarah on my side of the Great Wall, but my note on the kitchen table was gone. I went exploring, found her racked out in her bedroom, shook her shoulder. She half-raised her head, blinked heavily. "Thomas ... what time is it?"

"Quarter after eight."

"Oh, *damn.*" She sat up, brushed hair off her face, blinked again. Sleep lines over her left cheek. "I was just going to take a short nap ... damn it. Now I'll be up all night. I'm *never* going to get past this jet lag. Where have you *been?*"

Red neon Pissy Alert. When I was a kid and got home late, my mother asked me the same question in the same tone. She got the same answer I gave Sarah. "Attending to my business."

"Which is not *my* business. Fine." She swung her legs over the edge of the bed, reached for her shoes. "*Don't* tell me."

"Sarah, for Christ's sake. I'm a doctor. I went to check on Edna. I went to check on Frank. I came directly back."

Mean fish eye, but every word was true. No reason to tell her Schwartz went with me, or the full scope of our discussions. She'd only worry.

"When's the last time you made a house call, Thomas? And why in the evening? Why not earlier in the day?"

"Because earlier in the day I was busy—with my new apprentice. He's really got the knack." I pointed through the wall. "Want to see what he did? *Beautiful* work."

Also true, every word. Sarah processed it, couldn't find a hole, said a quiet, "No. I don't need to see it."

"That was actually why I went to Edna's," I said. "Jitters did so well here, I got a great idea. I took him, he fell in love with the automata, and now he's going to be Edna's right hand—and in the process learn automaton restoration. Let him spend time with Edna, time with me, and in a few years he'll be a master restorer of music boxes *and* automata."

"Wonderful." Whole lot less enthusiasm than you usually get with that word.

"Come on, Sarah. It's good for Edna; it's good for Jitters. Why do you have to be so pissy?"

"Why do I have to be so pissy? Let me count the ways. I'm two days back from my trip, jet-lagged, headache, buzzing ear, a mile-high pile of papers on my desk, a line out into the hall of people with problems that could not be solved until I got back. I finally come home at six-thirty, thinking maybe we can have a glass of wine and a nice dinner, and what do I find? A note from my husband, saying he's out on house calls. Is that enough?"

Wouldn't have helped to remind her that taking off a day or

even two to unlag yourself before going back to work really *isn't* incontrovertible evidence of moral depravity. Neither would it have been useful to tell her she got home late herself; I was just later. "No problem," I said lightly. "Here I am. Pick the restaurant, wine and dinner. Put on your shoes. Let's go."

"Forget it; it's too late. I'll just go in the kitchen and throw something together."

"Sarah, stop. A minute ago you were saying you wouldn't be able to get to sleep; now it's too late to go out to eat. Do you want to have wine and dinner, talk, unwind—or would you rather just sulk and feel sorry for yourself?"

Her eyes flashed, mouth opened, but she swallowed whatever she was about to sling at me. Say this for Sarah: when she realizes she's gone past pissy to unarguably unreasonable, she'll backtrack. "All right." Voice low, brown eyes grave. She slipped into her shoes, then stood up, stretched. "Let's go down to the Village, Carmine's."

"Carmine's it is."

9

A good doctor knows his patients, tailors treatment accordingly. Edna Reynolds was perfectly capable of giving her new apprentice both barrels right in the face if he didn't perform just so. And Jitters, not knowing Edna as I did, might not take it too well. The Bitch of Bleecker Street would be one thing, but Edna could be the Spouting Devil of *Spuyten Duyvil.* When I rang her bell next morning I was more than a little apprehensive.

After a moment the door opened slowly and I was looking into the amused face of my apprentice. "Edna said you'd be by first thing to check us out. Ain't much that lady don't know."

"She's usually one-up on me, Jitters. May I come in?"

The boy moved a step backward, let me pass, then closed the door behind me.

Breakfast dishes were still on the kitchen table, remains of juice, eggs, pancakes, coffee. This was not like Edna. Jitters saw me staring. "We were in a hurry to get back in the shop—Edna said we'd clean up before lunch."

"*Back* in the shop ..?"

"Well, yeah—we started last night, right after dinner, worked 'til about midnight. Edna said why didn't I stay over, sleep on the couch ..." He pointed at the sofa behind him, a crumpled sheet at the far end. "Then we could get going again first thing."

"First thing after breakfast."

"Yeah. We were done eating by seven-thirty."

"And Edna's—"

He pointed toward the open door at the back of the living room. "In the shop. Don't be surprised if she just, like, ignores you. She gets working, she don't like to mess around."

"I won't take it personally."

Edna sat hunched over the now-intact head of the Japanese tea-server. Without a word, Jitters sat beside her, rested the heel of his right hand on a small block of wood, picked up the head. No tremor. With his left hand the boy moved a small bottle of paint closer to Edna, who dipped a tiny brush delicately into the bottle, then ran a line of flesh-colored paint down the site of the glued crack. "We'll have to redo the whole face, Jit," she said. "See? Otherwise the join will show."

I cleared my throat. "Remember me? Thomas Purdue? I think we've met."

Jitters turned, then Edna. She nodded for him to put the head down on the table.

I rolled my eyes toward the living room. "I see you're doing nicely." Edna nodded. "Think we've got a permanent arrangement?"

"I don't think I'm in any position to make long-term plans."

Hear a warning bell at a railroad crossing, you're smart to let up on the gas, not try to beat the train to the intersection. "Just wanted to be sure the apprenticeship was working," I said. "Also wanted to tell you a little more than I did yesterday about your friend Wilcox."

"Hmmm." Edna knows me well enough. She looked at Jitters. "Break time, Jit. Let's go in the living room."

Edna and Jitters listened without comment as I brought them up to speed. "If what Frank the Crank said is true, makes it easier to understand why Wilcox has been on your back. He must be desperate for money."

"If Frank said it, it's true," Edna barked. "So the little bastard's being blackmailed—good. I hope they put his nuts in a vise and squeeze them to pulp. What a shame that poor sick old man didn't know better than to get involved with such a scuzz."

"Double-scuzz," I said. "Don't sell the late Barton short in the scum department."

"True enough. Not exactly a loss to mechanical music, is it? Well, I hope you can nail Wilcox; it'd be nice to get Mr. Hartmann's music box back for him. And I guess I really wouldn't mind if you got rid of Wilcox for me. He's called twice since I beaned him—"

"Why didn't you tell me?"

"I didn't need to; I was perfectly able to tell *him* what needed saying. First call, he threatened to file charges against me for assault with a deadly weapon—"

"Deadly weapon, huh? Wonder what a judge would do with an allegation that St. Cecilia played hit woman."

"I told him he was lucky I didn't shove the statue up his ass. Then on the second call he said he'd consider not filing charges if I'd consign my collection to him."

Jitters snickered. He was learning fast, not only about automaton repair.

"I told him I'd see him in court, hell, or anywhere else he wanted. He said I was making a big mistake."

I got up. "He's the one making big mistakes," I said. "Schwartz and I'll go back this morning, show him some red hots clotted in a piece of paper, tell him there are more where those came from, and say a few choice words about Prescott Dunbar. Then I'll let him know if he doesn't open up the back room and hand over Hartmann's music box his story is going to go public, big time. As it also will if he ever bothers you again or sets more goons on Frank. That should be the end of everyone's problems."

At that moment, Edna looked better than I'd seen her since her stroke. "Except his," she said. "But I'm not going to worry about that."

"Don't worry about anything," I said. "Go back to work. What do you say, Jitters—this arrangement working for you?"

Sly smile, sidewise glance at Edna. "Yeah, sure. She's pretty cool for an old lady."

"I'm out of here," I said, and was, fast.

Almost an hour until I was supposed to meet Schwartz, one of those useless scraps of time that slip through the lines of a schedule book. I thought about dropping in on Sophie but figuring travel down to the Village and back, there'd have been no time to visit. So I went into a drug store, sat down in a Ma Bell Claustrophobia Unit, dialed Soph's number, said hello.

"Oh, Thomas, I was going to call you. I did stop in at Edna's, and you were right: she's in a terrible way. I got absolutely nowhere. She said even an old serge suit has its bright side but it's still just an old serge suit, not worth shit."

"That's our Edna."

"I don't think it's a joking matter."

Wrong. The uglier the situation, the more it becomes a joking matter. Who laughs more, St. Peter or Lucifer? But no point getting into that with Sophie. "I called to tell you I think I've got the cure," I said. "That talented young man I found who's interested in music box restoration—I took him to Edna's yesterday, and he went nuts over her automata. He's going to work with her as an apprentice; the two of them have been going practically non-stop since last evening."

"What a fortunate coincidence. You just happened to take your young man over to Edna's, and he just happened to fall for her automata."

"*Now* it's a joking matter, Soph? No, of course it wasn't coincidental; I engineered it. So what?"

"Hummph. I'll bet there's a bit more to the story than that."

"There's a bit more to any story."

Moment of silence. Then, "All right, what can I say? I guess it was a good thing your prodigy turned up just when he did. And that you took him on."

"You don't let one like that get away. But now it's your turn. Go back to Edna's, meet Jitters—"

"'Jitters'?"

"His hands shake a little, but it's no problem. Go meet him, chat Edna up, tell her you'd love to sell any pieces she restores and any originals she wants to make. Give her a little incentive—a little *more* incentive."

"That'll be easy. I'll also tell her I'll make it a point to find restorable automata if she and your friend will take them on. Believe me, *I* can use the sales. A lady in her eighties operating out of her house is at a distinct disadvantage trying to compete with the likes of Lucas Sterne. But it makes me wonder, Thomas. You're such a buttinski. Who are you really trying to help out, Edna or me?"

Halt.

"You can play snoop or you can play ball," I said. "Go visit Edna."

Native energy in New York is a marvel of nature. All the way from Edna's apartment to Wilcox's shop Manhattanites zipped around me, chugged past the small clothing stores, antique shops, hair and nail salons. Singles, doubles, threes; arms, hands, lips in constant motion. By the time I covered the seven blocks to the Palais Royal I felt wired. All nerves on ready alert, antennae twitching.

Schwartz was waiting. I asked if he'd been there long.

"Just a couple of minutes. I got done early, figured I'd come on over and wait." Hitchhiker thumb toward the front door of Wilcox's shop. "But it looks like we're SOL again. This guy spends less time in his place than a man got a wife who never takes a bath."

"Shit." I walked up to the shop. Sliding metal barricade in place, door closed, lights out. I shaded my eyes, tried to peer through the display window. No idea what I was looking for, just too damn frustrated to turn around and walk away. I went to the far end of the window, peered again. If I'd seen Wilcox I'd've smashed the window, grabbed him by his lapels, shaken him until it was raining cinnamon red hots.

But sometimes you're lucky. As I scanned the shop someone behind me said, "Are you looking for Mr. Wilcox?"

I turned around. Schwartz was sizing up a skinny man with rimless glasses, bloodless purse-string mouth, and a pointy little nose. The striking pallor of his skin suggested either severe anemia or morbid fear of the sun. His few remaining strands of hair were combed across the top of his head, and he was holding a yellow tape measure in one hand. "Are you gentlemen looking for Mr. Wilcox?" he repeated, and waved his tape in a downtown direction. "I own the print shop next door."

"We had an appointment with Mr. Wilcox," I said. "At noon. To talk about furniture and such for my new apartment. I know I'm a little early—"

The thin man shook his head. "Oh, no, no—that doesn't matter, not now. I'm afraid ... well, let's say, sir, that Mr. Wilcox will not be keeping his appointment with you."

Bad vibes. Bad, *bad* vibes. "Oh? Is he ill?" I chirped. "Checked in with you, did he?"

More vigorous headshaking. "I'm sorry, but it would be more accurate to say Mr. Wilcox has checked *out*. He's dead."

"Dead ... oh *no*." I opened shock and horror faucets full blast. "That's terrible. Such a nice man."

My informant's face told me I was going too far.

"I was counting on him," I said. "What ... what happened, do you know?"

"I learned a little from the police. They came into my shop about an hour ago and asked me questions, like when I'd last seen Mr. Wilcox, and whether he'd left the shop alone yesterday or with someone else—"

"Did he?"

Little Mr. Purse-strings looked curiously at me. Tighten lips, loosen them, tighten, loosen, tighten, loosen.

"Leave the shop with someone else?"

"I didn't notice. That's what I told the police. The truth is, Mr. Wilcox and I were not close friends ... in fact I didn't care for him at all. He was not a good neighbor."

Welcome to the club, Pursey. "So he died ... last night?"

"Apparently late last night, the policemen said. One or two in the morning. And ... well, more than *died*, I'm afraid.

He was killed. Mugged and robbed. They found him with his watch and wallet gone, on a sidewalk near Gramercy Park—he lives in that neighborhood. So foolish ... in this city, to go out alone at night." He waggled his tape before my face like a stocking in the hands of a strangler.

"Guess I'll have to go somewhere else to get my apartment furnished—do you have any recommendations, Mr. ..."

"Bottomley. Samuel Bottomley. No, I'm afraid not. I own a print shop."

"Age of specialization. Thanks anyway."

Nearly twelve-thirty. Schwartz's biological alarm clock was clanging lunchtime, loud and insistent. We found a deli near 61st, all red-gray formica and mirrors, took a table at the back and ordered. As the waiter walked away, Schwartz caught my eye via the mirrored wall panel. "You think he really was mugged, Doc?"

"Walking around late at night near Gramercy Park—he certainly could've been. Or maybe he met someone there who killed him for other reasons. Or he might've been killed someplace else and dumped there."

"Mmm. Maybe that puts this Dunbar guy into the picture in a bigger way."

"How? If Wilcox is laying golden eggs in Dunbar's yard, why would Dunbar kill him?"

"Say Wilcox got the dough, paid Dunbar, and since blackmail or extortion or whatever ain't exactly legal, Dunbar figured Wilcox is enough of a crumb-bun it'd be better to shut up his mouth on a permanent basis. Like what you said Wilcox mighta done to Moss."

"I guess. Maybe we *should* talk to Dunbar. Frankly, I don't know where else to go from here."

The waiter set our food in front of us. Schwartz nearly dislocated his jaw getting teeth around the first half of a monster corned beef and chopped liver sandwich, set down the remains, chewed slowly, swallowed. Then he looked across the table at me. "Hey, Doc. Something just hit me."

"Something like what?"

"Like how about Wilcox really *was* goin' to wait Hartmann out to sell that music box—but Dunbar was pushin' him too hard. Maybe that music box ain't sittin' in the back room at Wilcox's shop. Maybe it's at Dunbar's." Schwartz dipped a French fry into ketchup, rammed it into the corner of his mouth.

"Could be ... but there's another possibility. Wilcox might've sold the box to someone else—he did mention a Deep Pocket to Hartmann. Then Wilcox paid off Dunbar. But considering the usual quality of Barton Moss' work, Deep Pocket easily could've been miles short of total satisfaction. He bitches to Wilcox, wants the box fixed right or his money back. But there *is* no money to give back—so Wilcox goes to Moss, Moss tells him the box is perfect and the new owner's a jerk. Barton pulled *that* line plenty. Now Wilcox is desperate. It gets hotter and hotter. Finally Moss goes for the pipe wrench, Wilcox stabs him in the back—"

"And then goes and tosses the joint? Why?"

"Good question. I don't know."

Schwartz tore away another chunk of sandwich, chewed thoughtfully.

"Whoever put those goons on Frank—Dunbar or Deep

Pocket—must've really braced Wilcox," I said. "At the two hundred-K level any unhappy is very unhappy."

A bolus slid down Schwartz's throat. "And Wilcox musta wanted big-time to get the heat lamp offa himself. But he can't say he got the music box from Lucas Sterne—Lucas knows too much. He's gonna pick somebody else in antique music, somebody who can't spill any beans 'cause he don't know any. Frank."

"Way I see it. Want to go see if Dunbar can shed any light?"

Schwartz glanced at his plate, then looked at me with gentle reproach. "Can I finish my lunch first?"

"Sure. Be bad if you faint from hunger there."

I was about to pick up my own sandwich—a meager three-inch-thick tongue on rye—when a thought hit me. Schwartz read my face. "Problem, Doc?"

"Small one. You remember where Dunbar's shop is?"

Schwartz searched the crevices of his memory. "Just that Frank said it was in fancy territory. But in this town that covers a lot of blocks. You wrote it down."

"Yeah, I did ... name and address. Then I left the paper on my night table this morning. Guess we'll have to go back and get it."

"Won't take that much time, Doc." Schwartz looked at my untouched food. "Come on, eat up. Else we'll be sittin' in here all day."

10

The paper with Prescott Dunbar's shop address on East 59th was where I left it, all right, on the night table next to the telephone, overnight repository for my pocket contents. The phone message light was blinking, one new message. I pushed the button.

The voice was Rudolph Hartmann's, but shaky, faltering. "Dr. ... Purdue ... please, can you come over right away? I'm ... I've ... I've been beaten up, a couple of thugs ... they were asking about my music box. I told them Wilcox stole it but they kept asking me where *I* got it and who repaired it ... I told them it had been in my family since before I was born and ... that ... Moss repaired it ... I know I shouldn't have, but I was afraid for Lettie. When they finally left they told me if I call the police they'll kill her ... I'm afraid to even go to a hospital ... I don't understand what's going on. Please, Dr. Purdue, call me as soon as you can."

The electronic voice said, "Eight forty-eight a.m." Just a few minutes after I'd left for Edna's.

"You don't understand, Mr. Hartmann?" I said. "Join the club."

* * *

Less than an hour later we were at the Hartmanns', in Lettie's studio. What the gorillas had done to a sick old man was appalling. He opened his shirt, showed us a red and blue map of bruises and cigarette burns. His arms and hands were the same. But unlike Frank he had damage above the neck: discoloration around his left eye, and a swollen upper lip; he pointed carefully to an impressive egg on the right side of his head. I palpated contusions, manipulated critical bony regions. "Be best if you *would* go in, have some tests—"

"Oh, I can't ... not with Lettie. I'm sorry, Dr. Purdue, but no."

"You're sure you never lost consciousness? That's important."

He shook his head vigorously. "This"—he pointed at the lump on his head—"and the eye and the lip happened when I ... guess I got a little wise with them. They asked me who I got the music box from, and I said my father, that some people know who their fathers were."

"No offense, Mr. Hartmann," Schwartz offered. "But if you don't mind me sayin' so, that wasn't exactly the smartest thing you could've said."

A reluctant smile spread from Hartmann's eyes and mouth. "I found that out fast—the one who was burning me went absolutely crazy. He pulled out a gun, hit me over the head with the butt, then punched me in the eye and the mouth. Fortunately the other one stopped him. He said they weren't there to kill me, just to get information. The one who hit me said, 'Okay, we'll *get* information—but I'm still gonna teach him some manners.' Then he put away the gun, and took a sewing needle out of his pocket." Hartmann extended his left hand, index finger out, pointed to a dark spot under the nail. "He stuck the needle in right there. I've never felt such pain."

Schwartz looked on the point of leaving a couple of pounds of chopped liver and corned beef on Hartmann's floor.

"There were two, Mr. Hartmann? What did they look like?"

"Mutt and Jeff. The bigger one had the gun; he was about my height, and maybe thirty pounds heavier. Around forty years old, I'd say, bald, needed a shave. He kept asking me to talk so they didn't have to keep hurting me. The little one was skinny, five-nine or so, with a scar on his left cheek. Dark eyes, smelled like he hadn't had a shower for a while. Oh, and he had a Spanish accent. He's the one who hit and burned me."

"Good thug, bad thug," I said. "I suppose they didn't say anything about who sent them?" Hartmann shook his head. "They didn't ask where the music box was? Just who'd worked on it and where you got it from?"

Nod. "I didn't tell them anything at all until ... they grabbed Lettie. But then ..."

Through all this, Lettie had been pounding at her pile of clay, muttering softly. Now she picked up on her name. "Lettie, Lettie on the jetty. Sweaty Betty, eat spaghetti." Her head lolled back, then snapped forward, and she flicked a small blob of clay against the stained wall in front of her table.

"That's when I told them about Moss," Hartmann said. "I hope I didn't—"

"How long ago were they here?"

"Late last night. They rang the bell, and when I looked out the window they said Thomas Purdue had sent them about my music box. I asked couldn't it wait 'til morning, but they told me you were hot onto something and needed information from me right away. So I let them in. And ..." He indicated his injuries with an unsteady finger, then started buttoning his shirt.

"They said my name? You're sure?"

"Absolutely. I wouldn't have let them in otherwise. I almost called you right after they left, but it was nearly two o'clock ... so I just made sure everything was locked tight, and waited for morning."

I looked at Schwartz. "Who knows I'm involved?"

"I'd say the guy who's sending out torpedo squads."

"Thanks, Broadway. A name'd be nice. Mr. Hartmann, last time we were here you told us Wilcox thought he could sell the music box to a well-heeled customer. Any idea who?"

Hartmann shook his head. "Sorry. He didn't say, and I didn't think it was my place to ask."

"Probably wasn't. But we need to start answering some questions. First Frank gets beaten up. Then Moss is murdered—"

"Because of what I said?" Hartmann reached back to lower himself into a chair. "Oh, *no.*"

"Oh no, to and fro. Black crow in Mexico. Gigolo in To-ky-o." Lettie crooned her rhyming singsong as she ran fingers through the gray mound on her table.

"Nothing to do with you," I said. "Frank was four days ago. Moss got it early yesterday afternoon—and I'm pretty sure Wilcox is our man there."

"Wilcox? How do you—"

I held up my hand. "For now take it on faith."

"You're going to talk to him some more?"

"I'd love to," I said, "but it's tough to carry on any kind of conversation with a corpse."

Good thing Hartmann was seated. "*Wilcox*? Someone murdered him too?"

"May've been a mugging. They found him on the sidewalk late last night, watch and wallet gone. What time were your visitors here?"

Hartmann looked at the ceiling. "Right around midnight ... just a little after. I watched the late news, put Lettie to bed, and was having a nightcap when they rang the bell. Was that before or after Wilcox ..?"

"From what I know, before. I think Wilcox killed Moss, then someone else killed Wilcox—and I'm guessing that someone is the same person who arranged to have Frank and you worked over."

Schwartz absently lifted his fedora, scratched the top of his head. "But your X-guy coulda iced Moss and set up a frame to fit Wilcox."

Oslerian Schwartz. The famous physician William Osler taught that multiple symptoms were more likely to be caused by a single disease than by several. "Possible, Broadway—but I just don't think so. If we go back to square one and look at this deal exactly the way it went down, I can see only one reasonable way to cut the baloney."

"Cut baloney, go to Coney." Lettie, right on the pickup. "Ride very merry merry-go-round, horses up, horses down, ride big Ferris wheel, big deal, *schlemiel*, breezy-freezy seat. Wheeeee."

How did Hartmann stand this all day long, all night? No irritation on his face, just sympathy and pain in his green eyes.

"Mr. Hartmann," I asked, "do you know a Prescott Dunbar?"

Surprise, connection established. "Why ... yes. Not well—he owns a gallery up near Central Park. Excalibur Antiques and Interiors." Little smile, chuckle. "A bit on the pretentious side—but he does have nice things. Why do you ask?"

"Because it looks as if he was on the outs with Wilcox. Have you heard anything about that?"

"No ..." Slow-motion headshake. "I don't think so."

"Anything about Wilcox selling him art fakes?"

"No ... no—but remember, I'm not in the loop anymore. I wouldn't be likely to hear anything."

"Not even that Dunbar might've been blackmailing Wilcox?"

"I'm sorry. No."

"Don't be sorry." I realized I was staring at the doll in the big black perambulator. "That's not a phonograph-doll, is it?"

Hartmann looked at sea. "A phonograph ... you mean some sort of record player?"

"Right. A small one, inside the doll. Edison made a phonograph doll in the eighteen-nineties; so did a Frenchman named Lioret. They both used top-quality French dolls, mostly Jumeau—"

"That's a Jumeau." Hartmann pointed at the doll in the perambulator. "One of their finest, a life-sized little girl."

"Really? Sure there's no phonograph? Because if there is, you could get a good bit of money in a hurry. A Lioret phono-doll as well preserved as that could bring five figures."

Hartmann struggled to remember. "I don't think so ... well, let's take a look." He picked up the lovely blonde-wigged doll with her saucy knitted cap. "Where would it be?"

"In the back—just separate the dress."

He did, peered inside. "I don't see anything."

Schwartz checked her out. "Just a doll, Doc."

"Too bad—well, worth a try." I tapped fingers against the pale pink silk coverlet over the perambulator mattress. "This *can't* be the original."

Hartmann chuckled, smoothed the doll's dress. "It certainly is. Look at the overall condition of the perambulator. That's why Lettie wanted it; you never find doll accessories in such fabulous shape. She paid top dollar and was happy at that."

I lifted the silk, ran my hand over the mattress, then down along the side ... well, how about *that*. "You'd get a better night's sleep on this than on most motel beds."

Hartmann rearranged the coverlet, then laid the doll gently on it. "Just as well there's no phonograph," he said. "Selling it'd be terrible; it was Lettie's joy for so many years."

Before long, someone *would* be selling Lettie's joys, but he knew that. I slipped my hand into my pocket, looked at Schwartz. "Broadway?"

"I'm here, Doc."

"Little late to go to Dunbar's now, and in any case I want to do some groundwork first. But we'd better get protection for the Hartmanns. Can you give Big Al a call—see if he can hop a redeye?"

"Big Al?" Hartmann needed clarification.

"Al Resford," I said. "A very good friend. With him here you and Lettie won't have to worry."

"Hey, but Doc—"

"I'm here, Broadway."

"You want to schlep Al all the way from England? I got other guys in town I could check with—"

"Let's call Al. This is getting nasty, and I know we can count on him. Besides, last time I talked to him, he said he's coming over next week anyway, some business; maybe he could come a few days early. Be nice to see him."

"Can't argue with that, Doc. But what about 'til he gets here?"

"Can you hang in?"

"Sure, you bet. Trudy and me ain't got nothing on tonight."

Hartmann gave Schwartz a skeptical up-and-down.

"Don't worry, Mr. Hartmann," I said. "You're right: Schwartz isn't carrying. But you and Lettie are safer here with his smarts than you'd be with an average-to-good hit man holding a tommy gun."

Hartmann smiled. "Do you give a guarantee?"

"Sure, why not? If I'm wrong you won't be in any position to collect. But don't worry: I'm not and you will be."

Early rush hour, gridlock on the sidewalks of New York. I tripped more than the light fantastic between the Hartmanns' and my office; past four-thirty by the time I got there. Waiting room empty; receptionists, nurses, my partners all gone for the day. No question, academic-doctor hours are a hell of a lot more congenial than those for the poor guys in private practice trenches.

I closed my office door, dialed the medical examiner's number. Then I waited, muttering, through a soupy-voiced electronic menu. I was afraid they might shut down for the day before I was done listening to voice-mail numbers for every ME, office administrator, and secretary in the department. Finally, "Hold please for the receptionist," followed by a click, then a woman's voice, obviously irritated. "Medical Examiner's Office."

"Dr. Thomas Purdue, Man Med Neurology," I said. "Please connect me to whichever ME did an autopsy today on Marcus Wilcox."

Papers flipping. "Yes ... that'd be Dr. George Overstreet. What did you say your name was?"

"Purdue. Dr. Thomas Purdue."

"Please hold."

The Emperor Concerto on a synthesizer. Ludwig would've gone positively homicidal. An excruciating half-minute later a deep voice terminated my suffering. "George Overstreet, Assistant Medical Examiner."

"Dr. Overstreet, thank you," I chirped. "I'm Thomas Purdue, professor of neuro at Man Med. You did Marcus Wilcox's autopsy today—can you give me a short rundown?"

"What's your interest?"

No hostility there, just professional curiosity. How to slant the verbal report. "One of my patients," I said. "I saw him last week, family history of Parkinson's, he was worried he might have early symptoms. I couldn't find anything—and then when I tried to reach him today to set up some followup testing, I found out he was dead. I hope I didn't miss anything ... he certainly didn't seem suicidal. If you'd be more comfortable, I can give you my number, you can verify it and call me back—"

"No, no. No need of that. Don't worry, Dr. Purdue, your patient didn't commit suicide unless he hit himself over the head with a blunt instrument. We don't have a final diagnosis yet, but I don't think the provisional will change. No problem telling you."

"Thanks," I said. "You've got no idea how much I appreciate it."

When Dr. Overstreet finished talking, I hung up and quick-checked the city medical directory. I dialed Medical Records at the Delancey Street Clinic.

Given my druthers I'd have gone straight up to Edna's, but knew she and Jitters would still working. Better to head home, chat a bit with Sarah, have dinner. Then I'd run out to Edna's, check my patient.

"I'll go with you," Sarah said as we cleared the dishes. "It's a lovely evening and besides: why should I sit here alone?"

I could've given her any number of reasons, beginning with the fact she'd hear information she wouldn't like, and ending with how badly that would complicate my life. But I just said, "I thought you were still jet-lagged and tired."

She stopped loading the dishwasher long enough to shoot over her shoulder, "I am—but if I stay here alone, I'll just fall asleep and then I'll be worse off. Besides, Edna's *my* friend, too. I'm worried about her."

"I understand—but still, it's a medical thing, quick checkup, come right back. I can be there and home in ..."

She straightened, cocked her head and stared at me like a bird on a phone wire, trying to make sense of the cat below who's trying to persuade her to come down and play. "Thomas, I'd swear you don't want me to go with you. What's going on?"

"What makes you think something's going on? You want to come? Come."

Sarah and I were barely through Edna's door when she let go on me. "Life's getting a little predictable, Thomas—every time I get a visit from you, here comes Sophie right after. Now she wants me to be a diddledamn automaton factory. She'll find automata for me to fix and her to sell. And if I'll make a new line of originals, she'll move them as fast as I can turn them out."

Sitting on the sofa, holding Edna's album of past glories, Jitters snickered. Edna glared at him. Sarah blinked at Jitters, then turned toward Edna. Get ready, Purdue.

"Why not?" I said quickly. "Food on the table, roof over your head. Keep you off the streets."

Edna was not amused. "Thomas, if you don't stop embarrassing me I'm going to do something you won't like."

That covered a lot of ground. No threat from Edna should ever be considered idle: if she said I wouldn't like what she had in mind, I was sure I wouldn't. But before I could say anything, Sarah took over. "Edna, we've talked about this. Thomas said he'd think of a way to help you, and if he finds something that happens to be good for two people, what's the matter with that? Sophie's past eighty, for heaven's sake, and we all know how her business has fallen off. She loves buying and selling; you love restoring. Stop being difficult."

Edna dropped her gaze, swallowed hard, chewed at her lip.

"Edna *is* getting on with her work," I said. "With a little help. This is Jitters, Sarah, the young man I told you about. Our apprentice."

Jitters shifted the album to the sofa, got up and shook Sarah's hand. "'Please' to meet you, Mrs. Purdue," he mumbled.

"Productive day?" I asked.

Jitters pointed toward the workshop. "We did a lot on the

tea lady," he said. "Then when we had to wait for paint to dry, we started on a hand-turn thing—"

"Manivelle," Edna said, more than a little sharply. "If you want to do this work, you'll learn the lingo."

A manivelle has no spring; its power source is the hand of its owner. As long as that hand turns the crank there's music and motion.

"Say it," Edna said.

"Jitters smiled shyly. "Man-ee-vell. It's got six little furry cats at a tea party, one of them's playin' a violin. Most of the tails're gone and some of the arms and legs. And the string linkages are busted. Edna was showin' me how to make new tails and arms and legs outa rabbit fur. Then we stopped for supper and just now she was showin' me her album. God, she's done some incredible stuff."

"Thomas, did you learn anything more from Wilcox?" In her embarrassment Edna made a dangerous hairpin turn in the conversation.

Without looking at Sarah I said lightly, "Not a thing."

"You did talk to him?"

"Well ... actually, no."

I tried to flash Edna a silent shut-up but her call-blocking system was on. "Well, why *not?* How the hell are we going to find out where that music box is? And what happened to Barton Moss?"

Edna looked expectantly from me to Sarah and back. I must've been crazy to think I could get away with this, should've told Sarah at dinner, could've done it yesterday or the day before. Now I was against the wall; nothing to do but go ahead. "I didn't talk to Wilcox," I said slowly, as if delaying the moment might improve the situation, "because ... he's dead."

Talk about stunned silences. "Dead," Edna repeated. No question mark.

"They found him on the sidewalk last night, near his apartment building. Hit over the head, watch and wallet gone. They think he was mugged."

"Bullshit," Edna snapped. "With all that's been going on? He was no more mugged than he was zapped by a space alien. First Frank gets worked over, then Barton Moss is stabbed to death, then Wilcox—"

"Barton Moss, stabbed to death?" Sarah's hand moved to cover her mouth, then slowly lowered. "Dead?" She looked ready to spring at my throat. "Thomas, I think you'd better tell me what's happening."

Now Edna saw—too late.

"I should have known," my wife snarled. "I go away for a week, you get bored and go looking for a little funsie trouble ... and of course you find it. Somebody beats up Frank, someone kills Barton Moss and Wilcox ... that's a name I don't know. Who is Wilcox?"

I wiped my hand across my face as if that would clean off what the fan had just sprayed on. "Wilcox ... Marcus Wilcox is—*was*—a nasty little man who ran an interior design shop over on Third. He was bothering Edna, trying to get her to consign him her collection. That's all."

"That's *not* all. Somehow he ended up dead and so did Barton Moss. And Edna said something about a music box being mixed up in this, which hardly shocks me. One of Edna's music boxes?"

"No," I said. "This is a very rare music box—"

The look in her eyes stopped me cold. Her lips went blood-less. "Keep talking."

"Combination revolver-plerodienique," I said. "Beyond rare, actually; it's probably unique. Belongs to a man named Rudolph Hartmann, who needs to sell it. Moss was going to restore it; then Wilcox was going to broker it to a wealthy customer—"

"I don't suppose this Hartmann is dead too, is he?"

If words could freeze, Sarah's question would've left me blue and motionless. "No," I said. "Just beaten up—"

"Like Frank."

"I didn't know that," Edna said.

"Happened since the last time I saw you."

I looked at my audience, six eyes more glazed than any pastry in a Dunkin' Donuts showcase. Up went my hands: peace. "Put on a pot of coffee, Edna. Let's sit down; I'll start from the be-ginning."

When I finished talking—leaving out only a small detail hav-ing to do with cinnamon red hots plucked from a pool of blood—Edna spoke first. "This story's running in circles, with Wilcox right at the center. Sorry, I can't believe he was mugged—"

"Me neither."

"So where do we go from here?"

I caught the *we*, decided to ignore it for the time being. "Not sure. The only other connection I've got is this Prescott Dunbar—and now with Wilcox dead, Dunbar can just shrug at any ques-tion I might want to put to him."

Jitters gestured with his coffee cup. "And if he really does got anything to do with who's gettin' beat up and stabbed, what if he decides you shouldn't walk out of there?"

Murmur of general assent. "Told you he was sharp, Sarah," I said.

Jitters blushed. Sarah, though, looked anything but impressed. But she didn't say anything so I went on. "I'd give an eyetooth to look around the late Wilcox's shop. See if the music box is in the back room—or if it's gone, whether I could find a sales receipt with a customer's name. Or see what might turn up in a drawer or a box. Something."

Now Sarah spoke. One word, my name. Loud, sharp, clipped. Everyone looked at her.

"What *is* it with you—and with *you*, Edna? With *all* of you? This isn't something you should be doing. It's police business."

"The police wouldn't put all these people together," I said. "And they already figure Wilcox was mugged, end of story."

"Fine. You can also figure end of story."

"Can't, Sarah. We *know* it's not the end. Somebody's still out there who's unhappy for some reason over that music box—"

"Yes, over the music box, that rare music box. In which you have absolutely no interest."

I shook my head. "At two hundred thousand dollars? I don't think so. What's important is there are people still in danger—Frank, and the Hartmanns."

"Tell the police. Let *them* provide protection. That's their job."

"Remember what the goons told Hartmann? If he called the cops they'd kill him and his wife. I promised him I wouldn't do that."

"And you never break a promise, do you?"

"Not if I can help it," I said. "And if I do I have a damn good reason."

"Like staying alive yourself? You told us Hartmann let these thugs in because they said *you'd* sent them. Your Mr. Somebody must know you're involved. Maybe *you're* next on the hit parade."

Time to play the ponies a little—but given this particular filly's track record I knew I had a sure bet. "Maybe so—but the fact remains, I did make a promise. If you think it's all right to break a promise I made trying to help someone, I'll at least listen."

Silence. All I heard was breathing. I knew I'd eventually hear more from Sarah, a whole lot more. But one horse race at a time.

"All right," I said. "I don't know what to do next. I've got an idea, though, need to think it through. Jitters, stay on and work with Edna for now. We'll catch up with your music box later."

On the subway, along the sidewalk, all the way back home, Sarah didn't say a word. As we came up to our building, who's standing there but that same street man, a look on his face like a cat whose owner forgot to give him food that day. He moved a step forward as if he were about to extend a hand, but then backed away. Sarah accelerated, pushed past him, took the concrete stairs up to the stoop in a flash. I stopped, relieved my wallet of another fiver, slapped it into the guy's palm.

"Thanks, Doc," he said, and I thought I saw light dancing in his eyes.

"Doc?" I echoed.

"Skinny lady on Three told me you were a doctor. The one with the legs. She said you live right above her, and you fix old music boxes."

That would be Helena Mascagni, the little ballerina with the big mouth. Helena's an intelligence man's dream. Flip her switch with a question and there she goes chattering, more animated than any automaton Edna Reynolds ever worked on. It never seems to occur to Helena that there are some bad people out there, and it's not bright to make it easier for them to rob, assault, or murder you.

As if reading my mind, the old man said, "I'm curious, that's all—just wondered about you. You seem like a nice guy; you've sure been good to me."

"Lot of people wonder about me," I said, glancing over my shoulder at Sarah, who was standing on the stoop, under the light, looking professionally impatient.

The street man chuckled. "Better go before you get two earfuls instead of one."

His eyes were clear, speech unslurred. He smelled dirty, he *was* dirty. No booze breath, though. If he'd disguised himself as a street man to tail me, you'd think he'd at least have used a bit of Thunderbird for mouthwash. And wouldn't have let me know he was gathering intelligence from my neighbors. On the other hand, what would make a disguised tail look *less* like a tail than spilling me one or two of the blander beans he'd picked up? I shook my head. Sometimes you can think too much.

"You don't know how right you are," I said, turning to go. "See ya."

"You never know how right you are," the man said softly, and waved the bill at me. Then even more softly, "Thanks."

Sarah went off before the door to my workshop was closed.

"Thomas, you are driving me over the brink! For months at a time you're reasonable; then something grabs hold and you're off, sticking your nose everywhere it doesn't belong. One of these times it's going to get cut off."

There's nothing down and dirty about Sarah; she's your classic *Homo institutionalis*, loves outlines, guidelines, baselines, any lines to govern and regulate behavior. "What grabs hold of me is called sympathy," I said. "Desire to help a friend. It started with Edna and Frank—"

"And spread to Barton Moss, whom you can't ... couldn't stand. And that Wilcox person whom you didn't even know 'til he bothered Edna—"

"Who's my friend."

She didn't even slow down. "And now those Hartmanns, who, I'll admit, sound pathetic—but they're hardly your friends. Why was it your responsibility to get into this mess on their behalf?"

"You didn't talk to them," I said. "You didn't see them. Somebody tells you they're starving in Africa or shooting babies in Eastern Europe somewhere, and out comes your checkbook. Or that the Holy Church Mission needs help spooning out grub. There's always a check or a ladle between you and your beneficiary. When I help someone I like to do it from up close."

"I'll say you do. How much closer can you be than to yourself? Don't tell me about Frank and Edna and the Hartmanns— they're all just an excuse. There's a music box involved here— by your own admission, a unique music box."

"Costing two hundred thousand dollars. I'm not poor, but I don't play in that league."

"I know you. You're hardly above a little interleague play now and then, if that's what it takes."

"That's going too far."

"Is it? I don't think so." Loud sigh. "All right—I'll admit your loyalty to your friends is admirable; so is your interest in people, one at a time. That's why you're as good a doctor as you are. But why can't you just be a doctor?"

"Because I don't want to *just* be a doctor. Medical work's interesting, but it's not all there is."

"All there is apparently doesn't include me. I've been back three days and I've hardly seen you."

No point picking up on that line. Sarah's a fastball hitter: throw her your best heat anywhere near the plate, and she'll knock it over the wall. Time for a nasty slider. Get myself out of this inning, put her on the bench for a while.

"Sarah, listen. You heard what I said before: I'm stuck. Let up a little. If the horse is dead, why should we argue over where I might want to ride?"

"You also said you had an idea. I know you. If you want to go riding and the horse is dead, you'll find a way to bring him back to life."

"Fine. If you see me getting back up on old Lazarus, you can start shouting again. But for now can we bag it?"

Sarah seemed to droop. "You're going to be the death of me."

"Nah." I leaned forward to kiss her cheek. "You're tired, that's all. It's near ten; why don't you go sack out? Good night's sleep, maybe you'll feel better."

Smile, if a bit wan. "I can't argue that."

I watched her disappear through the kitchen, waited a few minutes, then strolled to the workbench and reached past the bright, shiny pieces of Jitters' music box to push the start lever on a small circa-1845 box by Ducommun-Girod. At once came the sound of the "Sextet" from *Lucia*, lovely, light, delicate as a gently-stroked harp. I tried to imagine what Jitters might see and feel. If only the visual components of my apprentice's sensory response could be learned, his heightened emotional capacity developed. Sure. Maybe with a little practice I could also share the visions of Mozart or Michelangelo. Jitters had a gift; I didn't. Simple as that. As the cylinder clicked to a stop and the last tender chord faded, I felt a vague dissatisfaction clearly tinged with envy.

No sound from Sarah's rooms. I walked over to the sofa, picked up the phone, dialed my father's number.

Second ring, he picked up. "You want *what*? To come over *now*?"

"We've both been up a lot later than this over patients, Dad. I need another consultation."

"About Edna?"

"Related. It won't take long; would you mind?"

"Of course not. You know I'd never say you can't come talk to me."

I knew it, all right, counted on it. I thanked my father, hung up the phone, then walked back to the workbench and picked up the envelope of photographs Hartmann had given me. Very quietly, I let myself out of the apartment, went downstairs, got the Beetle, and drove off to Hobart, to my father's house. Time for a crash course in miniature paintings.

11

After Sarah dragged herself off to work in the morning I cleared the table, loaded the dishwasher. By now, Al Resford would be at the Hartmanns' and Schwartz well into his morning's picking. I decided to get Jitters' work-in-progress off the bench, put in a few hours on my Reymond-Nicole, then bring Schwartz and Big Al up to date on what I'd learned the night before from my father.

But you've got to be flexible. Just past nine, the phone rang. Edna. "Thomas, get your ass over here. Now."

Trouble again, capital T and all, but different this time. On her previous call, Edna was a nurse needing the okay for a body bag. Now she was my school principal, telling me to get to her office. This minute.

Now what? Did Jitters give her lip, too much or the wrong kind? Did he drop a work project? Screw up a valuable automaton beyond redemption ... wait. Oh no. Did he steal a valuable automaton?

"Right now?" Two little words in fine silvery tremolo.

"Any reason why not?"

"No, ma'am. I'll be right over."

***

One little surprise after another. As Edna let me in, Jitters waved hello, but he was not the only other person present. Sophie Soleski was there too. So was Cleveland Gackle.

Gackle regarded me calmly from beneath the most exuberant pair of white eyebrows I've ever seen on any mammal other than a Scottish terrier. A little smile flickered at the corners of his mouth. Lounging in an armchair, wearing his customary stained workshirt—engine grease, best I could tell—and baggy khaki pants held up with suspenders, he tipped a deferential nod in my direction. "Edna says we're doin' another job together."

My head started to pound. As lockpickers go, Gackle is no less than brilliant, but the man's got a maddening habit of refusing to give an unequivocal answer to a question, *any* question. Ask your crib cracker whether he can get through a door without leaving evidence of forced entry, it's at the very least disconcerting to hear him say, "Person never can be sure. Probably I can ... but then again maybe not."

I looked around the room. No one said a word. "Couldn't prove it by me, Pete," I said. "Maybe we are, but then again maybe we're not."

Why Pete? Gackle's full name is Cleveland Alexander Gackle; he was born the day Grover Cleveland Alexander fanned Tony Lazzeri with the bases loaded to sew up the seventh game of the 1926 World Series. Gackle Senior, a big baseball fan, named his bouncing son for the hero of the day, whose nickname—God only knows why—was Pete. See?

"Sophie came by last evening," Edna said. "After you left. We had a nice talk."

"We're going to work together, Thomas," Sophie chimed

in. "Edna and I. Buying, selling, restoring, making automata. With Edna's talent ... *and* your young friend's, there ... and my connections, we should make ourselves some pretty pennies."

Sophie started in the music box business more than a half-century ago, and even if her sales had fallen off in recent years, she was still, as she put it, well-connected. Not only in New York but throughout the U.S. and Western Europe, the name Soleski was synonymous with fine-quality music boxes. Give Sophie the goods, Sophie would sell them.

"I'm sure you can," I said. "And make no mistake, I'm glad to hear it. But I'm also sure that's not why Edna ordered me over here."

"There *is* a connection, Thomas," Edna said. "You've been kind to Sophie and me ... and Jitters. We decided it's time *we* gave *you* a little help. I told Sophie all about what's been going on."

"Including the music box. My, a plerodienique-revolver, I've never in my life seen anything like that." The sparks in Sophie's eyes were those of a woman fifty years younger.

"You haven't heard anything about one being sold here recently, have you Soph?" I asked.

She shook her head. "You may be certain if I had, I'd remember."

I was certain. "I haven't heard a thing, either—which tells me it wasn't sold to anyone in NYMBCA, probably not even to a nonaffiliated New York collector."

"That's what we were thinking," Edna said. "But maybe it wasn't sold at all. Maybe it's still in Wilcox's shop, locked in the back room."

Locked in the back room: ergo Gackle. "Possible," I said.

"But if Wilcox did sell it, I think I know why it wasn't to a music box collector." Quickly I went through what I'd learned the night before from my father about miniature paintings.

"So we need to get into that shop," Edna said, "and find one of two things: the music box itself or the name of the person who bought it. I called Pete and Sophie last night and told them my idea. Then we all went by and cased the joint."

They cased the joint. Ma and Pa and Auntie Barker, and the Machine Gun Kiddy. "You *all* went by and 'cased the joint'?" I gave Jitters the hot eye. My apprentice suddenly found something interesting on the floor at his feet.

"Jitters—" I began, but Edna silenced me with a look that would've melted brass gears in a clock.

"Leave Jitters alone," she barked. "If you want to get sore, get sore at me. Now, here's what I thought, Thomas. Jitters'd go up on the roof, check for a skylight—"

"A skylight! Edna, just how did you happen to know—"

She let go a real put-me-in-my-place snort. "Two days and nights working with Jitters, and you think I wouldn't manage to nail the skinny about how he and you really did get together?"

"I should've known."

"Sure you should've. And by the way, he also did say he'd promised you no more skyjobs. I told him it'd be all right if it was for a good cause ... and I'd take responsibility. He's my apprentice, too."

"In restoration work."

"Bull. Apprentices are part of the family, you know that. They live with the master and his wife and kids, do whatever needs doing. So here's what I figured: while Jitters was up on the roof, Pete'd check out the door and locks. Then tonight after dark we'd all go in and hunt for the music box and receipt books. Find either the box or who bought it."

"But Edna—breaking and entering, right on Third Avenue? With great big plate-glass windows across the front? How in hell are you going to—"

"Chill, Thomas. That *was* a problem but it's not anymore. Shut up and listen, you'll understand. We got to the shop and what did we see?"

"A little old man and eight tiny reindeer?"

I thought she'd give me holiest hell but all I got was a crafty smile. "Half right, wise guy. The shop door was open, lights on inside, and a little old man was walking around, looking, with a spindle-shanked old woman. I told Pete, Sophie, and Jitters to wait around the corner; then I went in and said I was there to see Marcus Wilcox. You can just about picture it."

I could picture it very well. What I couldn't picture was what was coming.

"They just stood there staring, so I told them I was supposed to meet Marcus Wilcox here, and where was he? The man said, 'You had an appointment with Mr. Wilcox ... at nine o'clock at night?'"

"'If it's any business of yours,' I said. 'Marcus and I both are pretty busy all day, and would you mind telling me what the hell's going on?' The two of them looked at each other, then the old guy coughed and said, 'Mr. Wilcox is, I'm afraid ... well, deceased. He was mugged the other night, and killed.' So I did my best Edna Barrymore bit, hand to my throat, plopped into a chair, finally said oh my, how awful, how shocking, and by the way, who *are* you people? The man introduced the lady, and guess what—she was Marcus' *mother*, for Christ's sake, Doris Wilcox. And he was her lawyer, Wendell Gooding, of Peterson, Gooding, and Blah-blah. That was all I needed. I got up, grabbed Mrs. Wilcox's hand, told her how sorry I was, that I'd done antique fabric work for Marcus for years. She sat down next to me, started talking, and guess what again? She's an antique dealer in a little place upstate, Horton's Falls, been in the game since the Flood, brought little Marcus up in the trade, but Horton's Falls wasn't good enough for him, he had to come to New York, and now ... well, she was looking over the inventory, wanted to take the good small stuff back to her shop—but there *wasn't* much small stuff. She figured she'd have to find a dealer here to come and clean the place out. By that time Mr. Gooding was starting to twitch, so Mrs. Wilcox got up and thanked him for bringing her by the shop off-hours; now at least she knew what she had to deal with. After Marcus' service tomorrow afternoon—that's today—she'd start asking around. Then we went outside, Gooding locked up, and gave her the keys to the door and the alarm system."

"I was wondering how you were going to shut off the alarm if we broke in," I said.

"So was I," Edna said wearily. "But now we don't have to think about it. I didn't have a plan before—but I sure as hell have one now."

I prepared to launch a wisecrack, but saw my father, tall, stern, gray, standing next to Edna. *She needs to feel necessary. Do you think you can manage not to be too clever for her good?*

"You have a plan?" I said. "I'm listening."

Dad smiled, something he does far more often in my imagination than when he's actually on stage.

Edna cleared her throat. "Here's the pitch, Thomas. Tonight, when Mrs. Wilcox leaves her hotel to go to dinner, Jitters rips off her purse. You chase after Jit, get the bag back for the old lady; then you and Soph take her out to eat and listen to her story, why she's here, what she's got to get done. You tell her you've got a friend who can empty that store in nothing flat; you'll bring him over in the morning if she'd like. I'm betting she'd like in a big way. Then tomorrow, while Schwartz is writing up the inventory, you, Soph, and Pete search the place, front room and back. Find either the music box or a record of sale. How's that sound?"

Gackle raised a brown-stained forefinger, souvenir of his longstanding love affair with Mary Jane. "You're a sharp cookie, Edna. Wish I'd met you forty years ago."

By comparison to Edna, the Cheshire cat would've looked like a candidate for high-dosage Prozac. Nice change in just a couple of days. "Well, Thomas?" she asked.

Another hot-eye for my apprentice. "You *are* a talented young man. How many more job skills do you have that I don't know about?"

Before Jitters could do more than stammer a couple of syllables, Edna swept between us, turned all guns on me. "Goddamn it, Thomas—go after that kid one more time, you'll be singing soprano the rest of your life. This is *my* idea. Talk to *me* if you don't like something about it."

Picture a thirty-foot cabin cruiser that just tried to cut off a battleship. "All right, Edna, sorry. I'm impressed, I really am."

"But?" Reading me like a kindergarten primer.

"One thing bothers me: if this deal goes sour you're on the line for some real unpleasantness. And frankly if we need to move fast to get away—"

"Sophie and I would be a drag on you?"

Jitters moved a couple of steps away from Edna. "In a word, yes," I said. "What'd they clock you ladies at last time you ran a hundred-yard dash?"

"I don't know," Sophie snapped. "It's been a while since I've had to run one. When you get older, you learn to use your head to get around trouble. Have patience, my dear, you'll find out soon enough. But if I do get nailed, that'll be my problem, not yours. I've never been a stool pigeon."

Sophie's faint *mittel*-European accent behind those last two sentences would've been hilarious were it not for the indignation in which the words were soaked.

Edna aimed an index finger at me. "Put it this way: Sophie and I are not about to spend our golden years dicussing our digestion and being careful to stay off the streets after dark. We're going ahead with this plan, Sophie, Pete, Jitters and me. I hope you'll play, too—you know better than any of us what to look for. But if you don't want to come along, stay home. I'll call you after we're done."

"Edna, you're not being reasonable. All of you are taking a risk for something that's not really your—"

Edna was on me like gangbusters. "Thomas, you know what? You sound like Sarah."

Talk about low blows.

"You didn't waste any time getting over here when Wilcox was giving me trouble, did you? And how many times over the years have you bailed Sophie out? You've done well by Pete, and—"

She needs to feel necessary, Thomas. You asked my advice; didn't you listen?

As Edna pointed at Jitters I pulled out my handkerchief, waved it. "All right—count me in."

Edna chuckled. "Great. You'll talk to Schwartz?"

"Soon as we're done here."

"We're done. Now: Doris is staying at the Imperial Hotel; that's on Lexington between Sixty-fourth and Sixty-fifth. Let's meet on the corner of Lex and Sixty-third this afternoon, say a quarter to five. Thomas, Sophie, Jitters, me. Small town people generally eat an early dinner. Then tomorrow morning, Thomas, Sophie, Schwartz, corner of Third and Sixty-first, quarter to ten. Pete, you'll be waiting near the shop by a quarter to twelve tomorrow. That ought to do it."

Schwartz was evaluating an estate on the west side. He blinked up at me from the living room floor, where he sat with a gigantic box of old picture postcards. The middle-aged woman who'd let me in, obviously heir to this inheritance, stood next to me. "Trudy told you I was here?"

"Sure, Trudy. Can you take a quick lunch break?"

Schwartz looked at the woman, who checked her watch. "I need to leave by three to get back to Jersey," she said in that clipped tone people use when they really want to say something else but know it would be unreasonable.

"Ah, no sweat." Schwartz scrambled to his feet. "It's what, not even twelve yet. Me and the Doc here'll just go down to the deli, have a bite, I'll be back inside of half an hour." He looked at me for confirmation.

"Half hour, easy," I said.

"And it won't take me more'n a couple hours after that. Have you on your way before two-thirty, okay, Mrs. Birnbaum?"

Mrs. Birnbaum nodded, lips tight. She'd rather see Schwartz keep working, said her face, but she knew she was verbally checkmated.

Schwartz didn't seem the least surprised by what I had to tell him. "That Edna—I don't think I ever want to be on the other side from *her*. Yeah, sure I'll play. Whole store full of goodies dumped in my lap? I'll take that kind of a gimme any day."

The waiter set our sandwiches in front of us. Schwartz two-handed his mountain of rye-coated pastrami, snapped off a monster mouthful, chewed thoughtfully, washed the bolus down with a swig of Cel-Ray soda. "I got a couple places I gotta visit tomorrow, but I'll be done by ten."

"Corner of Third and Sixty-first. *Quarter* to ten."

"Gotcha, Doc. Piece of cake."

Schwartz's sandwich was well along toward extinction. "Cheesecake, no doubt," I said. "Cherry cheese."

My little friend checked his watch. "Yeah, you bet." He half-turned in his seat to semaphore at the waiter. "He brings it now while I'm finishing the samwitch, I got just about enough time."

Lights blinking, cars swaying, the A train rattled me down the west side, past my usual 14th Street stop to Washington Square. From there a short stroll through the West Village to Hartmann's. *Hartmann's,* I thought. Not *Hartmanns'.* When we say someone's not all there, we're being more literal than we know. I was considering Lettie as if she weren't there at all. Shame on me.

She was there, all right, high-pitched singsong from the back room. Hartmann gave me a hearty shake and an eager look. "Are you making any progress?"

"I'm sure I am," I said. "Just haven't recognized it yet."

Behind Hartmann, comfortably filling an armchair, Al Resford chuckled appreciatively. "Same Thomas as ever, what? Never mind, Rudolph. I've no doubt but with enough rope and a little time to use it, Thomas will bring your attackers to bay." The bulky Englishman worked his way out of the chair by degrees, came forward for the prescribed handshake. "Pleasure to be able to work with you again, Thomas."

I was sure the pleasure, not to mention the advantage, was mine. Big Al Resford, a long-time friend of Schwartz's, is a major figure in the subterranean districts of London's antiques and art world. I can't tell you exactly what Big Al does most of the time, and if I could, I wouldn't. Schwartz warned me early on to enjoy his company, avail myself of his talents, and ask no unnecessary questions. Al's round face, mild light blue eyes, affable demeanor, quiet speech, and pear-shaped body stuffed into a dark three-piece suit give him the appearance of a jolly British teddy bear, but you'd be a bloody fool—take that as you will—to underestimate this unprepossessing hybrid of Alfred Hitchcock and Zero Mostel.

"I'm glad you could come, Al," I said, then added, "believe me," as sincere a tag line as you'll ever hear. "I assume you and the Hartmanns are getting on?"

"Oh yes. They're as lovely hosts as one could wish. I was able to book flight within a few hours, got here by late evening, ac'shly. Broadway briefed me, then went on home. We all got a

fine night's rest; then this morning Mr. Hartmann showed me
his workshop—most interesting. We've seen no sign of trouble."

"Good." I pulled pictures from my pocket, Hartmann's fabulous plerodienique-revolver, fanned them out like playing cards.
"Here's the source of our trouble, Al."

He leaned forward, scrutinized each picture. "Oh my—I
see. Yes, indeed." He straightened, smiled again. "Considerable
temptation, I'd say."

"Very considerable—a probable one-off, appraised for two
hundred thousand dollars." I slid the pictures back into my
pocket. "All right. I'll be in touch." I moved toward the door.

Al tapped absently at his jacket pocket. "I say ... Thomas,
Rudolph ... is there a tobacconist in the neighborhood—I like
the occasional cigar." Mischievous smile. "I promise to smoke it
out of doors."

Hartmann pointed vaguely east-southeast. "Just a half-block
down Washington Street."

Al looked confused.

"I'll walk you there," I said. "Mr. Hartmann: give Al your
key. Lock the door behind us, don't look out the window for
any reason, and if anyone rings the bell just lay low. Al'll be
back in ten minutes."

As we turned the corner onto Washington Street, Al said, "I
presume this is what you were thinking, Thomas? Bit of a chat
in private?"

"Right. What did you think of those photographs?"

"Ah, yes. Truly impressive ... lovely woodworking, stunning
mechanics, but what will bring the real pennies is that painting

inside the lid. Clearly a Sinclair, probably on silk. Astounding detail, but of course that's to be expected."

"Great! Exactly what I thought."

"Really? You surprise me, Thomas. I'd not have thought art lay within the boundaries of your expertise."

"Secret weapon." I smiled. "My dad's an amateur painter; when I showed him these pictures last night he didn't hesitate a second. 'St. John Sinclair!'" I pronounced the first two words Sinjin, as the English do. "Just another young commercial portraitist until he went to France, discovered miniatures, and developed a style featuring detail like no one before or since. But he died young, and long before the First War he was forgotten. Then, not ten years ago, someone wrote an article about him—"

"Michael Rothstein, *Art and Artists*, spring issue, 'ninety-three." Al's eyes gleamed; his smile was now highly mischievous. "Values of paintings are like those of currencies: determined by ongoing, wary agreement. What's dismissed in one place and time may be highly valued in another. William Blake, don't you know, worked his whole life as a book illustrator and painted on Sundays. He couldn't sell those Sunday paintings, couldn't give them away. After his death, they sat sixty years in a trunk in the basement of the British Museum; then the trunk was sold ... to Dante Gabriel Rossetti. Which is the only reason we have Blake today. So yes: Rothstein did the same sort of posthumous favor for poor Sinclair. After that article, the value of all his work went, as you would put it over here, ballistic. Something such as this, on silk ... well, I should estimate pr'aps a half-million of your dollars at a well-publicized Sotheby's or Christie's sale."

We stopped outside the tobacco shop. "Now you see why I asked you to come over. The Hartmanns do need a bodyguard, yes. But I thought your ... other skills would be at least as valuable."

"I imagined 'twould be something of that sort. Jolly fine. But we don't want to stay out here too long, do we?" He turned to go into the smoke shop.

"Does it bother you, Al?—Mrs. Hartmann's behavior." He looked back at me, waiting for more. "The singsong," I said. "I don't know how Hartmann stands it."

"Oh, heavens no." Al chuckled. "It's background music—what do you call it here?"

"Muzak?"

"Oh yes. Poor lady's maunderings are far less offensive than the acoustic swill they serve on elevators. No, I must say, I barely hear Mrs. Hartmann, bless her soul."

12

Plan on hold until a quarter to five. The Devil makes work for idle hands; wouldn't want that to happen to me. I went to the workbench, started dampering my Reymond-Nicole comb. Needle-thin teeth separated by hairlines, tiny brass pins in tiny damper recesses, wire so fine as to be barely visible. Finicky, fidgety work demanding intense concentration—just what I wanted right then. I'd thought enough about Edna's plan to be comfortable with it. No need to spend the afternoon playing it over in my head.

By four-fifteen I had twenty-one more dampers placed and shaped, time well spent. Now, time to spend well in a different way. I scribbled a quick note to Sarah, told her I'd be back late, left the note on the kitchen table. Then I charged out, hustled through Union Square, jumped aboard an up-town Number 6 Lexington train.

Edna knew her onions: small town folk are early to bed, to rise, to eat. Just a few minutes past five, an elderly woman walked down the three marble steps out of the Imperial Hotel, across the street from the four conspirators. The woman turned onto the sidewalk, headed south. Edna nudged me.

She didn't have to. I'd have recognized Doris Wilcox

anywhere, spindle-shanks and all. Howdy Doody's little gray-haired mother, a slight woman in a black-and-white polka dot dress, self-consciously keeping pace with the smart-stepping New Yorkers around her but without their aggressive body movements. Get where she was going—presumably a restaurant—as quickly as possible, and in one piece. We'd need to activate our operation before she reached her destination.

"See you later," Edna whispered. "Can't let her spot me."

Sophie, Jitters and I strolled to the corner, keeping Mrs. Wilcox in sight through the bumper-to-bumper cars, cabs, trucks, buses. Green light, we crossed, then stepped up our pace. Coming up on 63rd she was half a block ahead of us. Pedestrian traffic was thick, both good and bad. Easier to camouflage our maneuvers, but more of a chance some misguided good Samaritan might tangle us up.

But people who wait for perfect conditions usually have short curricula vitae. We closed the gap to our quarry, crossed the street behind her.

"This block," I said.

Sophie's face told me she understood. Jitters reached into his pocket, snapped open a mean-looking knife, hid the blade inside his left hand. "Jitters, be sure you don't ... hurt her," I whispered.

Jitters smiled, tolerant regard of the professional for the sweaty amateur. Then he stepped forward, swung to the inside of the sidewalk, came up on Doris Wilcox from her left—the side on which she held her purse, right hand reached across to grip the shoulder strap, left hand supporting the bag from below.

Jitters made his move, quick knife-slash, then another. Then he was off down the sidewalk with the purse, Elroy

(Crazylegs) Hirsch dancing between defenders with a football tucked into the crook of his arm, goal line far in the distance but no doubt he was going to get there.

Beautiful to watch, but I wasn't there as a spectator; neither was Sophie. We charged up to Doris Wilcox, who was standing transfixed, too startled to scream, staring at the length of black leather shoulder strap in her right hand. Only one person, a middle-aged man in a light suit, seemed to have noticed the snatch; he waved an arm, yelled, "Hey—stop him," and took off in pursuit. That wouldn't do. As we approached Mrs. Wilcox I slipped my foot in front of the would-be hero's leg; he grunted, went sprawling on the sidewalk. Quick mumbled "Whoops, sorry" in his general direction, then I turned to join the two elderly ladies.

Doris Wilcox was recovering both color and composure; she looked ready to let loose a good loud screech for the authorities. Sophie cut her off. "We were right behind you," Soph announced. "Saw the whole thing. Thomas—see if you can't catch that little thug."

"On my way," I said, then called back, "Wait here for me."

I took off down the sidewalk, not nearly as elegantly as Jitters, but fast enough to get the job done. Sophie would now be telling Doris I was a track and field star in college and still ran daily, did the occasional marathon. She'd bet I'd be back with the purse in just a few minutes.

She'd be right, of course. Down to 62nd I zipped, then charged west. I crossed Madison, ran uptown half a block to the Regina Hotel, took the marble stairs three at a time, chugged through the lobby to the registration desk. The proprietor, Mr. Espinoza, gave me a big smile and a conspiratorial nod toward the doorway behind him. "You' frien', he back in the office there. Ever'thing's jake, Doaktore. Nobody come after him."

Espinoza was his usual resplendent self in a flamingo-pink shirt and off-chartreuse polyester trousers. Where he buys clothing like this I couldn't begin to tell you. As he lifted the wooden panel to his right I ducked through, slowing just long enough to pat him on the shoulder. "Thanks, Nozey," I said. "You're making my day."

"Glad when I can help, Doaktore. Like I tell Edna when she call yesterday, you guys got my IOU forever."

I found Jitters lounging on a slatback chair behind an old oak secretary-desk, Doris Wilcox's pocketbook in his lap. "Went good," he said as I rushed through the doorway. "Move like that, nobody even knows something happened 'til you're six blocks down the sidewalk."

The voice of experience. "Looks like skyjobs really weren't your only source of income."

"Hey, Dr. ... Thomas—"

"It's okay, Jitters, just kidding a little." I pulled my shirttail out of my trousers, popped off a button midway along the shirt-front, reached up to tear loose the left side of my collar. Then I extended my hand. "Let's go—I've got to get back."

Jitters thrust the purse in my general direction; I grabbed, caught the strap near a cut end. Like a volleyball on a string, the pocketbook sailed up over my head, then recoiled sharply at its apogee. An object flew out, crashed to the floor, shattered. Purse dangling from my hand, I bent to look.

Jitters' face was smeared with concern. "Shoot, I'm sorry ... didn't even know it was open. I shoulda been more careful."

"We both should've ..." I picked up the largest fragment.

"Little blue vase—looks like Wedgwood. Pick up all the pieces; we can think it out later. I need to go."

Jitters started retrieving shards as I moved toward the door. "Got a gray powder on it," he shouted, but I didn't dare take any more time. If Sophie ran out of ways to keep Doris Wilcox quiet we'd be face to face with a first class mess. I flashed Nozey a quick wink, ducked back into the lobby, ran out.

Sophie and Doris were right where I left them, on the sidewalk in front of a dress shop, looking for all the world like a couple of elderly women discussing their children's latest accomplishments. People moved past, paying them not the slightest mind. As I ran up, waving the pocketbook, Soph cheered, turned to Doris. "See, I told you he'd get it back."

Doris took the pocketbook, thanked me gravely. "That was *very* kind, young man, thank you ... but oh, dear. Your shirt. You're not hurt, are you?"

I laughed. "Not at all. When I grabbed the pocketbook away, he grabbed back at me, ripped my shirt. Then he took off."

While I talked, Doris rummaged through the purse. She looked up, stone-faced. "There was ... something's missing," she said. "An eight-and-a-half-inch light-blue Wedgwood jasperware urn. Single white handle, with a flared top like a candlestick. You didn't happen to see it, did you?"

Oh, shit.

"Actually, yes," I said, slowly. "Everything happened so fast ... but now you mention it, the punk had it in his other hand when I caught him. He was going through the pocketbook, I guess looking for money and whatever else he might be able to turn a buck on. After I got the pocketbook away from him, he took off down the street ... with the urn."

Doris Wilcox looked stricken. "That urn had my son's *ashes* in it."

What did Jitters say as I ran out of the Regina's office—something about a gray powder? All I could do was stare at Mrs. Wilcox. Sophie obviously couldn't manage any better.

"He died a few days ago," Doris said. "I had the service today. I was the only one there, just a few prayers; then they cremated him and put his ashes in the urn. I'm a Wedgwood collector, you see."

I saw, all right. What I didn't see was what to do about what I saw. "The kid must've known he could sell it to an antique dealer," I said. "Which may not be bad. New York's a big place, but people tend to work in neighborhoods, and Sophie and I know the antique circles pretty well. I collect and restore antique music boxes; she sells them. Got a card, Soph?" I held my hand out to Doris Wilcox. "Thomas Purdue."

Mrs. Wilcox's grip was surprisingly strong, considering her build and what her mental state had to've been right then. "I'm Doris Wilcox," she said. "From Horton's Falls ... that's a little town, about halfway between here and Buffalo ..." She took the card from Sophie, studied it. "Well, for heaven's sake." Her face relaxed into a smile. "What a small world. I'm an antique dealer myself. Wilcox's Fine Antiques, quality china and pottery, glass, some furniture. No junk. Nothing—absolutely *nothing*—under a hundred years old."

Talk about feeling like garbage. I pictured Mrs. Wilcox walking through her shop after learning of her son's death, scanning shelves for the most suitable receptacle for his ashes, finally settling on a good Wedgwood urn. Now that urn was in approximately thirty pieces, and the gray powder so recently her son was wafting through the exhaust system of the Regina Hotel.

But the show's got to go on. I took Doris Wilcox's arm in one hand, Sophie's in the other. "We were just on our way to dinner," I said to Mrs. Wilcox. "Please come with us. It'd be—"

She waved me off. "I couldn't do that, not possibly. You've already been so kind—"

"Nothing of the sort," Sophie declared with full Hungarian imperiousness. Point beyond discussion. "Thomas—let's take Mrs. Wilcox to Randall's. It's nearby, and so nice."

"Settled." I led my two elderly charges northward up Lexington.

"Well, I must say: I never expected treatment like this in New York," Doris said. "You have no idea how grateful I am."

Randall's is one of those little mid-town watering holes with high mahogany booths all around, snowy white table-cloths, huge mirror-backed mahogany bar at the rear, waiters with black jackets and unstained white shirts. Mostly Italian food, but a good selection of steaks and fish. Doris began to relax as soon as we were seated; by the middle of her third martini her tongue was nicely lubricated. Horton's Falls, she told us, was a major R&R spot for the well-to-do from the late nineteenth century until the Great Depression. She'd lived there all her life, owned her shop for close to forty years, knew every-one. And everyone knew Doris Wilcox would treat them hon-estly when they wanted to turn their tangible residuals of The Gilded Age into ready cash. Her son Marcus worked with her for a while, but went off twenty-two years before to make it big in New York. And now ...well, Doris didn't see any need to ship her son's body back to Horton's Falls. He didn't want to live there;

why should he be dead there? She picked out a favorite small urn, one decorated in relief with the domestic employment scene by Lady Templeton—whoever she may have been, I didn't ask. Then she got on a Greyhound to the Apple, went to Marcus' lawyer, settled her son's affairs. "I thought I might rent a truck," she said. "Load in Marcus' merchandise and take it back home to my shop." She saw me looking at her oddly. "Well, who the hell do you think loads and drives my stuff when I do antique shows? My husband's been dead forty-two years, no great loss." Elfish gleam in her eyes, good old alcohol. "I'm one damn tough old broad."

Through my polite heh-heh-heh I warned myself to be careful. Play down to this one, she'll whack me from here to Chicago.

Doris sighed. "But Marcus has ... had mostly furniture—who *buys* such great big things in New York? They couldn't possibly fit into apartments."

Sophie chuckled. "You'd be surprised, Mrs. Wilcox—"

"Oh, *Doris*, dear. Please."

"Doris, then. Some of these apartments are bigger than houses. There're plenty of people here who've got the money *and* the space."

"Hmmm." Doris sipped martini. "Well, they don't have either in Horton's Falls, not for stuff like that." She paused. "No point dragging it back home. I need to get a dealer to take the lot, empty the shop; then I can just close the books."

She tilted her head, drained martini number three; I signaled the waiter to bring number four. Doris shook me off, nearly giggled. "You'd have to carry me back to my hotel."

I was going to say something light, try to keep her drinking, but the waiter, a serious gray-haired man with a closely-trimmed mustache and a natty red and black checked tie, walked up and asked whether we'd like to order.

"Yes, I think so." Doris looked at Soph, then at me; we answered with nods.

"Sure," I said. "Veal piccata's especially good here—or if you like fish, their Atlantic salmon stuffed with crabmeat is wonderful. That's what I'll have."

"Make it two," said Sophie.

Doris shrugged. "Make it unanimous."

The waiter scribbled, bowed, picked up the menus and left.

Doris visibly collected her thoughts. "What was I saying? ... oh yes. Before Marcus' service today, I tried calling some dealers about buying his inventory. But people here are so rude—they either put me off outright and hung up the phone, or told me they'd have to get back to me ... but most of them didn't even take my number. Frankly, I'm not sure *what* I'm going to do."

The words Soph and I were working toward.

"Well, dear, New York really *is* different from Horton's Falls," Soph said. "Most dealers here won't take the time to hunt around, and they don't want to schlep heavy things. They depend much more on pickers than you do upstate." Soph's eyes widened. "Say ..."

I'd swear I saw a fishing pole in Sophie's raised right hand, the line suddenly vanishing into Doris' mouth.

"... I have an idea ... but I wouldn't want to presume."

Queen Sophie of Greenwich, dignity personified.

"Oh, no, no." Doris was practically beside herself trying to dispel that ridiculous notion. "Please—go on. You know antiques, you know New York. If you can help me, I'd be ever so grateful."

"It's just, well ... we know someone, Thomas and I." Soph turned demure brown eyes on me. "A little man named Broadway Schwartz. There's no better picker anywhere—and honest. In one day he'd have your merchandise priced; next day the shop would be empty. And you'd have a fair wholesale value in your pocket ..." Soph lowered her voice, "in cash."

Those last two words were not lost on Doris. She took a few seconds to digest the information. "Would he come on such short notice?"

Soph deferred to me with a silent gaze.

"Don't see why not," I said. "Remember, he wouldn't just be doing you a favor; it'd be a good find for him. If you want, I'll be glad to call, ask if he can come by tomorrow morning ... say about ten? How does that sound?"

Doris' eyes filled, probably at least in part due to the multi-martini bomb. "That would be wonderful," she said. "I'd really like to get this settled and get out of New York as soon as I can. What happened to Marcus ... and now, *this*." She held up her purse.

Sophie patted her hand. "We understand, dear. Tell you what—instead of meeting you at the shop tomorrow, why don't Thomas and I—and Schwartz—pick you up at your hotel. Say a quarter to ten?"

That breached Doris' ocular dams; two small streams started down her cheeks. She pulled out a hanky, dabbed water away. "You are *so* kind, both of you," she said. "I just don't know how to thank you."

The waiter pulled up to the table with a huge metal tray full of fragrant plates. "Enough business for now," I said. "Dinnertime."

***

Past 8:30 when I got home, wondering which path Hurricane Sarah was going to take. But Sarah wasn't there, just a small note on the kitchen table where I'd left my own message a few hours before: *I'll be back about 10:30.* That was it. No Dear Thomas; no Love, Sarah. No question, deep shit.

Two hours, enough time to do some dampering on Mr. Reymond-Nicole's challenging comb. I must have been distracted; the work went along by stammers and starts. But by ten I had all wires in place and shaped. I got up, stretched, strolled into the kitchen for a drink.

I was rinsing the glass when I heard a door open, then slam shut. High heels marched *staccato* toward me through Sarah's rooms. When they stopped I half-turned around.

Sarah stood just inside the kitchen door. Glaring would hardly begin to describe the way she was looking at me.

"Been out for a nice evening, have we?" I said.

"*One* of us may have been," retorted the Ice Matron. "The other would've if she hadn't gone alone."

"Gone alone?" I turned full around.

"To a concert. Christopher Parkening, all-Scarlatti. At Lincoln Center."

I pulled my little appointment book out of my shirt pocket, flipped pages quickly to the date. Nice blank white paper.

"No, you didn't forget," Sarah said with excessive weariness. "I was looking through the *Times* today at lunch, saw the ad, and decided to call. The weekend performances were sold out but they still had good seats for tonight."

"Why didn't you—"

"Call you? I thought of it. But I decided it might be nice to surprise you. Just come home, pick you up, go to dinner and the concert."

She never would've admitted, probably didn't even re- alize, she was telling me a story, a pretty good one in fact. Sarah loves early music; two hours of English madrigals and round-songs is her idea of an evening in the waiting-chambers of the Lord. For me, it's an eternity of waiting for exit doors to swing open. There's nothing wrong with Scarlatti that any half- way decent meth lab couldn't set right; I've told Sarah that. So why should she call at lunchtime, thereby giving me a good five hours to come up with an excuse not to go? Better to just walk in at five and catch me without a prior engagement.

"Sarah, I'm sorry—really I am. But don't get sore because I can't read your mind."

She'd set the best trap she knew how and I wiggled through it. But admit that? No way. "Where *were* you to- night? What were you doing?"

"I was out to dinner with a lady friend," I said, then quickly added, "Sophie Soleski."

"Out to dinner with Sophie." Disparaging cluck from Mother Hen. "Thomas, I'm disappointed. You can do better than that. Sophie loves to cook for people who love to eat— like you." She set a foot forward, narrowed eyeball sockets. "Okay, then: two questions. Just *why* did you and Sophie go to dinner? And who else just might've gone with you?"

"We took a new friend from out of town. Little supper in the Big City. That's all."

"That's *not* all. What was this friend's name?"

"Doris."

"Doris What?"

Check. Stall. "Sarah, I'm your husband, not your little boy. 'Who'd you go to dinner with? Doesn't she have a last name?'"

"I know she has a last name; I simply asked what it was. I'll bet she also has a music box, doesn't she?"

Interesting question. The music box then a ward of A Person Unknown was the property of Rudolph Hartmann, had been all along. In no way was it ever in the legal custody of the late Marcus, subject to inheritance by any of his heirs. "She does not have a music box," I said to Sarah. "Are you satisfied?"

"Not on your life. I still want to know her last name. *And*, if she doesn't have a music box, I'm betting she has something to do with a music box ... Wait a minute. Something to do with a two hundred thousand dollar music box? With Barton Moss? And Frank, and that Mr. Hartmann ... Thomas, you're dodging all around your new friend's name, that Doris-From-Out-Of-Town you and Sophie needed to take to dinner tonight. What was her *name?*"

"We didn't *need* to take her to dinner. We wanted to. We met her on the sidewalk, she'd just had her purse snatched. I caught the kid who did it, gave her back her purse, but as you can imagine, she was still awfully upset. We decided it'd be a nice thing—"

"Oh sure. A nice thing! Thomas Purdue happens to be on site to foil a pursesnatcher and take the victim out for dinner afterward. It just couldn't be, could it, that this pursesnatching was a setup, a way for you and your playmates to cuddle up to this particular lady for some particular reason?"

Check. Damn, she was getting good. "Sarah, come on, cool it. Your blood pressure must be off the charts."

"Thomas, I want a straight answer. One word. What ... was ... this ... lady's ... last ... name?"

Check and mate. "Wilcox," I said, hoping it'd slide by her.
Fat chance.

"Like *Marcus* Wilcox? Who is also dead—something to do
with a rare, two hundred thousand dollar music box?" She
stomped over to me; all she needed was a leather belt in her
upraised right hand. "Sit down." She pointed at the kitchen chairs.
"Then talk, and talk straight."

When I finished my story, Sarah studied me for a moment. "You just exhaust me," she said so quietly I could barely
hear her. "You have such an interesting job; you make diagnoses, prescribe treatments, teach medical students, do re-
search. You could be chairman and run the whole department—and we both know you already *would* be if your col-
leagues didn't think you were such a flake. Bad enough you
spend so much time on those silly music boxes. But this new
game, this playing detective—"

"I haven't done so badly."

"Not yet. But you will. And when you do, your career—
all your careers—will be over in a hurry. So many people
could benefit from your help, and you're not there for them. It's
criminal."

"Like I wasn't there for Frank when the ER called? And
how about poor Mr. Hartmann? He nearly went down on his
knees, said I was his only hope."

"Stop it. You're not going to baffle me with your bullshit on
this one. If Mr. Hartmann didn't happen to own a rare music
box he'd still be looking for his savior, and you'd be looking for
a tastier situation for your so-called talents. You love to do exactly as you please, go where you want, when you want. Ignore
those aggravating schedules ordinary people need to put up with.

Mix someone's troubles with a music box and it's Thomas-on-the-Spot, off in a flash to play detective. Your life's just eternal fun and games, play-play-play. Damn it, grow up."

When Sarah goes to psychosocialworkerspeak it has the effect of a goodly pinch of itching powder dropped down the back of my shirt. "Better to play detective than go through life being a wet blanket with an attitude."

That did it. Up on her feet, clean military about-face, and off she stomped, back through the kitchen.

Two long-time partners doing their dance. Sarah, knowing exactly how to bring forth the reaction that in turn will send her galloping righteously off aboard her high dudgeon. And me, speaking the prescribed response, as reliable as one of Edna's automata. Sore as I was at Sarah, I was sorer by far at myself. Check, checkmate.

13

A few minutes before ten next morning, Doris Wilcox slipped a key into the front door lock of the Palais Royal, turned the knob, swung the door open ... and off went the alarm. Loud, steady beep-beep-beep, as commonplace in the city as an ambulance siren. No one on the sidewalk even slowed to look. I took the alarm key from Doris, reached to the nickeled box above the right upper edge of the door, pushed in the key, turned it. Silence. I shut the door, threw the bolt.

Three foxes and a farmer looked around the chicken coop. "Stuffy," Doris said. "I'll turn on the air conditioning." She marched to the back of the shop behind the desk. "We'll need to work fast to get through all this in one day."

Schwartz grinned, waved off her concern. "You got Broadway Schwartz on the job, you got no worries. All big stuff—be outa here before three, easy. You can take it to the bank."

Sophie gestured toward the back room. "Why don't we start there—we wouldn't want any surprises late in the day."

Good old Sophie, right to the chase, smooth as flan. Doris nodded, pulled keys from her pocketbook, peered at the labels. "Here ... storeroom." She slid the key into the lock, turned the knob, pushed.

A musty smell came forward; allergic Schwartz wrinkled his nose. I reached past him to pull the string on an unshaded lightbulb.

The room wasn't nearly as crowded as I'd expected; it took less than a minute to see that the object of our search wasn't there. Just wooden furniture.

Doris looked around, sighed. "Thank you for coming on such short notice, Mr. Schwartz," she said. "In fact, thanks to all of you. I just don't know how I'd have done this otherwise."

Schwartz was already at work, cranial calculator humming. "Hey, Mrs. Wilcox, no sweat—figure it's my pleasure *and* my business." He pushed a yellow lined pad at Sophie, held up a handful of small white numbered paper squares. "Be faster if you help. I'll go from piece to piece, put on labels. You write down numbers and descriptions. Like taking dictation."

"I think I'm capable of that."

Schwartz walked to the far end of the room, stopped at a big desk, paused just long enough to lift his fedora and run fingers through his dark hair. Like turning on a switch. Off he went, rattling particulars rapid-fire to Sophie: Number 453, partners's desk, Philippine mahogany with blotter-pad work areas, circa 1880, condition very good, minor scratches and scuffs. Tape measure out of pocket, zip, zip, zip: 60" wide by 48" deep by 29" high. "Got it?" he called automatically as he turned to the next item, Number 454, oak coatstand, probably American, circa 1890. Soph scribbled furiously, regret for her recent cavalier assurance all over her face.

Schwartz was a truck rumbling down a mountain road, gathering momentum. I had to work at keeping my eyes off a green

Mosler strongbox squatting against the wall just inside the door. Patience, I told myself. The time will come.

By a little past noon we'd finished the storage room and gone through about a third of the shop. Schwartz was describing a vast teak armoire when Sophie suddenly swayed, leaned against a big oak desk, said, "Broadway ... wait just a minute, would you, please."

Everyone turned to Soph, who looked a bit vague. She felt her way backward into a Morris chair, dropped her pad and pencil, lowered face into hands.

"Sophie—what's the matter?" I asked.

Doris covered her open mouth. Schwartz trotted over to the chair, took Sophie's hand. "Hey, Soph, you're cold like ice. What's up?"

"Nothing ... just a dizzy spell," Sophie mumbled.

"Sophie ... did you skip breakfast again?" My best doctor's voice.

Soph looked up at me, naughty girl.

"Sophie's diabetic," I said to Doris. "And she won't eat regularly, no matter what I say."

"If I'm not hungry—"

"Come on." I took her by the arm, slowly raised her to her feet. "There's a restaurant right down the block. Can you make it that far with us helping you?"

"Yes, Thomas. I'm not exactly at Death's door."

I steered Soph toward the sidewalk; Doris supported her from the left. Schwartz, however, hung back. "Hey, Doc ..." We all stopped, turned to look at him. "We take off for lunch, I ain't sure I can get done today. I know Soph's gotta get her food, but ..."

"Well, *I* know what we can do," Doris said. "Mr. Schwartz—"

"Broadway."

"Broadway, then. Why don't you stay here and keep working. Thomas—if you'll help me get Sophie to the restaurant, I'll sit and have lunch with her. You can come back to the shop and work with Broadway. If you don't mind."

"Not at all," I said. "Good thinking, actually. I'll get you seated, make sure they give Soph a quick glass of orange juice. Then Schwartz and I'll take care of everything here while the two of you have a nice, leisurely lunch."

Barely ten minutes later I was back at the Palais Royal. Schwartz chuckled as I came through the doorway. "Nice, leisurely lunch, hey Doc? The more leisurely the better."

"Sophie'll take care of that," I said. "She *is* good, isn't she?"

"She could be on the stage. If I didn't know it was a game, I'da been scared spitless for her. Would Edna have loved seein' that show, or what?"

"None of us'd love what would come next if Doris ever sees Edna with us," I said.

"No kiddin'. That Doris is some kinda pistol herself. Didn't take her a minute to figure out what to do about Soph."

"I knew she would. Bring up a kid like Marcus and live to tell about it, you've got to be a fast thinker. And since going to the restaurant with Soph was her idea, not likely now she'll get suspicious." I pointed at the yellow pad. "Better get back to work, Broadway—I'll go see how Gackle's making out in the storage room."

Cleveland Gackle was bent over the safe, fingers and ears

to the dial. Our apostle of agnosticism stopped just long enough to regard me from beneath the white bushes of his eyebrows. "Let me guess," I said. "Maybe you can open it ... and then again, maybe you can't."

Gackle tried to look withering but couldn't keep the corners of his mouth from turning upward. "Go on, Sonny," he said. "Do something useful, like see what you can maybe find out there." He handed me a large cloth tote bag from the floor next to where he was kneeling, then turned back to the safe.

Out front, Schwartz was about halfway finished, inspecting each item in turn, muttering to himself, pencil zipping between hand and back of ear as he wrote descriptions on his pad and stuck numbered labels onto the pieces. He was doing his job, as Gackle was doing his, and Sophie hers. Now I had to do mine.

Seemed logical to start at Wilcox's desk, a piece of furniture you'd expect to see in a photo with J. P. Morgan or Teddy Roosevelt parked behind it. Dark wood polished to high gloss, sea-green workpad, three drawers on either side of the knee-hutch, central drawer above. I tugged at the big middle drawer: locked. So were the six side drawers. "Pete," I shouted toward the back room. "Need your help with the desk."

Before the echoes of my voice died away, Gackle was on his way through the door and toward me, pulling a ring of metal picks from his pants pocket. Quick glance at the small lock on the central drawer, zip with a pick, twist, pull, open.

Gackle was already on his way back to the safe. "Wait a minute," I said. "The side drawers—"

He reached out to yank at the right top drawer then skewered me with his eyes. "Open the middle drawer, the others unlock automatically," he said. "Christ on a crutch! It's one thing I need to change your diaper; do I also have to wipe your ass? Leave me be a minute and I might just get that safe open for you."

No offense intended, none taken. Just Gackle's way. I started rummaging through the middle drawer. Receipt book, half-used, by dates the current one. I scanned every pale-blue page with its grandiose Palais Royal logo at the top, saw no record of sale of any music box.

I dropped the receipt book into the tote bag, went back to rifling the drawer. Keys, paper clips, pencils, pens, tape measure, booklet of patent dates, some photographs of furniture. I took the keys and pictures, closed the drawer.

Why did Wilcox keep that desk locked? Not because of anything I'd seen so far. I opened the top left drawer—full of reference books on antiques. I checked each one, fluttered them open to look for hidden papers. Nothing. The middle left drawer held lined yellow pads and file folders, more nothing. I grumbled, opened the bottom drawer ... and hit pay dirt.

Hanging files. I flipped through folders, saw one labeled Hartmann; another, Reynolds. I started to look inside but told myself there'd be time for that later. For now, just get the goods. I lifted the 20-odd files three at a time from the suspending rods, slipped them into the tote bag.

The right side of the desk was a washout, unless you'd consider a top drawer crammed with bags of cinnamon red hots to be significant. The middle drawer held phone directories, unused receipt books, and lists of antique dealers, but no annotations to turn my thoughts in any particular direction. The bottom drawer was empty.

Not nearly enough material. I peered under the green blotter pad, found nothing. A few papers were scattered over the top of the work area, one with a woman's name and a phone number, another with the name of an east side antique shop, followed by *lot of tea caddies, nice, 18 c.* There was a reminder to "call accountant." Didn't seem like much but I added the papers to the contents of the bag.

I ran my eyes across the desk top. Cigarette lighter. Half-empty bag of red hots. Stapler. Electric pencil sharpener. Rolodex. Wooden box of pens and pencils. Letter opener ... wait a minute. Rolodex? *Fat* Rolodex. Wake up, Purdue! The card file held a couple of hundred entries in Wilcox's crabbed handwriting. Hartmann-Rudolph was there, as were Maar-Frank and Reynolds-Edna. I dropped the Rolodex gently into the bag, then shut all the drawers and stood up.

Would Doris notice the Rolodex was gone? How about the pieces of paper?

Have to chance it.

I wandered through the showroom, looking for I didn't know what. I found no hidey holes, no secret compartments behind paintings on the wall, no storage cabinets, no anything. I was beginning to wonder whether this excursion was going to be worthwhile after all when I heard Gackle call from the back, "Got 'er, Doc. Come take a looky at what's here."

Schwartz looked like a cat who'd just caught sight of a fat robin across the lawn. He and I were in the back room in seconds. My immediate reaction was to be disappointed all over again; the safe was largely air space. But good things do come in small packages. At the rear was a pile of money, rubber-banded groups of hundreds, twenty to thirty thousand dollars by quick estimate.

Gackle grabbed a second tote bag, flipped it open. I tapped his shoulder, shook my head no.

Our lock man's face told me I had some fast explaining to do.

"We're here for information, Pete, that's all. Money belongs to Doris—the old lady, Wilcox's mother."

Air Gackle appeared on the point of takeoff. I reached past him to lift a handful of manila folders and large brown envelopes from the bottom of the safe. Then from behind me came, "You boys *have* been busy, haven't you?"

Schwartz went stiff. I whirled around. Manila folders and pieces of paper fluttered to the floor around us. "Jesus, Sophie!" I craned my neck toward the open doorway. "Where's—"

"Doris? Give me *some* credit, would you, please. Would I barge in like this if Doris were here? She said she needed to check with her lawyer today and sign some papers, so I told her why didn't she cab over there and do it. If we finish early we can sit and wait for her."

A nasty thought wormed its way into my head. "Soph ... you don't think she's—"

"Caught on? No. It was all friendly, very relaxed. We're practically old buddies, she and I." Sophie lowered her eyes. "In fact it almost makes me feel bad, what we're doing here."

"I know," I said quietly. "I've been feeling like that ever since Jitters and I scattered her son's ashes all over Nozey's floor."

Gackle cleared his throat. "What are we, on a job or a social rescue mission? We don't get movin' here, maybe we can get her to help pick up all this stuff."

Depend on Cleveland Gackle to say what needs saying. The four of us went down on hands and knees, started sliding papers into folders. Then from outside in the shop I heard a prissy voice. "Hel*lo*? Anyone here?"

We froze into a touching tableau of group guilt. That voice—Little Mr. Purse-strings; what the hell was his name? "Samuel Bottomley," I whispered hoarsely. "Goddamn print shop owner next door. He's seen Schwartz and me—Soph, Pete ... get rid of him."

Gackle and Sophie were nearly to the door by the time I finished talking. Schwartz reached for a loose paper. I grabbed his arm, put a finger to my lips.

"Yes?" I heard Sophie say as she vanished around the corner into the shop. "What can I do for you?"

Marvelous. With her imperious *mittel*-European elocution, swept-up iron-gray hair, and ramrod spine, Soph could be formidability incarnate. Take more than little Samuel Bottomley to get *her* on the defensive.

"I ... I ... you see ... I own the print shop next door ... and I saw the door open and thought—"

"Very kind of you, Mr. ..."

"Bottomley. Samuel Bottomley. As I said, I own the print shop—"

"I'm Doris Wilcox," Sophie said. "My husband, Pete."

In the brief silence I could see handshakes all around. Schwartz looked like someone was tickling him, cootchy-coo. I put my finger back to my lips.

"We're Mr. Wilcox's parents," Soph said. "From upstate, Horton's Falls."

"Oh ... oh, I see." Mortified Mr. Bottomley, trying to melt into the floorboards.

"We had services for Marcus yesterday," Soph went on, "and we are now in the process of settling his affairs. Including the shop. It was very kind of you to look in, Mr. Bottomley, thank you."

"Oh, yes, yes. I just wanted ... you know. In this city ... a person can never be—"

"Absolutely. We'll be glad to get home to Horton's Falls, you may be sure. Now, I'm sorry but we really do need to—"

"Oh, yes. Certainly. I understand. It was very nice to meet you both—"

"Yes, thank you. I'll see you out."

Door opened, door closed, but neither Schwartz nor I moved until Soph and Gackle came rushing back into the room. I'd wondered why Pete hadn't said a word through the entire exchange; now I saw. Tears coursed down his cheeks; his face was flushed, eyes reddened, muddy. But as he took in my gawk he snickered. "Always been able to cry on demand, just like I was peeling an onion. Got me outa more messes than you can imagine." He dropped to his knees. "Come on, let's get these papers in the bag and get me outa here—before she really does walk in on us."

Sophie lowered herself gracefully to the floor beside him, started scooping up folders. What a pair. Daddy softens the mark, Mom punches him out. A perk of the elderly—people *believe* them. Some oldsters meet condescension with indignation; the smarter ones just chuckle up their sleeves and walk away, leaving their opponents wondering how to get that shiv out from between their shoulder blades.

In less than five minutes it was all in the tote bag. Gackle scooted out to Edna's, bag in hand; we'd meet him there as soon as we could. Sophie went back to helping Schwartz catalogue the stock. I cruised the shop, looked for other hiding places, but by the time Doris Wilcox strolled back in, a little before three, I'd found nothing.

Schwartz turned bright eyes on Doris. "Nice stuff—won't have any trouble gettin' it sold and outa here. But one thing I do gotta tell you, er ... some of it's repros—"

"You don't have to tell me," Doris snapped. "I've been in the business more than forty years. I know antiques. I know fakes. And I know ... knew my son."

"Well, but the good news is, they're *good* repros." Schwartz in fast forward. "*Darned* good repros. I can sell 'em to the 'antiques of tomorrow' shops, no sweat. 'Course, I won't get what I would for the McCoy—"

"Just do what needs doing, as quickly as you can do it," Doris said. "You don't have to explain anything."

Schwartz backed off a step, adjusted his fedora. "Okay, great. I'll head out now, start hittin' the dealers, finish up in the morning. How about I give you a call at your hotel tomorrow when I got the dough?"

Doris couldn't thank the three of us enough.

We locked the shop. Doris gave us each a kiss on the cheek, then took off eastbound. Schwartz headed west. Sophie looked at me, I at her, our eyes mirroring the other's self-reproach. One more time, as if in slow motion, I saw that Wedgwood urn sail up out of the purse and crash to the floor.

"We ought to make it up to her, Soph."

"Make it up ..?"

"Wilcox's ashes."

"Just how would you propose to do that?"

"Get another urn. Put something in it. Seal it with wax. Tell her Schwartz found it in a neighborhood shop, and bought it back for her."

"Do you really think that's necessary?"

"Necessary, no. Desirable, yes."

Sophie grimaced, grudging silent agreement. "We can stop at Leo Kaplan's on the way down to Edna's."

"Leo Who's?"

"Kaplan. Over on Madison. He's the biggest Wedgwood dealer in town; if anyone has an urn to match the broken one, he will. What did Doris say ... eight-and-a-half-inches tall?"

"Yes. Light blue jasperware, single white handle, flared top like a candlestick. With figures on it by some lady ... wait a minute ... ah! Lady *Templeton*, 'Domestic employment scene.'"

"Hmmm ... all right. I'll do my best. But what are we going to put inside?"

"I'll take care of that. You go to Kaplan's, get the vase. Or urn, whatever. Meet you at Edna's."

When I got back to Headquarters, Jitters, Gackle and Edna were sitting around a card table in the middle of the living room. "Lot of material, Thomas," Edna said. "Most of it at least a little ugly. And I think one or two very helpful."

"Oh?"

She passed me a piece of paper, a copy of a receipt made out to Mr. Ferris Tyler just eight days before. One antique music box, two hundred thousand, paid in full. "This was in the safe?" I said. "Not in a receipt book."

Gackle nodded. "Mixed in with the stuff you threw all over the room."

I made a dive for the Rolodex, flipped cards to Tyler, Ferris. "That's our man ... two addresses. Home on Beekman Place; office on West Forty-eighth."

"Money," Edna murmured.

"Paying almost a quarter-mill for a music box, I'd say so." I slipped the Rolodex card into my wallet. "Guess Mr. Tyler's on my agenda for tomorrow morning. Anything else?"

Edna reached across the card table, pushed a button on a small cassette player. "Try this. Wilcox must've had a recorder on his phone."

The hiss of the tape played off in my mind against the sensation of a half-remembered melody trying to work its way to the surface of consciousness. Through crackles I heard an unfamiliar but very angry voice. "I've been as patient as I'm going to be. You have two days now—and I don't mean two days and one hour—to pay up. In full, every goddamn cent. You hear me?"

"Prescott, be *rea*sonable." The unforgettable whine of Marcus Wilcox. "I'm sorry about the fakes; I didn't know ... it was a ... well, a misunder*standing.* I can give you back the thirty-two thousand you paid me, today, right now this minute. Then we'll be even."

"Not to my mind. You know what I want; I won't take a nickel less."

"Come *on*, Prescott. Where do you think I can possibly get—"

"Two hundred thousand dollars? That's your problem. If I don't get it within two days, you're finished—I'll send a letter to every designer from here to Paris, telling them exactly what kind of scam you tried to pull on me. Then you can just close up your shop and go lie in the gutter where you belong."

"Prescott, *why?*" Wilcox again. "Why do you want to do something like this? What's in it for you?"

"Satisfaction, you lousy little slimebag. A ton of it." *Slam!* Few seconds of crackles, then silence.

Edna waved an accordian folder. "We found that in here, in the Creditors Section. Dunbar, Prescott. Excalibur Antiques and Interiors."

"Frank said he'd heard this Dunbar might've been blackmailing our friend," I muttered, then took the tape from the player, slid it into my pocket. "Wilcox probably tried to turn the squeeze on Dunbar—wonder how far he got. And who else he owed money to."

"Huh!" Gackle snorted. "Maybe you oughta ask who he didn't owe money to."

I took the accordion folders, flipped through the papers inside. Gackle had a point. There were perhaps thirty letters, all from people to whom Wilcox apparently owed money, mostly for restoration work and consignment fees. Two names caught my eye. The first was Rudolph Hartmann; Wilcox owed him nearly a thousand dollars for matting and framing jobs. The other was Edna Reynolds, designer-automata and fabrics. I whistled. "Edna—more than five-K?"

This was definitely a first, probably also a never-again. Edna caught with a mouthful of humble pie and not a napkin in reach. "I was embarrassed to tell you," she said. "It was 'Just trust me a little longer, I need just a little more time ... a little more money. Then I'll be able to pay you back the whole thing.' What can I say? The son of a bitch was good. He really nailed me."

I skimmed the rest of the material, sad souvenirs of a life tossed away under the influence of an overinflated ego and overweening laziness. Photographs of a younger Wilcox with an attractive dark-haired woman and a little boy. A letter from a woman-artist whom Wilcox had apparently pushed a bit too hard for money and carnal favors: she caught on, and what she told him about his ratings both credit and sexual made my mind squirm.

"More than a couple of suspects, aren't there?" Edna said. "You could start with me."

I turned off her suggestion with a smile. "I've got to think Tyler and Dunbar are where it's at. The goons who beat up Frank and Hartmann were trying to trace back the music box, which tells me Tyler wasn't altogether satisfied with his purchase. And Dunbar blackmailing Wilcox? Wilcox had to know if it got out he was selling fakes, he and his pathetic little ego would've been wiped clean. He might've paid through the schnozz 'til the well went dry, then Dunbar decided to put him out of the way."

Knock knock.

Edna sighed, pushed away from the table, got up, walked heavily to the door, pulled it open. Sophie swept past her like the Battleship *Missouri* coming in on high tide.

I sent my chair flying backward as I jumped to my feet. "Soph—did you get that Wedgwood urn?"

For answer she pulled a mass of plastic bubble-wrap from a paper bag, set the package on the table, carefully unrolled the wrap. Without a word she held up a small vase—light blue with a white handle, flared top, and decorated all around with white figures of a woman and small children at play. Domestic employment. Bingo.

"Sure looks like the one we dropped," I said. "Jitters?"

The boy nodded thoughtfully. "Didn't get that good of a look at it ... but from the pieces I picked up off the floor I'd say yeah."

I took a zipper-locked sandwich bag out of my pants pocket,

then carefully tapped its contents, a few ounces of gray powder, into the urn.

Edna's fingers tapped a riff on the table. "I know I'm going to regret this, but—"

"Ashes," I said. "I stopped by the Man Med Experimental Primate Center, had a word with a friend—"

"Thomas!" A full dose of Sophie's continental indignation compressed into one word imbued my name with unprecedented magnificence. Everyone stared at her, awestruck. Jitters looked on the sharp edge of dissolution—well, sure. Imagine the splendor of the images he'd just seen.

"What did you think we were going to use?" I asked. "We can't seal up an empty urn: first time Doris shakes it she knows. Better if I burned a tree limb in my fireplace? She'll take home this jar with monkey ashes and think it's her son. How's she ever going to tell the difference?"

No one wanted to toss the first snicker. Little coughs, averted faces. I handed the urn to Edna. "Jitters, where's the top piece of the original?"

Jitters trotted into the repair room, came back holding a round light-blue ceramic chunk, fractured at its narrow neck. Inside was a plug of wax. I motioned him toward Edna. "Your specialty," I said. "Get the wax out of here, into the new urn. I'll tell Doris that Schwartz found it at one of the neighborhood antique shops."

Edna was clearly short of convinced. "It seems like a cruel thing to do."

"Crueler than sending her home to wonder the rest of her life where her son's ashes ended up? Whether the purse-snatcher pulled the wax and flushed him down the toilet? This is the best I can think of to set matters right."

"You could've told her the truth."

"What? That we set her up to have her purse snatched and—"

"No, of course not. You could've said that while you were chasing the thief the urn flew out of the pocketbook ..."

She ground to a halt on the friction of her realization. That wouldn't have been the truth, just another story, one not nearly as good as mine. It would've left Doris forever seeing her son's paltry remains wafting from the East River to the Hudson on New York's gentle summer breezes. Hardly as comforting as a Lady Templeton Wedgwood vase full of monkey ashes. The fuss people make over the glory of truth! If I had my way, the worst criminals would be sentenced to a life of straight, clear, undecorated truth, stories strictly forbidden. But that would never fly past our lawmakers. What punishment could be crueler and more unusual?

Edna set the replacement urn on the table with the documents, took the original shard from Jitters, zinged a dart in my direction from the corner of her eye. "Matches," she snapped, and as Jitters took off toward the kitchen, she tapped the pottery fragment sharply against the table top. It split in half, freeing the wax, which Edna set into the top of the new urn. "Jitters!" she called back over her shoulder. "Come on with those goddamn matches; we need them today, not tomorrow."

Tomorrow Tyler, I thought; it'll take a while to deal with him. But Dunbar ought to be quick. That elusive melody surged in my brain, then just as quickly receded. I grabbed the Yellow Pages off the shelf of Edna's little phone table, found Excalibur under *Interior Decorators and Designers*, dialed the number. A woman answered: "Prescott Dunbar's Excalibur Antiques and Interiors."

"My name is Thomas Purdue," I said. "I'd like to talk to Mr. Dunbar, please."

"May I tell him the nature of your business?"

"Absolutely. I need to discuss a certain phone call he made recently to Marcus Wilcox."

Dunbar was on the phone almost instantly, sounding anything but pleased. "Make it quick," he snarled. "It's almost closing time. What is it you want?"

"Just to ask you a few questions," I said. "In person. I'll come right over, won't keep you fifteen minutes." He began to object, but I said, "I can talk to you or the police, same difference to me. Your druthers."

"Make it quick." He slammed down the receiver, loud enough to make Gackle roll his eyes like Eddie Cantor.

While I was on the phone Edna rewrapped the urn in its bubble-plastic, then slipped the package back into the paper bag. "Here. Marcus the Monkey. All yours."

I took the bag, moved toward the door. "See you tomorrow. I think I know how this all fits together—and after I've talked to Tyler and Dunbar I should know for certain."

14

Forget that stuff about interior designers being wispy little men with faint blond mustaches, or old farts with big bellies and pompous voices. Prescott Dunbar looked like Saturday's Hero at Princeton or Yale who'd kept in shape since his last foray into the end zone some twenty years earlier. Eyes of gray flint, granite skin, high, sharp cheekbones, mid-line chin cleft a la Kirk Douglas. Light, wavy hair expertly styled, fingernails neatly trimmed under clear polish, tweed jacket with leather elbow pads, shiny black Mephisto shoes.

He was not pleased to see me. As I came into his shop, just a few minutes past five, he closed the door behind me, flipped the OPEN sign to CLOSED, then started walking toward the rear. Not a word.

I followed him through his plush shop; by comparison the Palais Royal looked like the London Almshouse. Fancy furniture of all periods, expensive-looking glass and china. Hanging from the ceiling in mid-room, a magnificent sparkling crystal chandelier which could've been straight from the lobby of the Radio City Music Hall. I sneaked glances at the yellow tags on merchandise; descriptions and dates only, no dollar signs. Price stickers in *this* establishment? Perish the thought, how crass. All the better to size you up, my dear, and use my well-developed sliding scale to estimate just how much traffic you'll bear.

Still without a word, Dunbar led me through a door marked *OFFICE*, then closed it. The lair of *Arachne elegans*, soft walnut paneling covered with tastefully-framed paintings. Big mahogany partners desk, wall of bookshelves filled with reference works on art and antiques, light-blue Oriental carpet between desk and bookshelves. My host didn't invite me to sit; I didn't presume. Just laid my plain brown wrapper and its porcelain contents on the corner of the desk, and waited.

Dunbar leaned against the visitors' side of his desk, still trying to size me up. Finally he said, "You told me you'd take only a few minutes."

"I've got some questions about Marcus Wilcox," I said quietly.

Dunbar's expression suggested I'd raised one leg and blown a loud, fragrant note on my Netherlands trumpet. "Stupid, obnoxious little bastard," he said.

I smiled. "I assume you mean Wilcox."

Dunbar didn't come close to returning the smile. "Take it any way you like, Mr. Purdue. Who are you that I should even listen to your questions, let alone answer them?"

"Just someone who has some friends—older people—who were also screwed by Wilcox," I said. "I'm trying to help them. Specifically, I'm looking for the whereabouts of a particular music box Wilcox stole and sold. A big one, very rare, a type—"

Dunbar shook his head. "I can't help you. I never handle music boxes, not any mechanical items. They're forever going wrong; then I have to waste my time looking for someone to make them right." He shifted his feet and backed away, as if to say the interview was over.

"Wilcox didn't tell you anything about a very unusual music box he had a line on?" I asked quickly. "Or whom he might have as a buyer for one?"

"No. Why should he?"

"Maybe because he owed you a good bit of money and wanted you to know he'd be able to pay you soon."

Dunbar looked like a man in need of an emergency root canal.

I pulled out the cassette, held it in his direction. "Two days to settle accounts," I said. "Not two days and one hour. Just what was on account?"

Dunbar's head retracted between his shoulders, giving him the appearance of a muscular buzzard. "Where did you get that?" he snarled.

"Doesn't matter. Look, Mr. Dunbar: I'm only interested in helping my friends get back their property. There's word around the trade that Wilcox sold you some repro artwork as original, and you were unhappy enough to want to get back more than your money. Not that I care, but if you *were* blackmailing Wilcox, he might've—"

"Mr. Purdue, that is a nasty accusation."

"One more time, Mr. Dunbar. I'm not interested in *you*—"

"And if I *were* blackmailing Wilcox ..." He walked around the desk to come face to face with me. Expensive cologne, applied with a ladle. Eyes bulging, cheeks flaming. Index finger rigid, jabbing into my face. "I say, *if* I were—why would I be stupid enough to kill my pigeon?"

Reasonable question; I'd asked it myself. But why did *he?*

I'm no Bible-thumper but the Good Book does have some good lines, one to the effect that only the evil flee when no one pursueth. *Did* Wilcox use the tape to try to cut Dunbar off at the pass?

"I wouldn't know," I said. "That something you'd like to talk about?"

He looked as if he were considering a grave matter, fingers of his right hand scratching at the cleft in his chin while he gazed absently into space past my head. Then he hit me.

It was a beaut, a short right hook directly to my eye, followed immediately by a left to my jaw. I dropped the tape, folded to the floor, and thought fuzzily of Jitters as I watched a glorious kaleidoscopic light show. On hands and knees I shook my head, trying to clear fog.

As if from a long distance I saw Dunbar pick up the cassette. "You're about as good a fighter as your slimy little friend." He seemed to be speaking from the far end of a tunnel. "Keep meddling, you're going to get a lot worse." He sneered. "Like for example ..."

I raised my head enough to see him draw back a foot. No question of his target: my left kidney was directly in the line of fire. As the foot came forward I lurched to his left, grabbed with both hands just above the shining Mephisto, and yanked sharply to the side. Dunbar grunted, dropped the tape, then did a nice backflip, his head landing just beyond the edge of the Oriental carpet, making a very satisfying thud on the wooden floor.

Conventional wisdom is contemptuous of him who hits a downed man, but I decided good old CW could deal with Big PD if he happened to get back up in a hurry. Adrenaline's wonderful stuff. Shoving through spiderwebs, I was on Dunbar the instant he was down, pushed my knee hard into his solar plexus. More successful even than I'd intended: as well as hearing horrible crowing noises as he tried to draw air into his chest, there was the agreeable sound of at least one rib cracking. Ought to slacken his sails nicely.

I picked up the cassette, slid it back into my pocket. My left eye was pounding, my eyesight damn near cyclopic. I thought briefly of giving Dunbar a good sock in the nose, mess up those handsome features just a bit. But the notion struck me as petty, even cowardly. That broken rib ought to be a good enough souvenir of my visit, never mind the damage to his ego.

Maybe I'd learned something useful, maybe not, but I'd obviously learned all I was going to. Strong argument for splitting while the splitting was good. Down on the floor, Dunbar fought frantically for breath. The thought of giving Prescott Dunbar the Kiss of Life was a beat-all gagger, but Purdue's law allows for no appeal. I sighed, leaned against the wall, watched my opponent writhe, heave, wheeze.

Another minute or so, Dunbar's breath started coming more easily, stridor lessening with each insuck of air. Once the bastard regained his wind I was definitely going to be outgunned. "Mess with *me* again, see what *you* get," I barked, and was pleased to pick up on respect, even a bit of fear in his eyes.

Move, Purdue.

Fortunately as I turned, my eye caught the little brown bag I'd set on Dunbar's desk. I grabbed it, then ran. Through the door, out of the shop.

Back on the sidewalk I checked my watch: not quite five-thirty. Rush hour in full bloom, 57th Street mobbed, people pushing every which way. From the corner of 5th, deafening noise, even by New York standards. Two cops were holding up traffic in all directions; drivers leaned on their horns, screamed out their windows. A moment later a police emergency car flew through the intersection—and the two cops scrambled to the sidewalk. Traffic gushed crosstown with the green, life back to New York Normal.

I took a moment to scope my face in a bakery window; I winced. Gingerly, I felt at the bones through the swelling around my left eye. Probably no breaks but I'd be smart to get back home, put some ice to it. Maybe Sarah'd be working late. I could hope.

As I approached my building I saw a now-familiar man move away from the curb and walk toward me. No outstretched hand, no line of bull. Just a quiet, "Good evening, Doctor."

I pulled out a fin, put it into his hand. He couldn't seem to take his two eyes off my left one. "You should see the other guy," I said.

The mildly sympathetic smile of the captive audience spread across his stubbly face. "Are you all right, Doctor?"

"Basically, yes, thanks—bit uncomfortable but no serious damage. All in the line of duty."

That seemed to throw him off balance. "You *are* a doctor, aren't you? Not a cop? Plainclothes?"

All of a sudden, concern in his voice to the point of alarm. But no guile in his eyes, not a hint of slyness. I shook my head. "Nothing exotic, I'm afraid—just a little private altercation."

He nodded, raised the hand with the fiver. "Thank you again. I hope you feel better."

"You're welcome as always," I said, as he turned away. "I'm sure I will."

Maybe not immediately, though.

Definitely not immediately. Sarah must've heard me come in. As she walked around the corner from the kitchen she let out a scream. "Oh my God. What happened to you?"

She ran toward me but stopped halfway. "Wait a minute ... this has something to do with that business over the missing music box."

It wasn't a question. I gave no answer.

She pointed at the couch. "Go lie down; I'll get an ice bag. And then you can tell me about it. *All* about it."

Sometimes you've just got to go with truth, ugly and unadorned. Sarah knew too much about both the game and me. She listened while I lay on my back, talking, ice bag over my eye. When I finished she said, "That's it? The whole of it? If you've told me everything, say yes. If not, tell me the rest."

She drives me absolutely crazy. "Yes. Truth, whole, nothing but. Complete rendering of same, up to present."

"Up to ... I should have known."

Any Met diva would give a year's income and a hundred glowing reviews to be able to carry off so magnificent a modulation from sympathy to outrage. "*Thomas*—you're *not* finished."

I sat up, let the ice bag fall into my hand. "Of course I'm not finished. I'm—"

"Not while a killer and a valuable music box are still lurking out there."

"Couldn't say it better myself but I'd say it without the sarcasm."

"Oh!" Up on her feet, clenched fists waving in front of her face. "What *is* it with you and your dangerous little games? Look at your eye. You're going to end up dead."

"*Everybody* ends up dead, but why spend your life worrying about it? You've played my games before, even enjoyed yourself. Why don't you—"

"No!" Hair lashed across her face as she whipped her head side-to-side. "You're *done* sweet-talking me. My career in crime is over."

"Crime? Since when is helping people in need a crime?"

"When it's helping yourself because you're in need of another music box. Enough of your damn stories. You're your own best audience."

"Charity begins at home."

"Just my point. In *your* home, not mine. And speaking of that ..."

Uh-oh.

" ... this Jitters kid of yours—it sounds as if he made a nice professional job of that purse-snatching. You're not going to tell me it was his first."

"I don't know what number it was."

"But higher than one. You brought him into *our* house and left him here alone. There'll be times when he and I will be here but you won't. What do you really know about him?"

"That he couldn't bring himself to sell a valuable music box I put in his hands, no strings attached. That he has a one-in-a-million gift. That it would be a crime to *not* give him every chance. All right?"

"Not in my mind. You're amazing, you really are. To the rest of the world a major neurological abnormality is a handicap. To you it's a gift."

"Sarah ... listen to me. Please? I can't tell you how much I envy that kid. He lives in a garden in the middle of summer, gorgeous flowers every place you look. Next to his, my world's an evening coming on in December. Some neurological defect! If I don't do everything in my power to help Jitters make good use of his gift, I don't deserve to be on earth."

She chewed her upper lip, spoke slowly. "All right ... if that's the way you see it, that's what you have to do. But don't I count? I come home after a week away, I'm jet-lagged, popping antihistamines—"

"I'm sorry—really. Any time you want, I'll get an ENT guy to see you—"

"Don't be purposely dense. That's not what I'm talking about and you know it. I can make my own doctor appointments, thank you very much. Just like I wangled a couple of tickets for a wonderful Richard Stolzman concert tonight at Lincoln Center. I thought—"

"Great. Let's go. Why not?"

"Why not? Do I have to give you a mirror?"

"They're going to refuse to seat me because I have a black eye?"

She checked her watch. "It's after seven already; the concert begins at eight. There's no time for dinner—"

"There's no time to waste." I sat up, flipped the ice bag onto the coffee table. "Go on, get dressed. Ten minutes, I'll be ready.

We'll cab over, then after the concert get a little dinner in a little restaurant. Very romantic."

Talk about the ultimate fish eye.

"Sarah, if all you really want is to be pissy, *be* pissy. But then don't complain about *my* behavior. You want to go to the concert, though, I don't have a thing to do tonight. There's music, fine food ... twilight, balmy midsummer air. Come on, let's seize the night. Stop arguing; go get dressed."

She was already halfway to the kitchen passage, stomping, pulling her blouse up over her head. "Why couldn't I have married someone *normal?*" she shrieked.

"Think about it," I called back, then murmured to myself. "And I'll think about why *I* did exactly that."

15

A few minutes after nine next morning, I called Ferris Tyler's office, told his receptionist I needed to talk with Mr. Tyler about his new music box. Less than ten seconds later, "This is Ferris Tyler," boomed through the receiver. "To whom am I speaking?"

"My name is Thomas Purdue," I said. "I understand you're not altogether satisfied with an expensive music box you got from Marcus Wilcox. I may be able to help you."

"How very nice." Could've been a snotty comment but it rang sincere. "What might you wish me to do in return, Mr. Purdue?"

"I'm really not sure," I said. "Maybe something, maybe nothing. But I hope you'll talk to me, in person. At your earliest convenience."

"In this matter my earliest convenience is yours. Can you drop by my office?"

"About half an hour?"

"Absolutely. How long do you think you'll want?"

"Can you clear the morning?"

"I can and I will. I'll look forward to seeing you, Mr. Purdue. In about half an hour."

***

I thought about my encounter with Dunbar, wondered whether I was foolish to stroll unprotected into Tyler's office. I could take Big Al along—but might that put Tyler off? Nor did I really want to leave the Hartmanns unguarded for so long. I settled for calling and telling Edna where I was going, and that if she didn't hear from me by noontime she should get concerned. Flimsy net for a tightrope walker, but better than none.

Tyler's office was in a gray stone building on West 48th, half a block east of Seventh Avenue. I went through the revolving door into the lobby, checked the directory on the wall next to the three elevators. The firm of Tyler, Jacobs, Rennick, Sloan, Specialists in Industrial and Patent Law, occupied the third and fourth floors. No shallow pockets in any of those offices. I got on the elevator, got off at Three.

To my surprise I exited not into a hallway but a huge atrium, secretaries and receptionists everywhere, glass-framed cubicles along the rear wall. To the right, a brass-railed stairwell swept gracefully up to a brass-railed balcony, at the far side of which I could see a line of glass doors. Wall-to-wall carpeting, the kind you sink into up to your shoelaces. Mr. Deep Pockets, nothing. Mr. Bottomless Pockets.

A bright-eyed, coal-haired young woman in a circular kiosk just inside and to the right of the elevator exit greeted me with bright red lips, professionally parted to show straight gleaming white teeth. "May I help you, sir?" She had trouble not staring at my polychrome left eye.

"Yes, thanks. Thomas Purdue. I have an appointment with Mr. Tyler."

"Oh, *yes*, Mr. Pur*due*." Eyes suddenly full-open. "He said to bring you up the instant you arrived." She was already moving out of the kiosk toward the stairs. "Please come with me, Mr. Purdue. Our attorneys' offices are upstairs."

"Cream rises."

She smiled, ultra-polite response to ultra-important client. Tyler's door stood ajar. "Mr. Purdue is here, sir," the young woman called through the crack. She pushed the door open, then closed it behind me.

Behind his two-ton walnut desk Tyler looked fidgety. He jumped to his feet as if goosed, hustled around, gave my hand a single pump. "Thank you for coming, Mr. Purdue," he said. "This matter really *is* terribly important to me." All the while, he studied my shiner.

"I wanted to see how a tattoo'd look before I did anything permanent," I said.

He smiled, indicated one of the two chairs across from his desk. "Sit down, Mr. Purdue."

Tyler was younger than I thought he'd be, coming up on the Big 5-0, one of those bloody damned men who always look perfectly turned out. Three-piece tailored gray herring-bone suit, two pieces on him, jacket on a coathanger behind his desk. Red silk tie. Pepper hair with just enough salt to flavor, neatly trimmed mustache to match. I'd have bet my best Nicole music box that his weight fluctuated strictly plus or minus two pounds around the actuarial ideal for five-eleven, medium build. I could spend half my waking hours working on my appearance; Tyler'd roll out of bed in the morning, yawn, pass a comb through his hair, get dressed, and make me look like a bum. Easy to hate a man like that.

Like a monarch assuming his throne for a royal reception,

Tyler lowered himself into his tufted maroon desk chair, then leaned forward to face me earnestly. "You said you might be able to help me, Mr. Purdue—regarding the music box I bought from Marcus Wilcox. I hope you can."

His tone was open, no trace of condescension. He broadcast confidence; he invited confidences. Be careful, Purdue.

"You bought a plerodienique-revolver box," I said. "In a beautiful burlwood case, on a matching stand. For two hundred thousand, cash."

Light amusement in his eyes. "The purchase price is right. As to the jargon—what did you call it?"

Was he for real? I thought so. Which made me pretty sure I *was* on the right track. "Plerodienique-revolver," I said. "Combination of two of the rarest types of music boxes in existence, likely the only one of its type ever made. You didn't know that?"

"It rings a bell—if a faint one." Left eyebrow migrated archly upward. "That puzzles you? You assumed that's why I paid what I did, which I gather is a lot of money for a music box."

"A whole lot of money," I said. "And at first, yes, I did assume that's why you paid so high. But I think I was wrong."

Tyler nodded. "One of my law professors used to enjoy maneuvering his students into basing an analysis on a false or unsubstantiated assumption. His punchline was, 'Assumption is the mother of disaster.' But before I go further, why don't you tell me who you are, Mr. Purdue? And how you've come to be involved in this matter."

"I have a friend," I said. "An old man with a wife deep into mental deterioration and going downhill. The last several years, he's been selling off his possessions to keep them in food and rent money. That music box was in his family for years, he hated to sell it, wanted to get top dollar, so he talked to Marcus Wilcox. The mechanism needed work, so my friend and Wilcox found a restorer who turned out to be just a little unscrupulous. He went under the table with Wilcox, then did the repairs, called my friend, told him the music box was stolen, gave the box to Wilcox; Wilcox sold it to you."

"Why didn't your friend go to a lawyer?" Tyler asked. "It certainly sounds as if he had grounds for legal recourse."

"Two reasons. One, no money. Two, no time. He recently found out he's got untreatable cancer; he hoped the music box would bring in enough money to keep his wife in care the rest of her life. Which Wilcox knew—it was part of his *original* plan: Tell the old man the box was gone, then wait him out."

"That's revolting." Tyler shook his head. "But Wilcox was a revolting man in every way."

"But then Wilcox suddenly needed to raise some big money, fast, so he *couldn't* wait ... and you got the call to buy the music box."

"Hmm." Tyler scratched at this chin. "Who is your friend, Mr. Purdue?"

"I don't want to say ... not quite yet. Another friend of mine got a nasty little working over; someone was trying to find out where Wilcox had gotten the music box. I'm assuming ..."

Tyler frowned.

"... the person behind the attack was Wilcox's buyer."

"I'm sorry to admit that assumption is correct, Mr. Purdue. Wilcox told me he'd bought the music box from a dealer named Frank Maar. Knowing Wilcox, I thought it might be a lie, so I told my agents not to go overboard. They were far more energetic than I wanted them to be."

"They were also pretty energetic with my elderly friend," I said.

"Your friend got beaten up? The old man?"

"Sure did. Two men, asking about this particular music box."

"That's news to me, Mr. Purdue. I don't even know who your friend *is*."

"Then, there's the matter of the restorer—"

"Barton Moss." My turn to be surprised. "Wilcox mentioned his name." Tyler grimaced. "'The best restorer in New York, if not the entire country.'"

"Lot more than a slight exaggeration. And he ended up dead. Not to be rude."

"Not at all. But I had nothing to do with that either. By the time my agents went to pay him a visit, he was no longer in talking condition. And since then I've been at a dead end ... sorry. That's why I'm hopeful now, Mr. Purdue. How did you find your way to me?"

"I know Wilcox's heir," I said, "who let me look through his shop. I found the sales receipt for the music box, along with your address and phone number, and a little money—"

He waved me off. "It's not the money I'm interested in. Are you an antiques dealer, Mr. Purdue?"

Wakeup Time. "Actually, it's Dr. Purdue; I'm a professor of neurology over at Manhattan Medical. I collect and restore antique music boxes as a hobby, so my elderly friend decided to come to me for help," I hedged. "Clue me in, Mr. Tyler: you didn't care about the music box, fine. What did you care almost a quarter of a million dollars about, care enough to have a good and honest man tortured?"

Tyler leaned back in his chair, cocked his head, studied my face. I met his gaze. Waited.

Suddenly he sat up, leaned forward again. Decision made. "All right, Dr. Purdue ..."

His voice didn't change but his eyes did. In life's card game, lawyers trump antique dealers but doctors trump lawyers, "... not to offend you—but your passion simply isn't mine; music is of no interest to me. In my eyes, that marvelous, unique music box is no more than a giant frame."

"For the painting inside the lid."

Slight nod. "Yes."

I took a moment to eyeball the elegantly-framed watercolors, inks, oils on Tyler's walls. The man's interest was catholic: he had realistic work, surrealistic, cubist, impressionistic, a couple of antique portraits. "Wilcox knew about the painting, then?" I asked. "What it was worth?"

"Of course—at least in dollars. But as a collector yourself you know value can't always be properly expressed in tangible currency."

We both smiled, mutual understanding now firmly established.

"The painting is by a man named St. John Sinclair, Dr. Purdue—a young Englishman who went to France in the eighteen-sixties, developed an interest in miniatures, and therein found his genius. Unfortunately he didn't live long enough to produce a great body of work; there was a fight in a bar over a woman and poor Sinclair ended up with a knife in his heart. If I tell you he died in eighteen seventy-two and the music box painting looks like one of his very last efforts, would you call that consistent with the age of the musical works?"

"No doubt at all. The music box dates from right about eighteen-seventy and it's a treasure, obviously made for a wealthy, musically-discerning client. The painting was the manufacturer's last, perfect touch."

"Well, there you are, then. My chance to own an ultimate Sinclair, painted on silk. Irresistible. I paid in a heartbeat."

"So what was the problem?"

"Excuse me. I should have said, to own an *authentic* ultimate Sinclair ..." Tyler paused, perfect effect, "two hundred thousand dollars did seem a bit excessive for a copy."

I saw three whirling columns of fruit. Left column clicked to a halt on a ripe purple plum, then middle, finally the right. Nickels poured out of the slot into my lap. "Don't *you* take offense," I said. "But you *are* sure it was a copy?"

"Absolutely. An excellent copy. I'll admit to being victimized by my own collector's cupidity: buy quickly, carry it away before the dealer has a second thought. But as soon as I got it home and looked at it calmly, I knew. I went right back to Wilcox, of course, and of course butter would've melted into gold in his mouth. 'Copy? Why, that couldn't be. Surely you don't think ...' But surely I did. I thought I'd better check out Frank Maar and Moss, just to be sure, but I expected in the end to be dealing with Wilcox. He does have a track record for that sort of thing."

"Like selling fake art to Prescott Dunbar?"

Little smile. "The tip of a very large iceberg. Wilcox was easily unscrupulous enough to try to sell the same painting to at least two customers. Put a good copy into the music box, sell the music box to a sucker, sell the real painting to someone else. But the sucker caught on and squeezed him ... hard."

"Hard enough to kill him? Sorry, but ..."

"Don't apologize. It's a fair question, but the answer is no. Think about it, Doctor: my only interest was in getting the painting—the original painting. With Wilcox dead, my trail is cold."

Hard to argue his logic, but when passion dominates, logic abdicates. "Could your agents have gone just a little overboard with Wilcox?"

"Absolutely not." Fist onto desk by way of punctuation. "After the unfortunate incident with Mr. Maar, I made certain nothing like that would happen again. Besides, nothing like that was needed with Wilcox. The slightest twist on his arm set his tongue wagging at both ends. I suspect he went to the buyer of the original, tried to get it back—whether by refund, theft, whatever—and was killed for his trouble. Did you find a receipt for the sale of the original painting?"

I shook my head. "If there was one we'd have seen it. But maybe it wasn't exactly a buyer. An original ultimate Sinclair might be a nice blackmail payment."

"Hard to imagine it being refused." Tyler stretched, locked fingers behind his head. "Does your friend have proof of ownership of the music box? An insurance policy?"

"No insurance—couldn't afford the premiums. How about pictures, though?" I pulled the rubber-banded photos out of my pocket, passed them to Tyler. "Pre-restoration. Before Moss and Wilcox got their grubby hands on it."

"I can see, yes." Tyler studied each photograph, nodding as he flipped from one to the next. One picture seemed to grab him harder than the others. He gazed at it, smiled, then held it out to me.

"Closeup of the painting," I said. "Nice."

"Also interesting." Tyler shot his left cuff, looked at his watch. "Do you have time to come to my apartment, Doctor? Before we go any further I'd like to show you the music box."

Might I have a few moments to permit Wotan to give me a short guided tour of Valhalla? "Sure I've got time."

The bit of smugness around his mouth told me he'd read my mind—but the expression was tempered with sympathy. Two good ol' collector-boys; we were gonna get on fine. Tyler picked up the phone, punched a single digit. "Polly ... yes. I'm going out; I should be back for my two o'clock appointment."

As he replaced the receiver I pointed at it. "May I?"

"Of course."

I dialed, waited. When Edna said hello, I chirped, "Hi, dear—just wanted to let you know. Mr. Tyler and I are still working; we're going over to his place now ... yes, I'll call you from there when I'm finished." Then I hung up.

"You're cautious, Doctor." Tyler's face said he'd just slammed a low whistler across the net, right at my feet.

"Once slugged, twice cautious, Lawyer," I said, and as surprise spread over his face I laughed. "Call me Thomas."

He chuckled. "Fair enough. Then I'm Ferris."

Of course—as he himself might have said. Ferris, Ferris Tyler. Bingo. The melody that'd been playing so faintly between my ears since the last get-together at Edna's suddenly became a full-throated crystalline lyric.

We cabbed to Tyler's humble abode, a full penthouse in an

elegant 'twenties brick and stone building on Beekman Place. Past the fawning doorman, up eighteen stories in the wheezing elevator, through a short hall, into the apartment.

He let me stand a moment in the living room to acclimatize to the rarefied atmosphere. The living room was huge and light, floor-to-ceiling windows giving on southern Manhattan and the East River. To the west, doors opened to bedrooms, bathrooms and kitchen. Near the south windows stood a full-sized open Steinway grand; someone living there must've liked music at least a little. Next to the piano a small piecrust table held a photo of a younger Tyler with his family. Mrs. T. was clearly a class number, lots of teeth and wavy blonde hair; the kids, a boy and a girl—of course—were end-stage adolescents, chips off the female block. No one else was home right then, but Mrs. Tyler had left a hint of expensive perfume that I picked up on, lost, then found again as I slowly gawked my way around the room. Easy to see ghosts who lived and visited here in the 'twenties, 'thirties and 'forties, dashing men in impeccable evening dress and elegant women with snowflakes glistening in their hair, eyes shining as they glided on the arms of their escorts into the building and upstairs for an evening of music and animated conversation. Nice history, if you can afford it.

Which Ferris Tyler clearly could. Industrial and Patent Law paid damn well or Mrs. Tyler came with a hope chest full of doubloons. Or both.

Coming around the corner to the east window, I walked past a green leather sofa to a gorgeous walnut-cased music box on a matching stand. Behind me, I heard Tyler chuckle. That music box was sending me a wireless communication, just as its painting must've sent one to Tyler. No trouble imagining what went through his head when he realized the painting was a fake. Imagine *my* feelings if he were to open the lid right then to reveal a tawdry little 18-note musical movement made yesterday in Japan, rather than a unique mechanism epitomizing the genius of some Swiss manufacturer of a hundred and thirty years ago.

Tyler reached over my shoulder, lifted the lid, pushed the stay hinge into place. If I'd been a cardiac patient on a monitor in an ICU, they'd've red-coded me. Six shiny brass cylinders set into a carousel, Cylinder Number One in line with the teeth of the musical comb, ready to play. At the center of each cylinder, a dark sleeve-line, the tell-tale mark of a plerodienique. My gizzard danced in perfect time to the irregular drumbeat in my chest.

"Each cylinder plays a complete overture from some opera or other," Tyler said. He opened a drawer in the table, took out a black leather rectangle onto which was mounted the attractively decorated tune card I'd seen in Hartmann's photo. "But I've only heard one cylinder, the one Wilcox played when he showed me the box. I'm afraid to turn the damn thing on."

The look I gave him must have been a doozie; he actually backed off a step. "Sorry," I muttered, as I bent to read the program.

"No problem." Another sympathetic chuckle.

The program was indeed the same as in Hartmann's picture: *William Tell, The Thieving Magpie, Semiramis, Zampa, Alessandro Stradella, Ines de Castro.*

"Look here," Tyler said, and pointed at the framed painting set into the lid.

I studied the painting, an exquisitely detailed depiction of a village in a valley before a majestic mountain range. I could count windows in the white walls of the buildings, read the time on the clock in the tower of the church in the background. A path led back toward the mountain, another into the foreground where a young man worked a patch of lush land behind a brace of oxen. A girl with a basket of laundry on her head turned to look at him, while on the dirt road behind her, a boy, hat held respectfully in his left hand, carried on a conversation with a well-dressed gentleman astride a brown and white horse. The scene gave me a sense of *déjà vu*, then I realized it was no illusion. Not only had I seen this place in photographs, I'd been there. This was St. Croix, birthplace of the Swiss music box, as it looked a century and a quarter ago.

I shook my head. "What'd Sinclair do—work under a magnifying glass? You could step right into that painting. How the hell do you know it's a fake?"

"You're overlooking the obvious."

I glanced from the painting to him, then back.

"Compare it with your photos."

I pulled out the stack of pictures, flipped to the one of the lid painting. As I held it next to the actual I suddenly felt very foolish. "The glass is broken," I said. "At the left lower edge. But it's not broken in the photograph."

"Right—just as I never really listened to the music, you never really looked at the painting. That broken glass was the tipoff, and I should've paid more attention to it at Wilcox's. But I was so excited I discounted it: old setting, been around, glass got cracked. After I brought it home, though, I realized there was no dirt in the crack, and with a loupe I could see fresh slivers inside. Besides ... look closely. That glass isn't anywhere near a hundred and thirty years old—it's perfectly smooth, no bubbles ... so ..."

He tugged at the lower edge of the wooden frame, which responded by coming free. The smaller glass fragment dropped neatly into his hand.

"... the frame came off just as easily then as it did now. Someone had been there before me, removed the original painting and glass, then replaced the frame over a new painting with new glass, using the same nails and holes in the lid." Tyler laid the small piece of glass on the table. "Watch this."

He spread his palm over the larger glass remnant, pulled downward. Glass and painting slid into his free hand. He motioned with his head. "Look at the clean edge around that glass—it could've been cut yesterday." He took the exposed corner of the silk gingerly between thumb and index finger, peeled it away from the glass. "It came off just like that the first time I did it," he said. "After more than a hundred years, a silk painting under glass should be stuck tight. Then, when I looked closely at the painting I could see subtle differences from Sinclair's style; I also noticed the painting was unsigned. Sinclair always signed his work, low in the right corner. With the frame on, it was easy enough to tell myself the signature was beneath the frame. So I went back to Wilcox, who said he and I never discussed the painting. He showed me the box, I bought it. He never warranted the painting as a genuine Sinclair—so if it turned out to be a copy, that was my tough luck. I wouldn't have argued—*if* the painting really was original to the music box. But the switch was obvious and recent, and Wilcox was just the man who'd do such a thing. So I decided to push him ...

and now, here we are. You said you might be able to help. What've you got in mind?"

"Make you a deal," I said. "You want the painting, couldn't care less about the music box. Return it—with the copy—to my friend, so he can sell it as is. In return, I'll find you the original painting."

Enigmatic little smile. "You do know, don't you, that the fact I bought the music box from a licensed artwork dealer gives me a valid legal claim."

"Sure I know. Like I know if you decide to go to court, you'll win—especially considering my friend's health. He won't challenge you. But if that's the way you decide to play, I'll give him the painting when I find it. Then he can sell it. From what you've told me, he ought to get more for it than for the music box."

Tyler nodded. "Have you ever thought of going to law school?"

"Never. Too damn many binding precedents."

He laughed. "What's in this for you?"

I pointed at the music box. "Reward me with a tune."

Tyler's smile at first cynical, went sheepish. "You're the expert. Go ahead, play it.."

People are often afraid to play their antique music boxes: they don't want to "wear them out." But old music boxes are like old people. No exercise, their joints go stiff. They should be played every day.

I pushed the start lever and listened, entranced, as the air filled with a glorious arrangement of a melody I'd never heard, the overture to the opera *Ines de Castro*, by a composer I'd never heard of, Giovanni Persiani. Have to check my references ... but for now, enough to let the lovely melody with its gentle counterpoint and bright piccolo trills flow sweetly by.

The cylinder clicked to a stop after its fourth revolution. Music faded; Tyler touched my arm. "Suppose I play your game—I return the music box to your friend. When do I get the painting?"

I looked at my watch. "You said you have 'til two?"

Nod. "What are you thinking?"

"It's eleven-thirty. Let me make a couple of calls. Then we'll need to wait about an hour, maybe we can have lunch. After that I'll tell you what I've got in mind."

Tyler chewed at his cheek. "All right ... but it damn well better be good." He pointed at a white phone on a round glass table. "Go ahead."

I grabbed the phone, dialed, waited. At the hello, I said, "Yes, this is Thomas. Let me speak to Al, please."

Big Al was on the line almost instantly. "I need your help," I said, then gave him Tyler's address. "Tell our friend to keep his doors—and windows—locked, not to open up for *anyone*. Be here at ... oh, quarter to one."

Then I called my father. The phone rang four, five, six times. "Answer, goddamn it," I muttered. "Answer, answer, ans—"

"Dr. Will Purdue."

"Dad!"

"Thomas?"

Who else? "Yes. How are you?"

"A little surprised—I don't usually get calls from you at midday. What is it?"

"I need your help. Can you come in to New York for an hour—now?"

"Thomas, are you all right?"

"I'm fine, Dad, just need some help from you." I repeated Tyler's address. "Can you be here by a quarter to one?"

"If you need help I'll be there."

I could see him nod solemnly. Emergency calls were always just that to Dad; he never tried to figure them in advance. Go in, guns blazing, time later for questions. Sometimes, tough questions.

But I'd have an hour to talk to Tyler, and by the time my father arrived, my ducks would be lined up nice and neat. "Thanks, Dad," I said. "See you soon."

Tyler headed for the door as I hung up. "There's a good German place over on Second, just off Fifty-second. They have outdoor seating; we can be there in five minutes."

I was halfway out when I stopped. "Whoops, almost forgot; one more call." I trotted back to the phone, dialed quickly. When I heard Edna's hello I said, "Everything's under control, dear, no problems. See you later."

16

The doorbell rang; Tyler pulled at the knob. There stood my father and Big Al, eyeing each other with open curiosity. I pictured them walking into Tyler's building simultaneously, riding up on the same elevator, going down the hallway to the same door. "You're both in the right place," I said. "My father, Will Purdue ... Al Resford, my good friend from London. Al's saved my life, Dad, once literally, more than once figuratively."

Dad's brief glance told me the salt with which he was taking my remarks was having a nasty effect on his blood pressure. But he gripped Al's hand. "My pleasure, Mr. Resford."

"The pleasure is mine, I assure you." Al's eyes glittered with mischief.

"And Dad, Al: this is Ferris Tyler. He owns an exceptional music box with what should be an exceptional piece of artwork framed inside its lid. That's why I asked—"

Dad leaned forward, touched me tentatively below the left eye. "Thomas ..?"

"Accident, Dad, I'm all right. No fracture."

I led the three men toward the plerodienique-revolver. "Look here." I pointed at the square of silk lying atop the closed music box. "This was inside the lid, under glass. What do you think?"

Al and Dad studied the painting. "Sinclair," Dad ventured. "Those photographs you showed me the other night ... yes, I *would* say St. John Sinclair. But there's no signature."

"Agreed, and more." Al leaned over the painting, gently brushed an index finger across its surface. "Be helpful, what, to inspect it under a bit better conditions. But I'd stake a great deal on its being a copy, and a recent one at that."

"What Mr. Tyler was thinking," I said.

"Mr. Tyler's expertise is respected throughout the international art world," said Al. "Were I at variance with his conclusions I should be forced to reconsider mine. But pr'aps you might bring us up to date on the ... shall we say, circumstances?"

I zipped through a *Reader's Digest* version of the situation to that point. As I described Edna's scheme, complete with purse-snatch and the way we engineered Doris out of the shop so we could search it, Al and Tyler both looked amused. Dad's expression fluttered between horrified and grudgingly impressed.

"It's been a shot in the arm for Edna," I said. "Between working with Jitters and brainstorming us to where we are, she's her old self again. But now I ... we ... need your help, Dad. Can you paint a copy of that faked Sinclair, make it look even more like an original? If you—"

"Let me understand this, Thomas." Dad looked nearly apoplectic. "You want *me* ... to paint a forgery?"

"In a word, yes," I said, speaking very quickly. "If you'll do it, I'll arrange a little party and set this matter straight, once and for all. Get Mr. Tyler the painting he's paid for, the music box to its proper owner ... believe it or not, get everyone who's been involved in this business exactly what they deserve. Your call, Dad."

For reply, a familiar soft, deliberate hum. I watched Dad's decision circuits oscillate through binary flips, faster than I could count. Finally he said, "That's the straight story? Nothing altered? Nothing held back?"

"That's it, Dad," I said quietly. "Complete and accurate ... to the best of my ability."

His expression was that of a baby trying to pass a particularly painful gas pocket. "You're an ... exasperating man," he said, sounding as if he were paging through a mental thesaurus. "Which shouldn't surprise me. You were an exasperating boy. Once you got it into your head that both teams win when they play baseball in heaven, there was no stopping you."

Tyler looked mildly embarrassed. In his neighborhood you washed even slightly-soiled linen in strict privacy. Al, however, chuckled appreciatively.

Dad paused just long enough to scan the audience, then looked back at me, leveled a finger. Gray eyes hot between narrowed lids; I felt six years old. "I don't want to cause your friend to relapse, Thomas. Will you promise me we'll destroy my forgery as soon as it's served its purpose? That it will not survive the evening of that party?"

A moment's thought. "Not without your consent."

"I'd never give—"

"I promise, Dad."

Another moment's thought. "All right," he finally murmured. "Yes ... I'll help."

He extended a hand; we shook like two hardheaded businessmen finally closing the deal that all the smart heads in town said could never be done. "All right if I set up the party for Friday?" I asked. "Night after tomorrow?"

"I think so ..." Dad took a little brown-covered book from his shirt pocket, flicked it open. "Yes. Friday'll be fine."

"Mr. Tyler?"

"Friday's perfect." He grinned like a lottery winner. "My wife has a charity auction that evening—you know, win a night on the town with a basketball player or a talk-show host. I've been praying for some important business to come up."

Nice having a reliable connection to the celestial switchboard.

Tyler's face went serious, every trace of humor suddenly blue-penciled. "But I'm telling you, Thomas, and I hope you're listening: if I don't leave that party with my painting, I'll leave with your scalp."

"Thomas' schemes always have been worth my time," said Al. "And I must say, they've been highly entertaining in the bargain."

Dad remained silent, his features stern, almost grim. Al finally broke through the fidgety standstill. "Mr. Tyler—might we pr'aps have a brief look at this remarkable music box?"

Tyler gingerly picked up the painting in his left hand, lifted the lid with his right.

"Oh my." Al, hunched forward from the shoulders, a rotund buzzard. "Quite a grand mechanical creation. Not many of these around, I'd venture."

"Probably no others," I said. "Painting aside, it's an extremely valuable instrument."

Dad glanced at the music box, then looked back to the painting in Tyler's hand. One man's shoe leather is another's tenderloin. Al smiled at me.

Outside, a quick goodbye, then Dad marched off toward

the Port Authority Bus Terminal. As he vanished around the corner, I asked Al whether he had any idea who might've painted the Sinclair copy.

"Been wondering about that, don't you know." Al spoke slowly, pushing past the inertia of heavy thought. "No reason to go outside one's backyard to get such a job done ... and in New York, who comes to mind? Ben Chester ... Philip Andrews ... Stuart Panora." He pulled a small notebook from his jacket pocket, flipped pages. "Yes ... all in Manhattan."

"Let's go visiting," I said.

Ben Chester lived just a few blocks away, in a third-story walk-up on Second Avenue, pathetic by comparison to Tyler's digs. Postage-stamp living room, bedroom, mini-kitchen—in real-estatespeak, a dollhouse.

Chester didn't look particularly pleased to see us, but I wondered whether he was ever pleased to see anyone. His key word was droopy: belly, shoulders, jowls, corners of mouth all sagged as if in perpetual discouragement. As he opened the door, he gave Al a perfunctory nod of recognition, then mumbled, "Howyer, Hedgey. Wot brings y'here?"

Threw me off, until I remembered in certain circles in his home country, Big Al is known as the Hedgehog.

Al took a moment to study Chester and his surroundings. The artist wore a filthy smock over a grubby white shirt, held a paint brush in his right hand. At the far end of the room stood a partially done canvas on an easel; just to its left, another easel held a finished painting, one of the French impressionists, I thought. It took little in the way of artistic perceptiveness to notice a striking resemblance between the two canvases.

Al chuckled. "Same old Ben, eh? Business better on this side of the pond, is it?"

In the bedroom, a figure stirred on the bed, grunted, rearranged itself. Chester went acutely antsy. Lips twitched, fingers trembled; he set his brush down on a table without apparent regard for the finish. "It's all right, Hedgey," he muttered, "I'm getting by."

"Bobbies haven't tumbled over here, eh?" Al turned to me. "Ben left England a few years back in ... shall we say, a bit of a rush. He'd sold quite a nice piece of work to a customer who turned out to be both more knowledgeable and influential than Ben had imagined." Al looked back at Chester, who by now appeared ready to give his kingdom, such as it was, for a handful of Thorazine tablets. "Ah, Ben, you got greedy ... and worse, careless. I trust you're being more discreet these days."

Poor Chester, waiting for the shoe to drop, afraid where it might fall. Mouth sagging open, he nodded silent acknowledgment.

Big Al beamed jolly cheer at the now-writhing painter. "Good-o! Common sense, there's the important thing. Knowing when to speak and when to remain silent. Now, Ben ..."

I thought Chester might drop to the floor.

"... have you done a Sinclair recently?"

"A what? A Sinclair? No ... no, Hedgey, I ain't. Honest. I ain't done a Sinclair since ... well, not over here at all, not a one. Honest."

Two honests in one proclamation, uh-oh. Like prefacing a remark with, "I'll tell you the truth." He's lying, I thought.

To my surprise Big Al smiled, said, "Very well; thank you, Ben." Then he tipped his bowler, opened the door, went out into the hall. I followed him quickly, heard the door slam behind us, the lock being thrown.

We went down the stairs, out into the sunshine, started walking down Second Avenue. "Ben and I go back a long way," Al murmured. "Pity he needed to emigrate as he did; he was most helpful on a number of occasions. I expect we can scratch him off the list—not that he's above lying, understand. But he knows well what will happen if I find he's lied to *me*."

I didn't ask which list Ben might be scratched off if Al ever did uncover him as a liar. Just said, "Where now?"

"Andrews ... Philip Andrews." Al consulted his pocket notebook. "West Eighty-third Street. Lead the way."

I led Al up Broadway through a richly multi-ethnic neighborhood, sidewalk crowded with older people pulling wire rolling baskets filled with food from the local supermarkets or from Zabar's, the *primo* gourmet palace at Broadway and 80th. As we approached 83rd, though, more and more of the carts were loaded with blankets, sleeping rolls, odd personal possessions. Some of the cart-pullers held hands out to us, quavered, "Spare change, sir ... please ... anything." I gave a few of the supplicants a little money. Around the corner, on 83rd, Al gently pressed a bill into the hand of a toothless old woman with a ratty knitted maroon cap over greasy gray hair. The woman hobbled away. "Horrid," Al said, then as if to clarify the object of his repugnance, murmured, "One must provide."

Philip Andrews greeted us with considerably more cordiality than Chester had. He was slim, blond, and smiley, his speech clearly New York, but he seemed to know Big Al. "To what do I owe the honor?" he asked, focusing entirely on my companion.

If Andrews' breeziness bothered Al, he didn't show it. "Been a bit of unpleasantness recently over a Sinclair miniature—a miniature copy, that is," he said calmly. "Very well done, it was. I thought of you right off."

"Heh-heh. I suppose I'll take that as a compliment." Andrews shifted a step away from Al.

"You might also take it as a question," Al said. "But since you choose to be obtuse, I shall be more direct: During the past month, have you painted a copy of an elegant Sinclair miniature—to be even more specific, one whose subject was a Swiss village scene?"

Andrews shook his head, blond hair tossed this way and that. He laughed lightly. "You're not working for the cops now, are you, Al?"

I held my breath. Al's mild expression didn't change. He just said, "Will you please answer my question, Philip."

Another shake of the straw-topped head. "No, I didn't copy a Sinclair. But why're you asking? What's going on?"

Al took a deep breath, let it out with a soft um-*oom*. He looked around the room, all very casual. Then he strolled toward the far end of the apartment. Beneath windows, a line of paintings stood on the floor, propped against the wall. Al studied them like a visitor to a gallery. Not quite midway along the line he stopped, stooped, picked up a small, splashily color-ful rendering of flowers in a glass vase on a wooden table. He looked at it closely. Andrews scratched his head.

Suddenly, Al glared at Andrews. "What's going on is lying," Al said. "Which I do not appreciate in the least." He pulled a lighter from his pocket, snapped it open, moved the flame to the edge of the painting. "I shall ask you again," he said. "Have you recently painted a copy of a Sinclair miniature? Yes or no, please."

Andrews looked frantic. "I told you already, Al, no. I haven't. Hey—"

Andrews' voice became a shriek as Al held the canvas at arm's length, then moved the flame onto the corner. Paint sizzled, dripped to the floor in black globs. Orange flame coursed upward, engulfing the image. Andrews charged across the room, arms waving wildly.

About two feet from the now-ruined painting he pulled up short, staggered back a step. Al was pointing a handgun at his chest. I never saw the little cannon come out: one instant it wasn't there, next instant it was; the lighter lay on the floor near Al's foot. I flattened against the wall.

"Not a step closer if you please," Al said to Andrews. "Yes, that's right." He dropped the burning remains, extinguished the flame with a bug-squashing motion of his foot. Keeping Andrews in sight, he bent to pick up the lighter, then crouched sideways over a second painting, this one of a crowd at a seashore, striped umbrellas dotting the beach. "I'll ask again, Philip. Have you recently done a Sinclair miniature?"

Andrews spluttered, coughed. "Al—I told you, no. That's a week's work you just burned. Come on, please ..."

His voice petered out as Al flicked the lighter alive, then set the seaside into conflagration. We watched the scene vanish; the only sound was the crackling of burning canvas. Al moved to the next painting, a portrait of a young woman dressed for a ball one hundred or so years ago. "I'm quite patient, Philip," Al said. "There are enough paintings here to keep me amused for a good while. Eventually, of course, they *will* run out, and you might give a thought to what I shall do then for diversion."

Andrews went pasty, cheeks splotched circus-clown style. "Al ... I ..."

Big Al held the lighter to the corner of the third painting, elevated his pistol just slightly. "Pr'aps you're simply a slow thinker, Philip. Now, did you or did you not recently paint a copy of a Sinclair miniature?"

Andrews collapsed altogether. He sank to the floor, first kneeling, then in a sort of exhausted-Buddha position. "Nothing wrong with doing a copy," he whined. "Guy comes in with that miniature on silk, says he wants a copy for his wife's birthday. So I paint a copy—I don't sign it—and I put a sticker-label on the back, says, 'St. Croix, by St. John Sinclair. Copied by Philip Andrews.' Then the date. Not my business, is it, if he takes the label off."

Al smiled, slipped the gun back inside his jacket, then dropped the lighter into his pocket. "Thank you, Philip. Your honesty is refreshing."

Back on Broadway, weaving through mobs of people and pull-carts, I asked Al how he knew Andrews was the one. "Didn't really," he said. "But at that point 'twas even odds, and I do know Andrews to be fast, superb on detail, and reliable ... in his fashion. I also know he's a bit of a brass-cheek, so I thought it might take some persuasion on my part. As it did."

"But what if he'd kept saying no? You wouldn't have really ..." I made a bang-bang motion with my thumb and forefinger.

Al smiled. "No purpose to that. No, we'd have just gone to pay a call upon Panora ... and if *he'd* denied knowledge we'd have gotten the three artists together–at which point, I assure you, the truth certainly would've come out."

One more concern. "But Al–to burn paintings?"

Uncle Al beamed me a healthy slug of tolerant amusement. "Did you notice how closely I looked at those paintings? Do you remember Andrews' saying I'd cost him a week's work? Really, Thomas–you must give me more credit."

Half an hour later Al and I were sitting in the Hartmanns' sparsely-furnished living room. Over the background of Lettie's crooning, Mr. Hartmann listened intently to my update. "Tyler must've got your name from Wilcox, same as he got Frank's," I said. "He admitted setting up the knock on Frank, but wouldn't take credit for you. One thing to put muscle on an antique dealer, but I think he doesn't fancy the way a jury might react to a well-known, respected multimillionaire art collector who allegedly tried to cut losses on a bad purchase by having a sick old man knocked around. I also suspect Tyler's goons got a bit rough with Wilcox–anyone could lose patience in a hurry with a creep like that. Whether they killed him accidentally or on purpose I don't know, and I'm not about to lose any sleep over it. You and Lettie are probably safe now–but let's keep Al here 'til everything's settled. Just in case."

"That's no problem." Hartmann's face flushed with good fellowship. "It's been a pleasure having a house guest. Someone to ..."

Talk to, obviously. Well, why not? Must get tiring, listening day and night to jabberwocky, your every word transformed into rhymed nonsense and pitched back at you.

Al jumped right in. "We've been having a fine time, Thomas: Rudolph's shown me his workroom and I've learned a great deal about matting and framing. *Most* interesting. I shall be glad to stay."

"We've arranged to bring back the music box on Friday," I said to Hartmann. "Have a little celebration, champagne, some good food. Sound all right?"

"It sounds wonderful," said Hartmann, grabbing my hand and giving it a full-blooded pump. "I just don't know how I'm going to thank you."

"Never fear." Mischief glowed in Big Al's eyes. "Thomas will think of a way."

Back in my workshop, I called Edna, quickly filled her in. A couple of days' recess sounded like a good idea, time to stand back and look over the plan. One misstep, the whole thing could fall to pieces, leaving me in a position more embarrassing than most of those shown on videos delivered to your home in plain brown paper.

Whoops. *I* had something in a plain brown paper bag, didn't I? A small Wedgwood urn full of monkey ashes.

I pulled the Yellow Pages out of my bottom worktable drawer, thumbed through Hotels until I found the Imperial. Then I dialed the number and asked for Mrs. Wilcox's room. No answer. I left her a voice-mail: call me.

Not fifteen minutes later the phone rang. Doris. She was there with Mr. Schwartz; he was about to pay her off from the sale of the shop merchandise. She didn't know how he'd done it: the shop was empty, stock fully accounted for, eighty-three grand in her purse, ten percent commission in Schwartz's pocket. "For a job like that he really should take more. I *know* the antique business and I've never seen anything like it."

"Don't worry," I said. "I'm sure he's satisfied."

"You've all been so kind." Catch in Doris' voice. "I don't know how I would've managed without you."

"Not at all. Listen, why I called before—I want to give you back your ..." at which point my voice faded.

Talk about missteps! I was about to stride boldly into the biggest squishy brown heap I could imagine. Doris was there with Schwartz, wasn't she? Schwartz, who supposedly found the urn in a local antique shop and left it with me. But Schwartz didn't know any of this. I hadn't seen him since we left the Palais Royal the previous afternoon—before Sophie went to Leo Kaplan's and I traipsed off to the Primate Center.

"Er, you said Schwartz was there, Doris?"

"Yes. He was just showing me the accounting. But you said something about my—"

"Let me speak to Schwartz first—please."

"Yes, of course." Curiosity was clear in her voice, but she did as I asked. A moment later I heard, "Hey, Doc? What's up?"

"Broadway, listen carefully ... and don't ... say ... anything." Low voice, almost a whisper. "I've got the Wedgwood urn here, the one with Marcus Wilcox's ashes in it. The one you found earlier today in a shop near where Doris' purse was snatched, and then dropped off with me for safekeeping. The one you forgot to tell her about 'til now. Got me? Say yes or no."

"Yeah, Doc. Sure."

That's Schwartz. If one word is good, two are better and three are wonderful. "All right, then. I want to give her back the urn, sooner the better; then we're free and clear with her. Can you bring her down here when you're done with the accounting? Say yes or no."

"Well, yeah, Doc, of course. What do you think, I'd say no to something like that?"

And sixteen words is unbeatable. "Good, Broadway. I'm going to tell her you'll do it. Put her back on. And remember: we told you about the urn, and while you were going around selling her stuff, you kept an eye peeled in every shop near where her purse got snatched ... and you found it. Right?"

"Yeah, yeah, yeah. Hey, Doc—what do you think, I'm retarded?"

"Not for a minute. Now please—put Doris back on."

A second later, Doris' voice. "Yes, Thomas?"

"Sorry for the interruption. I'm pretty sure I've got your urn, the one with Marcus' ashes. Color, size—it's exactly what you described, sealed with wax at the top, and when you shake it you hear something rustling. Schwartz found it in a shop this morning, near where that kid grabbed your purse, and since he was running around selling Marcus' merchandise, he dropped it off with me. He says he's not busy now, so as soon as the two of you are done with your accounting he'll bring you down here."

"Oh, I couldn't possibly let you—"

"Relax, Doris. It's all arranged. Just leave your money in the hotel safe. Better you don't walk around New York with five figures in your purse."

"My God, I wouldn't *dream* of doing that. I'd have to be crazy."

"Just making sure. See you soon."

***

Half an hour later, clattering on the stairs outside. I set down my musical legacy from Reymond-Nicole, pushed away from the worktable, trotted through the vestibule, opened the door. Schwartz's fist was in the air; I was lucky to not get a shot in the snoot. "Heard you," I said. "Come on in."

Doris walked into the workshop, stopped, stared. "Oh, my." Her eyes moved upward, to the ladder-accessed sleeping platform. "That's right—you told me you restored antique music boxes. What a marvelous workshop ... and you live here, too. How perfect."

"It works." I went to the coffee table in front of the sofa, took the urn out of the brown paper bag, handed it to Doris. "I thought we had a good chance of finding it—better than in Horton's Falls. Kid in your neck of the woods steals an antique, he drives an hour down the pike to dump it. But in New York he'll just run in to the first place he sees, sell fast for cash, then disappear back into the city. For someone with eyes like Schwartz's it was a gimme."

"Piece a cake," chimed in the modest hero.

As Doris clutched the urn her eyes filled. I heard Sarah's angry reproof, silently argued it away. What should I feel bad about? Empty store, reclaimed funeral urn, kindness of strangers. It made the whole deal right.

I was about to tell Doris that Sarah would be back any minute and we'd all go to dinner, when a puzzled look came over the old woman's face. She held the urn up to light, squinted at it, then turned it over to study its bottom. Schwartz shot me a glance that said his antennae were picking up some very bad vibes.

"Thomas ..." Doris drew out my name for what felt like five excruciating minutes. "This isn't the urn I lost."

"It's not?"

She shook her head. "No. Marcus was in an antique urn, from the late eighteenth or early nineteenth century; this is a much newer one. It feels rough; old ones are smooth as velvet. And look closely: the white relief figures aren't nearly as well defined as they are on older pieces. Early Wedgwood is superb, but quality went downhill as time passed."

"Well, yes ... it was that way with music boxes too." I reached automatically to the coffee table, turned on a choice Bremond aria box, and what started to play but "O Fatal Hour Impending," from *Trovatore*. If what I felt right then in my innards ever made its way to my face, I was a goner. This had to be put to bed, fast—definitely before Sarah came in. "Doris, are you *sure*?" I asked. "A second vase, newer but otherwise exactly the same as the first, showing up in a shop just a block or so from where the first one vanished, with a wax seal and something inside, sounds like ashes when you shake it? You've been upset the last few days ... could you *possibly* be wrong?"

"No. Upset, not upset, I've been collecting Wedgwood for more than forty years, and I *know* how old pieces look and feel." Bite to Doris' voice I didn't like at all. She turned the vase over, pointed at some letters impressed on the white undersurface. "Look here: 'Wedgwood, Made in England.' That's what it says, doesn't it?"

"Well, yes—"

"The urn I brought from home was stamped 'Wedgwood,' just the one word. It was done that way until eighteen ninety-one, when new export laws required them to add 'England' to the stamp. After nineteen twenty-one, all pieces were stamped 'Made in England.' Like this one." She waved the little vase in my face.

Schwartz looked at the door as if it opened onto the stairs to Beulah Land. As I followed his wishful eyes I again heard footsteps outside, then the sound of a key in the outside lock. Sarah, great. I willed her to go into her apartment, change her clothes before she came over, maybe even take a little nap.

A key turned in my door lock. Door opened.

I wanted to dematerialize, just go poof into the ether. Sarah would've been a bargain. In barged Edna and Jitters. Our young apprentice was holding the Japanese tea server automaton. She looked wonderful—without doubt a whole lot better than I did at that moment.

"We've got—" Whatever Edna was going to tell me went by the boards as she saw Doris Wilcox gawk from her to Jitters and back. Doris glanced at the urn, then at me, then focused an increasingly baleful gaze on Jitters, who responded by clearing his throat and shuffling his feet. Slowly, his hand disappeared into a pants pocket. He wasn't going to come out with that knife, was he?

I started to frame a warning, "Jitters ..." but stopped as I saw he was holding a small brown pill bottle. Klonopin, his ultimate shake-stopper pills. His eyes flashed me a silent question.

"Go ahead," I said. "You'll never need it more than you do right now."

As Jitters gulped his pill, waterless, Doris turned her visual firepower on Edna. The two old women locked eyes.

No one in the room seemed to be breathing; you could've

heard a mouse burp behind the wall. Finally, Schwartz whispered, "*Vay iz mir.*"

Did any Fury ever turn more frightfully on an unpunished criminal? "I'd say that sums it up very nicely, Mr. Schwartz." Doris advanced on him; he backed away. I stepped quickly between the two. "Doris, wait—"

"Shut up. This has all been a little stage-play, hasn't it?"

I could see next day's headline in the *Daily News.* MAN MED DOC AND PALS HELD WITHOUT BAIL IN CLIP GAME. Then, in smaller print, *Wife says it's about time he finally got what he deserves.*

"Well ... sort of ..."

Doris brushed aside my pathetic parry. "But why? *Why?*"

She looked on the point of exploding, glared at each of us in turn. No one spoke. Then her eyes narrowed; thin lips snaked into a sly grimace. "I'll guess again," she said, looking straight at Edna. "I collect antiques, I deal in them, I know them. Schwartz ... if that really is his name—"

"It is," I said. "You know us all by our real names."

"Which wouldn't figure if you were out to rook me. But I was saying—Schwartz got damn good money for Marcus' stock, and he gave it to me, every cent for every piece, less an honest ten percent commission. The money's in the hotel safe; first thing tomorrow it goes into the bank two doors down and gets wired to my account in Horton's Falls. You sure as hell haven't fleeced me. So I have to ask myself, *why?* Why did Edna there set me up to have that kid snatch my purse? So you could steal a Wedgwood urn worth a couple hundred dollars? I don't think so. Do you know what I think?"

In the way every moment of a person's life is said to flash

before his eyes at the moment of death, every thought Doris might've had ripped painfully through my brain.

"*I* think all this crap is because of some trouble my piss-weasel son cooked up. Am I right?"

At "piss-weasel," I saw Edna's eyes light with sympathy, saw Doris pick up and return the signal. Edna punctuated the wordless communication with a barely-perceptible nod.

Doris gave the urn in her hand a look hot enough to melt potter's glaze. I thought she was going to hurl it through the nearest window, but instead she slipped it into her pocketbook, then dropped into the nearest chair and laid the purse on the floor at her feet. "Make a grab, you go home without your fingers," she said to Jitters. "And maybe some of your other body parts."

Jitters' face went the color of undercooked prime rib.

"Let me tell you all something." Doris' voice was beyond weary. "My son was no good, never was. He was a liar, a cheat, a thief. He filched candy bars from the confectionery when he was a boy, stole merchandise out of my shop when he was old enough to do that. When he finished school I brought him into the shop with me—I hoped in his own place he might shape up. Fat chance! He cheated our customers and consignors, he cheated people who brought items in to sell outright. He once got an out-of-state buyer to send a check for an expensive piece to a PO box he'd rented, then sneaked the piece off the shelf, shipped it, and swore to me it must've been shoplifted. I only found out because the buyer called to report breakage in shipping. Lazy little bastard hadn't packed it worth a damn."

Amid general lip-chewing and soft sighs, Doris paused for breath, then went on. "Saddest thing was, the boy really did have talent. He taught himself glass repair, actually did some nice work. He said he wanted to be a master glass restorer, so I sent him to Michigan to work with an expert, and when he came back he set up in the rear of the shop. But still, he always had to find the angle. Glass restorers have their customers sign a liability release in case the piece is broken in restoration—it happens."

We all knew the antiques world; we knew what was coming. Edna took a step forward, rested a hand lightly on Doris' arm.

Doris didn't skip a beat. She must've been waiting a long while to tell this to someone, *any*one. "One day Marcus told a customer he'd accidentally broken an item, and the man said he wanted to see the pieces. Marcus got huffy: didn't the man trust him? Actually, no, the man said, not as far as he could throw him. He said unless Marcus came up with some shards in a damn big hurry, he was going to the police. All of a sudden I knew. Every repair job Marcus ever broke was something impressive and expensive. But he *didn't* break them. He just told the customers he did, then sold the glass out the back door. Can you *imagine*? I told him to get out of my shop or I'd throw him out myself. That afternoon I called the locksmith and changed my locks; next day I had an alarm system installed—first one in Horton's Falls. I told Marcus if he ever set foot in the shop again, he'd go out with the cops. He laughed and told me I had nothing to worry about. All that had kept him in Horton's Falls was loyalty to his poor old mother, but now she'd made it easy for him. 'I'm going to New York,' he said. 'I'll open up there—a *salon*.' I told him a clip joint by any other name is still a clip joint, and the next Greyhound left in an hour."

Doris drew a deep breath, blew out two lungs full of spleen.

"My son liked people to think he was a big shot—but work for it? Forget that! Please excuse me if I don't seem as upset as I should, but I've been expecting this day to come for eighteen years, and now here it is. I've cried every tear I had for Marcus; there aren't any left. Tell me what he did. I want to know."

Edna, Schwartz, Jitters and Purdue: four naughty children caught with their red hands squarely inside the cookie jar. It wasn't up to Schwartz and Jitters to talk: they'd been invited into the kitchen by the two big kids. Edna and I stared at each other.

"I want to know," Doris repeated, words edged sharply enough to draw blood. "I don't want to go back to Horton's Falls and live the rest of my life wondering." She picked up the urn, pointed it at me as if it could shoot cannon balls. "Talk."

"Let's sit down," I said quietly.

I told Doris the story of Marcus, Hartmann, Edna, Frank, a music box, and St. Cecilia. When I finished, she pursed her lips, nodded grimly. "Thank you."

"Least I could do."

Sarah would've loved this.

"You're not done, though." Doris held up the urn. "Where did you get this, and why? And what's inside? I know it's not Marcus."

Sarah would've been ecstatic.

"Come on," Doris urged. "Whatever you've got to say, I've earned the right to hear it."

In a minute she'd be going for thumbscrews. "I was in too much of a hurry grabbing your purse back from Jitters," I said. "The urn flew out, smashed on the floor." I paused like a kid waiting for his whack after confessing an especially naughty deed—but was Doris smiling? She looked like my father at Tyler's: a two-week-old baby with colic. "I felt terrible, wanted to make it right if I could. Sophie went to a shop in midtown—"

"Leo Kaplan's?"

"How did you—"

"I told you, I've collected Wedgwood for more than forty years," Doris snapped. "Leo has the biggest Wedgwood shop in the city, maybe anywhere. Then what?"

Humiliation without end. "Doris, please. Don't ask. Let's just skip this one."

"Goddamn it, I *did* ask. Now *tell* me."

Explaining terrible biopsy reports to patients and their families is as heavy as it gets in medical practice, but this situation felt worse by several degrees of magnitude. Doris looked at me like a third-grade teacher who'd caught the class clown in mid-act.

"You really insist?" I asked.

"Quit stalling, Thomas. Give it to me, and give it straight."

I saw Edna nod, opened my mouth, willed speech past the constriction in my throat. "I went to the Primate Center at the med school where I teach," I said. "Got ashes from a chimp they'd just cremated ... put them into the urn and sealed it."

"I sealed it," said Edna.

Doris looked at the urn as if she could see through it and was analyzing the contents. "Monkey ashes," she finally said. "You characters put *monkey ashes* in here and told me it was Marcus."

Not a question, needed no answer, and got none beyond the most pregnant silence this side of a labor and delivery suite full of anesthetized parturients. Gradually, Doris' features softened. Then she began to laugh.

She started quietly, a chuckle that ripened into a snicker, passed rapidly into a guffaw, and finally became a full-fledged horselaugh. Without dropping a yuk, Doris set the urn on the table next to her chair, wiped at her eyes, kept laughing. She screamed, shrieked, roared.

I began to worry: was she hysterical? Would she eventually get herself together, calm down, go straight for a phone, call the cops? But laughter's contagious as yawning. One by one, the four of us followed Doris down the Hee-haw Path. We sat shaking in our chairs, clutching at the pains in our sides.

"Well! I'm glad to see everybody in such a jolly mood. What's going on?"

Sarah stood over us, hands on hips, glaring. "If everyone's having such a wild good time, there must be monkey business."

That did it. Off went The Boffo Gang, giggling, snorting, rocking in their chairs. Finally we began to catch hold of ourselves; belly laughs faded into chortles and stifled snickers. "I could hear you all the way out in the hall," Sarah said. "What on earth was so funny?"

"Nothing really," I said. "I made a comment that struck Doris silly, and we all started laughing." Then I remembered— Sarah hadn't met Doris. "My wife, Sarah," I said quickly. "My friend, Doris."

Doris extended a hand, said, "I'm so pleased to meet you, Mrs. Purdue. After all I've heard about you from Thomas."

"Mmm." Sarah looked around, tried to take stock. Doris was now the embodiment of decorum, but still, five people having such fun? *Something* had to be up. "Doris ..?" Sarah said.

Uh-oh.

"Wilcox," said Doris. "I'm from upstate, Horton's Falls. Your husband and his friends have been so kind and helpful to me."

I don't know whether Sarah heard anything beyond Doris' first word. My wife had the goods on me, knew what I'd been up to and with whom, could name names. A transcription of her thoughts right then probably would've sounded like an old, cracked 78-RPM record. Wil-cox, Wil-cox, Wil-cox ...

"*Marcus* Wilcox!" she almost shouted. "You're not his ..."

"Mother? Yes, I'm afraid I am, dear. Or was. That's what we were just laughing about." Doris picked up the urn, showed it to Sarah.

Don't ever think a situation can't get worse. Oh, for verbal Kevlar jackets. "This is perfect," Doris crowed, waving the little vase around her head. "A fake urn with fake ashes—*monkey ashes* for that matter. What better memorial could there be for Marcus?" Then her face went serious. "If I'd never met you people I'd have gone home with a lot less money, a lot more aggravation, and a vase full of ashes to pack away out of my sight. But *this* urn will go somewhere in the house where I can see it—and every time I do I'll remember all of you and smile. And now ..."

Oh, God. Now *what?*

"... I want to take you out to dinner. We all have something to celebrate."

All but one. Sarah's face was closing in on black. I knew what Doris had to celebrate but to Sarah the old woman's behavior must've appeared unseemly bordering on insane. Her son was murdered, somehow or other she lost his ashes and replaced them with those of an incinerated monkey ... and she was going out to *celebrate*? "Sarah, listen—" I began.

She shut me up with two outstretched palms, stepped away as if to avoid my contaminating her.

"Mrs. Purdue," Doris said. "I do hope you'll come with us. It would be—"

"I'm sorry," Sarah snapped, "but I'm afraid I'd spoil your party. I've got a nasty headache; I'm going to lie down. Nice to meet you." She turned and stomped through the kitchen into her apartment.

Doris was clearly embarrassed. "Did I say something—" she began.

Edna cut her off. "Yes, but don't feel bad about it. Sarah can be ... well, a little out of step with the rest of us. You couldn't have known. Thomas, tell you what: Get her to come to that party at the Hartmanns' Friday night. When she sees how nicely this is all going to work out, I think she'll feel better. And Doris—why don't you come, too? You're not really in that big a hurry to get back to Horton's Falls, are you?"

"Well, no, but I don't think—"

Edna leaned across the sofa to pat Doris' arm. "We'd love for you to come; why not? You're as much involved now as any of us."

"Besides ..." Doris' attention snapped from Edna back to me. "Whatever you say, we owe you. Without your help we'd still be stuck on square one, looking for Mr. Hartmann's music box. And without your ... understanding—"

"We'd all be wearing zebra suits." Schwartz can remain silent for only so long.

"You be *our* guest," I said. "*We'll* take *you* out to dinner tonight. Then we'll check you out of the Imperial, take you over to a wonderful little hotel on Madison, The Regina. Owner's our friend; he'll treat you like royalty. Next couple of nights we'll go to the theater, museums during the day, whatever you'd like. Our treat."

"Oh, my goodness, no. I couldn't."

Edna leaned over again. "We'd really like to," she said, and as Doris opened her mouth, Edna added, "We *want* to."

Try playing immovable object to Edna Reynolds' irresistible force. "All right," Doris murmured. Then her voice rose. "Except for one thing. Tonight's dinner is *my* treat. No argument."

"Deal!" I grabbed the phone, punched in numbers, heard, "Raygeena, a leetle hotel. Espinoza speaking."

"Nozey, this is Thomas. We have a friend here, Doris Wilcox, we'd like to put her up first class, three nights. What's the best room you've got?"

"Hmm." I heard pages being shuffled. "Well, I got the Royal Suite, bes' in the house. Leetle 'spensive, but for you' frien'—"

"Not a problem. We'll be by with her after dinner, see you then."

"Oh, Doaktore ..?"

"What?"

"Thees have anyt'ing t'do wit' that pocketbook and the busted vase?"

"That never happened, Nozey."

"What never happened, Doaktore?"

The mischief in Nozey's voice was like a clap of thunder after the lightning bolt of his words; fortunately it hit soon enough to stop me from saying something stupid. "Right, Nozey. See you in a few hours."

"Room be all ready, Doaktore. Ain't nothin' to worry about."

What, me worry?

While I talked, Doris wandered over to the worktable where Jitters had carefully set the tea server. "That's so lovely," she said. "Is it musical?"

Edna snorted. "It should be. But it was badly damaged, had a ... fall, and when Jitters and I got through restoring the automaton, its music wouldn't play. I knew Thomas was here, so I thought we'd come over and ask him to take a look at it. Jitters has a key, no need to bother Thomas by ringing bells."

"Bad manners to drop in without notice," I said.

"I won't do it again in a hurry," said Edna.

"You restore these," Doris' voice was heavy with awe. "How marvelous."

Edna and Jitters exchanged a secret smile. "Me and my apprentice there," Edna said, a tad Dietrich-toned.

"I don't know about anyone else," Schwartz chirped. "But *I'm* hungry."

What's new? "The Brasserie's reopened," I said. "Complete remodel. You like onion soup, Doris?"

"Love it."

"This is the best in the world. Broadway—whyn't you call Trudy, tell her to meet us there." Then I remembered. "Call Sophie too." I almost added, "and Gackle," but caught myself. By this time of day Gackle was probably well into an intimate evening with Mary Jane. Better to just figure seven for dinner was lucky, not push that luck.

Past nine-thirty by the time we finished eating and got Doris ensconced at the Regina. Half an hour later I turned off Seventh onto West 16th, and there was my private panhandler, standing opposite the steps to my apartment building. By the time I reached him I had the five-spot out, plus a couple of singles. "Late fee," I said as I pressed the bills into his hand. "Sorry to keep you waiting."

If he was amused he didn't show it, just answered with the usual nod and a quiet, "Thank you."

In the oblique light of the street lamp I looked at his seamed, grimy face. Something about him, a gentleness—a *genteelness*—and in his tired eyes mild reproof. Had this guy lived a century and a half ago, and hung around outside the New York Customs House, he could've been Melville's inspiration for *Bartleby*.

I took a deep breath, decided to play a long shot. "Tell Dunbar next time he messes with me he won't get up at all." I watched closely but the man's eyes stayed level. "Did you hear me?" I asked.

The answer came in a calm voice, dignified, free of guile. Political candidates would kill for the credibility of this sidewalk beggar. "Yes, of course I heard you. But I have no idea what or whom you are talking about."

"Whom" from a panhandler? Give me a break. But I was clearly getting nowhere, it was coming up on eleven o'clock, and I had another task waiting for me. "No problem," I said lightly. "See you tomorrow."

Was that a faint smile? "Thank you, Doctor."

When I hit the light switch in my darkened workshop, surprise! Sarah pushed herself upright on the sofa. She looked at her watch, then at me. "Nice of you to come back before dawn."

We won't be home until morning, I thought, but didn't sing it. "You were invited along," I said. "You didn't want to go."

"Of course I didn't want to go. I walk in and find five grown people hilarious over the fact that the ashes of an old woman's just-murdered son were lost—apparently because of some half-witted prank by the other four—and replaced by ashes from a cremated monkey. Put myself through a whole evening of that? I'd've had to be crazy."

I sat down opposite her. "Did you ever hear of context?" I said. "Or out-of-same?" When she didn't answer I went on. "I'd've been glad to tell you then, but if you'd like I'll do it now."

Arms folded across chest, lips thin and tight. Eyes narrow. "This better be good. Better than I think even you can make it."

I picked up from where I'd left off in my Ice Bag Confession the night before. The further I went the more disgusted Sarah looked, and when I finished she fairly exploded. "My *God*—I've never heard anything so reprehensible in my life. I can't say I'm surprised at you, but Edna? Or *Sophie*. And as for that Doris person—however bad Marcus Wilcox may have been, he was still her son. To be laughing about—"

"Laughing's one way of handling pain. Wilcox was rotten from day one, Doris wrote him off years ago, but yes, sure, it still must've hurt. As for the rest of us, call it relief. Couple of minutes earlier it looked as if we were all going to jail."

"You should've," she snapped. "I just can't *imagine* doing what you did."

"Why not? Because of what I did, an old lady's going home feeling good instead of bad. Knowing she helped right a major wrong her crook of a son committed."

"You think you can talk your way out of anything, and so far you've been right. But not this time, not with me. If you'd approached Mrs. Wilcox openly, told her what was going on, and asked for her help, I'd feel differently. But you had to con her, didn't you? Because that way it was *fun*. Thomas Purdue is just too clever to live in the world as it is. He has to make his life more interesting ... no matter how it may affect others around him."

"Listen—"

"To your latest story? I don't think I'm interested."

She drives me bananas. "Sarah, name me one person who's been hurt or left worse off by my 'fun.'" I waited, no response. "Go ahead. I'm listening."

Big sigh. "You've been lucky ... so far. But sooner or later one of your crazy schemes is going to backfire and something horrible will happen to an innocent person. Meddling where you've got absolutely no business, all the while talking like Mr. Sister Teresa! 'Oh, there's nothing in it for me. I'm just trying to help my friends.' But there always is something in it for you, a new music box, another toy. Just happens to work out that way; lucky Thomas. Lucky, *lucky* Thomas."

"Sarah, listen: I'm sorry you came home and found me in the middle of a game, but what should I have done? Jumped ship, left my friends holding the bag? Friday night it gets settled once and for all. Come with me ... it's going to be a party. A little celebration. If you see anyone get hurt without deserving it, I'll take an oath: no more. Ever."

"Oh, sure. As if I could believe any oath you might take."

"I'll put it in writing."

"As if you couldn't talk your way around any piece of paper in the world."

"Sarah, who's being unfair?"

"You're going too far, Thomas."

"Come judge that for yourself. Friday night."

She got up, stretched, walked slowly to the kitchen, then around the corner and out of sight.

She *would* come Friday night: I knew it, she knew it. And not only to see for herself whether the game would sort out well or I'd take a nasty pratfall. Sarah could be prissy, Sarah could be pissy, Sarah could be sore as a three-inch-wide boil. But Sarah would be there to pick me up if I did go down. That brand of loyalty they don't sell at Macy's. If only she didn't behave as though trying to brighten your corner were a capital crime.

17

Next morning, slow breakfast, trying to tie up a couple of loose connections for Friday night's show at the Hartmanns'. Suddenly a wire flashed a message. I put down my coffee cup, went into the workshop, came back with a tape cassette and portable player, grabbed the phone, punched numbers.

"Prescott Dunbar's Excalibur Antiques and Interiors," said the female voice at the other end.

"This is Thomas Purdue," I said. "I need to speak to Mr. Dunbar."

"Mr. Dunbar is with a client. May I have your number—"

"Please tell Mr. Dunbar I won't keep him more than two minutes ... and if he's got a problem with that, he'll be explaining the police to his client."

Dunbar was on the phone almost instantly. "Purdue!" he roared. "What in *hell* are you—"

"Be quiet and listen," I said, then turned on the cassette player, held it close to the receiver. "Come *on*, Prescott," Marcus Wilcox whined. "Where do you think I can possibly get—"

"Two hundred thousand dollars?" boomed the recorded voice of Prescott Dunbar. "That's your problem. If I don't get it within two days, you're finished. I'll send a letter to every designer from here to Paris—"

I clicked the tape off. "We need to talk about this," I said. "Just the two of us. Meet you halfway, Rhinestone Jim's, on Forty-sixth between Broadway and Eighth, twelve-thirty. You'll be there?"

For reply, a strangled, "Yes."

"Good. I'll reserve a quiet booth."

I washed my dishes, then headed for the workbench. Except for my appointment with Dunbar, I was on my own for the day. Sophie was going to shepherd Doris around the city, Edna had commandeered Jitters again, Schwartz was appraising an estate in Brooklyn.

Fifteen minutes at the bench was all I needed for the musical mechanism from Edna's tea server; then I set myself to communing with Mssr. Reymond-Nicole. I was on the homestretch, final damper adjustment. On most music boxes this is a routine operation, but nothing is routine about a Reymond-Nicole. Comb teeth are needle-thin with mere slits between them, so if a damper wire is set the least bit off-center, it may be picked up by a pin from an adjacent tune track, causing the very noise the restorer is trying to avoid. Matthew Arnold said the pursuit of the perfect is the pursuit of sweetness and light, but Matthew Arnold never redampered a Reymond-Nicole comb. I kept at it, picky-picky tweak-tweak, until it was time to go meet Dunbar.

I was early but he was earlier yet, already sitting in a high-backed booth at the rear of the restaurant. As the headwaiter showed me to the table with a flourish of his black-jacketed arm, Dunbar didn't say a word. Just glared.

"Nice to see you again ... and so soon," I said.

He didn't even blink.

Before this one-sided conversation could go further, an elderly waiter appeared, asked if he could bring us anything to drink. I told him I'd be fine with water.

"I don't drink with pigs," Dunbar said.

The waiter laughed, why not? This was the theater district, remember? The guy was at least seventy, could easily have gone back to the days of Berle, Benny and Burns. Just a couple of crazy friends, joking around. All right with me: Dunbar was getting mad and madder. Easier and easier for me to get even.

"I'll give you a few minutes to look over the menu," the waiter said.

Dunbar slapped the long page into the old man's hand. "I don't eat with pigs either," he growled.

I grinned at the waiter. "I *eat* pigs. Give me the barbequed pork sandwich, please."

The waiter laughed again, took my menu, hobbled away.

Dunbar looked ready to detonate. "Be quick," he snarled. "The smell in here could make me sick."

"Cool it," I said. "If you've got half a brain." I pulled the tape cassette out of my shirt pocket, waved it across the table at Dunbar. "Wilcox recorded your whole conversation with him, and no, this isn't our only copy. You've got two hundred thousand dollars you haven't exactly earned. Wilcox stole a valuable music box to get that money; now it needs to go back to the owner."

Dunbar cut short a sarcastic bray by gasping and clutching at his side.

"Little accident?" I asked.

He looked on the verge of bolting. "Sit tight, " I said. "You're going to return that money, or the owner of the music box will bring suit against Wilcox's estate ... and how long do you think it'll take for two bunches of lawyers to find out where the money is? They'll have it all over the papers; you'll hear this tape for days on the eleven o'clock news. Better start thinking about how to explain an undeclared two-hundred-K in cash to your neighborhood IRS auditor."

He balled his fists, leaned across the table.

"Look at it this way," I said. "Better *I* nailed you than the cops, the feds, or some professional blackmailer. Play ball with us and at least you'll come out even."

"What about the thirty-two thousand I paid Wilcox in the first place?"

"That's your penalty. Oh, and by the way: if you're wired right now, remember one thing: I go down, you go with me. You'll spend your next twenty years smelling me next to you on a rock pile."

He sank back into his seat, broadcasting hate. "When do you want the money?"

"Friday night, six-thirty. Be at your shop. Someone'll meet you, check the payment, then bring you to a party—"

"A *what?*" Back in my face again, choking me with his expensive stinkwater. Some nerve complaining about *my* smell. "Listen, Purdue: payback is one thing. But I'm not about to go to any goddamn party—"

"Yes you are," I said. "Part of the deal. Relax. You'll have a good time. Food'll be great." I smiled. "Company even better."

By the time Sarah came in after work I had the full mechanism reassembled, all dampers set reasonably well. She walked over, stood behind me at the workbench. "You're here."

I blinked up at her. "Been here all day—except for a short lunch break."

Not a word. Just a big fish eye.

"Look." I pointed to the gleaming brass mechanism, then the comb. "You think it put itself together and set its own dampers?" I snatched the magnifying visor off my head, jabbed a finger at my bleary eyes. "Look at *these*. Yes, I've been here working, all day. Now go change your clothes. I got Lincoln Center tickets for tonight, classical guitar. John Williams, all works by Sor and Guiliani. Dinner at the restaurant of your choice."

"You were here all day but you got Lincoln Center tickets."

Not a question but I answered. "Sure. I used this wonderful new invention, the telephone. Marvelous contraption—just dial some numbers, then a nice young woman takes your credit card information and says your two eighty-five-dollar tickets will be at the will-call window—but you need to pick them up at least fifteen minutes before show time." I shot my cuff, held my wrist up in front of Sarah's face. "Which means we have two and a quarter hours to eat and get over there. Go change; let's move. You've already broken the record for most consecutive hours being a pain in the ass."

Sarah's eyes went like Frisbees; her cheeks flared.

I rested a hand on her arm. "I knew you'd want to hear this concert, so I bought tickets over the phone. You don't want to give due credit, don't. But at least don't behave as badly as you tell me I do."

Her eyes softened. She bit her lip, walked away through the kitchen.

Sarah loved the concert. For the first time since her return she invited me to sleep in her bedroom. "You really can be so nice when you want to," she said. "I only wish you wanted to more often."

"I always want to," I said. "But when you think I'm not, is that necessarily—"

Sigh. "Stop right there. I don't want to hear about how a short circuit can be in a transmitter *or* a receiver."

Gloriosky! She *does* listen to me.

"Let's not argue."

"I'm not prone to argue."

In the morning, back to Reymond-Nicole, one last loose end for next night's get-together still buzzing in dark corners of my brain. The old master must have taken pity on me because when I set the comb into place, screwed it down, and listened to the three tunes, I heard remarkably few of the squeaks, squawks, and chirps that signal mis-set dampers or improperly aligned cylinder pins. I thought the treble came through a bit over-bright, so I loosened the screws and nudged that end of the comb a hair's-breath farther from the cylinder. Then I re-played the tunes, one by one, listening carefully, adjusting a pin here, a damper there. This is *terminage*, last job for the manufacturer 160 years ago, last job for the restorer today. One by one, the unwanted sounds vanished.

Finally, just past noon, I flipped off my visor, sat back in my chair and pronounced it good.

Like finishing a painting, a novel, a symphony. Now, what? I looked around the room: plenty of work waiting. But no volunteers, understandable. Would *you* want to follow Joe DiMaggio into the batting cage?

All of a sudden I knew.

I wrapped the Reymond-Nicole and the tea server for safe travel, put them into a carton, locked my door, charged down the stairs and outside. I paused long enough to give Bartleby his daily fin, then burned leather down 16th toward the Union Square subway station.

Waiting for the light at Sixth Avenue, I glanced back— and saw Bartleby shuffling along, two shops up from the corner. Ratty white shirt, dark pants, unkempt gray hair. Probably on his way to his bar *du jour*.

But as I walked into Union Square Park he was still there, trying to blend into a small crowd. I scooted down the stairs to the subway, stood on the platform, shifted from one foot to the other, spotted him lurking behind the token booth. A Number Six train came in; I pushed my way aboard. Bartleby shot through the turnstile with amazing speed and agility for such a geezer, zipped into the car directly behind mine. As the train rumbled out of the station I caught sight of a bit of his face through the glass in the end doors of the cars. I got off at 68th, started up Lex to Edna's. Yes, there he still was, a half-block behind me.

I ran into the Warburton vestibule, pushed the bell, heard Edna say, "Yes?"

"Thomas," I called. The buzzer sounded. I charged past the door, made certain to push it shut behind me, ran into the elevator, muttered encouragement as it made its painful, halting way to the fourth floor.

Edna was waiting at her door. "Here." I pushed my carton into her hands. "Be right back."

"Thomas ..?"

I got to the elevator just as the doors were closing, snaked my way inside, rode back down to the lobby, walked out onto the sidewalk. No sign of Bartleby, nuts. Did he wander off once I was inside?

Just have to find out.

I strolled up Lex, across 70th, past 71st ... and whom do I see back there, doing his best to look inconspicuous in a swarm of neat summer suits and fashionable warm-weather frocks? Talk about sore thumbs—this one was red hot and dripping pus.

Go, Purdue.

I turned quickly, trotted back toward Edna's, keeping track of Bartleby via peripheral vision. He froze, gawked, but before he could reverse fields I was up to him. "Hey, Bartleby," I called out, and clapped his arm. "Long time no *see*." I made a show of checking my watch. "Well, lookee this—what say we do lunch? Come on."

I clutched his arm, started walking him down the pavement past astonished faces on all sides, but no one made a move or said a word. Good old New York. He started to wiggle; I tightened my grip. "Just keep walking," I said, *sotto voce*. "Make a run, scream, do anything, I'll kill you." Let his imagination tell him the rest.

Odd conjoined twins, we marched up to the Warburton, buzzed the bell, walked through the lobby. Give my companion this: caught in the act, he lost none of his calm dignity, didn't even try to avoid my eyes. All the way up in the elevator, he stared silently into my face. As we approached the fourth floor it was I who cracked. "Who're you working for?" I snapped. "Tyler? Dunbar?"

He didn't say a word. For him to know, for me to find out ...

Well, shit.

"Come on," I said, politely as I could, then led him down the hall, knocked on Edna's door.

She opened up, dog-eyed my companion, then me. "What the hell—"

I guided the old man into the apartment. Edna closed the door. "Jitters here?" I asked.

She inclined her head toward the workshop room.

"Get him."

She walked away, limp almost unnoticeable now, returned almost instantly with her apprentice. The boy stopped cold when he saw who was with me. The old street man, on the other hand, howled, "Jitters!" and ran across the room to embrace the boy.

"Thomas, what the hell *is* this?" Edna asked.

"Little family reunion," I said. "This guy's been hanging around my place for days; I caught him following me here." I pointed at the carton, now on Edna's table. "Had to drop off my stuff before I could nail him—and then in the elevator, I remembered the first time I ever saw him. Right before I ran up to my place and found myself staring at Jitters and his shaky little popgun."

Jitters and his grandfather looked ready to bolt for the door.

"You were the lookout, right, Grandpa?" I said.

Jitters was practically doing an in-place cha-cha, but didn't reach for his Klonopin. The old man nodded.

"Let's sit down," I said.

Jitters guided his grandfather to the couch, sat next to him. Edna and I took chairs to either side. "Guy told Grandpa and me you were some big-time collector, real valuable stuff," Jitters said. "So we figured maybe we could make a huge hit. I did the skyjob, Grandpa waited outside for me to give him the okay through the window and buzz him in."

Grandpa looked at me, eyes leaking shame. "But when you ran inside and Jitters didn't signal or come out, I took off."

Jitters snorted. "Hey, Grandpa—no reason you shoulda got nailed too."

"*I* can't keep calling you Grandpa," I said. "You're Mr. Levitsky?"

"Gus. Gus Levitsky." The old man wiped the back of his hand across his mouth. "I ran back to Rivington Street—and found our belongings on the sidewalk. Bastard landlord'd moved it all out and changed the lock. I took what I could carry to a shelter for the night. Next day I unloaded it at a hock shop."

Jitters couldn't stay still another second. "When *I* got back to Rivington Street that night, Grandpa must've been there already; wasn't nothing on the sidewalk. I hunted for him all the two days before I went to work with you on the music box, bummed food, got doorways for at night. Then Edna told me I could stay over with her, she didn't ask no questions—"

Grandma Edna smiled benignly. "So you didn't have to tell me no lies. Pretty obvious you were on the street."

Jitters blinked, smiled shyly.

"Losing my apartment and my belongings was one thing," Gus said. "Jitters was something else. I was afraid you'd turned him in ... or even killed him. I found out what I could from your neighbors; a few times I followed you. I thought you might take me to Jitters."

"You weren't around when he came in to work, eight o'clock in the morning?"

"Huh!" Gus snorted. "*You* try getting out of a shelter before prayers. I thought I had a shot a few days ago—after you and your little friend with the black fedora gave me a handout I ran across the street, hid behind a car. When you came out with Jitters, I followed. But then you went down into the subway—"

"A little after five on a weekday in Union Square," I said.

Eyes still on Jitters, Gus nodded. "I lost you before you were all the way down the stairs. At least I knew Jitters was alive, and he looked all right—but I was still scared. Where were you going with him? And why? I hung around your apartment, sometimes followed you when you went out, but after that once I never saw Jitters again. I was getting desperate ... so I decided to follow you today and see what happened." He disparaged himself with a chuckle. "Guess I'm not prime gumshoe material."

"You're also not prime street man material," I said. "The way you talk, the way you act ... doesn't compute. What're you doing on the street?"

With a shake of his head the old man spread sadness across the room like salt flying from a shaker. "Natural progression of events, Doctor. 'Forties Communist, 'fifties pariah, bum ever since ... wife committed suicide ... daughter—Jitters' mother ... shot in a bar one night when Jitters was six ..."

Jitters shifted in his seat, draped one arm lightly over his grandfather's shoulder, a move so casual I wondered whether the boy realized he'd done it. Gus honked. "Long story ..." A whisper, barely audible.

"Which you don't have to tell," I said, then pulled bills out of my wallet, leaned over to give them to the old guy. "Here you go. Get some new shoes, pants, couple of shirts, shave and a haircut. Then go up to the Regina Hotel, Madison between Sixty-second and Sixty-third. Owner's named Espinoza; tell him Thomas said you need a room with two beds. Take a shower, rest up. When Jitters is done working for the day, he'll come up and take you out to dinner, tell you all about what's happening. He's a young man with a very bright future."

"Never mind 'take you out to dinner.'" Edna obviously had ideas of her own. "Go ahead, Gus—do what Thomas said. Only come back here about seven for dinner." She turned a crooked grin on me. "I wouldn't miss this for anything."

As the door closed behind Gus, Jitters looked ready for a heaping plateful of Klonopin. I took him by the elbow, walked him toward the workshop. "Let's see what you characters are up to now."

They had a new patient on their operating table, a monkey, twelve inches tall, dressed in ragged silk, holding a little mallet in each hand. He'd been removed from his place behind a xylophone on a black-painted oval wooden stand; an intimidating tangle of gears, pulleys, and wires showed through the hole in the base.

"He's supposed to play along with the music in the stand below him," Edna said, "but all his linkages are rotted, some gear damage too. Needs the full treatment: mechanical, cosmetic, but he'll be a honey—eyes'll open and close, head'll nod, mouth and lips'll move as if he's singing."

"Yours?"

She shook her head. "I wish. He belongs to Chris and Carolyn

Hamner; they got him at a flea market in Europe last year for practically nothing, he was in such rough shape."

"More damaged goods ... say, why don't *you* go to Europe, Edna? Pick the place clean."

Edna snorted, then looked across the worktable at Jitters. "Bet *you'd* like that."

Shy smile, shrug. "Sure." Shakes gone.

"Bet you're both wondering why I really came over here," I said, then led them back into the living room, pulled the tea server out of the carton, unwrapped it, set it on the table in front of Edna. "Nothing serious—just a couple of wood slivers in the governor, must've flown in and stuck there when the piece hit the floor. I took them out, cleaned the gov in the ultrasound. Works fine now." I pulled the start knob.

Oriental music began to play as the young woman poured from her pot into a cup on a small table, then into a second cup in her hand. She turned, smiled, offered the cup to me.

Edna nodded approval. "What do I owe you?"

"The cost of a coronary bypass which I damn near needed when you came in and Doris saw you."

"Yeah, well," Edna chuckled.

Jitters snickered.

"But why I'm really here ..." I unwrapped the Reymond-Nicole, set it on the table between the monkey and the tea server. As Jitters leaned forward I opened the lid.

The boy's eyes bulged, lips extended into a circle. Edna craned her neck to peer inside the case. "Oh my." No mistaking the reverence in her voice. "Reymond-Nicole. Yours?"

"I'm glad to say yes. Picked it up last year in a shop in Pittsburgh. It needed a lot—new leads, cylinder repin, total redampering, broken spring, love and kisses to the governor ... but a Reymond-Nicole ..."

I turned the winding key, pushed the start lever, all the while keeping my eyes on Jitters.

Most music boxes play a minute or less per tune, but Reymond-Nicole governors are geared for long play, rotating the cylinder at only about one-third customary speed. The first tune was the overture from Rossini's *Italian Girl in Algiers*. If I'd spoken to Jitters I doubt he'd have heard my voice. As the second tune began, the overture from Weber's *Euryanthe*, Jitters' enthrallment deepened. His consciousness seemed totally defined by the chords, melody, counterpoint and dainty trills rising into the air, then falling gently on his ears. But count on Rossini for the last word. The third tune, a duetto from *Elisabetta, Regina d'Inghilterra* was no more than five bars underway when tears began to flow down Jitters' cheeks. No sobbing, no snuffling or heaving of shoulders; picture a statue weeping. As gorgeous as the music sounded to my own ears I knew I was hearing no more than a pale copy of what Jitters heard, and I felt envy as never before. As the delicate, precise music played on, the rush of water down Jitters' face became twin streams, then rivers, finally cascades. When the mechanism shut off at the end of the tune and the notes faded, Jitters stood motionless, making no attempt to stop the flow of water.

"Oh my," Edna whispered. "It's unbelievable. From another world."

"Jitters, what did you see?" I asked softly.

He spoke without moving. "First tune like flags, purple and gold, waving gently ... very gently. Next one, columns, you know ... like on the porches of those old houses down south. Marching columns, orange, black, real bright blue. And the last one, oh ..." His head shook ever so slightly from side to side. "Green and yellow curtains, so soft ... like a film. With tiny little red points, wrapping around me, wouldn't let go. Didn't *want* them to."

I rested a hand on Jitters' shoulder. "This is close to the ultimate in music boxes," I said quietly. "Work hard, be serious; pretty soon you'll be turning scrap metal into music boxes like this."

Jitters looked from the Reymond-Nicole to the monkey xylophonist, then quickly back to the music box. Caught between a cushion and a soft place. "No need to choose," I said. "Work part-time with Edna, part-time with me."

Jitters gazed into the distance, smiled gently.

"Aren't a lot of decent music box restorers around, even fewer for automata. You'll have a waiting list the rest of your life, people lined up around the block. You won't get rich—"

"Let him play some more of your little games," Edna said, "a few nice tax-free bonuses, he won't starve."

Jitters waved toward the disabled dolls and animals waiting their turns on Edna's shelves. "Too bad there ain't no books about fixing these ... like the books Thomas has for music boxes. I liked readin' 'em the other day when I was workin' there by myself. Kinda filled in the blanks."

"I've been thinking about that," Edna said.

We looked at her, waited.

"I could work from the material in my repair log," she said. Put a book together while Jit's off fixing music boxes. *Collecting and Restoring Musical Automata.* By Edna Reynolds. It'd make me feel good, knowing I'd still be bugging Jitters' little ass when I'm not here anymore myself."

"That job'll take you a while," I said. "You'll need to cash in your ticket for the Midnight Special."

Jitters looked confused. "You're gonna go on some sort of train trip?"

Edna nodded. "I *was* ... but Thomas is right. With all I've got going here, I really don't have time for that now. I'll just flush my ticket down the ... wait a minute. Thomas—you already did that, didn't you?"

"Sure. I knew you wouldn't be needing it."

Anger flared in her eyes, but subsided as she glanced at the monkey on the table, then at Jitters, finally back at me. So softly I could barely hear, she started to speak. "My father used to tell a story about an old teacher who held up a piece of glass and asked his student what he saw. 'All the people around me,' the student said. Then the teacher held up a mirror. The student said, 'I see only myself.' 'Yes,' said the teacher. 'What a difference a bit of silver can make.'"

Taut lines sprang up between Edna's nose and the corners of her mouth. She was on her feet now, vintage Edna, full steam ahead, clear the track. Jitters turned an anxious glance in my direction.

"*You* look at the world through clear glass, Thomas," Edna said. "For which I'm damn grateful. Nursing homes make fortunes off old people whose kids and friends won't look away from their mirrors even long enough to say goodbye. It's nice you're also a very smart man, but ..." She shot her right hand a caustic look. "That's not nearly as important. Without a kind heart and a generous spirit the best diddledamn human brain on earth's not worth a pail of warm spit."

I might've been embarrassed but was too busy processing

Edna's story. *Look through a piece of clear glass ...* Bingo, thanks, Edna. Last loose end in plan about to be snugly tied.

I checked my watch. "Got to run an errand, then meet Sarah. See you at Hartmann's tomorrow night."

The young woman at Barrow's Antiques, on Lexington south of 61st, seemed to think I was a bit off the wall when I told her what I wanted. She waved a finger toward the rear of the shop. "If we do have anything like that it'll be on the floor over there; you'll have to just look through the piles." She consulted her watch, as if to remind me the store would close in less than forty-five minutes.

"Got a tape?" I asked. As her face went blank I added, "Tape measure. Ruler. Anything that measures."

She shook her head slowly. "I don't think Mr. Barrow keeps—"

"Forget it." I took a dollar bill out of my wallet, waved it at her. "A dollar's exactly six and an eighth inches long, two and five-eighths inches wide. That'll do."

She told me without speaking she couldn't care less and that come five PM the shop would close and I'd be outside.

But I was on my way again with ten minutes to spare, my purchase tucked under one arm, my Reymond-Nicole under the other. I'd applied my dollar bill more than thirty times before I hit the jackpot. When I went to the counter to pay, the young woman beetled her eyebrows. "I can't let you take it apart—you gotta take the whole thing. Frame and all."

"No problem." I smiled. "Seems appropriate."

Friday evening, half past five. Schwartz, Tyler, Jitters and I lugged the revolver-plerodienique and its table from Tyler's apartment into a rented Ryder truck at the curb, drove to Hartmann's, offloaded. Then Jitters and I returned the truck to Mr. Ryder and went home to pick up Sarah Stoneface.

Lovely night, warm but not humid. People seemed to move more slowly than usual, faces relaxed, some even smiling. Summer magic in New York. By the time we got to the West Village Sarah looked almost congenial.

Hartmann admitted us, red-faced, beaming. With his barrel chest and dark green three-piece suit he looked like a jovial bullfrog. "Mrs. Purdue ... *Mrs.* Pur*due*." He took Sarah's hand between his two giant palms. "I am *so* pleased to meet you. Your husband ..." He turned his head to gaze on me like a master pianist congratulating his protégé for a career-making performance. "Thomas, I am forever in your debt."

I waved him off. "Person to thank's Mr. Tyler—if he hadn't been willing to return the music box, I couldn't have done a thing. *He* deserves the credit."

"For returning stolen property?" Tyler boomed from behind Hartmann. He raised a glass of amber liquid in my direction. "I don't think so. I bow to you, Thomas."

Sarah's face said she was barely managing to hold back a nasty attack of logorrhea. Better start paying her more attention. Tomorrow.

Hartmann walked toward the back of the room where a long white-clothed table struggled to hold Schwartz's extravaganza of champagne and other high spirits, soft drinks, and deli sandwiches. "Want something?" I asked Sarah.

"A glass of red wine?"

"I'll get it for you."

"I'll come along."

Passing Hartmann, I noticed he was staring beyond the refreshments, toward the rear of the apartment. "Problem?" I asked.

"Oh ..." Concern weighted his eyes. "It's just ... well, with all the *schmoozing* I can't hear how Lettie's doing. When she gets upset or distracted she can make a holy mess in a hurry."

"Bring her out here. Then you won't have to worry."

"Thomas ..."

"What? Would she get frightened?"

"No ... she never seems to notice where she is or who's around. But don't you think ..."

"She'd put people off?" I shook my head. "Tell you what. Let me get Sarah a glass of wine, then I'll help you move Lettie, her table, her doll and her pram over there." I pointed at an empty corner to the side of the food counter. "You won't have any trouble keeping tabs on her."

Sarah harrumphed. "First things first. I'll help bring Mrs. Hartmann out and get her comfortable. *Then* I'll get my wine."

By seven-thirty, Lettie was in her corner, working clay, giggling, mugging, pointing a finger here or there, babbling happily in echo of the conversation. "Mr. Hartmann's been looking after her *himself?*" Sarah whispered.

"For at least the past few years."

Now there's a man to be admired, said her eyes. All right. I've long since given up trying to be Sarah's hero. Just being her husband's a full-time job.

Lucas Sterne was last to arrive, slithering through the doorway in his customary crow suit: black turtleneck with trousers to match. The room was buzzing. Trudy, Schwartz, Gackle, Edna, Sophie, Doris, Jitters and Gus—the old man a whole lot spiffier now, nice new shirt and pants, hair neatly cut—sat in a circle of rented bridge chairs, making points with jabs of their fingers. Near the refreshments, Hartmann and Tyler stood in less-dynamic conversation. Hartmann's eyes kept up an almost-rhythmic beat, darting glances at Lettie in the corner, but the old woman seemed content, if a bit loud of voice. My father and Sarah sat on the sofa under the windows, talking quietly. Frank the Crank, looking well-recovered, earnestly chatted up Prescott Dunbar, the only person in the room who appeared at all uncomfortable, elastic bandage visibly wrapped round and round under his shirt. Dunbar met my eye—the good eye—once, as he walked in with Al, a little after seven, carrying a large briefcase. He didn't appear at all pleased to see me, and I caught the eyeball message Big Al sent his way: Behave! Dunbar nodded a staccato yeah-yeah, then marched to the far side of the room, where Frank collared him. That'd occupy the bastard for a while.

An hour passed, attacks on the refreshments became fewer and less extensive, conversation shifted from buzz toward drone. Then, over the background noise came the voice of Frank the Crank. "Hey—Mr. Hartmann. What do you say we take a listen to this music box, caused all the trouble?"

Good old Frank, right on schedule. He stood in front of the revolver-plerodienique, big grin cracking his face, eyes agleam with elfish sparkle.

Hartmann held out his arms, a priest at the altar of the Temple of Music. "*Would* you all like to hear it?"

"Yes!" chorused the congregation.

Little shrug of acquiescence, tiny smile. Hartmann opened

the lid to a surge of craning necks and ooh-aahs. Only Sarah stood back, coolly disengaged. Hartmann pushed the start lever; I heard the opening notes of the overture from Rossini's *The Thieving Magpie*. Sarah's eyes sent me a wordless message: How appropriate.

Entire overture, beginning to end, but with clever orchestrations never heard in any opera house. Except for the music the room was silent. Even Lettie Hartmann stopped babbling, some troubled region in her brain temporarily soothed out of the compulsion to invent and repeat verbal nonsense. I made a mental note to talk to Hartmann about investing in state-of-the-art stereo.

When the music stopped, our host made ready to close the lid. Edna waved a hand. "Play all the cylinders, Mr. Hartmann ... please. This is a once-in-a-lifetime treat."

General applause sent Hartmann to the winding lever, which he cranked back and forth as Lettie crooned, "Dunce in a wife's lime feet."

Hartmann disengaged the carousel lock, rotated the mechanism to the next cylinder, refastened the lock. Then he pushed the start lever. As the first notes of *Semiramis* began to play, the buzz in the room stopped as if someone had thrown a switch. We listened to each cylinder in turn, not a sound in the room other than music and Lettie's occasional clay-noise, slap, bam, flup. The final rousing notes of *William Tell* faded to the accompaniment of little sighs and a softly-mumbled "marvelous." Someone—Doris, I think—thanked Hartmann warmly. Our host smiled, nodded acceptance, then reached to close the lid.

"Just a minute," I said. "Look what I've got."

18

What I had was everyone's attention.

I held up a large brown envelope, opened it, pulled out a cardboard sandwich, split the tape, slid out a 5x7 piece of glass. To turn up the perfect item I'd pawed through more than thirty old frames on the floor of Mr. Barrow's shop. "See the wavy lines," I said to the crowd. "Old glass."

"Cold ass, sold gas," Lettie echoed. Slam. Flup.

I pointed toward the lower left corner of the glass. "When Mr. Tyler showed me the box the other day, I thought why not replace that broken glass? This piece is exactly the right size, right age. Make it look a whole lot nicer."

Hartmann looked like a windup toy with a jammed motor. His jaw opened, snapped shut; hands moved abortively toward the music box, then jerked away.

Dad said, "I don't think we ought to do that, Thomas."

"Why not?"

"Because after all these years, the painting's going to be stuck fast to the glass. We could ruin it."

Through a murmured buzz of enlightenment came Tyler's magisterial voice. "No worry there, Dr. Purdue. The painting's a fake, remember, a recent one at that. We shouldn't have any trouble at all."

"Well, then." I took a Swiss army knife from my pocket, moved past Hartmann, insinuated the slim blade behind the lower panel of the wooden frame around the lid picture. Quick twist of my wrist, a sharp pull, and off it popped. I edged glass and silk painting downward, pinching the exposed corner of silk between thumb and forefinger. But before I could start working the painting away from the glass, my father restrained my hand. "Thomas, *stop!*"

The urgency in his voice silenced everyone but Lettie. "Call a cop, Pop. Sing doo-wop."

"Look." Dad aimed a finger directly above where I was about to pull. "S. Sinclair, the artist's signature. That's no fake." He pulled gently at the unprotected bit of silk. "See how firmly the painting's stuck to the back of the glass. In those days they used balsam as an adhesive. Pull harder, you'll leave half the paint behind."

Hartmann looked like a landlubber aboard a small fishing boat on a rough sea.

Edna reached to rub a finger over the back of the painting, fiddled with the edge of the fabric. "I can't tell for absolutely sure," she said. "But I'd bet a ton of money that's hundred and fifty year old silk."

Tyler hopped up and down like a rabbit on Dexedrine. He pointed at the signature, then jabbed his finger skyward. "But ... but this ... isn't possible!" He spun around, glared furiously at me. "You saw yourself ... the other day ... What the *hell's* going on here?"

I sneaked a peek at Big Al, right behind Tyler. Very reassuring.

"I've got an idea." Everyone looked at Dad. "Balsam's an excellent stickum," he said. "As it ages it doesn't color or get crackly. It's easily dissolved with naphtha, which shouldn't do anything to paint. We could apply naphtha one small drop at a time, blot it, peel away a bit, then put on another drop. That might work very well."

"If we can find a chemistry supplier open at eight p.m.," I said.

"It should be easier than that." Dad's face said he'd nailed his wise-ass son. "Lighter fluid's pure naphtha. All we need is a container of ordinary lighter fluid, available at any grocery or drugstore. Unless someone happens to have some in their pocket."

"Pocket, hock it, sock it in the courtroom docket," Lettie crooned, as heads shook no all around the room. Not a smoker in the crowd? *O tempora! O mores!*

"I think a bit of lighter fluid can be arranged."

Big Al became the center of attention.

"I picked some up along with my cigars the other evening, at the smoke shop down the street. I'll get it from my suitcase ... easy enough."

Al lumbered toward the back of the room. Tyler cleared his throat. His lips ratcheted into a scowl of concern. Beads of water oozed from the skin of his forehead. "I don't like this," he intoned. "Yes, the glass is broken, but imagine if we ruin the painting. I'd rather—"

"I wouldn't worry, Mr. Tyler." Dad at his best, explaining to a patient that an operation, though not totally risk-free, was certainly in his best interest. "Naphtha *doesn't* dissolve paint, but in any case we'll go at it slowly, very carefully."

Al reappeared, holding a small red and white cylinder. Dad took it from him, accepted the painting and glass from me, then sat down at a small end table. The group converged around him.

"Dr. Purdue, you damn well better know what you're doing." No mistaking the threat in Tyler's voice, but every eye in the place except Lettie's stayed on Dad, whose concentration looked unbroken; he didn't even seem to hear Tyler. Dad bunched a pocket handkerchief in his left hand, opened the container, turned it upside down, carefully let a small drop fall into the handkerchief. "Ah—just right." He picked up the glass and painting, poised the container over the broken corner. "Let's start here: there's an entry point ..."

"Entry, gentry in the sentry joint." Slap, wham.

Rudolph Hartmann, linebacker bent on sacking the quarterback, blasted through on my left, nearly knocking me cockeyed. He grabbed the glass and painting out of Dad's hand. Dad looked up at him, shocked.

"You must be crazy," Hartmann shouted. "An original St. John Sinclair, worth half a million dollars—and you're going to pour *lighter fluid* on it?" He retreated a step, bumped into Big Al, who nonchalantly plucked the object of controversy out of Hartmann's hand. Hartmann glared; Al blinked mildly. Hartmann was big, Al was bigger.

But Hartmann was no wuss. "Give me that," he snarled at Al.

Al shook his head. "I think not. I for one have explicit faith in Dr. Purdue's judgment." He reached around Hartmann, returned the prize to Dad, then positioned himself squarely between Dad and Hartmann. He glanced at Tyler. "Go ahead, Dr. Purdue," he said. "I'll make certain there will be no trouble."

Hartmann swiveled his head wildly, then bolted for the telephone. "I'm going to call the police," he shouted.

"Go right ahead." Big Al, soul of geniality. "By the time

you've no more than been connected, the job will be finished." Al peered over Dad's shoulder. "Looks as if you're successful so far, Dr. Purdue."

"So far, so good," Dad said in the automatic manner of a person with his attention fully engaged in something other than speech.

Hartmann let out a howl like an animal with a foot caught in a trap. He lowered his head and barreled back toward Dad, a Mack truck on legs. Big Al shifted his weight; Hartmann hit him with an "ooph."

"You looney!" Hartmann shouted, struggling in Al's embrace. "Let me *go*. An original Sinclair miniature ... *mine*. I don't know how you found it, or when you put it back into the frame. But you're not going to destroy—"

"Bad boy, destroy the toy."

Hartmann writhed; Al held him in place. "'Twasn't difficult," Al said. "More than enough time to search it out whilst you were asleep."

Hartmann was livid. He jerked this way, twisted that way, but Al was more than his match. "All right, all right," Hartmann cried. "I had a copy painted and switched it with the original, glass and all. But I was in too much of a hurry and broke the corner of the replacement glass. I didn't have another ... had to get the box off to Moss ... I was running out of time ..."

"Sit down, Mr. Hartmann," I said gently, and guided him into a chair. "Sarah ..." But she was already on her way to the kitchen, came back in a few seconds with a glass of water. Hartmann took it from her, drank deeply, then thanked her quietly.

"Feel better?" I asked.

Nod.

"All right. Grab a chair, everybody, sit down. We'd all love to hear the real story, Mr. Hartmann. From the beginning."

As Hartmann scanned the room, the defiance on his face gradually melted. Finally he murmured, "I've wronged a lot of people. But I really didn't intend ..." He bit fiercely at his lower lip, waved feebly in Lettie's direction. "I needed money ..."

"Money for my honey-bunny."

Sarah looked about to cry.

"... and I knew this music box was valuable. Just how valuable I had no idea. I'd known Wilcox for years; he sold some of Lettie's work. I did matting and framing for him. Not that I liked him ..."

Everyone tried to look anywhere but at Doris.

"Well, I told Wilcox I wanted an appraisal. He suggested Mr. Sterne there—"

"I'd never seen a music box with a painting that had any independent value ..." Pause, embarrassed smile from the man in black. "At least I'd never recognized one. So the appraisal was on the basis of the music box alone."

"Which I knew," said Hartmann. "But I didn't say anything to Wilcox, just let him think I hadn't picked up on the painting. He and I went to talk to Barton Moss—who did not inspire my confidence—but what choice did I have? Moss said he'd do the repairs for about five thousand dollars; Wilcox said he'd take a twenty percent commission to sell the box quickly for full appraisal price. So I persuaded Wilcox not to waste his time going with me to take the music box to New Rochelle. Then I got the painting copied—"

"By Philip Andrews," said Big Al.

Hartmann just stared at him.

"Oh yes. Easy, that. Only a few artists over here are capable of such work; no trouble tracking it to Andrews."

Hartmann put me in mind of a rapidly deflating tire. "I rented a small truck, hired a couple of strong young men to load the box and table in, and unload them at Moss'. But ..."

One of the saddest smiles I've ever seen, followed by a sigh. "Then the whole scheme blew up in my face. Moss called to tell me the music box had vanished from his workshop, along with some others. He'd notified the police but ... well, you know the story from there."

"Sure," I said. "Wilcox was every bit as dishonest as you were. He gave Moss a little money or a lot of booze or both to get the music box into shape, turn it over to him, and feed you a cock-and-bull story about a theft. They were going to lay low, wait for you to die, then sell the box. But Wilcox suddenly developed an urgent need for money—didn't he, Mr. Dunbar?"

Dunbar took a step in my direction. Al moved between us, inclined his head toward Dunbar, who ran his hand lightly over his rib binder, then moved the step back. Al smiled benignly. "Go on, Thomas."

"So when Dunbar squeezed Wilcox, Wilcox called Tyler—"

"And told me he was about to get a fine antique music box with a magnificent oil-on-silk," Tyler said. "I told him to call me when he had the piece in hand. Just a few days later he called, said he had it, and if I wanted it I needed to do a deal right then. Otherwise he'd call client number two. I spent the rest of the afternoon turning securities into cash, then I went to Wilcox's. I didn't stop to think about that crack in the glass 'til after I had the box home. When I realized what was up I went back to see Wilcox ... who of course swore he didn't know anything."

"Lousy little piss-weasel!" Doris snapped.

Tyler didn't know whether to laugh or look embarrassed. "I told him if that was true, then I needed to know where *he* got the box. Remember, at that point I hadn't heard anything about Moss and restorations. Wilcox told me Frank Maar brokered it to him. And Mr. Maar, I'm sorry for what you've gone through; I'll make it up to you."

Frank turned dark eyes gleaming with humor onto Tyler. The creases at the corners of his mouth turned upward, ran into his hollow cheeks. "Thanks, Mr. Tyler—that makes the situation a horse of a whole different cowboy."

Time to grab back the stage. "In one way, though, it worked out well," I said. "Frank made the connection between your music box, Mr. Tyler, and the one Lucas said he appraised a few weeks before. That's what led me to Wilcox, then Moss and Hartmann."

At the mention of his name Hartmann slapped a hand to the side of his head, classic migraine pose. "That's when I knew I had real trouble—first you and Schwartz came asking questions, Thomas, then next night, Wilcox. According to Wilcox, Moss'd had an idea. He'd repaired the music box, told me it was stolen—so why didn't Wilcox sell the box quietly, and they'd split the take? You should've *heard* Wilcox: oh, he'd *never* do anything like that to me, heaven forbid! He said he drove right out to New Rochelle, paid Moss for the repairs, picked up the box, sold it that day to Tyler. So now he and I should've been golden. But Tyler raised a stink about the lid painting being a copy, so Wilcox went back to Moss, who denied knowing anything about a fake. Worse for me, Wilcox believed Moss and why not? What would a slob like Moss know about art and paintings?"

Hartmann's voice faltered; he swiped a handkerchief across his beefy, sopping forehead. "Wilcox accused me of ... well, of doing exactly what I did do. Having a copy made of the lid painting, putting the copy into the frame, and making off with the original."

"Which you were going to sell on the QT?"

Defiance made a partial comeback over Hartmann's face. "When I had to. A piece of art like that ..."

You sell your mother before you sell a piece of art like that, I thought.

Hartmann sighed extravagantly. "Wilcox got angrier and angrier. He said he'd sold the music box to Ferris Tyler, and by now he ought to be on Easy—"

"I ... sold ... it ... to ... Ferris ... Tyler," I said, loud, slow, each word clear and distinct. "Big wheel in the art world. By now I ought to be on Easy Street. Cut the baloney!"

Lettie stopped pounding clay, turned around. Wide-eyed, open-mouthed, a child just come downstairs and seeing the tree on Christmas morning, she let go a laugh capable of turning circulating blood into snow-cone filler. Her arms whirled in grand circles. "Cut baloney, go to Coney. Ride big Ferris Wheel, big deal, *schlemiel*, breezy-freezy seat, Wheeeee."

Hartmann looked at me, then nodded sadly. "She said that the second time you and Schwartz came here, didn't she?"

"Sure did. Damn lines kept banging around in my head— but they didn't come into focus 'til maybe the third time I heard Mr. Tyler say his name. Wilcox tried to con you, didn't he? Told you he was going to pay you your share just as soon as Tyler's check cleared, but then Tyler started raising hell. 'If it's a forgery, it's got to be you, Rudolph—give me that goddamn origi-

nal. If Tyler stops payment on his check, where'll we *both* be?'
How close am I, Mr. Hartmann?"

"Practically word for word."

"But you knew once he had that painting you'd never see a
nickel. Go on. What happened next?"

Sigh, dejected headshake. "I told Wilcox even if I had
the painting I'd never give it to him—not after the way he
tried to screw me. He came right up in my face and screamed,
'Are you questioning my integrity?' I laughed, which was the
wrong thing to do. He grabbed me with one hand, swung
with the other. I was surprised how strong and quick he was.
He got in three or four good shots, finally knocked me down;
then he went after one of those bronze bookends over there."
Hartmann pointed toward a shelf under the window, where a
row of paperbacks stood between figural reader-bookends.
"I got back up on my feet; he swung the bookend at my head.
I dodged, then hit him a pretty good shot to the chops. He
raised the bookend to take another swing, but all of a sudden he just fell ... as if he'd been shot. I thought I'd knocked
him out but when I bent down to look closer, I saw he was
dead. No pulse. No breath on a mirror—"

"But wait." Edna, square on the uptake. "They found Marcus
on the sidewalk, on East 18th Street. How did he get there?"

Keeps getting worse and worse, said Hartmann's face.

I pointed at the perambulator in the corner. "Mr. Hartmann
took him for a walk."

"How did you know?" Hartmann asked in a colorless voice.

"First time I came over here, the doll's hat was on with the
pompom to the right. But when Schwartz and I ran over after
you called to say you'd been beaten up, the pompom was on the
left. I didn't think either you or Lettie had been playing with it.

Then, guess what I found between that nice straw mattress and the side of the perambulator?"

Hartmann stared at me, clueless, full of dread.

"Three cinnamon red hots. I took two out. Still one there, if you want to check."

Hartmann exhaled extravagantly. "Damn Wilcox and his lousy, smelly candies. I was afraid to call the police: could I have made them believe it was self-defense? And what if Mr. Tyler saw the story in the papers or heard it on the news? One way or another I'd have been cooked. I knew I had to get rid of Wilcox in a hurry, so I took the doll out of the perambulator and put him in. That perambulator's almost three-and-a-half feet long, Wilcox was a small man ... and being just-dead, he was all floppy. I turned him on his side, bent his legs up, scrunched his head down, and he just fit. Then I covered his body with a blanket and pulled the wool cap over his head."

I kept my eyes squarely on Hartmann, didn't dare look at Schwartz. Or Edna, or Frank, or Sophie, for that matter.

"But I couldn't leave Lettie here alone," Hartmann continued. "I told her to come along, we'd take the baby for a walk. Wilcox lived only about a half-hour away; I thought we could find a quiet side street in his neighborhood and dump him so it'd look as if he'd been mugged and robbed. Getting out of our building was easy, and all the way to Wilcox's neighborhood we had only one bit of trouble. We'd just crossed Fifteenth, Lettie was singing "Rock a Bye Baby," and a woman going the other way leaned over to look inside the perambulator. 'Oh, his poor little face is all covered up,' she said. 'He'll suffocate.' When she went for the cap I gave her a shove, told her I wasn't going to let her get germs all over my grandson. She got insulted, stomped away, and just a few minutes later we were on Eighteenth. The street was deserted. I told Lettie we were putting the baby to bed, pulled Wilcox out of the perambulator, dropped him on the sidewalk, and stole his watch and wallet. When Lettie and I got home, I put the doll back into the perambulator ..." Rueful smile in my direction. "... not quite carefully enough. I hid the watch and wallet; I was going to throw them into the garbage ..." He looked at Doris. "I'll give them to you, Mrs. Wilcox."

Al pulled a gold watch and a black leather billfold from his jacket pocket. Hartmann's jaw clunked into full gawk.

"Oh yes," Al said mildly, placing the two items gently into Hartmann's lap. "All those hours people usually waste in sleep can be put to profitable use." He inclined his large head toward Doris Wilcox.

Hartmann followed cue, handed the valuables to Doris.

A soft murmur chased through the little group. Feet shuffled. Sarah looked a millimeter from a gut bust.

"I decided I'd better cover myself," Hartmann said. "What with the damage Wilcox did on me during our fight. I took a couple of the pills I got after some dental work a few years ago, then banged my arms and legs against the oak table there. Then I ran down for a pack of cigarettes, and burned my arms and hands. Next morning, I called Thomas and told him I'd been beaten up by a couple of thugs looking for a plerodienique-revolver music box."

Tyler scratched at his head. "I was so sure Wilcox had made the switch I told him I didn't want a refund; it was the original painting ... or else–"

"Assumption's a real mother," I said.

Everyone but Tyler looked puzzled. "Touché, Thomas," he

said. "It's just hard to believe Wilcox really *didn't* know anything was wrong until I came after him."

"All he wanted was to get the merchandise out of his hands and the money in, ASAP," I said. "What did he care about music boxes or paintings? I'll bet between the time he got the box from Moss and when you bought it, he never even opened the lid."

"How could he not have noticed while he was showing me the box?" Tyler mused.

Doris let go a snort of impressive grandeur. "Maybe he did. But do you think he'd have said anything *then*? And risk losing the sale?"

Hartmann looked like the dishrag after last night's dinner party. "I have no right to throw stones at Wilcox," he muttered. "If it weren't for my dishonesty he'd never have come here, we wouldn't have fought, and he'd still be alive."

"Not necessarily," I said.

All eyes moved from Hartmann to me.

"Wilcox died of what's called a delayed subdural hemorrhage; the medical examiner found both old and fresh blood inside his skull. In other words, he got a head injury some days before, bled a little, then went around with a time bomb of a blood vessel in his head. When Wilcox started the fight with you, it probably sent his blood pressure high enough to blow the vessel. Sorry, Mr. Hartmann; you're not quite as deadly a fighter as you thought."

I knew what was coming, looked over my shoulder at Edna. Her appearance resembled Hartmann's a moment before. "An injury some days earlier?" she said. "Like a crack over the head with a ... bronze statue?"

"Maybe," I said. "But we'll never know. How many fights did Wilcox *have* over the past couple of weeks? Edna, one; Mr. Hartmann, two ... He tried to pick a fight with Schwartz in his shop. Barton Moss? Maybe good old Barton gave him a crack on the bean before *he* went down for the count. And Mr. Dunbar: what was that you said the other day, right after you slugged me? Something about my being as good a fighter as my 'slimy little friend'? You were squeezing Wilcox at least as hard as Tyler was—did Wilcox try to squeeze you back by playing you a certain taped phone conversation?"

Dunbar dropped his briefcase, took a step in my direction. "You're not going to—" he shouted, then suddenly followed the briefcase to the floor.

Big Al leaned forward to extend a hand. "Beg your pardon, Mr. Dunbar. I believe I've tripped you up, terribly sorry."

Clutching his side, taking care to look away from Al, Dunbar slowly got to his feet. His hands were like birds set to sudden flight. "If you think you're going to pin that on *me*, Purdue, think again. I'm calling my lawyer—"

Big Al fastened eyes on Dunbar. One wrong move of the bird-hands and they wouldn't fly again for weeks.

"Only thing anyone can pin on you is a tail," I said. "Which is my point—if you'd just listen. No way of knowing when or how Wilcox happened to have that first hemorrhage. One fight or another—or maybe he really *was* mugged on the street, but a few days earlier. Whatever, he brought the second, fatal bleed on himself; I think we should leave it at that. As we should leave the original painting with Mr. Tyler, who bought it in good faith."

Hartmann's eyes hardened, lips went tight. His jaw muscles cycled through a seizure-like contraction-relaxation pattern. "So that's the deal," he muttered through his teeth. He looked long-ingly at Dad, who was still holding the signed Sinclair in one hand, container of lighter fluid in the other. "Why don't you just tear out my heart and liver and be done?"

No trouble picking up on the despair in Hartmann's eyes. With a word he could be free of some very serious criminal charges, but don't forget what he said about selling the painting on the QT. He'd do it when he had to—but that time would never come. When all Hartmann's money ran out, after he'd sold all his possessions and he and Lettie were on the street begging, that half-million-dollar painting would be in a plastic envelope, inside Hartmann's shirt, directly over the left side of his chest. If you're not a collector, I can't explain it to you. If you are a collector, I don't have to.

"Your choice, Mr. Hartmann," I said. "Last chance to make an honest man of yourself. But if I were you I'd take advan-tage of Mr. Tyler's generosity. Force him to file charges, you'll lose both the painting *and* your freedom."

Hartmann took just long enough to glance at Lettie in her corner, then looked back at Tyler. Finally he turned to Dad. "All right," he managed to say. "Give him the painting."

"If I may so venture," Big Al rumbled, "'tis not *that* painting you wish to give Mr. Tyler. He paid for the original; that's what he should get."

Hartmann, bug-eyed, rose from the chair, took the painting from Dad, extended it toward Al. "But ... this is—"

"A forgery," I said. "Signature and all. Look closely; smell fresh paint? Dad did it from Andrews' copy, then forged Sinclair's signature from one of Mr. Tyler's originals. Then he separated the copy from your replacement glass—easy enough—and bonded his painting to the glass with balsam. He really *is* good, isn't he?"

Sarah, fists clenched at her sides, stared at Dad like someone who'd walked unannounced into the exam room at God's podiatrist.

"Had to be done," I said. "Because of how clever you were. Al found Wilcox's watch and wallet but not the original Sinclair. Why don't you get it now and give it to Mr. Tyler."

Hartmann scanned the audience, sixteen witnesses to his detailed confession, and his face went the color of a gigantic plum at harvest time. He slammed Dad's forgery into my hand, then stormed over to the coffee table, laid "Lovers" on its side, pulled a small knife from his pocket, and pried away the ebony base.

"I looked there," Al said. "Inside that sculpture."

Hartmann made a valiant attempt at looking smug, but moral victories don't count for much when you've lost the war and your face is being rubbed into battlefield mud. Starting with the knife, then working carefully with his fingers, he peeled away the old green felt from the underside of the base and gently removed a paper envelope, just about five by seven. He slit the envelope with the knife and presented it to Tyler, who nodded thanks, then tapped at the closed end of the envelope. A painting fell into his free hand. He leaned toward me to compare it to Dad's. Low whistle, then a little salute. "You *are* good, Dr. Purdue ... very good."

"And you were right about this being the deal, Mr. Hartmann," I said. "But only half-right."

He followed my glance to the music box. So did Sarah. She could've been a mannequin at Madame Tussaud's. *Here it comes,* screamed her face.

"You set out to sell a music box with a painting for its assessed value," I said. "And that's exactly what you're going to do. Mr. Tyler paid for an original Sinclair painting; now he has that painting ..." I paused as Hartmann groaned. "In exchange, he's agreed to relinquish the music box for you to sell to another buyer. I can't afford to pay that kind of money in a lump sum, but ..."

Sarah's cheekbones threatened to tear right through their flaming cover of skin. "But *what?*" came the silent shriek from my wife.

"Let's start at Lucas' appraisal, two hundred thousand dollars. You offered Schwartz and me a reward for finding the box, forty thou. Take my half off the two hundred, I should pay you one-eighty—but then you still owe Schwartz his twenty, right?"

Hartmann inclined his head slowly, most tentative nod you'll ever see. "So..."

"So to make it easy I'll settle with Schwartz for his share, and pay you one-sixty...just not all at once. I'll give you a monthly payment - we'll work out the amount—'til you've got the full hundred-sixty, appraisal value less reward. That's the other half of the deal."

Under the weight of this last bit of verbal accounting, snap! went the spine of Sarah the Camel. "Thomas!" she screamed. "You don't know the meaning of shame! 'So much a month' ... and how many months did you tell me Mr. Hartmann *has?* Three? Six?"

She caught herself, literally bit on her tongue, but her expression as she looked at Lettie, happily pounding clay in the corner, said it all and eloquently enough. *And that poor woman, how long can she have? Why don't you steal the music box? Get your slimy pals to help you run out of here with it? That would be more honest than what you're trying to do.*

Hartmann locked stares with me. No question, his eyes had heard precisely what mine had. "Tell her," I said gently.

Misery without end. He actually squirmed in his seat. "I do need the money, Mrs. Purdue," he almost whispered. "But I don't have cancer. I thought saying I did might be an incentive to Wilcox to get the music box sold quickly ... *and* I thought it would move Thomas to help me get it back. But he obviously saw through me."

"Wasn't sure at first," I said. "I called the Delancey Street Clinic from my office, checked your records. You're healthy as a horse. I'd say odds are pretty good you'll be here to collect my last payment."

Hartmann glanced at Sarah, then looked quickly away.

"I'd also bet that music box *will* take care of Lettie the rest of her life," I added, more quietly. "But if it turns out I'm wrong, don't worry. We'll talk. We'll *talk*."

The old drink-buyer and doer of lunches segued from a pained frown into a throaty chuckle. He clapped my arm lightly. "Guess I'm really coming out of this mess pretty well."

"All considered," I said. "But we're not quite finished ... Mr. Dunbar?"

Prescott Dunbar glowered. I wasn't sure but I thought I saw Al give him just the slightest nudge in the side. Dunbar winced.

"You brought the money?"

Dunbar motioned toward the briefcase at his feet.

"Good. Give it to Al."

Dunbar hesitated ever so slightly, then handed the briefcase to Big Al, who accepted it with the politest of nods, set it on the coffee table, snapped it open. Those close enough to see inside let out a collective gasp. Schwartz took off his fedora, mopped his forehead with a sleeve, clamped the hat back on. "Whew. More frogskins than I've seen in one place in a while."

"Two thousand hundred-dollar bills," I said. "Which Tyler gave Wilcox, which Wilcox gave Dunbar. Who's now giving them to us. Figure half as the Dunbar Scholarship—that'll see Jitters and his grandpa through his aprenticeship. Gackle gets ten; another five or so'll cover my own expenses for this game. The rest goes to Al." I pulled a cassette from my pocket, handed it to Dunbar. "In exchange, Mr. Dunbar gets this tape from Wilcox's safe; we've destroyed all copies." I paused, tried to hold back what wanted to come next, couldn't. "Unlike what I'm sure he'd have done if our positions were reversed."

Dunbar's move toward me was arrested by Al's hand laid across his shoulder. "We'd best move on, Thomas ... Mr. Dunbar," Al said lightly. "Grudges are notoriously unprofitable, what? Time to forgive each others' trespasses."

Dunbar looked like a schoolboy caught in the act of throwing spitballs. I suspect I looked the same.

Al reached into the briefcase, counted out a pile of bills, extended them toward my father. "Artists must be paid, Dr. Purdue."

My father took a step backward, as if the money were generating uncomfortable heat. "Artists, yes," he said. "Forgers, no."

"A fine point at best." Al smiled genially. "But circumstances must be considered, and without your fine work we'd not have been able to ... er, confuse Mr. Hartmann *and* safeguard the original Sinclair. For you not to share in the benefits of our little activity would be most inappropriate." He moved forward, pressed the money into Dad's hand. "I insist."

I watched Dad's stern ethical principles do battle across

his face. Worse for Dad, his ethics were operating off a handicap. He'd forged a work of art, helped perpetrate a fraud. Could he bring himself to believe that refusing the money would really leave him standing purified among sinners? Or would the refusal come across as no more than a pious hypocrisy?

Dad looked at the pile of green paper, then at me. His expression was that of someone catching sight of half a worm in the apple he'd just bitten into. "This is more than I'll get for all my paintings together in the gallery show."

"Tell me it's a fair world, Dad."

He didn't want to chuckle, but he did. "All right—but on one condition. We burn my forgery. Now, here, tonight. As you promised." He snatched the can of lighter fluid, reached for his painting.

I grabbed his arm. "I *didn't* promise to burn your painting—only that it wouldn't survive the party without your consent. Listen, Dad: burn Andrews' fake instead. Then write a note, date it, say your painting was done as a faithful copy of the original which became separated from the music box and is now in the collection of Mr. Ferris Tyler. I'll put that note behind the painting in the frame. I don't want Philip Andrews' damn copy in my music box; I want your work. I'd rather have that than the original."

Did I see Dad's eyes fill? Probably my imagination. Without another word he grabbed the Andrews copy and the lighter fluid, then walked over to a metal wastebasket. He sprayed fluid generously onto both sides of the painting, dropped the silk into the basket, took a blazing match from Ever-Ready Schwartz, flipped it into the wastebasket. Fire flared, then only ashes remained.

Doris Wilcox cleared her throat, rummaged in her purse,

came up with a check which she handed to Edna. "This'll settle Marcus' unpaid bills. The shop's empty, thanks to Schwartz ... thanks to *all* of you. Even after I pay off every one of my lousy son's creditors I'll come away with more than fifty grand off his stinking business. *I'm* satisfied."

Edna looked at the money, shrugged. "Guess I am too, then." She folded the check briskly, one-handed, slid it between two buttons of her blouse, glanced at Jitters. They both smiled.

"What a touching scene."

Sarah's words, drenched in vinegar, shut everyone up but Lettie. "Touching scene, Constantine clutching Josephine," the old woman screeched, not missing a beat at her clay.

Which seemed to enrage Sarah further—if that was possible. She stamped a foot, slammed a fist down on the oak end table. "You ... *all* of you," she spluttered, swiveling her head to be certain to distribute a choking dose of contempt to every person in the room. "Thomas said this was supposed to be a *party*, but I've been watching a little theatrical, haven't I? Every move orchestrated in advance, which everyone knew but Mr. Hartmann and me. The painting going to Mr. Tyler, the music box to Thomas, Mr. Dunbar giving that money to Al ... you planned every step, knew exactly what was going to happen. Right, Thomas?"

"Well ... yes. But—"

"But, but, but. With you there's always a but. Three letters that excuse any criminal behavior you can think up."

"Sarah ... most of the time you've got it right." Cool, assured Dr. Will Purdue with an overwrought patient. "But usually is *not* always—not in medical practice, not in the world beyond medicine. Face it: sometimes you need to stretch rules;

occasionally you need to bend them. And very infrequently"—quick hot-eye in my direction—"you need to break them. Better that and your patient lives than to follow usual procedure and he dies."

Dad paused; I thought he was finished. But then he said, very quietly, "One of the lessons I learned from my father."

My grandfather was also a doctor; he died when Dad was a teenager. I could count on one hand's fingers the number of times I'd heard Dad talk about him.

Nobody moved, no one breathed. Sarah's stern gaze softened ... but only for a moment. Then her features contorted and her face became a mottled dermatologic jigsaw puzzle of stupendous rage. She clutched at both temples; I thought she really might yank out handfuls of her hair. "No!" she shrieked. "It's wrong. Any way you look at it, it's *wrong*. Lying's *wrong*. Stealing's *wrong*. *Blackmail's* wrong—that's what you're all doing, you're blackmailing Mr. Dunbar there. Never mind *he* was blackmailing Mr. Wilcox. Two wrongs do *not* make a right."

"What happens when you multiply two negatives?" I asked. Shouldn't have but I did.

Good thing looks really can't kill, or Dad and I would've been stretched out side by side on the floor. "The fruit really doesn't fall far from the tree, does it?" Sarah screamed. "Fine. Have your fun—but without me." She grabbed her purse, stomped toward the door. A couple of steps from her destination, hand ready to grab the knob, she suddenly stopped, then turned slowly, an unworded question on her face. She raised a hand to her temple. Uncertainty faded into blankness; she crumpled.

Dad and I charged through the partygoers. Sarah's labored,

noisy breathing told us she was at least alive. Dad grabbed a wrist, counted. "Pulse fifty-four." Gently, I tried to flex Sarah's chin toward her chest. "Three-plus neck rigidity," I shouted to my father.

"I'll call nine-one-one," murmured a ghost-faced Schwartz.

Sarah's condition remained unchanged for the few minutes it took for a city ambulance to scream up and whisk her, Dad and me off to Man Med.

19

Two in the morning before Dad and I got back to the Hartmanns'. People were draped over chairs, stretched across the floor, curled on the sofa. Lettie lay on a loveseat next to her clayworking table, breathing slowly, her head on a doubled pillow and a knitted comforter covering her body.

Only Dunbar was missing. "Said he figured the fuckin' party was over," Frank muttered. "What's the word, Doc?"

"Aneurysm," I said. "Weak spot in a blood vessel in the brain. You're born with it, go forty or fifty years, then bang. May've happened tonight because of how upset she got."

"Sounds a lot like Wilcox." Schwartz always first at matching pennies.

"A whole lot," Dad said. "In both cases there was a weakened blood vessel—one because of an injury, the other genetic—"

"For heaven's sake—is she going to be ... all right?" Sophie's voice trembled, but her gray eyes were steady.

I moved my hand like a vertically-challenged priest. "Don't know, Soph. They took her right to surgery, called in Connie Fortgang, best vascular neurosurgeon on the staff, got all the blood out of her brain, artery tied off in minutes. Not a sure bet but she'll probably make it. Real question's in what condition."

All around, grim faces. Edna looked at her right hand and arm, then back at me, guilty, as if she'd done a filthy deed.

Gus approached me slowly, dignified as ever. "I can't tell you how I hope your wife has a full recovery," he said slowly. The old man's gaze was level, unflinching. "You and Edna have managed to do more for my grandson in a week than I did in twenty years. How do I thank you?"

"You just did," I said.

Gus shook his head. "There's an IOU outstanding, a big one. I'm not about to forget it—don't you."

Edna took three quick strides, put an arm around my waist; for just an instant she looked as if she'd got an unexpected strong whiff of vinegar. Then her expression changed. Like a passage from Brahms' First Symphony, unequivocal declaration punctuated by an impassioned major dominant chord, then modulation into a muted, heartwrenching minor key. "You know something, Thomas?"

Uh-oh. "What?"

My father was looking at Edna and me as if each of us had his full attention.

Major dominant back across Edna's face. "Barton Moss, Marcus Wilcox ... *Sarah* ..." She raised her left hand, snapped fingers. "But here's Gus, seventy if he's a day, writing big-time IOUs. There's Mr. Hartmann, betting six figures he's going to be around to pick up the money for his music box. Well, *I've* got a few open accounts, too. Goddamn Midnight Special's going to have to wait a while for me!"

Majestic in her wrath, the old woman cocked her head to regard Jitters with a fierce tenderness. "Kid, you better come to work with running shoes on," she said in a harsh undertone. "And I mean every day."

"Huh!" Jitters straightened his back. "I was *born* with runnin' shoes on—ain't no little old lady gonna run *me* into the ground." His bravado was affectionate and—considering his youth—oddly touching.

Not yet light in the sky as we trudged out of the Hartmanns'. Al would stay the rest of the night with Rudolph and Lettie, then put his stack of green paper through a proper laundry and catch a flight to Heathrow. He shook hands solemnly. "Please do keep me informed." Hartmann echoed Al's concern. I assured them both I'd be in touch.

Tyler herded Schwartz and Trudy into a cab: faster, easier, safer to Beekman Place and Yorkville this time of day than the subway. I put Edna, Jitters, Gus, and Doris into another cab uptown. Cleveland Gackle shambled over to Eighth Avenue to catch a bus. Frank the Crank and Sophie went off toward their homes in the Village.

My father and I walked slowly across Perry, turned uptown on Eighth. New York's predawn lull, silence almost palpable. A sharp report—backfire? Gunshot?—from somewhere to the west blew the stillness to atoms, sent me flinching. Few steps farther a shadow swung across my path; I lurched away. Dad took my arm, pointed toward the street with his free hand. "Pigeon. It flew down from a windowsill."

We crossed the street. A man propped against a trash barrel held out a palm in front of his expressionless face. I pulled change out of my pocket, put it into his hand. Without a word he dropped the coins into a ceramic cup at his side, then extended the hand again. Like one of Edna's automata, but I didn't smile.

A metal grate in the sidewalk shook and rattled beneath our feet; a puff of wind whipped cinders into my face. I blinked, rubbed at my eye.

Dad shook his head. "Trains never stop running here. All day, all night."

"You can catch the Midnight Special twenty-four hours a day," I muttered.

Dad looked at me curiously. "Didn't Edna say something about ..." Then he started to sing quietly, as if to himself. "*Let the Midnight Special ... shine its light on me. Let the Midnight Special ... shine its ever-lovin' ...*" Pause, just that long. "Thomas, the Midnight Special has come and gone for today."

Mild, early monring air, classic New York summer night, but a penetrating chill ran the length of my spine. "Dad ..?" He turned, waited for me to go on. "You're not going home now, are you?"

"That's what I *was* thinking, yes. Haven't I had enough excitement for one day?"

"But it's a quarter to four. You'll sit for hours in Port Authority. Come back with me, sleep over. In Sarah's rooms." No reply. "Then in the morning we can go check on her."

Dad's eyes softened. He gripped my arm, started guiding me up the sidewalk. "I'd like to do that."

My father's always had perfect pitch for the human voice. He heard me say "Dad—don't leave me alone right now," then replied by thanking me for my kind invitation. I suspect he's never thought of it quite this way, but good doctors are good storytellers, and Dad's as good as they come.

***

We dragged into the vestibule. I pulled out my key, glanced at Sarah's closed door and suddenly got clobbered by a thought: *She may never open that door again.*

I dropped the key, swayed, clawed at the knob.

"Thomas, what is it?" My father swept an arm around me.

"I blew it." All I could say.

Still supporting me, Dad bent to pick up the key, opened the door, worked me inside. Before he could ask any more questions I said, "I'm all right," but the weariness in my own voice startled me. I pulled away from Dad's arm, went to the workbench where I'd left my Reymond-Nicole, pushed the start lever. Tune Three began to play, the duetto from "*Elisabetta, Regina d'Inghilterra.*" Glorious chords dropped at my feet; complex contrapuntal effects bounced dully off my chest. Might as well be on an elevator or endless telephone-hold. What *happened* to that magnificent comb and cylinder? A striking minor modulation that never before had failed to send every hair on my body quivering to attention hung in the air like cooked spaghetti.

The cylinder clicked to a stop.

The song is gone.

My fault, *my fault.*

"Dad, I *blew* it," I howled. "Sarah's aneurysm never should've burst."

Gray eyes suddenly heavy with concern, lips twisted into a silent, worried question.

Out it poured, verbal hemorrhage, not a chance of holding any part back. "She came home from her sister's complaining of a headache, buzz in her ear; I've *never* seen her so irritable for so long. I kept thinking, she's not herself.'"

Now he knew. I didn't have to say another word but couldn't shove in the plug. "I told her it was a blocked ear from the flight; she should take antihistamines, nasal sprays, headache remedies; it'd go away. But I never examined her, never even stopped to *think*. That buzz in her ear—blood flowing through the aneurysm, ready to blow. I had plenty of time, could've gotten her in for a quick vascular repair, no bleeding, no brain damage ... my God, Dad! Talk about a textbook case of medical negligence."

During my outburst my father seemed to age ten years. Eyes heavy with pain, he extended a hand toward me, seemed to want to speak but didn't. I waited.

Finally words came, slow, soft. "Thomas, you're a first-class doctor. What you've done for Edna, for that boy and his grandfather ... you weren't in a hospital or a clinic but you *were* practicing medicine. Yes, you blew it with Sarah, blew it badly, and you're going to have to find a way to make it right ..."

Dad's voice faded; his eyes were focused somewhere far away. He dropped a fist lightly onto the worktable. "But even the best, the *very* best, screw up ... I think I owe you a story, Thomas. Not tonight, though; what you need now is sleep. Like people, most situations look their worst at four in the morning. Tomorrow ..."

I could hear gears humming in the decision-works of his mind. "*Sweetest little feller ...*" He pulled himself just a bit straighter, rubbed hands together. "Tomorrow we'll go check on Sarah ..." Pause. Whatever he'd decided, it wasn't easy for him. "And then we'll have lunch ..."

"*Have lunch?* Dad, are you—"

"And I'll tell you that story."

He put a hand to my shoulders, propelled me toward the ladder-steps. "She'll be all right now," he said quietly, but with utter assurance.

I looked back at him.

"I was talking about Edna," he added, far more rapidly than he usually speaks.

"Dad, you could use some sleep yourself. Go across to Sarah's—"

"I will ... soon." A moment's hesitation, as if words were being dragged forth against their will. "We'll see how it all looks in the light of day."

He started walking toward the workbench. I dragged myself up the ladder, tossed my clothes onto the floor, pulled on pajamas, slid under the light blanket. The bed seemed to soak me up, mattress drawing aches from my back and legs. "See how it all looks in the light of day." Daylight, sure antidote to predawn gloom, morning's bouncy fortitude a time-release capsule to carry us through the nasty little surprises of our waking hours and the sure slug of anguish in the night beyond.

A sound from below told me Dad was sitting in my wicker rocking chair, his slow back-and-forth motion translated by the wooden flooring into a gentle rhythmic creak. He must've been heavy in cogitation, humming accompaniment to the chair. *Sweetest little feller ... everybody knows.* It pulled at my chest as the music of the great Reymond-Nicole himself had been unable to do a few minutes earlier. Good. I was still alive.

Next I knew I was on a carousel, Sarah beside me, our horses going up, going down, 180 degrees out of phase. The big band organ in the middle of the merry-go-round took up Dad's pensive hum, worked it over, transformed it, pumped it out in brassy, joyous double-time: *Let the Mid-night Spe-cial shine its light on me. Let the Mid-night Spe-e-cial shine its ever-lovin' light on me ...* Brass ring coming up fast; I grabbed, missed, toppled. Sarah yelped, reached for me. The carousel spun madly. I lost all balance, clutched the heavy leather reins, held on for dear life as my feet flew outward into impenetrable blackness. Exhilaration gave way to terror as I saw Sarah wrap her left arm around her horse's neck, dig in her heels, lean as far as she could to extend her free hand to me. "Don't fall!" I howled, and as our fingertips touched I woke, sweat-drenched and heaving, into mid-day blaze pouring through my new skylight. The clock next to my bed said 11:35.

I flopped back onto the pillow. The phone beside the clock had been silent all night: no news, good news. Right again, Dad. The Midnight Special's come and gone for today, Sarah not aboard this run. Edna still here, all the rest of us ... Hours yet to go before that big rattler pulls back into the terminal to pick up another load of passengers.

I reached across the table next to the clock, pushed the start lever of my prize Francois Nicole rigid notation music box; as the air filled with the master's haunting arrangement of the overture to *Don Giovanni*, I threw off the blanket, leaped to the floor. Lot to do before sundown. Go to Coney. Ride a pony.

Cut baloney! Get Dad, go check on Sarah.